Decline and Paul

a comédie noir

by

Brian Joplin

Meltman Associates 2018

All enquires concerning this book
should be directed to:-
meltman7777@gmail.com

ISBN No: 9781798444986

DECLINE AND PAUL

1: *Tanked up in Tolverton*

"Bugger!" I exclaimed in exasperation, turning back to the dreary side street as if surveying it would somehow lessen the distance to be retraced. Not that the problem was unusual, at least for me.

Even so, quelle pain! Earlier that morning, given the dense grey wool which seems to cluster permanently over Wales, and considering the long mile between here, outside school, and my lodgings in Abercorn Rise, I had invested a good proportion of my paltry resources in – apologies if this seems terminally middle-aged – an umbrella. A stout umbrella, mind. Not one of those flashy specimens with parti-coloured segments, or, worst of all, the telescope type that turns inside out at anything more than a whisper.

No way – this was ash-stemmed, with jet black fabric and a brass ring, formidable of aspect. Let the heavens open any time they liked, here was an ally to see you through storm and shower with dog-like faithfulness and assiduity.

And what had I done? How had I marked my good fortune in locating such a paragon? By losing it within an hour! Mislaying it as I tend to mislay most things.

Mea mega culpa and three times three until, after the initial shock and self-chastisement, reason began to assert itself. Tolverton, though old and distinguished, was hardly what you could call a metropolis. Nor had my foray that first morning been extensive. The bus station for a timetable & chocolate McVities, Timothy White's for razor blades, Mostyn's for picture hooks, and finally the post office in Naseby Square. It had to be in one of them.

Or, on second thoughts, how about the place I'd unearthed it? Evans, the town barber who, as well as cutting hair, disbursed snuff & cigars, flies, rods, malaccas and all things cane and arcane to the local gentry – of which, in the Tolverton scale of things, I was now judged to be one. Despite my puppy youth, despite being perplexed, despite being about to be, if the lowering sky was anything to go by, thoroughly drenched.

Typical! I thought wanly. A fine start to my teaching career. To present myself for lunch at the Headmaster's for all the world like a drowned rat. Or as sodden and woebegone as one of those unfortunates who pass their nights in shop doorways or under railway arches. Maybe that was my destiny, my ultimate haven: a sooty railway arch with nothing for company but a hound on a string and a copy of Shakespeare.

Unless, of course, I could get it back, my black and comely. And maybe, at that, there was time. No spots had yet fallen and it wanted half an hour or so to sherry. But where on earth should I start looking?

The post office? Unlikely – I'd only popped in to wire Julian that I'd be back in Oxford next Sunday and to keep his diary free. Some chance! Don't guys like Julian revel in it, that queue a mile long for their favours? Still, one has to try.

More likely was the bus station where I'd spent a good ten minutes attempting to understand the accent of the good lady presiding, and to decipher her most intractable of timetables.

Oxford and back on a Sunday? You must be joking! Out eastwards, fine – home via the coast, fine. But what's your reward? Bugger all. One hundred and seventeen meagre minutes. Hardly time to wipe your nose. And scant time indeed amidst the dreaming spires.

Or, more to the point, in Julian's bed.

Let's face it, OK? Is one's first day in one's first job ever going to be anything but hell? Away from friends, away from familiar places? I had accepted a post at this, what seemed to a Londoner, remote outpost of education for several reasons. One, my Oxford 3rd which despite its bravura excluded its possessor from schools situated anywhere halfway scintillating – another my Puritan father's insistence that I pay off all college debts pronto, and in full, without resort to him. So here I was, day one, having endured the long, long trek down from Mrs Kent's b & b, about to enter the Tolverton Common Room for the first time – there to inquire for my teaching schedule, and thence, perforce, embark on an embarrassing and probably fruitless lost property quest.

One thing was certain, with no salary till October and less than a tenner in Barclay's, any replacement was out of the question.

Which, then, first? Search or staffroom?

Fortunately I was saved from dither by a sharp flurry of rain, evidently set to develop into the kind of steady downpour which would make the refuge behind me, as prospects go, almost pleasant.

Not a soul was about and bereft of its denizens Common Room seemed even more chaotic and dingy than it had at interview. Dominated by a huge billiard table, the work section presented an impenetrable jungle of threadbare armchairs, boxes, books stacked here and there in crazy heaps, cups, canes and a brace of incredibly inky Gestetners – whilst the lobby cum cloakroom, ostensibly reserved for loos and shower booths, proved even more amazonian. Muddy boots, jock straps, college scarves, sou' westers – you name it, there they were piled haphazardly on the slatted benches, together with fusty towels and long-discarded nether vanities from Marks & Sparks. From ancient iron wallhooks hung droves of academic gowns of varying age and hue, all of course dustblown, and below them – joy of joy – thanks a million, oh ye Gods – a huge brass urn crammed so full of umbrellas that they resembled the dismal leaves of some melanomic aspidistra. Most it's true were holed or broken or both, but one or two at least had life left in them.

Ace – problem solved!

Lunch with Dr Amberley and spouse – and Robin, their charmer of a son about to start at Douai – thus ended up by no means the damp squib it had promised to be, and by half past two I was striding upwards and homewards, dodging pools of surface water, humming an air from *The Pirates*, all cares banished thanks to the effects of good claret and Mrs Amberley's exceptional (cum)quat brulée. Searching for lost artefacts and compiling lesson plans could wait for the morrow. All that mattered now was a long siesta on a comfortable divan with Julian, albeit in imagination only, stretched out beside me. Or maybe we'd conjure up some evanescent tyro for a threesome!

Feeling the effects of the long climb, I stopped at the corner of Abercorn Rise to catch my breath. Hands on hips, a quick gaze back to where the school lay in miniature below, snug between its two rivers, the emerging sun starting to lend a spot of cheer to that harsh Victorian stone. Maybe I'd made a good choice after all. Maybe what lay ahead would turn out more nirvana than disaster.

Anyhow, who could tell? As for now, priorities – bed and a porn mag, if I'd remembered to pack my back numbers of H & E, at that time, all those years ago, the only Gentleman's Aid readily available from Smith's. Then afterwards a saunter out as long as the skies remained favourable. Or a swim – that would be OK too. But was there a pool? Unfortunately the school's, as I'd been advised, was still of the outdoor variety and thus usable for about two hours a year in high summer. A replacement was planned but what use was that to me, now, today? Surely there must be somewhere in town, mustn't there? Even in a one-horse place like Tolverton.

Queries, queries – but just as I was about to turn again towards my lodgings, a loud toot assailed me from behind, plus the unmistakable screech of tyre burn.

There, askew and stationary in the main road, stood an elderly and very muddy Rover 14 whose driver was beckoning me with a crook of the finger. His flat tweed cap and ebony cigarette holder seemed curiously at odds with the collar which proclaimed him a clergyman, though there was no mistaking that voice. All font and forgiveness, these were the tones which sweeten versicles and soften the grave, mellow but quietly imperious, imbued above all with an indefatigable air of camaraderie.

"Hi there!" he called. "Bryant, isn't it?"

And then I remembered him. From the interview board. The Reverend Something Something Marchpane, Chaplain to the school *and* almshouses, as he'd insisted on styling himself. There was no mistaking that cigarette holder – nor those eyes of milky blue, alive, indeed awash, with amusement and a sort of Boy Scout zeal.

But what could he possibly want with me? Now, this moment? Noticing that traffic was building up behind, a bus and a couple of saloons already, with more in the distance, I hurriedly returned the wave and stepped off the kerb.

"No use waiting there," he said. "The 2.40's gone and the 3.10 goes round by Feyhill."

"Feyhill?" I replied, glancing back in puzzlement and noticing with horror the bus stop by which I had inadvertently lingered.

"Other side of town from the school," he beamed. "Not our cup of tea at all. Jump in – I'll take you down."

"Er…"

"No problem. I'm en route myself. In a manner of speaking."

By now the queue had grown by two vans and a tractor, whilst to my consternation what looked like a hearse sailed wraith-like into view round the far bend.

"Really, I couldn't put you out…" I said feebly, with dwindling hope.

"Nonsense, glad of the company – take care with that door, though."

"But…"

"It sticks."

There was nothing else for it – care was duly taken, and in utter disbelief I found myself starting to be whisked down the same hill up which I'd trudged so laboriously minutes before.

Even now, I suppose, an older or – let's face it – more resolute man would have explained matters in a trice and been let out in some convenient lay-by. But what novice can bear looking like an idiot? And, besides, here we had clearly one of those clerics who thrive on doing good. To him this counted as an act of charity which had saved me a tuppenny bus fare. Who was I to dent his halo?

The Rover proved extremely noisy at speed, an oddly pervasive hiss rendering conversation difficult, and it was quite a relief when, after a minute or so, my host braked hard, popped out the trafficator and swerved slowly left into a narrow and bumpy lane.

"Could you," he asked brightly, avoiding a pothole, "oblige?"

"Beg pardon?"

"The doodah," he replied indicating the yellow arm by my ear. "Always the same in wet weather."

"Oh, right."

"It sticks."

After a prolonged struggle with the window, I succeeded in returning the arm to its slot, by which time we'd halted outside what had once been a windmill, but now served as a garden centre. Invited to help wedge two huge wet sacks into the back seat, how could I refuse? Or fail to cover my new overcoat with broad smears of compost? But no matter.

Off we set again, this time on a circuitous route round by the Tolver to where an ample lady was waiting patiently outside the Rex cinema.

"Clemmie, my dear," began the pulpit tones, "this is Mr Bryant who's missed his bus. Bryant, my wife."

Handshakes, platitudes, change of seat into the back beside the sacks now seeping freely. But no matter.

Off we set yet again, a mild irritation beginning to vie in me with curiosity as they began to chat. How much more of such domestic bliss would there be? Kids to be collected from the nursery? Dogs from the vet? Paraffin from the oil shop? Dry-cleaned knickers from some godforsaken branch of Sketchley? With a nod at the roof, I thanked my lucky stars I'd been born queer. Let others sustain the human race: for me, the table for one, a stoup of Gevry-Chambertin '59, and a good long silent Trollope.

Even this smug mood was quickly eroded, however, as the source of the car's hiss began to reveal itself. On the rear wheel arch my side, a tiny hole had rusted through, from which issued not quite Coleridge's mighty fountain, but nevertheless spray. Road spray. A thin but persistent stream of cold brown bilge. Fantastic! Should one try stemming it with one's thumb? Great – cuff and arm soaked in mud! Should one try ignoring it? Superb – general devastation Krakatoa style!

Just what I needed!

"All right in the back there?" called the cheery voice.

"Couldn't be better!" I replied, shrinking as far right against the sacks as their bulk permitted.

"Not long now."

An estimate whose inane subjectivity at any time tends to irritate, but which, under circumstances like these, ranked as provocation of the most extreme kind. Nevertheless I limited myself to a brief growl – and so it was that, around half past three, after further stops at Boots and a market stall in Over Tolver, stockists of what Marchpane assured me were "the most cracking sausages in the county", I was deposited on the steps of Common Room once more, comprehensively besmirched and pretty disconsolate.

"Any time," cried the dulcet voice as a hand flapped and he sped away.

"That'll teach you, my lad," chortled Watson, the Second Master, coming up behind. "Never accept lifts from clergymen. Marcho bought that wreck, you know, with the grant for his demob suit. Fact, I assure you. Absolute fact. And it wasn't new then. Daresay he's waiting for the next war before he buys another!" A broad hand on my shoulder sweeping me inside, he surveyed my disarray sympathetically. "Never mind – when it's dry that'll soon brush off. Comfortable are you with Mrs Kent? A good soul – used to be matron in Rhodes at one time. Where your flat's to be when Docherty vacates. Sorry about Docherty, by the way. A good soul, but these boffins… Now, tea. Where's tea? Anything I can do, just let me know. Operate a Gestetner can you?"

And off he darted, leaving me to survey my new domain. Rather more populated than earlier, doubtless at the imminent prospect of food and drink, the room now accommodated five inmates beside myself and Watson, or, as I'd gradually realise, about a quarter of the total staff, not including part-timers such as Jephson. Stretched out on an immense sofa was a gaunt figure asleep, whose daubed and spattered smock shrieked Art. Next to him, by the window, a guy sorting through stuff on what I'd later realise was the mail table. Two others were playing a desultory game on the baize whilst chatting to a third in rugger kit. Though I couldn't see his face, those legs were enough to convince me that good things might well be in store.

It had not escaped my notice that the showers in the lobby were equipped with neither doors nor curtains!

Today's contingent was completed by a rotund figure at a nearby desk copying out sheets of numbers which I could just recognise as – and mind you I'm not boasting or anything – Stedman's Triples. It was later to transpire that his name was Ormulak, and that he'd escaped from Warsaw just before the onslaught. For now, he was just a small fat man with a rather gloomy face.

"There will be no tea today," he murmured shaking his head. "Always it is the same with Chris. Tea starts on Friday when the boys return. Always he forgets. No tea today."

"OK," I retorted. "Still, that means no calories either. Every cloud, you know."

He nodded. "Not that you youngsters need worry about such things. Not at your age."

"What, waists and stuff?"

"I used to have a waist," he smiled sadly. "Now I have wisdom. Was it a good exchange? You tell me." But before I could answer, he moved his chair round to peer my way more closely. "Herr Bryant, is it not? Did you know you're the first recruit here for four years."

As it happens, this was news to me, and, moreover, news with implications. For the moment, however, I contented myself with a non-committal shrug.

"Oh indeed," he continued, jerking a thumb at the god in shorts, "young Frobisher there was the last. One of *the* Frobishers – but he doesn't like it mentioned. Battle of Cadiz, very famous in naval history."

Not wishing to contradict him, I just smiled.

"So," he mused, placing a plump hand on his knee, "you must be prepared. Four years is a long time. People will sniff round you like something from a zoo. Something strange and rare. They will try to net you for this and that. The choir, debating, bells, cross country. You must learn to say no."

"To everything?"

"At first, yes. Or you will be swamped. The rugger, the cricket…"

"The campanology?"

"Ha," he cried with pleasure, tapping the sheets. "So you ring?"

"Not quite," I replied cautiously, backing a step. "My father did, and there's this old novel…"

"But you'll learn," he beamed, rising from his chair in rapture. "You'll learn quickly, my friend. Baxter and I will take you in hand. Now the first step is to…"

"Tea, where's that tea?" queried Watson, reappearing from what must have been his office. "Oh, Ormulak, in here a minute, if you would. We must finalise that rota for Inspection Day. Come along, come along."

As the door closed behind them, Frobisher turned my way, surveying me with a lean laconic gaze. "Saved by the bell," he murmured, "if you'll pardon the pun. I'm James. This pair of squirts are Tiny and Carver." Two cues waved as he held out his hand.

As any member of the tribe will vouch, when your skin touches that of a golden guy, it matters not a whit whether he's queer as well. There's a buzz. A kinetic buzz. Like static or the crack of a Wimshurst machine. And make no mistake, even if straight, he feels it too. Sure, he can't admit it – except maybe by some sort of glance or quirk of the lips – but it courses through his body too. He feeds on it, OK? That waist, those legs and shoulders, those veins – everything feeds on it, takes its confidence from it, grows in stature like an organ note at the end of a voluntary. Sans doubt!

We shook hands.

Simultaneously, our mouths opened – to what? Issue an invite? Suggest a rendezvous? Or just, you know – establish parameters?

Sorry for the sophistication!

Anyhow, what the heck! At that exact instant, the door crashed open and the moment, if it was a moment, was lost. Suborned, as you might say, by a phalanx of large ladies bearing large trays. One of tea, one of cake, one of bread and butter already slightly curled.

"No jam, Renee?" cried Watson once more sailing forth with Ormulak in tow. "Where's the ruddy jam then?"

"Jam tomorrow, Mr Watson, sir," she retorted placidly. "Term starts tomorrow. Now who's to be mother, then?"

Rather surprisingly – at least to my mind – it was James who volunteered, and, with cups full and plates full, conversation turned to what friends had warned me would be standard Common Room fare. Prospects for the Llandovery match, prospects for the Monmouth match, prospects for the Brecon match. Prospects for the House leagues, Junior leagues, Under 15s, Under 16s – Under 99s for all I cared!

Unable to take much more, I gulped down my tea and managed to sidle away without anyone noticing – only to meet Tiny in the cloakroom doing up his flies. Had I heard right? Tiny? The guy was huge.

"Right then, we'll see you, shall we?"

So was the voice.

"See me?"

"The Fox at six. Can't miss it, left at the graveyard. Own arrows, is it?"

"Actually…" I began.

"Or maybe you're not unpacked. No problem. Jimbo's ducked out. Time of the month."

"Tough luck!" I shrugged, unaware that males had times of the month, unaware that pubs permitted archery, unaware of anything really except that just before six I must turn left at some graveyard (unspecified) and take things as they come.

Things turned out to be pints, vast foaming pints, just as arrows turned out to be nothing more romantic than darts. And as for things & coming – well, first a word about The Fox, a far outpost of Garne's Oxford & Burford brewery. The only way I can do it justice is to describe it as pure Skelton. Thatched, stone paved, below street level, its single low-ceilinged bar boasted little by way of frivolity except a triangular fish tank containing a shoal of what, but for their jostling here and there at every shadow, would have resembled miniscule bulls-eyes. The counter at the far side was long and dark, and behind it stood half a dozen barrels on trestles, each chocked and tilted at its own peculiar angle. Above hovered a shelf displaying a bottle or two and some packets of Players whilst on the counter itself lay a Perspex-covered tray containing a single cheese roll.

That cheese roll was to become an obsession with me during my time at Tolverton. There were apparently never two for sale – certainly never three – but neither did the tray ever languish empty. Nor did I ever witness anyone auccumb to its blandishments. Sometimes the cheese was dark, sometimes the cheese was pale. On market days a sprig of parsley would lie athwart its dusty crust. But otherwise, as an institution, it never varied. Plump and improbable, it reclined there in solitary state, defying even the most starving of punters with its sheer hauteur. Clearly, were the worst ever to happen, the skies dark, and thunder threatening, woe betide both Fox and ravener!

Nevertheless I swore to myself the most profound and secret of oaths. That on my last day in Tolverton I would brave the Furies and not only order the thing, but consume it with a flourish down to the last crumb.

That I was, ultimately, denied this recklessness, that my pledge turned out never to be fulfilled is, of course, a matter for somewhat later in these pages. One year and almost three months later, if you must have it precise.

And precision – though of the oddest kind – was, as it soon became clear, the keynote of this strange pub. For no glass was ever filled from just one tap. Five of the six barrels contained the same ale, one of only two sold there. Crafting wallop had clearly become an actor's art with Cedric the landlord. A gurgle from here, a gargle from there – and the froth would be held up to a candle to be inspected. Then a long effusion from a third tap, and sometimes a fourth, would bring matters to a head. At which the creation in all its glory would be presented to you on a salver as if vintage port, whilst your one and threepence was collected with a knuckle to the forehead and a low deferential bow. Two if you came from Dr Amberley's.

After negotiating the dimly lit alley between St Tywyn's and the cinema, I was not a little chuffed to find myself at The Fox, bang on time for my first social in this new world. Bang on time, that is, as I understood it.

"Late is it, then?" barked Tiny, though not unkindly. "You'll have to buck your ideas up, boyo. None of this slacking now."

"Really?" I replied nonplussed. The clock said ten past six, didn't it? And wasn't Lady Troubridge – indeed every book on etiquette – witheringly clear on the propriety of not arriving at an evening date except between nine and eleven minutes past the specified time? Wherein had I erred? What exact faux pas had I committed?

All I could assume was that London rules ceased to count at that lofty border five miles away – but what on earth replaced them? Should one arrive ten minutes early? Or an hour? Or what? But though these questions irked, something far more ominous was beginning to dawn on me. For the table, besides its overflowing ash tray, was clearly playing host to no fewer than half a dozen huge glasses. Two empty, two nearly empty and two, by the vacant chair, horribly and stomach-churningly full.

Disaster! And for that matter – was Tolverton time two hours early, or was one expected to pour a pint down one's throat every seven minutes, regular as clockwork?

Callow though I may seem for confessing as much, up to that moment I had never been confronted with glasses so utterly Norse. The silver tankards at college had held a chaste third of a pint – and boy didn't the buttery staff frown daggers on the rare occasions one ordered two! Likewise at The Ram & Stag where halves had been the general rule. Halves drunk thoughtfully and sedately, indeed so sedately that one rarely ended an evening more than half a crown out of pocket.

Now it was a rather different prospect which loomed: the contents of my purse destined for Cedric's till, the contents of my gut destined for Cedric's flowerbed. Does puke improve begonias? I remember quite clearly asking myself the question as I took my first draught of the abominable brew which passed for IPA in Tolverton and those parts. But at least, I comforted myself as my intestines began to swell and glow, at least there's something they've forgotten.

With a bit of discipline, disgrace might be avoided where beer was concerned. No way with the darts. Thank God they've forgotten the darts.

Not a bit of it! Gut full and unsuspecting, I must have been close to coma when suddenly, an hour or so from closing, Carver slapped the table. "Time, gentlemen!" he declared, reaching inside his jacket and tossing me a slim leather case. "By the bye," he added without a trace of insobriety, "these are an heirloom or something. Make sure you let him have them back in the morning, right?"

"James?" I queried.

"Oh quite! James, James, Morrison, Morrison, Wetherby, George…"

"Shut the hell up Tiny!"

"…Duprat!" Tiny's attempt at a Chelsea accent was rendered all the more hilarious for the touch of malice which lurked behind its incompetence – but I was too disturbed to laugh. I'd begun, as the hours slipped by, to get the measure of this prize pair, and, concomitantly, a growing conviction that the evening would end in humilation. For hadn't most of the session so far involved character assassination of one kind or other?

There exists, Blake assures us, a class of men whose sole delight is in destroying – and for my money, Tiny and The Carve, fell fair and square into this category. Perhaps Messrs Amberley and Watson could be considered fair game for their jibes, especially in a haze of inebriation – though to bite the hand that feeds you struck me then, and does so now, as poor sport granted its ease – but unforgivable was their stigmatisation of anyone at all out of the norm. For instance the foreigners on the staff, especially Ormulak and Otto Kerns, his fellow Pole, or colleagues with some disability or other such as Rice with his one lung, and Tom Fairfield whom later I came to know well despite his plastic cheek and neck.

Worst of all, however, was their mimicry of Marchpane, his cigarette holder and clipped manner of speech. Not for them the homely soubriquet of Marcho, universally adopted by the rest of Common Room. To them he was Macho, and the source of all unrest and evil at the school.

"I tell you," had insisted Carver, stubbing out his fifth cigarette, "the man's a menace. Just doesn't fit into a place like this. I mean, for instance…" He turned to Tiny. "When was the bugger last on the touchline? Bear me out, when?"

"Search me, boyo. I've only been here three years."

"There you are." A nicotined finger stabbed menacingly my way. "The man's a parasite, see? A sodding parasite. No concept of team. No idea what really matters in a school like Tolverton. Besides which, he's a poofter."

"What?" I exclaimed cautiously. "How about his wife? I've met her."

"Lucky you!"

"Never heard of the closet, man?" Tiny wrinkled his nose in disgust. "It's those sly buggers – they're the worst of the lot."

"Ought to be castrated?" I ventured dryly,

"Too right," agreed Carver, oblivious, like all fascists, to irony. "Take Macho, for instance. Masquerades as a clergyman, but do you know what? He wears…" Here a red face bent close to mine in confidence. "…silk underwear!"

"And always taking lads off in that old banger, he is," asserted Tiny. "What might a man of his age want with young boys, then?"

"Or young men," nodded Carver, putting his hand on my knee. "Take my tip – never accept a lift from him, the old bastard. Oh, and after lunch, never accept an invitation to coffee."

"Gilly's right." Tiny nodded. "Avoid it like the plague, that vestry."

"What's the problem?" I asked naively. "Indoctrination?"

"From a pagan like him?" Carver's sneer seemed almost to consume himself, like the Cheshire cat. "No, it's his filthy coffee. You can guess what brand he uses, eh Tine?"

At which both collapsed in ribald laughter, from which Carver was the first to recover. "Take my word – it's bloody disgusting. And do you know where he washes his teaspoons…?"

And so it had gone on and on. Envy and vituperation churned into a heady brew which might well have influenced some youngster less accustomed than I to the taunts and imprecations of the hairy-legged brigade. As it was, I'd had other matters on my mind, and not just that odd reference to Marchpane's coffee, though quite where the harm lay in Maxwell House or Nescafé was beyond me.

No, my bane all through the evening had been that large round disc of bristleboard over the grate, lit by a lamp, the distemper behind it resembling some leftover from the Somme. And now, it seemed, my worst fears were about to come true. As I hesitantly balanced one of the darts in my palm, Tiny called to Cedric for his weapons and the Carve's.

"Game's called Heckle & Jeckle."

How appropriate! I thought.

"To open you have to throw a double seven. Youngest starts." Carver snapped on the light.

My heart pounding, I stepped to the crease and stood there swaying slightly. The board was little more than a blur after all this beer, but adopting the stance I'd seen on TV and praying to whatever god takes this ghastly sport under its wing, I launched my arrow in the air – it fell to earth, well, not quite in Berkley Square, but somewhere even more exalted. Plump in the middle of the double seven, no less.

Joy unbounded! Nothing much mattered after that for I was the hero of the hour. Double seven on his first ever throw! Who in the annals of Tolverton could match that?

Eventually walking together up to Common Room, we gradually became all too aware that rain was staging a determined reprise. "Nightcap, then?" suggested Tiny. With much tact I declined, but was then struck by an afterthought.

"The cab rank – you know. Is it anywhere near?"

"At this time of night?" The Carve roared with delight. "You'll not find anything this side of Hereford." No offer of a lift in his own car. No solace with assurances about lightness of rain or shortness of walk. Just his accustomed pleasure at another's discomfiture.

"If it's a brolly you'll be needing, just help yourself to one from the rack." Rather more accommodating, Tiny unlocked the thick oak door, but almost immediately stepped back, flourishing something in his hand. An umbrella. And not the specimen I'd replaced in the urn after lunch, but a new one. A spiffing one. One with a brass ring gleaming round its neck.

Attached to it was a large official Royal Mail label: c/o Mr Bryant at Dr Amberley's.

"There now," said Tiny. "Left it up at the post office, you must have."

"But how did they know me? Who I am? Where I work? The whole thing's extraordinary."

"Not extraordinary at all." Tiny shook his head. "This is Tolverton, see? Like a bloody great Spider's Web, with the school at its hub. Every move you make, five minutes and it's public knowledge. Best to bear that in mind from the start."

With this sound advice ringing in my ears – but sadly, as events turned out, too little heeded – I began a rapid trot back up the hill towards Abercorn Rise. The lights across the river from Over Tolver made the prettiest of pictures but I was in no mood to dwell thereon. Certain movements in my gut vouchsafed that, ere long, I should need the services of Mrs Kent's downstairs loo – its washbasin or lavatory pan, whichever was the nearest.

Moving as fast as I could, desperate not to make a spectacle of myself in front of the traffic, I held the tide in check as far as the Abercorn turn, and beyond. But, key abandoned in the door, I'd had no sooner lurched onto the smooth pristine expanse of Wilton than suddenly my gorge welled up, categorically refusing further co-operation.

Quick – there it is. The loo door. Just time. Reach for the knob – turn it for God's sake, turn it, turn the bloody knob!

It stuck.

Fortunately He who fashions all things, the Prime Moevere himself, in his infinite wisdom so designed the umbrella that not only would it ward off rain, but, inverted, serve other useful purposes.

Over which we will draw a veil. Save to say that even now, when a shower causes me once again to unfurl said fabric in all its swarthy splendour, it's that faint whiff of Dettol which brings back old memories. The sights and sounds of my first day, long distant – and of faraway Tolverton and the odd folk that swarmed there. And foremost in the parade, not the backbiters and hypocrites with all their coarse stridency, but, fondly, the figure of the most excellent and equable, if gloriously weird, Marcho.

Moreover, let's be absolutely clear about it, never ever, even in one's direst, most caustic moments, Macho. OK?

Well, at least – hardly ever!

2: *Saved on the Sabbath*

Hands shaking, I viewed the slip of paper just pulled from my pigeonhole with more than a little consternation. Could this be right? Could this really be for me? Unfortunately, the initials in the corner made matters as clear as crystal.

PRB/Rhodes.

No getting away from it. My death warrant. And absolutely nothing to be done about it.

It was break on Saturday, and so far things had gone, how shall I put it - middling to well? My first lessons on Friday afternoon had passed without incident, jam had indeed arrived for tea, whilst by good fortune an evening appointment with my Housemaster-to-be had allowed me to decline a second invitation from les enfants terribles – and without any but the most transitory pangs of conscience.

Before me now, the canvas had seemed to lie clear. A free period followed by the doddle of library supervision. Then lunch. Then the rest of Saturday to myself. To walk, swim, read, fantasise over Julian – whatever. The sun was out again, the air keen and fresh – one of those autumn afternoons to revel in, and revel in by myself.

Or so I'd hoped.

This flimsy duplicated scrap changed all that. Terse and tabulated, with an air of what Shelley would have deemed "cold command", it comprised a rota for weekend rugger supervision, and – how totally asinine! – there on the first Saturday appeared the initials of yours truly in the column headed Senior Colts 'D', pitch 5.

Senior Colts? What the blue blazes might they be? And how about D? Delightful? Deplorable? Time would tell.

At my own school, Branwell Upper, soccer had been the game whereby the hearties had justified their miserable lives, but, despite its brutishness, it had had one merit: it was easy to dodge. As long as you changed into boots and kit, and clustered round the goalposts or similar, the staff at Bran's had been perfectly content. So one group might be busy emulating Stanley Matthews or, in later days, Tosh Chamberlain, whilst another would be earnestly discussing the sonatas of Scarlatti and whether Truman should go further and bomb Uncle Joe as well – or, for that matter, vice versa. We were a very liberal establishment!

Clearly, at Tolverton, a different obsession held sway, namely rugger, and one which was not, I suspected, to be taken so lightly – though quite what the point was of inflicting a complete novice on boys who'd been playing it for years escaped me. I mean, what were its rules? What were its conventions?

Still, there was no getting round it. Gruesome though the prospect was, in a couple of hours I must, with whistle, hie me across the river, there to take charge of thirty young predators avid for blood. It was enough to put one off one's cottage pie!

The lads would be boisterous, the field a swamp after yesterday's deluge, and in all probability laced with dog shit – worst of all, my glaring ineptitude would be revealed to Eric Amberley, ex-Blue & vigorous altruist, who was reputed to take his Saturday constitutional round the various pitches, cheering on the losing teams.

My only consolation was that it might have been worse. I might have been carded for the Sunday stint when, one by one, Tolverton played the local state schools. A pretty pickle that would have been. No Oxford, no Julian, and a full seven days before there'd be the slightest prospect of getting my leg over with anyone anywhere.

So it was that around two, still thankful for small mercies, I stood in my bedroom at Abercorn wondering what to wear for the coming ordeal.

Already an hour ago I'd seen Carver in riding boots and a stetson whilst other tubby and balding colleagues had been jogging round campus in track suits or shorts & jerseys, yet somehow they all presented a spectacle (and olfactory presence!) no man of taste would wish to emulate. I did in fact possess a pair of jeans and a kind of jerkin thing, bought for dinghy sailing, which would presumably have passed muster. If, that is, I'd been in any mood to compromise. As it was, I selected a blazer and white ducks, plus overcoat, plus college scarf and – why not? – my choice umbrella.

Best to start as one means to go on.

Thus equipped I set out, taking care to descend by a side road lest some antique Rover should just happen to materialise from nowhere and pirate me off in search of rare mushrooms or the last charcoal burner this side of Rhyader. At the memory of that spray, and the hiss which accompanied it, I shuddered. That raw unremitting hiss, like some marauding hornet! Today the roads were dry but something told me that, if the odd puddle or two did by any chance survive, Marcho would somehow and unerringly locate them and dash through their wash like Moses quelling the Red Sea!

I'm not usually superstitious but it was starting to dawn on me that normality stopped dead, right on the English border.

Waiting my arrival was a sprinkling of teenagers, still sleek in their Costa Brava tans, half of whom had been herded close together under an elm as if by a sheepdog. Actually it was their Housemaster, Owen Murdoch, whose tutor I was destined to become once Docherty had got his act together. Not that I'd so far encountered Docherty, nor altogether believed in his existence except, perhaps, as a species of Jorkins, dusted off whenever the authorities got into a fix.

By contrast, Murdoch was not only real but inconveniently ubiquitous. Slight of stature, sporting an RAF moustache though he'd flown nothing more warlike than a kite one year at Aberystwyth, he presented a figure at once peppery but faintly ludicrous. His accent, for instance – well weird, a lingo which might have belonged to an Irishman domiciled too long in Scotland, or a Scot domiciled up his own arse, I could never decide which.

Today this was compounded by his garb: a pair of floppy faded shorts which reached halfway down his calves, surmounted by a nylon windcheater in fierce red whose hood rose to a height and point not unworthy of the Ku Klux Klan. To say he looked like a garden gnome, especially one which had gone a bit wrong in the kiln, would not be far from the mark. So you'll understand how hard I found it to keep a straight face as I returned his wave.

"Might I present ma Rhodes squad?" he began in that peculiar constipated voice of his, gesturing elmwards. "Ye'll find Johnson a reliable lock when he puts what passes for his mind to it, while wee Travers there – well, he'll do at fly half as long as he makes sure not to trip over his hair, eh?"

The two lads thus lionised grinned savagely and looked at their boots.

"Thanks for the info," I responded cautiously, wondering whether to ask him for a loan of his rulebook, but curbing the thought in a trice. Just imagine it, the barbs in Common Room, not to mention The Fox. Barbs which would have reverberated down the years, accruing embellishments as each new season passed.

'Once had a chap here who thought scrimmage was a bloody card game – no kidding – played by virgins at the vicarage!'

Not quite how one would wish to be remembered.

"One thing to be vigilant aboot," persisted Murdoch, drawing me aside, his voice subdued. "Check they dinna dodge the showers afterwards, understand? I'm not having ma Hoose smelling like an Addis Ababa urinal, got it? Boys and soap, they're like opposite poles, unless you keep an eagle eye on the whole pack. Make sure they get well and truly scrubbit."

Keep an eye on them? Sounded like heaven on earth, but before I could inquire how far it was meant literally, he clutched my shoulder as, in the distance, a familiar figure hove into view. "Hell's teeth," he grunted. "Not the padre – he'll have ma guts for garters! Been pestering me all week for chapel lists. I'll have to make tracks. Finding our feet all right, are we? If there's anna way I can help, dinna hesitate. Big or small, just ask. That's what I'm here for!"

Breaking into an ungainly trot, he managed a few steps before turning round for a moment. "And dinna forget," he cried. "Scrubbit – well and truly!"

"No problem," I signalled, before rounding on my charges. "Right lads," I barked, my wits racing. The Stanley contigent, apparently abandoned by Binks, their Housemaster (sensible man!), scrambled to their feet and joined the rest. "Press ups, OK?" Sounded efficient, would keep them quiet, stroke of genius! "In your own time – let's get to twenty – now! One and two and…"

"My word, how impressive!" beamed the new arrival, greeting me with a wave of his Sobranie. "Promising bunch, are they? Stars in the making?"

"Who knows?" I shrugged modestly. "We've quite a useful fly half. And, er – a lock, you know."

"Splendid, splendid. Though somehow I hadn't seen you as one of the throng. The embrocation wallahs, that is."

"No?" I retorted wryly, recalling Carver's imprecations in the pub. "Nor me you. Quite a surprise, finding Holy Church over here."

"Ah," he twinkled, "but I've an alibi. Or at least an excuse."

"Better be a good one," I countered in the tone of mock admonition on which he seemed to thrive.

At this moment, however, a young voice piped up. It was Travers, red-faced under his delightful mop of gleaming, coppery hair. "Twenty done, sir. Want me to repeat?"

"No, that's enough," I replied thinking rapidly. What a metabolism the lad must have! "Tell you what, take charge. As the others finish, form them into their teams, pick leaders…"

"Captains, sir."

"Whatever – just get, er – started."

"Borrow your whistle, sir?"

"Right" – tossing him the lanyard – "get a move on, OK?" I turned back to my visitor who had been observing all this with an amused grin.

"Touch of the RSM?" he observed. "Mind out or you'll end up a Headmaster."

"Beloved by all!" I nodded. "But no changing the subject, thank you very much. Let's have it, this mysterious alibi of yours, and pray make it…"

"Improbable?" he smiled, flicking ash onto the grass. "Nothing so exotic, I fear. I'm just on an errand. From Clem."

"An errand?"

"To ask you to lunch tomorrow up at Buggleskkely, that's all." At which he broke out into a broad smile which somehow promised ribs of beef and gooseberries and stilton and all good things English. Mead in the glass, Elgar on the radiogram. Vases and vases of gladioli radiant in sun.

I groaned inwardly.

Just my luck to be asked when already booked. And asked, moreover, to what would clearly be a feast – one could hardly imagine Marcho presiding over anything frugal. But how on earth could I accept? True, Julian hadn't wired back to confirm, but neither had he ducked out. A date's a date, and there was nothing for it but to decline in such a way that I might be asked again at some later time. Like so many things, Buggleskkely Villa must wait.

"Fantastic!" I began. "I'd really love to, but I'm afraid I've sort of already agreed to head over to Oxford. You know, meet up and…"

He cut me short with an amiable pat on the shoulder. "Quite right, quite right. Observe the decorums – that's what they're there for. Spot on! Girlfriend, is it?"

"That sort of thing."

"Bonnie lass?"

"For heaven's sake – d' you have to sound like Murdoch?"

"Perish the thought!"

We twinkled in unison, after which, having repeated the invitation for later that term, he became suddenly pensive."

"Oxford!" he murmured. "You're in for it. What a haul! Coming back's all right, but going… Dear oh dear! Two hours on some dreadful bus then that brute of a line over the Cotswolds. Little more than walking pace if the rail's greasy, despite double-heading."

"Double heading?" I blinked, in awed ignorance.

"Obligatory, I fear, obligatory. Of course, if you'd been born five years earlier, you could have gone the whole way direct." And he waved his stick at a long line of brambles between the pitch and the river which did indeed smack of that indignant melancholy which tends to linger over abandoned railways. "Ten, and it would have been even quicker via Lydney and the bridge." This time the stick indicated a distant viaduct so graceful it seemed to have been there since the Romans.

"A hundred and ten, and I expect I could have gone by canal!" I quipped.

"Oh you could, you could," he replied earnestly, his eyes shining with passion. "The most exquisite of journeys. A trow downstream to the Thames & Severn, then Lechlade, then…"

In full flow, he seemed to hesitate, collect his wits, and return reluctantly to the drabness of contemporary life. "Of course," he said, "I'd drive you over myself if it weren't for…"

"Thanks a lot," I interposed quickly, remembering the deluge, that hornet buzzing round my knees. "That's very kind but really – I don't mind buses at all."

"You're sure?"

"No problem. Views from the top deck and all that. And you can meet quite interesting people, if you're lucky."

An assertion I remembered somewhat ruefully a little after one the following day as the single-deck coach – no upstairs on the Sabbath! – ground its noisy way over the border.

And as to luck, if, I'm afraid, was most definitely the operative word, for the company's clientele on this particular departure consisted of none but myself, a photo geek intent on snapping every scrap of thatch we sighted, and a very young courting couple. Young and evidently sex-starved. Their antics, on a rear seat across from mine, served as an apposite and rather excoriating reminder of just how long it had been since I'd sipped from the same cup – and it was quite a relief when, at a remote crossroads, they alighted, leaving me to munch my sandwich and reflect on the fireworks to come.

Julian had arrived at Arnos a year after myself, preceded by quite a reputation. Not that Oxford at that time hosted all that many Bransbians, but those it did, to a man knew Julian. An actor who also played for the 1st X1, an exhibitioner in Classics who also sang with a boy band, he was one of that admirable breed which in former times had both built and lost an Empire – that is, the dedicated, and oblivious, all rounder.

OK, our modern bland Americanised world has no time for anything so colourful, but in those days it was hip, it was cool, it was the image to achieve if achieve it you could. And Julian Copeland did. Or rather, given his muscular physique and unblemished looks, it came to him as just one facet of a popularity he'd enjoyed since first noticing that people tended to look his way rather than anywhere else.

And, unusually for those prim times, it extended to matters amatory. On the whole his inclination was simple: to go to bed with anyone whose interest in him was intense enough. Why not? As a prefect at Bran's, for instance, he'd fathered a son – the whole thing hushed up, of course, and the girl sent abroad – while in his gap year he'd not only survived a short and explosive affair with an elderly Count (possibly bogus) who ran a vineyard near Cagliari, but landed himself a contract modelling underwear in Romania. Even today, travellers in the more remote parts of that benighted land can find their morning brightened by Julian in Y fronts grinning at them, somewhat tattered, from grim, untended hoardings.

Our parting in June had been attended by the usual promises to write – neither of us had – and an ill-defined plan to visit one or two Etruscan digs which were just opening up on the Turkish coast. This I had eventually accomplished – he had not, having landed the role of Poins with the National Youth Theatre for their summer season in London.

Hence my present avidity: not just a natural keenness to meld with a lover from whom one's been too long absent, but also – curiosity. To see if six weeks in the West End, under the spotlight, had changed him for better, for worse, or in any way at all.

A quick sum indicated that six weeks amounted to close on a thousand hours. What proportion, I wondered, had been spent on stage, what on the casting couch? And if the latter percentage was high – given his charm it was probably mammoth – was there any point in my being jealous?

Correction: had I any right to be jealous?

After all, I was no Quasimodo myself. And if my quirky youthfulness had won me a contract at this quirky school in Wales, why shouldn't he exploit the even more quirky world of Binkie Beaumont and the sublime Noel? Sure, the theatre required slightly different talents to academe, but the basics were the same, let's face it. Since when did a good-looking teacher get stick from his class? Since when did a James Dean fail at the box-office?

Time would tell. After all, I'd have a full hundred and seventeen minutes to winkle out the gory details, wouldn't I? Ample opportunity given the customary Copeland lack of reticence, especially when nude. Moreover, since term had not yet started – he was up merely by virtue of being a member of the college XV training squad – he'd have had no time to get entangled with any precocious young freshmen. No problem – I should find myself with a clear run.

It was just after a quarter to five when I dodged through the lodge, and round the grotesque statue of King Edywy in copper green which dominated Arnos' apology for a front quad. Looking up, I checked my watch against the chapel clock. No room for mistakes. I must leave dead on six fifteen to be sure of making the last connexion westwards.

Like other athletes of his standing, Julian had been allotted rooms in a functional, inelegant new building known disparagingly by its inmates as The Pritch – not after some intimate disease, but a Bursar on whose former coachhouse the block had been erected. Nevertheless, what it lacked in charisma, it more than made up for in facilities such as en suite shower rooms, telephone points and central heating. Old Oxford was not, however, entirely neglected: for each room was approached through double doors. The inner and the 'oak', an outer defence which could be closed, or 'sported', when its owner was engaged in work or some other activity demanding privacy.

For what, I asked myself, noting that Julian's oak was firmly sported, did one need privacy at teatime on a Sunday afternoon? As but one answer could present itself to a mind like mine, I softly lifted the latch, found as expected my way unbolted, and pushed brusquely through both doors.

It's difficult to be sure which body I focused on first: Julian's, busy and steam-shrouded in his shower cubicle, or the youngster's in rugger shorts, sprawled on the bed, singlet in one hand, *King Solomon's Mines* in the other.

"Hi," said the latter, looking up from his book. "After Julian?"

"Sort of," I replied, adding mentally, Which makes two us, Buster, n'est ce pas?

Well, what could be more obvious?

And wasn't it reminiscent, as things go, of my first score chez Copeland the previous November? I'd got back around eleven from a late-night showing in Kidlington – *Good Companions* with the delectable John Fraser – only to find Julian in bed, holding court to no fewer than five hopefuls clustered round on whatever stools, pouffes etc. they could find. Since I had actually been invited, since I was no mere chancer with my tongue hanging out, I'd parked myself on the end of the bed, resolved to face out the lot of them. Fortunately my quiver of anecdotes is fairly substantial and anyone can make his conversation boring enough if he tries.

Boy, did I do boring!

One by one, stifling their yawns, they'd slipped away until only Reynolds and I were left. An awkward tosser, Reynolds – the sort of turd who never knows when to give up. Half midnight passed, then one, but just as I was about to embark on a lengthy dissertation re the difference between amplitude and frequency modulation in radios – even more mind-numbing than a chant at terce – Julian himself decided to take matters in hand.

For some time he'd been fidgeting a bit beneath his sheet. Like, stretching, stroking his arms, that sort of thing. Now, abruptly, he sat upright in bed and announced, "I am fucking thirsty." Reaching for a glass, he thrust it at Reynolds. "Simon, be a darling. Pantry's over the landing, on the left."

"Oh," retorted Reynolds faintly, clearly overwhelmed by the dusky six-pack so suddenly displayed in front of him, "but couldn't…?"

"And bring some biscuits. Jock often forgets to lock the cupboard."

Exit Reynolds. Straightaway Julian had jumped out of bed, he and I simultaneously heading for the oak, one bolting the top, the other the foot.

Nor had the Copeland subterfuge been altogether a total porky. Thirsty he most certainly had been – but not for water. His tipple was of an altogether less tame kind, although, despite the speed at which he pulled off my clothes, despite the initial frenzy of his tongue, what followed didn't quite accord with the overture.

Assuming they're highly sexed and well endowed, when most guys come, their loss of control is total and explosive – not so with Julian. One moment he was into it all, enjoying the shag, relishing the rhythm just as you'd expect – the next, there on his belly it glinted. The stuff. Nothing in between. No yelp of pleasure, no sudden acceleration, nothing at all special. Three albumenic gouts as if materialised by some music-hall conjuror. He might simultaneously have been chewing porridge or reading a logarithm table for all the ecstasy he displayed. Or put it this way – Eliot's 'not with a bang but a whimper' was clearly written after bonking with some earlier Julian.

Sans doubt!

Anyhow beggars can't be choosers, and on the whole our ups had exceeded our downs – or at anyrate been better than nothing. Now here I was, a year later, having to fight the battle all over again, just like before, but this time with one foe instead of five. One inexperienced little creep of a curly-haired freshman. Right-ho – let battle commence!

Except – well, somehow there wasn't much creeplike about him. On the contrary, his manner could not have been more bright and pleasant and apparently free from guilt. Obviously a feint! Cunning little shit!

He propped himself up on an elbow. "Fancy a coffee or anything?"

Proprietorial, huh? Knows where the Nescafé's kept already, huh? Tosser! "No ta," I smiled winningly. "Bad for the complexion."

"Sorry – we finished all the wine up at lunch."

All the wine? Orgies already and term's not even started! "So," I queried, hiding my antipathy with consummate skill, "live here, do you? I mean, on this staircase?"

"Not likely. No, Keble's my dungeon – or, rather, will be come October. For the time being, I'm just…"

At this moment, Julian backed out of the shower, towelling his head and hair with customary vigour. Though his long lean back was a magnificent sight under any circumstances, just now my eyes were fixed elsewhere. Holmes-like! On the interloper!

When Julian turned, precisely where would the youngster look? Or perhaps, how would he look, how would he react? With that embarrassment, however slight, with which an Englishman confronts another's nudity for the first time? Or that familiarity – that cosy ease with which you contemplate a well-known and well-loved set of credentials?

Julian turned.

All too easy. No contest at all. The lad fell into the trap, zonk, zonk, zonk. Hook line and sinker! "Surprise, surprise!" he said, flicking the other in the balls with his singlet. "Visitor from Porlock! Want me to do your back?"

Worser and worser! They'd obviously been shagging for years!

"Porlock? What the fuck…?" Out from his towel peered a bedraggled Julian. "Oh, Paul! Hi! You made it then!"

"Obviously."

Neat, that touch of asperity – slight but acid!

OK, Copeland's greeting had been genuine enough, warm sort of, but what did he expect? That I'd accept the situation, accept his acolyte like this, without putting up any sort of fight or redoubt?

"Good to see you!" Tossing his towel to the youngster, he stuck his arms in the air.

Those arms! Those veins!

"So then," he continued, "introduced yourselves, you two, have you?"

"Give us a chance," I replied, if anything more nettled as unlicensed fingers began to brush those shoulders. It was I that should be foraging there, not some wanker of a novice, for all his coiffure and freshness of face.

"Give us a chance?" Julian blinked. "Since when did we get so geriatric? Buck up Bryant! Toby, meet Paul who's deserted us for Wales. Paul, meet Toby, my bro."

"Brother?" I couldn't contain my surprise.

"Sure. What did you think? Oh, don't be fooled by those curls. He fucks like a dingo, don't you Jugs?"

"Except on ember days," grinned the other modestly.

Copeland junior! Though I could hardly let it appear palpable, my relief was intense and ultimately, I suppose, funnelled itself into the intense, unbridled bed session which followed – after, needless to say, Toby's departure. Even Julian appeared moved by my exceptional enthusiasm, and actually contrived to manage a slight cough before coming. For what seemed the most profound half hour in the universe I went at it like a refugee from the *Satyricon*, so that sleep, when it came, dropped over me like some dewy coverlet from Parnassus.

I awoke to the dusky aroma of Earl Grey, Julian, already dressed, and stunning in black tie, stirring the teapot.

"Hi, gorgeous," I said sleepily, feeling a bit like one of those basking sharks that float past Ireland as if in honey, "off to a Ball or something?"

"Rugger do," he grinned, pouring out two mugs. "By the way, here's that Virginia Woolf you lent me – bit over my head, I'm afraid."

"Thanks," I said, catching Mrs Ramsay mid-air – and putting on a brave face though, in my experience, a lover returning your books, can presage only one thing. And it's not that you're going to shack up together for the next fifty years!

He sat on the end of the bed. "So what train are you catching?"

"Plenty of time." I yawned, ostentatiously deep and heavy. Keen to get rid of me, was he? We'd see about that! "No hurry till the bell for Chapel."

"Cretin! Forgotten already, have you? There's no Chapel, nor early Hall out of term. And if there were, there wouldn't be."

"Wouldn't were?" I repeated hazily.

"Because of the rugger dinner, you clot! No Chapel, no Hall, no bell. It's twenty past six."

"Twenty...?" I sat bolt upright. Nine minutes to Rama! Just possible if I were already out and haring down the Broad. As it was...

In Guinness Book time, I was clad, hugged, and running for dear life. Forlorn it was as hopes go, but one had to try. Missing the 6.29 meant no connexion at Didcot, no bus for Tolverton, and spending the night God knows where. With zilch in my pocket, it wouldn't be the Ritz, that was for sure.

Hope revived as I sped over the canal bridge. There, far ahead, was an engine getting up steam. Maybe it's a Risborough, I thought. Maybe it's a Risborough running late, with mine behind. But even as I tried to fool myself, a phantom porter seemed to smirk in my face as he bowed. "No Risboroughs on Sunday evening, zur. Not since Mafeking, zur."

I was still two hundred yards away when the coaches began to move, slow at first but soon a blur. So what? If anything my adrenalin boiled higher. Here were taxis, and the junction a mere twelve miles away. I'd no idea when the Newport left, but it was worth a go.

We made it – just! Tossing my last half crown to the cabbie and ignoring his protests, I raced on to the platform the precise moment the express started to move, wrenching open a door and jumping into a compartment, which was, as luck would have it, empty.

"Safe!" I crowed, preening myself in relief. "Safe as houses!" I crowed, throwing myself full length on to the hard dusty cushions.

Foolish youth. Did Akela never warn you? That trusting yourself to an evening train on an English Sunday is about as suicidal as letting piranhas into your hip bath?

That soi-disant flyer was delayed at Swindon by signals and at Chippenham by a late running local from Calne. Fishplates were under repair before, and a semaphore gantry beyond, Bath. Finally we were kept ten minutes under the Severn, imagining that any moment the bore might come crashing through and incarcerate us in a watery mausoleum.

That thence we made up time and arrived at Newport a mere eighteen minutes late was little consolation. The Tolverton bus had long-since gone, leaving me penniless in a strange town, with forty miles of dark fields and hillocks between myself and my bed.

Or rather, almost penniless. Fishing out a few coppers, I gazed at them: not even enough for a cup of tea. Indeed there was only one thing they could buy – but carumba! Why hadn't I thought of it before? Murdoch – that offer of his the previous day. What was it he'd said? If there's any way he could help, just ask? Something of that order.

Why not put him to the test? Fortunately I'd tucked a list of Common Room numbers into my wallet only the day before.

Well, then. I was a member of his House, wasn't I? Almost. Under the Murdoch wing, in a manner of speaking?

What's more, now I came to think of it, wasn't he the proud owner of a Jag, a fast coupé which, according to the Carve, he never tired of showing off? Wouldn't he jump at such a chance? Putting her through her paces and rescuing a friend? Killing two birds with one stone?

As for needing help – as I stood there in that dank, deserted bus station I felt there could be no soul ever born who needed help more than I did.

Four coins dropped echoing into the slot. Finger on button A, I waited an age, my foot tapping impatiently. It was no more than a few minutes past ten. Surely no knight-errant ever retired this early.

Knight-errant? Instantly, an image flashed at me, of Murdoch sitting upright in bed, resplendent in a huge red nightcap, trimming his nose hairs in a mirror – a cartoon so impudent that, despite my predicament, I broke into an abrupt giggle which couldn't not have been heard at the other end as the receiver, all of a sudden, clicked into life.

"Rhodes House?" I queried, swallowing hard. "Is that you, Mr Murdoch? Owen? Paul Bryant here."

"There's no any need to shout, laddie. I'm not deaf, and I'm quite capable of recognising a colleague's voice."

"Sorry."

"Yes?"

"Well then, apologies for bothering you of course, but…"

"Quick aboot it, now. Ma mug here'll get cold. Nothing worse than tepid cocoa."

Don't you believe it! said I to myself, but meekly answered, "Well, it's like this. I thought I'd better let you know I'm sort of – stranded."

"Stranded?"

"I'm afraid I've accidentally missed the last bus. From Newport."

"Accidentally? Ye'd hardly do it deliberately, wouldya noo? Talk sense, ma friend."

"Sorry."

"It's all verra remiss – I wouldna make a habit of this if I were you."

"Oh, no?" I replied idiotically. This was not beginning auspiciously. "I mean…"

"Yes?" You could almost smell the acid of his impatience melting the bakelite.

"Well, I thought it best to let someone know."

"Why me, laddie?"

So there it was. So much for the milk of human kindness! Anything at all – wasn't that what he'd said? Crap! In fact, megacrap! But I wasn't going to let the bugger off the hook that easily.

"Don't you remember yesterday?" I said, trying to sound plaintive.

"Saturday, aye. What aboot it?"

"Oh, er – nothing." Predictable! Quelle creep! No way was he going to give an inch, the turd! I had to change tack. "Look, Owen – this is a hell of a jam!"

"That's the way of the world. Ye've made your bed. Noo you must lie on it."

"If only I could."

"What?"

"Lie on my bed, OK? Or yours. Or anyone's!"

"Bryant," retorted the tinny voice, "it's a wee bit late for witticisms, dinna ye think? Have ye tried the Salvation Army?"

A suggestion of such monumental absurdity, that I could only reply, "Wow, brilliant. Thanks for that – you've saved my life!"

"Glad to be of use."

Reflecting what a waste of time irony is, I took a breath before proceeding. "Mind if I ask you a favour?"

"Och aye?" Extreme caution, as if expecting to be asked to lend sixpence to a leper.

Wishing I could send a million volts down the phone line, I continued: "Maybe it's infra dig, but I'll ask anyway."

"Noo look here, Bryant..."

"Apologies for the imposition, OK? But it's like this..." I could hardly contain my delight at his discomfiture, as he contemplated the road south, forty miles of twists and turns.

"Let's be reasonable, laddie..."

"Tomorrow..."

"Bryant, I'm warning ye!"

"... if I'm not there first thing, could you possibly alert the Head for me? Tell him I'll make it back as soon as I can?"

Now came a protracted silence as relief seemed to flood down the wire in waves. Then he cleared his throat: "Why not? I can do that for ye, Paul. Of course. Happy to oblige, ma friend."

"Thanks," I retorted archly, "a million. Do the same for you one day. Sweet dreams!" And I slammed down the phone with a bang.

Well – I wasn't going to beg. Not to some bastard of a pixie with a big head and no brains!

OK, amour propre preserved – but still the night was cold, and I was getting bloody hungry.

These grand gestures! How sterling they feel while being made, how hollow a minute later. What on earth was I to do now? I was flat broke, this was way before the days of credit card and my cheque book, for what that was worth, lay ten leagues away beyond man's life, snug in my sock drawer.

As it happened, earlier in the summer I'd seen one of the first of those Hollywood road movies which were to become all the rage years later as the sixties began to swing. The sort of picaresque thing where a couple of dudes hitch their way to California, pick up girls, do coke and stuff, till one ends up dead, the other a movie star.

To be frank, neither prospect – and I mean neither – seemed particularly appealing at the moment. Moreover it hadn't escaped me that thumbing a lift at night in Wales might prove rather more difficult than amid orange groves, with your shirt open, and the sun ablaze. What option had I though? What else could I do but give it a try?

Selecting the most likely road – Usk, I think the sign said – I turned to face the headlights, and tried to put out my thumb. Tried hard. Tried as hard as I could, but, like Marcho's trafficator, it preferred not to budge. Hunching my shoulders, I turned back to the shadows.

A minute or two screwing up courage, then I tried again. Same result.

English reticence! Tightness of arse, tightness of brain, tightness gulling one's whole being into a useless respectability which gets you nowhere. Bugger it! Bugger!

A third time I tried. This time the thumb came out, but in a half-hearted sort of way. Besides which it had now started to rain again. What I must have looked like I've no idea. Only not James Dean or Steve McQueen with their slick boots and audacious grins. If only I'd had a saddle over my shoulder. Tight blue jeans and a chunky chain round my neck.

I suppose I must have kept it up for a while. A few lorries, a few cars – the more they passed, the more I felt like some obnoxious tramp – until, wet through and utterly despondent, I could stand it no more. Something snapped. Crawl on my belly if I must, I had to get home.

About half a mile back, I'd noticed a place advertising cabs. Not at all prepossessing, in fact rather seedy, it nevertheless had one virtue: it was open. Half running, half stumbling, I got there just as eleven was striking.

"Where to, mate?"

"Look," I said panting, "I'm a master, OK? At Tolverton. You've heard of Tolverton School."

"No."

"I'm a teacher there."

"You – a teacher? Come off it – you're not old enough to be a bloody prefect."

Flattered, I managed a bit of a smile. "Look, I've missed my bus and I've gotta get back there."

"Tolverton?"

"For my sins."

"Let me see, then." Consulting a tariff hung up on a nail, he gave a long portentous sniff. "That'll be seven pounds one and six, I'm afraid."

"What!" The price sounded enormous, a huge slice of my first month's wages yet to come.

The guy shrugged. "Forty or more there – back again empty? It's a bargain, mate. Tell you what. Seven quid for cash. In advance."

"Ah," I blinked. "I was coming to that. I'm afraid my cheque book's at home. Will it be OK if I pay when I get there?"

"Pay when you get there?" His face creased in amusement. "What the hell d'you take me for? Anyhow, we don't accept no cheques from strangers."

"For Christ's sake…"

"Look mate," he said tartly, "I don't know you from Crippen, do I?"

Repressing yet another urge to smile, I leant a hand on his desk. "I've told you – I teach at Tolverton."

"Prove it," he replied, rotating his phone in my direction. "Hang about, hang about", as I grabbed the receiver. "Fourpence first."

"Add it to the bill?" I pleaded.

"You must have seen me coming," he shrugged, waving me to go ahead.

I was halfway through dialling Murdoch for the second time, when I paused. By now he might well be on top of Phyllis, enjoying his biennial shag. And anyhow, his was hardly a voice to inspire confidence in anyone, let alone a provincial cabbie. There must be someone better.

Of course.

"Tolverton five three," answered a sleepy voice. "Marchpane here."

"Sorry to disturb you, but it's Paul Bryant…"

"Hullo there."

"I know it's late but I'm sort of stranded. The Newport train got in late…"

"…and you missed the bus. What a hoot!"

"Not really," I muttered. "It's like, I'm in this taxi office, and they need proof…"

"My dear, don't move an *inch*. Forget about cabs, I'll be there as quick as lightning. Can I pass you over to Clementine? Give her directions while I throw some clothes on. Newport, you say? I can do that in half an hour."

"But I only…"

"I quite understand. Just you hang on there. Bye the bye, how did it go?"

"Pardon?"

"Your tryst, of course. Curate's egg, was it? You sound a bit down."

"On the contrary," cried I, starting to revive. "Oeufs Benedict, as it happens. With truffles!"

"Splendid, splendid. Now remember – not an *inch*."

Only once or twice in the whole of my life, have I relished a journey more than that night's. Clem had somehow found time to make a flask of tea and cut some sandwiches of the most heavenly mushroom paté mixed with slivers of smoked ham. These she administered to me while the March chattered about this and that – before getting the old Rover up to seventy on the straight stretch past Monmouth despite the gusting rain.

And when at last I settled back sleepily and was allowed to rest, I noticed the strangest thing. Sure the puncture in the arch was still there, sure its spray was unabated. But now it *sounded* kind of different. Like a samovar simmering gently, its steam shafting up from the hob. Like some Persian lamp, hushing forth incense in its garden of a tent.

Contentedly, I stretched out my fingers and watched them brown and glisten as I curled them this way and that in the benison, the unbelievable benison, of that incredible chocolate fountain.

For one thing at least was beyond dispute – and well worth the angst and turmoil of the last few hours. At last, unplanned and all the better for it, I'd clearly made that rarest and most precious of things. A friend for life.

3: *Out on the Briny*

"You know what," announced Tiny, pushing his empty glass at James and scooping up about half a ton of peanuts, "you should take driving lessons, boyo. The Selby School of Slaughter."

Driving lessons? Moi? At a guinea a time?

It was a week since my first pay packet had arrived, prompting complex calculations under a midnight lamp. After my loan repayment, after hire purchase on my typewriter, after my rent to Mrs Kent, I found I could allow myself just four pounds a week without doing a Leonard Bast. Following him over the abyss, that is. And, like, take this evening – a couple of rounds at The Fox, what would that cost me? Roughly ten per cent of that princely sum, never mind if there were a midnight visit to the chippie.

Driving lessons? Out of the question! Of course, like most youngsters, I knew the rudiments from watching my dad dodging cyclists down King Street and so on. But as for mysteries like double declutching and reversing round a haystack, they would have to wait.

Yet Tiny, as always in his rough-hewn way, had a point.

It's almost impossible, in these days of mobiles and jet planes and the internet, to convey just how isolated at that time one felt in a place like Tolverton. TVs were still prohibitively expensive, my landlady discouraged use of her phone – which anyway was a party line, so half the town might be listening in – and as for the post, that, as I'd soon discover, might take days to get through once the first snow fell.

One had to be able to get out! Not necessarily to Oxford – my first experiment had knocked that idea on the head, and anyhow there'd been no word from Julian – but somewhere. Somewhere where one might meet guys. Swansea, maybe? Surely a place named after so noble a bird must harbour bars of the right persuasion – or perhaps Barry. Not that I'd ever been to either, but at least the latter sounded camp.

Half term would be upon us in a fortnight. Plenty of time to suss them out. Plenty of time to show Julian he wasn't the only fish in the firmament.

Yet even such relatively short journeys presented problems. Rural trains were becoming a blissful memory whilst what buses survived were slow and designed for pensioners and bumpkins. And even these, as we've seen, dwindled pitifully at weekends.

Tiny was quite right. Unless I passed the test and got myself wheels, I was finished. What a prospect! Desire and equipment withering, in tandem, to bugger all.

There's glory for you! No money, no sex, no future!

It's thus understandable that, a morning or two later, when Marcho peered round his *Church Times* and asked, "Fancy a trip?" I was all ears.

"Anywhere special?" I asked. "Venice? Marrakesh?"

"Much better," he twinkled. "Ilfracombe."

Now I don't know about you, but an English seaside resort in October is hardly my idea of paradise. What talent there was will either have hibernated till spring, or be loping around well muffled up in parkas and scarves. Pubs, restaurants, the whole boiling's bound to be either closed or desolate, the only signs of life flickering from the esplanade wind shelters. Those ghastly structures where geriatrics huddle deciding which bingo parlour to grace next.

"Sounds great," I retorted, not very convincingly. "What on earth are you up to there? Preaching and stuff?"

"Not at all – it's just that they've finally announced closure, the devils."

"They?"

"British Railways – whom d' you think?"

At which point the penny dropped. That conversation on the playing field hadn't been a send-up, or just a one-off. The guy really was a railway freak. And somehow it fitted. It was right. I could imagine him outside Paddington, perched on his shooting stick, dog collar gleaming, gaily writing down engine numbers and waving at guards on milk trains. Or at Public Enquiries, giving learned evidence as to why the branch from Fal Vale to Churley via Much Binding in the Marsh should not be closed and converted into an eco trail.

Religion and railways: the two great lost causes of the 20th century. Proper religion, that is, and proper railways!

"Right," I said, thinking hard. Desperate as I was, did I really want to puff up and down behind some decrepit tank engine all afternoon? Sure, there might be compensations. More of Clemmy's exquisite sandwiches, for instance – I could still taste those mushrooms! Or a young stoker, stripped to the waist as he heaved coal with all the might of his sinewy limbs. Nevertheless, as some sixth sense insisted, in such an enterprise it was ultimately boredom which would rule.

Besides which, where was this Ilfracombe exactly? Somewhere in the West country, I knew that much. But how far?

How long would it take? My slim knowledge of the rail network after postwar butchery sufficed merely to warn me that a jaunt of 10 miles as the crow flies, would probably burgeon to 200 by train!

As if sensing my reservations, the good padre lowered his paper. "Fortunately, the last runs coincide with half-term," he said brightly. "No rush to book. Tomorrow will do. Sleep on it, why don't you? Sleep on it and let me know."

Sleep on it – one of the most absurd expressions in the language. Why on earth should we suppose that snoring over a dilemma is more likely to resolve it than tossing a coin? All it gives you is more time to worry, more scope to consolidate your indecision. In my case it prompted me to do some research.

Megamistake!

At first I couldn't believe them. The atlas, I mean, and Bradshaw. Taking the shortest practicable route, via Bristol, Taunton & Barnstaple, involved a journey not far short of a hundred and fifty miles including at least four changes, probably more. Hours and hours of clackety clack and soot in your eyes – not to mention however long the Rover would take to get us to a railhead.

A trip, had he said? No way – it was a bloody expedition.

Yet how could I let the old boy down? Clearly he yearned for company. To disappoint a guy who'd been so good to me would quite rightly be deemed bad form – unless, that is, I could come up with some excuse. Not your common or garden fib but one ingenious enough to fool what, I had begun to suspect, was the quite astute mind enjoying itself behind that daft cigarette holder.

Next morning I was late in common room, judiciously dodging him while be conducted junior school Matins. Still unsure how to extricate myself from Ilfracombe, I needed more time. As much as possible.

Scenting steam, I strolled into the lobby, hoping it would be Frobisher.

It was.

"Hi, James," I smiled as casually as I could – not that it mattered. Like others of his kind, he was only too willing to entertain an audience. If I'd gone down on my knees and licked his hairy toes, his only reaction would have been an affectionate nod or gesture. As it was I just smiled. Tacit acknowledgement of his muscles and fabulous neck.

"Cutting chapel?" he said, kneading shampoo into his scalp.

"Why not?"

"Why not indeed. It's only Tiny in the pulpit so we've heard it all before."

"Right," I nodded, fascinated by the rivulets of white froth coursing over his shoulders. Down round his neckchain and pendant, and thence drip, drip till they met their very ample match – which, I'm glad to say, suffered none of that abject indecision ascribed in rhyme to the Grand Old Duke of York!

How tedious, that one can never remember which grows upwards, stalagmites or stalactites…

"By the way," he continued. "All that bullshit in the pub the other night. You know, while Carvo was taking a leak."

"Oh – like, driving lessons, you mean? The test?"

"Take no notice of Tiny. Believe me, you'll pass first time."

"Without lessons?"

"Guaranteed."

"OK," I countered. "D' you mind my asking how you're so sure?"

"Tell you afterwards. After you've passed."

"Fair enough."

"All you need is a bit of practice – and a fat lot of that you'd get from Selby. He's the only instructor in town and totally useless."

In the face of such certainties I thought it best not to probe. "Thanks for the tip," I retorted.

"Best thing is to borrow a jalopy, get up into the forest and jigger round the back lanes. Nothing to run over there except peasants and the odd cat. Borrow my wife's if you like. Car I mean, not cat. Just a little Singer run-around."

"But surely…"

"Don't worry – for the time being Sue's no use for it. Getting too big to fit in, if you see what I mean."

Involuntarily, he glanced down with a look of pride.

"Congratulations," I nodded, joining in his admiration. "And thanks for the offer. But, I mean – how about…?"

"The Fuzz? What if they stop you? Most unlikely, but you can borrow my licence too if you want. Just get the signature off pat in case you do meet some little tick of a bossyboots. Not that there's a problem. Just mention you work for old Amberley."

"So what?" I asked, intrigued by this whiff of Edgar Wallace. "Why should that make a difference?"

"Search me!" he said, laughing. "Unless – could it be that the Chief Constable has a son who happens to aspire to Cambridge?"

"What, Walmsley-Pope?"

"And who happens to have applied to the same college which nutured his Headmaster?"

I nodded sagely. "Voila!"

Well, there it was again, the Spider's Web – vehicle, roads, protection from the law. What more could a hoodlum like me ask? It was, of course, one of those offers it would be impossible to take up – but what fun it was to fantasise. Returning James's keys at midnight when he'd be in nothing but pyjama bottoms. Or getting him to come out with me, to guide my hand over a tiresome gear change.

All of which was delightful, except that for now it had delayed me too long. In came Carver to hang up his gown, followed by about a thousand others, the rear being brought up by Leyland

Trewes – my Head of Department, or Doggo as the lads called him – and Watson who was shaking his head.

"Absolutely impossible. All the way to Great Malvern just for a lecture? Nonsense. The Head would never wear it."

"But it might be the last chance," pleaded Trewes abjectly. "He must be eighty if he's a day. It's a miracle he's lasted this long."

"It's a miracle he ever got into print in the first place."

"For God's sake, Chris. We're talking about the Poet Laureate."

"Titles, titles!"

"But surely my 6th formers ought to have the opportunity…"

"Rubbish!" rasped Watson with finality, "I tell you no-one reads him any more." He turned my way. "Aren't I right? Masefield? Ever read Masefield, have you?" Then to James. "Frobisher?" Without pausing for breath, he waved a dismissive hand. "Of course not, old hat, passé, waste of time! And Frobisher…" consulting his watch "…do get your drawers on, for goodness sake – it's only a minute to the bell and the cleaners will be in. Come along, come along."

Out he swept.

"Thanks for your support!" muttered Trewes plaintively. "By the way, Marcho's looking for you."

"Really?"

"Chapel steps. Better not keep him waiting."

Nodding reluctant assent, I made ready to depart but not before turning to wave goodbye to James. He'd paid no attention to Watson whatever, and was still standing there, towel over his shoulder, sort of frozen – but, as he looked my way, there was this expression on his face. Really strange. Wistful almost, as though he'd recalled something, knowing that he must soon lose it again. Kind of famished. Then, as our eyes met, he turned back into the cubicle and I – well, there was nothing for it but to hurry off, busy, the dutiful schoolmaster.

Given the configuration of the buildings, what possible way was there to bypass Roy? Worse still, just as I turned the corner, the bell for first lesson clattered into strident life.

"Ah, there you are, mon brave," The usual chintzy greeting.

Breathless, I saluted back.

"Thought any more about it? I need to book today, if possible."

Wondering vaguely what there was to book, I assumed the tone of regret one uses when refusing a glass of cowslip wine from a maiden aunt. "Yuh, well Roy," I began, "I'd love to come along but to be honest – it's a fair old way, isn't it?"

"You think so?" The pale old eyes expressed genuine surprise.

"By my reckoning, well over a hundred miles. More if..."

"There's something rather wrong with your slide-rule, I'm afraid old chap. Besides comparatively little is what you could call open water."

"Open...?"

"Nor would I have thought you were the type to succumb to sea-sickness, or for that matter..."

"Hang on – have we got our wires crossed or something?"

He spread his hands. "Car to Penarth, steamer across to Ilfracombe, trip on the line – then the whole thing in reverse, with dinner on the boat. What could be simpler? Out on the Briny, With the Moon big and shiny."

"Put that way," I grinned in relief, "it sounds terrific." So it was to be a sea trip across the Bristol Channel. Choice! But why on earth hadn't the possibility entered my obtuse head?

"What was all that about a hundred miles?"

"As you said, dodgy slide-rule."

"Very well, I'll reserve seats at lunchtime. By the way, do you know it's five past."

"Christ!"

"Better hurry along or Eric will be doing his party piece."

Breaking into a run, I waved farewell and launched myself into the cloister. Past Clive and across the green – no time to inquire what the Head's 'party-piece' consisted of.

I soon found out.

Eric Amberley was one of that now-vanished breed of Headmasters to whom the notion of discipline was so fundamental that it could be exercised without the slightest speck of tyranny: in other words, with a courtesy and tact which enhanced rather than lessened its impact. When, for instance, like today he found a form awaiting a late master, he would usher them into their room and commence teaching whatever subject was scheduled. He could, it was said, turn his hand to anything from Zoroastrianism to the topography of Tunbridge Wells, and on this occasion as I arrived, red and crestfallen, I found him in high spirits, taking the Upper Sixth through a particularly abstruse passage from *Troilus and Cressida*.

"Like a hangover, is it, sir?" suggested a bright spark in the front row. "After a thrash?"

"Can we confine ourselves to the English language, Jukes – or thrash may take on a rather different meaning."

Polite laughter – a nod from Jukes as if to say touché.

"The root's from oblivisci, isn't it, sir? To forget." A handsome but reserved and rather anonymous boy by the radiator, brushing a lock of hair out of his eyes – the sort of kid you might cast as Malvolio if you wanted to stage a conventional but not totally moribund *Twelfth Night*. There was certainly a marked touch of disdain in the way he regarded his Headmaster – and, for that matter, myself!

"Just so, Marsden and here's Mr Bryant…" at which I was summoned into the fray "…to aid our journey from semantics to sagacity. Mr Bryant?"

Thank God, I'd been scanning Act 3 that weekend. "Well," I said, taking a peek at Jukes's text and trying not to sound cocky, "it helps to remember that the verbal force here is sort of passive. So that 'alms for oblivion' are in effect alms to be forgotten, or put in this wallet in order that they will be forgotten – i.e. not rewarded, despite the advent of some future judgment day."

"And alms, Jukes, are…?"

"What connect," replied Jukes deftly, "your shoulder to your cubitum, O magister."

A howl of laughter in which Amberley joined heartily. "A bright class, Mr Bryant," he said amiably. "Carry on." Though, in a lower voice, as the door was opened for him, "Kindly call at my study, 4.10 today, prompt."

Silence until the gown had whisked out of sight. Then: "You're for it, sir!" A fair-haired lad behind Jukes, not unlike Julian's brother in looks.

"And so will you be, Macdonald," I retorted regaining my composure, "unless you do up that bloody top button. And you Benson, and take off that scarf, OK? Now then, back to 142. Carey, Achilles – Jukes, Ulysses – Foster, Patroclus. And no Tony Hancock accents, if you please!"

By ten past four, however, composure was in somewhat shorter supply, though as dressings-down go it could not have been more civilised.

"Interesting class that," observed Amberley, still in his gown and formidable under a grim portrait of Canon Spoonwall, the school's founder. "Though as for the play in toto – Bard on an off day, don't you think? Only slept through it once myself. Round about '35 at the Arts. As it happens, my brother was playing Ulysses. Yes – just before he joined the International Brigade. Oblivion, eh? How right Shakespeare sometimes is." A recollection seemed to cloud his brow momentarily, before he sat himself upright and laid a hand upon his desk. "Don't remember much about the performance," he continued more purposefully, "except that the curtain went up on time. Dead on time. Important that, don't you think, Paul? Gives an audience confidence. Makes them feel they're in professional hands. Hands that can be relied on – that have sorted their priorities out. Do I make myself clear? Always, always – the curtain up on time!"

"Absolutely clear, sir" – nails biting into my palms.

"What does Manilius say? 'Delinquere semel et frutrabitur exspectationes'? You're the expert, of course, but as for myself – I've always thought that rather harsh. As long, of course, as there's no – second lapse."

"There'll be no such thing, Dr Amberley. Of that I can assure you."

More chastened than if I'd been locked in the stocks, I was in no mood to meet anyone, let alone Marcho who, however, hailed me from his car. "Want a lift up?"

"Thanks anyway," I nodded, "but I've stuff to do in town."

"Right-ho – I've phoned for the tickets, by the way. And booked restaurant seats for the way back. Nothing like dining in a sunset. Cheer up! Just think of Ilfracombe."

And thus it was early one morning a fortnight or so later, I found myself on a rather windy quayside while Marcho unloaded knapsack, notebook and camera from the Rover's boot. It was the first day of half term and here I was shivering when I should have been tucked up, enjoying a well-deserved lie-in!

In those days, there was no direct service to the Quantocks. You left on a smart white paddle steamer for the short hop across to Weston-Super-Mare, there to await the coaster for Ilfracombe. Though more substantial, the latter proved to be neither smart nor white, indeed rather grimy. Indeed not dissimilar in hue to the ominous clouds piling up in the east.

"You've seriously booked seats for dinner?" said I, peering disparagingly into the dingy saloon with its deal forms and long oilcloth-covered tables.

"Fresh fish!" twinkled my companion. "Nothing like it. You just watch. They'll have the lines out all the way over."

"And if I fancy something else?"

"I daresay they can rustle up a stew or something."

"Stew?"

"Cassoulet then, if you prefer posh. Now hold on to this for me, and we'll find some deckchairs, eh? Port side, I think, for the best views."

Disconsolately, I followed him up the companionway, his knapsack slung over my shoulder. Very light and thin it seemed. Not much by way of contents – maybe a pamphlet or some maps, but certainly no sandwiches! Finding a nook, a slight platform between a hatchway and a pile of lifebelts, we opened a couple of chairs and settled down.

What an idiot I'd been to agree to this folly – a thought which, I suspect, was beginning to occur to more than a few of our fellow passengers as the vessel backed out into the swell. No way did they strike one as a particularly robust bunch; in fact, quite the opposite. Mainly elderly, mainly couples, they seemed just common or garden holidaymakers intent on a last gasp of ozone before the steamers went into annual hibernation. What other motive could there be?

After all, the ship itself, a former collier of some 700 tons, held little intrinsic interest. Besides the dining room and adjacent bar, a tacky hole dispensing mainly Guinness and Kit Kats, there was nothing. No fruit machines, no souvenir shop, no brass band over the loudspeakers – none of the usual amenities which make an English holiday such an incomparable delight!

Nor, by the look of it, was haute-cuisine the objective of these particular punters. Almost all clasped carriers or holdalls from which, every now and then, they would extract a thermos or a pack of sausage rolls. Unlike Marcho, the prospect of fish, albeit fresh from the grey green greasy Bristol Channel, seemed to leave them colder than cold.

To cap everything, it soon became clear that in all probability Roy and I were alone in our quest. Certainly there were no Bradshaws peeping out of pockets, nor evidence of stop-watches, locomotive manuals or any of the other paraphernalia which marks out your dedicated train geek. Few, I suspect, were aware that a railway survived at Ilfracombe – fewer still that its obsequies were imminent. Marcho and I might well have to shoulder, on this sailing anyway, a heavy burden indeed – as sole mourners and eulogists for yet another morsel of vanishing England.

Burden, did I say? From my companion's expression, you'd hardly have guessed. Bubbling with enthusiasm, he fixed his binoculars on the grey coastline. "Isn't this perfect?" he crowed. "You can keep your Karoos and Karakorams. Give me a stretch of Constable like this any day."

It was then that we struck our first wave!

I had just been about to point out that Constable made a lifelong point of eschewing seascapes, and that anyway the tumult of clouds above seemed rather more Turnerian, when a sudden mighty lurch rendered any such remark superfluous.

The old lady seemed to rear up abruptly and, for a second, hover, like a squirrel on alert, before simultaneously crashing forwards and rolling to the left. A deep moan arose from the plastic macs and tweed caps lining the rails, a requiem intensified as the bows plunged into two more deep troughs, sending spray high over the superstructure and starboard deck.

By now stewards were emerging with piles of sick bags which they dished out in twos to the clutching hands. "Force seven expected, reverend," shouted a weatherbeaten specimen, tapping Marcho on the shoulder. "Best get down the saloon while seats be spare. We'll have mayhem later."

"Not up here we won't!" replied Marcho grandly, waving both him and his bags away – the latter gesture to my mind unfortunate given the rising wind, darkening sky and, by now, pronounced pitching of the old coaster.

To cut a long story short, we suffered nigh on three hours of it, part spent sheltering in Combe Martin Bay – at least sheltering was how the tannoy described it – before a temporary respite allowed us round the last headland and into our mooring. By then the decks were awash with vomit, and the gangways packed with folk desperate to alight, vowing that never again would they set foot off dry land.

All of which was viewed by Marcho and myself with a complacent and, I'm afraid, rather smug disdain. Neither of us had been ill, neither even mildly disconcerted. Only one little matter clouded our horizons. The railway.

The last departure which would have allowed us down the line and back before sailing time, the 12.15, had long gone, whilst the 3pm was timetabled to linger a leisurely two hours at Barnstaple before returning. What it did do, however, was to make onward connexions to Bristol, Cardiff and London. A rumour to this effect having circulated the ship, the road up to the station was now thick with plastic macs and tweed caps, intent on paying any price rather than trust themselves yet again to the storm gods.

"Good-oh," chuckled Roy, rubbing his hands in glee as he handed our tickets to the Purser. "All the more room at dinner."

"You're coming back with us, then?" came the amused reply.

"And why not?" retorted Roy as once again the steamer hit the jetty with gong-like force, sufficient to shake the very concrete beneath our feet.

"Force 8 forecast."

"Excellent, excellent. Let the welkin roar!"

"Five sharp then."

As I had even less interest in railway yards than railway trains, it had been arranged that I should amuse myself around town for a couple of hours while Marcho took his photos and made his obeisances. We'd then team up at the museum before repairing to Cakes & Ale, The Tinker Bell, or whatever the nearest teashop chose as its oh-so seductive soubriquet.

Amusement, however, was even thinner on the ground in Ilfracombe than I'd expected. A gin or two and a pasty in some pub, five minutes in Holy Trinity checking out tomb poems, and I was already at a loose end. So what was it to be? The waxworks, a tour of the lighthouse, or the flicks? None seemed all that appealing until, outside the cinema, I noticed in one of the publicity stills a face I recognised. An attractive, sensitive face. John somebody, wasn't it? Charlton, Charlesworth? Of course – East! He'd got the jolly old glands going in *Tom Brown's Schooldays* – maybe he'd do the same in this *Yangtse Incident*. Since his name didn't even appear on the poster, his part could hardly be prominent, but something's better than nothing, so I fished out a couple of bob and in I zoomed.

The auditorium seemed to be your standard 1930s kind of thing, damp, with a faint scent of dung and few customers. I counted twenty or so, but there might have been more in the balcony. The film had already started and I settled back in my seat intent on savouring to the full whatever few seconds of Charlesworth had escaped the cutting-room floor – oh, and as additional solace, I'd raided the kiosk and furnished myself with a tube of Maynard's wine gums. How boyish I felt, chewing that rubbery confection – carbolic acid the flavour appeared to be, but who cared?

Even more boyish were my feelings when, after half an hour or so, the seat on my left was silently and creepily taken by a mac man.

D' you get my point? Nowhere else downstairs could two people be seen sitting next to each other, except a couple of elderly ladies in the third row. Around us yawned acre upon acre of empty seats. An absolute surfeit, one might say, of vacant places. This cove with his buff mackintosh could have taken his pick of any prime location in the cinema, stretched out, enjoyed the comfort of an entire block to himself. Watched the film in total and undiluted luxury as though the last man in the world. Or a Roman emperor.

Instead he'd chosen me!

Here we go! I thought. First the mac, then the knee. Does nothing ever change? There must be a manual they consult, or something.

As a lad in London cinemas, part of growing up had been learning how to deal with the mac men. Paedophiles I suppose you'd call them now. To us, they were simply saddos whose overtures could easily be avoided – once you moved your seat, they never followed – but who sometimes added frisson to an otherwise tedious movie. The technique never varied. First the mac, which would start to inch across, bridging his lap with yours. Then the knee, which would start to nudge your leg, causing, in my case at anyrate, intense erotic excitement.

The third stage, I was informed by boys more adventurous than myself, was the hand. Personally, well aware how dodgy my self-control was, I never allowed things to get that far. And as my informants were reluctant to go into detail, what transpired thereafter had remained a tantalising closed book.

OK – was this at last my chance to find out?

At first, the prospect was just something to be toyed with, a wild stupid joke. For Christ's sake, I was nearly twenty three, not some twiglet in short trousers! But, as happens so often with sex, two other factors insisted on having their say.

One, a sense of flattery – in the dark at least the guy had mistaken my slimness and unruly hair for that of a teenager. Ace! I could still pull – I was still in with a chance, viable, not past it!

Two, that stab – that sudden stab of sexual arousal that does its own thing when it wants, where it wants. Remember, it was aeons since I'd been with anyone, so who could blame me?

A sideways glance told me that the guy was passable: youngish, lean, clean, and close shaven. So when I felt the first touch of his leg it was like, I don't know – sort of out of this world. Irresistible. Total bliss. There was no way I could flinch. Nor at the second nudge. Nor the third.

At the fourth, I responded with slight pressure from my side – to be rewarded after a few seconds by his hand on my crotch, lightly, not threateningly, just enough for him to ascertain the state of play. Which was, I might say, more spectacular than anything I'd managed for months.

So this was stage three. Quo vadis, then, meinheer?

He took a quick look round, gave my nuts a deft squeeze which sent them crazy, rose and headed down the side aisle to the Gents. This was to the left side of the screen under an illuminated clock. And there in the doorway he paused, gazing back with that same primeval look James had blitzed me that day in the shower.

I sort of half got up – he nodded and went through. But as I made my way along the row, not at all concerned if anyone was watching, lo and behold, what suddenly flashed up before my eyes, vast, close, brilliant in black and white?

Charlesworth! Charlesworth on some warship or other, with sirens sounding.

I paused. It was the shortest of scenes but it was enough. There he was in a white top, innocent, virginal, confessing to an older rating his fears of the impending battle. Everything about him seemed clean and fresh and hopeful – and in total contrast to what awaited me. Sex in the urinals, love amidst the piss, the grubby noisome interface between flesh and spirit.

It was, as I say, enough. I turned and made for the foyer in a scurry of self disgust, wondering if Marcho would notice anything. At least, I consoled myself, I'd have an hour or so to get my face straight and drum up some sort of story. How much I'd enjoyed the view from the lighthouse, or the waxworks display. How much like Hitler Hitler had looked.

You can imagine my discomfiture when the hour turned out to be two minutes.

"Ah, there you are," he cried, coming out of Boots. "Providential, my dear boy, providential. Just look at the sky. I'll bet my bottom dollar that boat won't wait till five. Not if she wants to get home tonight, eh?"

No answer seemed expected so we pressed on to the quay where sure enough the boat was making ready to sail. Marcho put a foot on the gangplank before once more thrusting his knapsack at me. "Hold that, there's a good chap!"

"Hurry along, gentlemen," shouted the Purser. "We're just off – no time to waste!"

In the rush to get aboard. I hardly had time to notice that the canvas seemed to have swelled considerably in both bulk and weight.

"Force 8?" queried Marcho, gazing up at the black.

"Or worse. Inside, sir, if you please."

One bonus was that the barman was able to conjure up a bottle of sherry – revoltingly sweet, of course – and as we sat refreshing ourselves, a deep rumble signified the engines beginning to turn. "We're off," beamed Marcho, raising his glass. "Good-oh."

An odour had begun to permeate the room of baking fish and herbs and what smelt like some kind of cheese sauce.

"Ah," cried my companion, "dinner. Won't be long now. I'm famished, how about you?"

It was easiest to assent with a brief nod, but food was, as you'll appreciate, the last thing on my mind. I mean, what on earth would Marcho have thought had he known how close I'd come to making a fool of myself in that cinema? And what right had I, stupid idiot, to sit here pretending virtue in the company of someone who'd never, in his whole life, trodden in anything like such shit? I felt about two inches tall, and it was as much as I could do not to blurt out the whole story and have done with it.

End of career – probably. End of friendship – certainly.

"Not feeling queasy are we?" he suddenly asked, with a look of concern.

"Fine and dandy!"

"In which case, I'll just dash off to powder my nose!"

But as he left, and without noticing, his arm brushed against his knapsack, knocking it to the floor with a soft thud. Picking it up, I was again struck by its weight and bulk, and, noting that it was already partly unzipped, couldn't resist taking a peek inside.

With a gasp of surprise, I delved further.

There, nestling next to Arthur Mee's *Devonshire*, was none other than a flat enamelled plaque in brown and cream proclaiming 'Platform 2 for Mortehoe and all stations to Barnstaple Junction'.

A railway sign. The old maverick! And purloined before the line had even closed. With a chuckle of relief, I shook my head. Here had I been numbering myself among the damned, and not fit to lick his boots, when all the time he'd been committing wholesale theft and deception! Well, maybe not wholesale – but more actual criminality than ever I'd been responsible for. I'd no idea what such artefacts sold for on the black market, but I guessed it was a tidy sum. On the other hand, so what?

Priests, schoolmasters and others of that ilk – isn't society content to underpay them all their lives? Does it really matter if sometimes they make a bit on the side?

On his return, Marcho – or perhaps Macho really was more appropriate – appeared a tad surprised by my change in mood, but made no comment, instead suggesting we go up on deck for a while.

By now the boat was well away from shore and breasting into the full force of wind. We found ourselves a couple of stout stanchions to hang on to by the bridge, from thence like eagles surveying the scene. What few passengers remained had either huddled themselves in corners where they could throw up discreetly or were stretched out flat on deck, moaning in dirge-like distress. The wind was too noisy to make out their cries. Pleas for last rites maybe? Calls for euthenasia?

Certainly not requests for food which must have been the lowest priority of everyone on board, except the indefatigable Macho. And of course myself, to whom everything had begun to resemble some dotty cartoon where only the impossible reigns. An abrupt pitch to the right caused steam to waft our way from a nearby hatch – roast capon, and treacle, and boiled sprouts.

Roy clapped his hands in delight. "Time to go down," he cried.

"But," I remonstrated, failing to suppress another chuckle – what a glorious fraud the old man was – "it's hardly five yet. You can't have dinner at five."

"Then we'll call it High Tea," he replied magnificently. "Plaice, chips, bread and butter. Nothing could be finer."

Than to be in Carolina, I added mentally, my spirits continuing to soar in the face of life's manifest absurdity.

They soared still further the next moment when a mighty swell caught us astern and lurched us sideways within an inch of foundering. Above the cries of distress there rose a brash and deafening and prolonged clatter as racks and racks of plates and cups and saucers, bowls, jugs, ewers, tumblers and tureens, broke loose from their moorings and smashed themselves to pieces on the galley slats.

The March was aghast.

A final solitary crash seemed to confirm the obvious: that not a platter was left!

High Tea or Low Tea, one thing was for sure. Food there might be in abundance, but as for anything to eat it off…

"Looks to me," I murmured, putting an arm round his shoulder, "as if we're done for."

"Looks to me," he replied dolefully, "as if you're right!"

Had we been natives of Borrioboola-Gha or convicts on the run, I daresay we'd have scooped the food up in our hands and gobbled it down without demur. As it was, we simply peered down the hatch at the crazy mountain of white, Roy stoically, myself in wry joy at man's helplessness in the coils and conundrums of the human maze.

A mood which persisted all the way to shore, and the Wimpy bar where we finally ate. No Trimalchian feast for us – just burgers with salad and double fries. And Seven-Up instead of Chateau Reyville '54.

And as I stripped off for bed that night, what image was it my mind locked on to by way of lullaby? Marcho with ketchup tricking down his cuff? Charlesworth smiling sublimely from a fifty foot screen? The Channel at full blast, spitting green walls of water straight at our eyes?

No way. It was that look of primal hunger, under the clock, in the shower – that vicious pheremonic thirst which neither words nor thoughts can assuage. And which I thereupon let myself kind of make love to, albeit vicariously, under Mrs Kent's silk quilt for fear lest, I guess, someday some youngster might spot on my face too the same deadly signs, the same most wretched of curses – the leer of the unrequited male.

4: *Here's a Health unto His Majesty*

Even at first sight, it was clear that Mr Selby fell into that category shopkeepers term 'damaged goods'. Not that he bore scars or limped or even suffered from a twitchy eye – like that of my old Economics teacher whose affliction was so great that he seemed perpetually trying to proposition the dude next to you.

Though come to think of it – maybe he actually was!

On the contrary, Selby was a well-made little man, neatly dressed and meticulously shaven, in appearance not unlike the rural squireens with which the neighbourhood abounded. Yet there was this air which seemed to hang over him. An air á la Croaker – as though doom lay in wait, just beyond the next Belisha beacon. No sooner had he ushered me into his smart Cortina than I noticed the oddest of his peculiarities. Three or four times a minute he would take a swift slight glance to the left, then flinch – as though expecting a Cossack to leap through the window and attack him with a coal hammer.

Most disconcerting! It was a nervousness which couldn't fail to transmit itself to his pupils, especially when combined with another quirk. That of crossing himself in alarm as soon as your speed reached twenty. Not quite what you expect when you're shelling out a guinea an hour.

As must by now be evident, on the question of driving lessons, Mahomet had at last come to the Mountain. Or rather, been dragged there by circumstance. And what was the last straw, the crisis which had finally persuaded me to submit and don my crampons? Well, for that we need to go back to the end of half term, which had begun so spectacularly in that Somerset gale.

The rest of the week had, as anticipated, passed with all the razzmatazz of a coma or protracted bout of narcolepsy. I'd stayed with my parents in West London and had much enjoyed watching them fall asleep on the sofa during repeats of *Emergency Ward 10* or Fanny Craddock. I'd visited one or two old flames, now doused by marriage. I'd licked arse with my bank manager. I'd swum at the council baths, only to find the peep-holes between booths filled in and impenetrable. I'd even – and this shows the extent of my desperation – spent an afternoon at Chessington Zoo, reminding myself that there were actually creatures in this universe less fortunate than I.

By Saturday I was more than ready for the journey back, especially as I had to change trains in Oxford anyway, and had promised myself an unannounced call on Julian.

There's something very reassuring about dropping by unheralded. If your quarry's in, you can preen yourself that the Gods are smiling your way – unless, of course, he's enjoying position 69 with some young brat from the Buttery. If your quarry's out, you can reflect that at least he can't be deliberately snubbing you.

Mine was out. I did so reflect. OK, but that still left the question of what to do for the next hour or so, especially as none of my other acquaintance at Arnos was still living in college. No problem. Given the time and given the day, a not disagreeable solution soon jumped to mind.

One of the best kept secrets in Oxford then was Saturday evensong at Magdalen and the organ recital which preceded it. Scholarly music, no entrance fee, and a venue sublime enough to disconcert the most hardened of atheists. Arriving a tad late, I crept pew-wards to the strains of Mendelssohn's organ sonata no. 3, barely noting from my programme that the virtuoso was an organ scholar from Keble. Doubtless some cub with more ambition than expertise! Still, his stuff was diverse enough. Buxtehude, followed by Boyce, ending with a Fantasia on 'Yes, We have no Bananas' apparently composed by himself. How cute, I thought – an estimate repeated and doubly when the guy bowing to applause turned out to be none other than Julian's brother, Toby.

"You total fraud!" I cried catching up with him outside the quad. "But congratulations, anyway."

"Paul, isn't it? Hi."

"As I say, great stuff."

"Liked it, did you?" Adopting a pose like Beecham, he began to beat time. "Aus – gerechnet – bananen…"

"Frabjous," I nodded, casting a wary glance around for proctors. "But why the pseudonym? Toby Whatsit?"

"Oh, on the programme. Can't you guess?" For a moment, the light from a passing coach made his curls glisten like tinsel.

I shrugged. "Haven't a clue, I'm afraid."

"Then I'll just have to come clean, won't I? Admit the shit. How about over a drink?"

"A drink?" I echoed with a mixture of surprise and chagrin, checking my watch.

"And supper?"

Too much! Absolutely typical! Here was I being offered bliss on a plate, an evening out with one of the best-looking guys in the cosmos, and what must my answer be?

Reality, reality! My last connexion left in just under half an hour, whilst delaying till tomorrow would mean paying out all over again. Twenty six shillings, near as dammit! Although I tossed a quick mental coin – Heads: chance of nooky but abject penury, Tails: chaste bed but bankruptcy deferred – I knew in my heart of hearts I had no choice.

Not the one you'd have made? Fine, but this is my story, OK?

And as the express pulled out over Port Meadow, I have to confess that could I have jumped out without breaking my neck, I'd have certainly done so.

Certainly? Well, probably.

'But it's not going to happen again old girl,' I quoted to myself grimly as steam canopied the ponies in white, 'it's not going to happen again!'

Thus it was that today, just a fortnight later, I could be found climbing into a sleek green Ford, Highway Code in my pocket, avid for expertise.

"This," said Selby, "is what we call the gearstick."

There are some men born absolutely & specifically, fundamentally & irreversibly, not to be teachers, and Selby, as I realised in the first ten minutes, was one of them.

Sans doubt!

Not only was his method prosaic and best suited to Eskimos with an IQ of 50, but his instructions were muddled and unerringly dispensed well after the expiration of their usefulness.

"Left here – sharp left I meant, not the layby! Oh well, never mind. Better carry on to the roundabout and take the third exit. Two o'clock. Or is it the fourth? Anyhow, there it is, down there." And a shaky finger would indicate some halfway point between a lane to the Crem and the Tolver slipway.

But above all, it was his nervousness which really took the biscuit. Not only the flinching and crossing, but his tendency to vastly over-use the dual controls. One would be happily pottering along when, about a million miles away, a stationary milk float would come into view. Immediately, his body would tense and one would be deprived of both accelerator and brake as he slowed to minus 5 – just in case!

An hour was quite enough. Stalling in Naseby Square much to the amusement of the Saturday market, and fending off his inquiries as to my next lesson, I alighted ruefully. James's judgment had been spot on, as well as kindly meant. Why did I find it so difficult to listen to other people's opinions?

"Beware, beware!" cried Marcho, approaching from the direction of St Tywyn. "Put not your trust in Selbies. Oh!" Rotating to the statue, he raised his hat and made a slight bow. "Beg pardon!"

"Selby?" I queried, spirits returning. "Your alma *motor* too?"

"Ha, ha!" he nodded, turning back. "Mine too. But we must be charitable. Perhaps it improved him. His bit of a crash. Let's hope so for your sake."

"*Bit* of a crash?"

"Five or six years ago. The chump allowed some prize pupil or other to open up the throttle yonder, down the valley. Result? Collision, first with a truck, then the viaduct. Two birds with one stone, eh?"

"Poor sod – still, at least he survived."

"After six months in plaster. I hear he's a touch more careful now."

"That," I replied with a grimace, "is one way of putting it."

"Really?" Shifting the box he was carrying, he nodded. "Well, I thought I'd better not trust Clemmie and the girls to him anyway. Taught them myself. All passed first time."

Amused at this preening, but realising what might follow, I assumed an air of polite indifference. "Well done," I said. "Super. By the way…"

"I could of course do the same for you."

"Oh, Roy…" I began.

"Unless you've other plans, of course. There's no mystery to driving – hardly anything to teach. The main thing is never to lose your head. Oh!" And again he turned and raised his hat.

"Not to mention Kipling," I smiled, eager to keep my end up. "But seriously, I don't even own a car yet. As you know."

"Use the Rover," he cried. "By all means, train on my Rover. She's an absolute pet. Massive torque and a chassis like the Titanic. You can get her into top gear at fifteen and she'll sail along like a daisy. Oh dear…"

Hopelessly distracted, physics and metaphor both bleeping in protest, I too glanced up as the clock began to strike.

"I'll be late for lunch. My dear chap, could you possibly do me a favour?"

"Well, I..."

"Just drop this into Common Room for me, as you go by. It's no great weight. The fact is, Clemmie's at home preparing a secret treat. Stuffed marrow, which does *not* improve with keeping. I must be on time to be surprised. Take care!"

Glad of anything to get me off the hook, I made no resistance as he thrust into my arms the black tin box which he'd been cradling. The usual wave and he was off to the car park.

True, as boxes go it was no great weight – also, by poking one's fingers through the slit in the top, it proved not too difficult to carry. Even so, it was a considerable embarrassment lugging such an object through the streets with no idea of its provenance or purpose.

Nor was its mystery revealed until the following Monday when the weekly staff meeting was held at break. Watson whizzed through the agenda with his usual promptitude before removing his glasses. "Now gentlemen," he barked. "Any other business – and pray keep it brief. Chaplain, you've something for us, I believe?"

Placing the black box on the billiard table, Marcho took a puff at his Sobranie. "I'm glad to announce," he twinkled, "that, after settling all our promises to charities, the Chapel accounts have this year produced a surplus. Quite a handsome surplus. Twenty eight pounds three and elevenpence, as matter of fact."

During the desultory applause which ensued, James and I caught each other's eye and grinned.

"With the Head's agreement," continued the prelatical tones, "I've decided to devote this sum to a rather exciting project. Indeed, dazzling one might say – though, of course, in no way meretricious."

"Merewhatsit?" One of the Carve's devastating frowns,

"A supplement, no less. A supplement of hymns to be bound into our existing books. There! I thought that might surprise you."

"My God!" groaned Rice, hand across his eyes.

"But," protested Murdoch, "didna we invest in a new set only aboot five years ago? *Ancient & Modern*?"

A buzz compounded about equally of support and dissent.

"Just so, absolutely correct," agreed Marcho, raising his voice a little. "But time flies. Though hardly Ancient, can you really call them Modern, eh?"

Supportive laughter from the older staff. Watson glanced at his watch.

"Added to which," continued the old voice, "some of the wording is really most questionable. Number 183, for instance, on devils. 'And though they take our life…"

"Luther," nodded Otto to Ormulak approvingly.

"…Goods, honour, children wife, Yet is their profit small, These things shall vanish all'."

"If only!" muttered Rice, nudging me in the ribs.

"Now there's barbarity for you. How would you like your wife to have to sing that next Sunday?" He beamed at the serried faces, most of them sporting a look of pronounced wistfulness, before tapping the box with his cigarette holder. "So what I need are your suggestions – hymns only please, no smut – and here's a receptacle, as it were, for your convenience. Deadline? Oh yes, noon on Friday. Now the sort of thing I'm after, if I can elucidate somewhat…"

"Come along, come along," interposed Watson, watch in hand.

"Well, words with a cutting edge, as it were. Tunes which inspire. Hymns which will really set the boys on fire. Don't forget – Friday!"

"Is that man for real?" queried Rice as the meeting broke up. "Set the boys on fire? Alice in Wonderland!"

"On the contrary," leered Carver. "Just what's needed. A blow torch up the ruddy backside?"

Tiny cocked his head. "His, boyo, or theirs?"

"Cheer up, Harry," I smiled. "It can't do any harm, can it?"

But before Rice could answer, the Carve, face reddening all of a sudden, broke in softly but vehemently. "Bullshit! I tell you, I know his game. All that clap-happy, hug-your-neighbour tripe. That's what he's got in store for us. Cutting edge, my arse! Negroid drivel and tambourines. You mark my words!"

Unable to take much more, I started to edge my way towards James who'd been pinned into a corner by Ormulak and Baxter, both brandishing hand-bells. I'd not forgotten Frobisher's offer of a car, whilst the arrival that morning of a date for my driving test made it imperative I get a move on. No more nonsense with Selby nor monkeying about with obsolete relics, torque or no torque. I needed solid practice in a sane car – fifty point turns, emergency stops, hand signs to the left, and all the useless stuff which keeps examiners in business.

Unfortunately, before James could extricate himself, I too was bearded.

"So what do you think?"

"Roy?"

"My address – did it go down well, did I make myself plain?"

"Oh, very plain. I wouldn't worry about that."

"Excellent! Well, then – I trust yours will be first in the box. And maybe you'd care to give me a hand on Friday to sort them all out. After lunch? Before our lesson?"

"Our…?"

"A little quid pro quo? One good turn deserves another. I've arranged for Clemmie to get home by bus so that'll give us a full hour on the road before evening school. Oh, and the forecast's fine. Not a drop in the sky."

"Glad to hear it, but…"

"Not that that would present much of an obstacle anyway – if the electrics fail, you can always turn them by hand."

"Them?"

"The wipers. What else?"

"How useful…"

"Only one hand, of course, while you steer with the other."

"Look, Roy…"

"And she's equipped with a starting handle, you know."

"Amazing."

"And picnic window."

"Every luxury," I nodded holding up my hand and smiling my lamest smile. "Can't wait! About half past three, did you mean?"

Well, what else could I do? What excuse could I make? And after all, maybe it was a blessing in disguise. Frobisher, though alluring, was married. Very definitely and comprehensively married. Who knows what an idiot I might have made of myself on some secluded twilight road, with his torso next to mine, his aftershave in my nostrils?

Yes, all for the best, thank you Gods. The pallid deathbed best!

The rest of the week passed uneventfully except for a deputation led by Jukes and Carey (an unlikely alliance, to my way of thinking), a rare sighting of Docherty in the Biology garden, and, on Thursday, a phone call from my mother which incensed Mrs Kent by coming through at nearly ten.

"I know ma," I soothed. "That's just her manner. She doesn't mean to be unkind but ten here's like midnight to you."

"How appalling. I've always loathed Wales. Is it really as bad as all that?"

"Look, love, this must be costing you a fortune…"

It transpired that today had brought huge excitement to Ombre Close and all on account of yours truly. Firstly a phone call for me in the morning. Then a letter for me by the afternoon post. Unprecedented! But, she observed, how nice that people should assume I was still living at home! Whom had it been on the phone? Sorry, he didn't give a name – or a number. But he sounded foreign.

She remembered that particularly. Foreign and young. Oh, and it had been a trunk call, one of those where the operator answers.

The letter? No, that wasn't foreign. Quite an ordinary stamp. Should she keep it safe or send it on? No, it wasn't OHMS or anything like that. No, she didn't recognise the handwriting. The postmark? Wait a moment while she found her specs – that was better. Oxford, of course. What a very nice envelope. College? Well, not a crest she recognised and the motto was quite complicated – did I have a pencil handy?

Plenty of fodder, then, to keep my mind active as I slid into bed. The letter was obviously of lesser interest. It would be here by Saturday anyhow, and would almost certainly turn out to be some belated circular. Careers? Awards? Who cared!

On the other hand, that phone call – now that did set the old gonads churning! I began to rack my brains. So far my forays abroad had been hardly what you could call extensive. Conquests, even less so. And as for memorable conquests (i.e.leading to orgasm) megasparse!

So what candidates were there amongst the fantasy fodder? Lukas maybe, but how would he have got hold of the Ombre number? I was always careful over matters like that. Same thing with Sten, and that rent boy foisted on me in Lisbon – in the latter case there wasn't even time enough to learn his name. Hang on – how about Xavier, nicknamed Alexis after the G & S romantic lead? At least our liaisons, such as they were, had been in England. Or maybe that other Cambridge guy, what was he called…? Or…?

I yawned and reached for my *Health & Efficiency*…

By the close of Marcho's poll next day, though the atmosphere in Common Room had hardly reached fever pitch, there had been some cursory interest, with folk popping slips of paper into the box when they fancied others weren't looking. Even I was disposed to bolt my rissole in order not to be late in the vestry.

This was, in fact, my first summons to the inner sanctum and I couldn't help remembering that evening in The Fox – Heckle & Jeckle collapsing with laughter at the thought of Marcho's coffee. Nor was it easy to refrain from following suit as I now observed, on the tray, next to the tin of condensed milk, the key to that joke of theirs which had so puzzled me at the time. Namely, a vast bottle of essence with a kilted soldier on its label.

Of course – I should have guessed!

"'Camp' do?" queried Roy, entering with a hot kettle. "I find it easier on the kidneys than the powdered variety. Black or white?"

"Black for me," said I, just about keeping control. "Camp by all means! It's just my cup of tea."

Sorry about that – tea, Camp, OK? Not that Marcho, in his present fervour, would have noticed, even had the joke been genuinely hilarious.

"Good-oh," he beamed absently. "Now, nose to the grindstone!"

By about three, we'd sorted out the slips from the toffee wraps, stuck them in a folder, and were sitting in the Rover, myself at the wheel. Yes indeed, the comparison with Titanic had not been awry. Even before starting it was apparent that her deficiencies as a vehicle for a passenger were far outstripped by those as a vehicle for a learner. For one thing, the bonnet. Dull and unpolished, it stretched out far into the distance, roughly the length of a cricket pitch – thus making cornering more a matter of luck than judgment. For another, the tiny rear window, plus the absence of wing mirrors, bid fair to turn reversing into an act of pure suicide.

Not that Roy was all that concerned. Much more interested in the slips on his lap, he simply pressed the starter and declared, "We're off."

Dindling around the estate roads of Feyhill proved easy enough. At this time of day there was no traffic, whilst the Rover, though heavy to steer and elusive to brake, did at least, as Roy had suggested, possess bags of torque. You could slide her straight from second to fourth, and that at a mere fifteen miles an hour. To be honest, it was more like driving a canal barge than a car and I settled back in my seat, starting to enjoy myself.

Then it happened. Roy put away his slips, lit a Sobranie, and pointed to a turning just ahead. "Now," he said, "for the real stuff. Hard left and foot down!"

Real stuff? That turning only happened to be the access road to the town's high-speed bypass!

"For God's sake, Roy!" I shrieked, swerving at well over forty towards a solid wall of traffic. Touch and go, but I just managed to insert us between a car-transporter and a football coach decked out in red and yellow, hooting wildly and flashing its lights. "What on earth…?"

"There you are," he beamed. "Well done! Flying colours. So now you know my method, eh? Same as the sanctuary. In at the deep end. Kick-start the jolly old instincts."

"Roy," I retorted, "you're not out training some bloody thurifer, OK?"

"Well now, I wanted to talk to you about that…"

With a loud grunt, I stamped hard on the accelerator, losing his voice in the roar of the cylinders. Too much – you'd think a guy of his years would know when to back off!

Nevertheless, after the next ten minutes or so I found myself beginning to relax once again. By now we'd turned on to the B road for Brecon with a consequent thinning of traffic, and as we began to breast a series of hills I felt a sudden urge to sing. The day was warm, the old lady was handling well. Could anything be more exhilarating?

As if reading my mind, Marcho smiled a secret smile and reached for a large black knob just beneath the dashboard. No sooner had I begun to sweep up the next long slope than he turned it full circle and sat back beaming.

"Roy…!" I cried warningly – but nothing seemed to transpire. No braking, no shudder of gears, no explosion of ejector seat. Halfway up the incline we were doing fifty five, smooth as a glider, with no other cars in sight.

"Take it easy," came the command. "Steady as she goes and don't change a thing. Keep your head – you're in for some fun."

Fun? It was absolute rapture. For as the heavy car swept over the summit, without any intervention on my part the engine died away to idling and we started to freewheel down the steep slope.

"Foot off the pedal," shouted Marcho. "Now you can change gear without the clutch, and whenever you need power, just press the pedal again."

It was like flying. Unlike most cars, where the engine is always engaged except when stationary, this pearl of a machine was able to transcend such mundanities and swoop o'er hill and vale with all the grace of a swan. And legally too. All was well, insisted Marcho. She'd been built that way and the law couldn't touch us.

The device, by the way, known as a Freewheel and limited (almost) to Rovers, consisted of a Bowden cable connecting the knob to the clutch which could, in effect, when turned, remove the gears from the chain of command. Thus in town you could use the clutch as normal – on the open road you could bowl along like a greyhound with the shits.

And so was ushered in a fabulous few days in which Marcho and I sailed across half Wales. As soon as lessons were over, off we'd set with a pile of Clem's sandwiches, not returning until night put a stop to such capers. Nor was it all mere pleasure. Every now and then we'd reverse into a farmyard or I'd try an emergency stop (not, I hasten to add, with the Freewheel engaged!). But by and large we'd simply burn down the long empty lanes of the border with my spirits as high – as Curly puts it – as the 4th of July.

And further buoyed up, I might add, by developments in the Ombre saga. Though there'd been no more foreign phone calls, that mysterious letter had been duly forwarded and proved to consist of an invitation to a party. But what a party! End of term, theme Roman orgy, and at – wait for it – Keble! Not from the elusive Julian but his dishy young brother.

Choice! Ace!

Clearly, my star was in the ascendant – I could do no wrong! The ultimate awaited me just round the corner, OK?

Back to bread and butter – with a little negotiation (the Spider's Web again?) I'd arranged for my driving test to coincide with Visitation Day, the occasion when sundry fur-collared members of the Worshipful Company of Fustian Bollers, Trimmers and Weavers came down from London to see if their pet charity still existed. As this meant no lessons, it was an ideal time to face the examiner. No-one would miss me at St Tywyn or the grand buffet lunch and, besides, there was the weather. Somehow the Gods always smiled on Fustian day, and I had no wish to manipulate Marcho's wipers in the teeth of a gale.

For him too this would mark a red-letter date, namely the occasion when his beloved supplement would make its first appearance in public. And Lord how he fussed. On several occasions I'd seen him closeted with some colleague, or one of the girls from the typing pool, reading earnestly from what looked like a galley proof. So too in the car, he'd peer closely at a verse, spectacles on his forehead, scoring out this word, adding that, taking care to keep his clipboard tilted well to one side.

No hassle. When he wanted my opinion I assumed he'd ask for it, and sure enough, a few days from zero, he stalked warily into The Fox.

Having outraged Cedric by ordering ginger beer, he strolled over to our table – quite naturally it, like the rest of the pub, had fallen silent – and, coming up behind, put his hand on Carver's shoulder. Enabled, thus, to assume an expression of extreme nausea without causing offence, that gentleman crowed merrily, "Roy – wunderbar! What a nice surprise! Hunting down recusants, are we?"

"Not quite. Opinions, as a matter of fact."

"No boiling oil? No glistening axe?"

"Afraid not – nowadays we just bore people to death. Far more effective."

"Well said," smiled James amidst the general laughter. "Good to see you, padre. Have a pew. How's it all going?"

"Getting there, you know, on beam. We've almost reached our target, and what's more, en route discovered some absolute gems. *Calon Lan*, for instance."

"*Calon Lan*?" expostulated Tiny. "Bless you, I first sang that at the age of ten. Five Nations down Cardiff Arms Park."

"In English?"

"And get myself slaughtered? Talk sense, man!"

Meanwhile Marcho was all undiminished enthusiasm. "Now what I'm consulting everyone over is this. Our dilemma! Now what d' you think I've chosen as number 1 in the new supplement?"

"'Three Little Maids from School are We'?"

"Shut up, Tine," grinned James. "Go on, padre. Don't keep us on tenterhooks."

"Well, it's what I consider the most disgraceful omission from the old book. None other than 'I Vow to Thee my Country'. You know, by Spring-Rice."

"Oh quite!" joshed Carver. "To the tune *Chopsticks*?"

"So I imagine," continued Marcho with a warning glance at the HJs, "the problem is obvious. Which is our country? England or Wales? And besides, how about our Sikh and Chinese contingents? Dare we risk offending their own national loyAlvies?"

"Mustn't upset the turbans," replied James evenly. "Perish the thought. So what's to be done? D' you have a solution in mind?"

"I hope so," beamed Roy. "That's why I'm testing it out. Collecting yeas and nays from around the staff, as it were."

"Go on."

"Well, my idea is to adapt. Bring Sir Cecil into line with modern sensibilities. Give him what one might call a tweak."

"Sounds," growled Tiny, "bloody painful to me."

"All very reasonable," said I as James again raised a warning finger. "So how would this new version read?"

Marcho cleared his throat. 'Some vow to thee their Country," he began, All…"

The storm of protest and derision was unanimous, Baxter abandoning the dartboard, an arrow still in hand, Trewes and Fairfield joining in from the snug.

"You cannot be serious," cried the latter. "That is *so* wet! Marcho, you'll become a ruddy laughing stock."

"Become?" muttered Carver, rolling his eyes.

"Talk about travesty!" agreed Leyland. "What a nonsense!" I'd never seen him so engagé – or irate. "You might as well start debasing Shakespeare. How about, 'This blessed plot, this earth, this realm, this United Kingdom'?

"That, my dear Trewes," replied Roy blithely, amidst a storm of glee, "has a certain merit, you know."

"Marcho!"

"Oh yes – a Scotsman might consider it an improvement. What right have any of us to cause offence? Answer me that."

"Fiddlesticks! The whole raison d'etre of literature is *to* offend. Aren't I right, Paul? Tell the old fathead."

"In a just cause," I replied with reluctance, "yes."

A burn of emotion in his eyes, Marcho took a step backwards. "Thank you, gentlemen," he said, finding a stub of pencil and marking his book. "That's all I needed to know. Yeas nil, nays five. I shall announce the outcome on Monday."

Refusing to join in the laughter which accompanied his exit, I popped out by the other door and got to the car park just as he was starting up.

"Roy," I said. "I'd hate you to think…"

"I know," he twinkled, "I quite understand. Yeas one, nays four. It's never easy to nail one's colours to the mast in public, is it?"

"Oh, but that's not…"

"Lesson as usual tomorrow?" And off he swept, one tail-light guttering, the other a defiant bright red.

Which left me, as would so often be the case in the next year or so, utterly perplexed as to what he felt and what he assumed. And perhaps that was his intention. No – at this distance in time, one can be more positive. It *was* his intention.

To be born in this brutal world without a thick skin is to be a crab without a shell. Poor crab, when the beaks muster at sunset. Poor Marcho, had he not been protected by at least the next best thing.

Enigma.

Over the weekend, in odd spots throughout the campus, this quaint debate rumbled on: 'some' versus 'I' – of all semantic quibbles, apparently the most trivial, yet capable of arousing passion in the most unlikely breasts. And interestingly, neither was it the case that Marcho found himself isolated, nor could his party be called minimal.

By the Monday meeting there was the same sort of feeling in the air that you get on General Election night. It's all about machismo. No way will the outcome affect your life in the slightest, all politicians being cheats and liars, but even so you're tongue out with euphoria, agog at the sheer drama of the thing.

The room was packed. Even Docherty was there, even Baxter, even Ken Tarn sprawled beside his sofa, purple cheeked, smouldering ominously at its having been commandeered by Ormulak and the matrons.

As Fustian day was nearly upon us, various diktats appertaining thereto replaced the usual notices, after which the March was again waved forward.

Leaning on his tin box, cigarette holder in his top pocket, he gazed serenely over the mob. "Gentlemen," he began, "and of course ladies – " at which he bowed low in the direction of Miss Frame, Mrs Jarrow and the one we called Irish, perched beside Ormulak in their prim row – "I think I speak for us all when I say it's time for controversy to be put, as it were, to bed. This very afternoon, the printers begin work on our momentous supplement, which, I trust, will invest VD with even more than its accustomed lustre."

The odd "Hear, hear" and some shuffling of feet, plus faint guffaws from Carver and Tiny at some private joke. Watson reached for his watch.

"Some vow or I vow," continued the old voice. "Simple words, simple concepts, yet for a week or more they've divided us. Now I hope we can unite behind what I might term the victorious, er – camp!"

Mild applause, marred only by Carver and Tiny again doubled up – and by Tarn cupping a hand to ear and declaring loudly, "What's the feller on about? What victory?"

Cries of "Back to sleep, Ken" and so forth, with Watson beginning to look testy.

"They are discussing their silly trifle of a pamphlet," explained Ormulak, not bothering to whisper. "Just humour them."

"Pamphlet? What pamphlet?"

"Really, Ken!" barked Watson, stepping forward, his hand raised to quell the jeers. "Where have you been the last fortnight? We're debating new additions to *Ancient & Modern*, all right? Hymns like 'I vow to thee my country' etcetera."

"Additions?"

"Now Marcho suggests…"

"Hogwash!"

The effect on the room was electrifying as six foot three of painter's smock unrolled itself and stood erect.

Watson clutched his watch more tightly. "I'm afraid I don't quite…"

"Stuff and nonsense! Why does everyone in this place waste their fucking time on trivia like this?" And away he stamped into the workroom.

"Well," observed Watson, "what would we do without Ken? But time to get on, time to get on. Chaplain?"

Despite loud thumps from next door, Marcho nodded and opened his notebook. "Actually it was a quite a close run thing. Abstentions totalled six. Those in favour of retaining the original text totalled thirteen. Those preferring my improved version..."

"Thought so!" came a yell of triumph from next door.

"Those," repeated the scholarly old voice, "in favour of..."

"How idiotic can you get?" roared Ken, stamping back in, a red volume in his hand. "Look!" He held up the hymn book, open roughly two thirds through. "Number 579. I Vow to thee my Country. The fucking hymn's in the book already!" Thrusting the volume at Marcho, he strode out to wild applause – and mirth!

I've rarely seen academics abandon themselves to laughter in quite the way Common Room did that day, despite Watson waving his hands, and despite Marcho, a rather tragic figure, staring intensely at 579, his disbelief streaked through, however, with a sort of irrepressible zeal – as though like some middle-class Gorgon he could somehow change the letterpress into what he wanted, his vision of the universe.

And that was that. Despite the high ideals, despite the fervour, despite the twenty eight pounds. After all, what can withstand ridicule that public and that intense? Marcho's cherished supplement never saw the light of day, nor had the Worshipful Fustians any inkling of the maelstrom they'd so narrowly avoided as their Humbers rolled in stately fashion through the streets of Tolverton the following Friday.

As anticipated, the day dawned without blemish. Sunny, hardly any wind, it might have been May instead of November. As I stripped for the shower, I hummed to myself in contentment.

Roll call and stuff was soon despatched, a second deputation from Jukes and Carey – this time to found an underground magazine entitled *Ché* – was dismissed as swiftly as the first, and I settled down for a final thumb-through the Highway Code. Plenty of time. It was nine thirty before I was due to meet up with Roy, then a couple of hours' warm up before I faced D-Day, whilst he harangued the Fustians from his pulpit.

At just past nine, the annexe phone began to ring. "Bryant, where's young Bryant?" shouted Watson, resplendent in black jacket and pinstripes. "Come along, Bryant, come along – don't keep the Chaplain waiting."

"Paul," said the receiver pathetically, "I am *so* sorry. Bad news, I'm afraid. Not to beat about the bush, the fact is – I've a problem with my knob."

"Really?"

"Bother that Rover."

"How dreadful," I sympathised, the penny suddenly dropping. Thank God I hadn't started to recommend an ointment or something! "Is it serious?"

"Oh, it can be mended all right, but not in time."

"Not for my test?"

"Hopeless, I fear."

"But Roy..."

"I know, I know. Mea culpa, dear boy, mea culpa. Checking over the car just now, I forgot one must only turn the Bowden knob when the engine's pulling. As a result, the cable's snapped leaving the whole thing in clutchless mode."

"So? You've said it's legal. Can't I take the test as it is?"

"With rod brakes and no clutch? My dear, think of it, the Emergency Stop! Suppose he signalled in the square – you'd be halfway to Feyhill before the wheels stopped turning! No, no, it's out of the question."

Even before the apologies had ceased, my mind had switched to fast gear. It's amazing how crisis stimulates the grey matter, and as I replaced the receiver possibilities were already jerking past me like flick cards. OK , so all the married men would be using their family cars to ferry wife and brats to St Tywyn. Of the bachelors, neither Docherty nor Tiny possessed wheels of any kind whilst Baxter preferred a Norton. And the Carve? Well, his MG was so svelt and spotless that to entrust it to anyone else would be unthinkable.

Which left only…

Only?

"James, hi," I began sunnily, clutching the receiver hard. "Paul here. Look mate, I'm in a bit of a fix. Correction – one hell of a fix."

"Calm down there young Bryant. Just take a deep breath and start at the beginning. All shall be well, and all manner of thing…"

"Point taken. Right, it's like this."

As usual, the old adage seemed to steer one back on course and, not much later than the scheduled time, I found myself skimming along in his wife's little Singer towards the ring road. The hood was down, the sun was bright, and Frobisher was sprawled beside me, looking as though he'd just stepped off some Hollywood lot.

It's weird how some men sort of exude sex in the most everyday of actions – like brushing their hair back or turning their head – and without necessarily meaning to. Without any kind of guile. It was like that with James. For instance, during the three point turn, how he lit his cigarette with all the starry panache of *Now Voyager*. Or later, when we'd stopped for a breather by the lake in Emmet's Wood, how he stretched himself before languidly reaching for a shirt button and tugging it, oh-so slowly, open.

"Fancy a dip?"

Caught unawares, I gaped in amazement. "Middle of winter?"

"Race you!"

"You must be joking."

"Am I?" He smiled – as it all flashed before me like flick cards again, what it would be like: his stripping off, his diving off the jetty, his coming up for air in a rush of spray. And wrestling with him, kicking in that icy sting, writhing in the clasp of those strong arms, being ducked, fighting back, with one hand to his pulsing neck…

Nude with Frobisher!

And how could I have possibly foreseen it, the irony? The exquisite irony? All those times I'd stood in front of the blackboard, vainly struggling to think up an example of prolepsis, and here was one coming to life in a daydream!

"When it's warmer then," he grinned, reaching over to press the starter, and adding, "By the way, have I shown you this?"

His finger indicated a brown lever like the handle of a bicycle pump.

"Um," I remarked, shaking my head, still on cloud nine.

"It's a special feature," he explained as we got under way. "A clutchless drive fitted only to Singers, allowing them to freewheel down hills. See, if I pull out this lever…"

"For Christ sake" I shrieked. "Spare us that! Anything but that…"

All of which – the turns, the stops, the faux sex, the déjà vu – conspired to make this the most bizarre pre-test stint imaginable. At length, however, I found myself shaking hands with my examiner, and feeling a vague but powerful sense of unease I couldn't quite put my finger on. It was just before the half hour.

"Well I never! A Le Mans, isn't it?" inquired Mr Swanage peering doubtfully at the little tourer. "About 1934?"

"About that," I concurred.

"Used to have a '34 Riley myself. Scrapped it years ago." He looked up at me sternly. "It is safe, I suppose? Steering, brakes?"

Only as I eased us out into Abbey Lane, with the sound of the school band floating over the rooftops, did I begin to relax sufficiently to realise whence my discomfiture stemmed. What it was that I'd found so disconcerting these last few minutes.

I needed a pee!

Not sort of desperately – not yet. But who could tell what the next half hour might bring?

I suppose a more confident individual would have pulled up at the cattle market – taking care, of course, to look in the mirror, engage the handbrake and switch off the motor – and announced, "Won't be a tick – must have a jimmy riddle." Thereby, in all probability, earning himself brownie points, especially if the examiner had declared, "By Gad, I need one too."

As it was, I tolerated. And the toleration grew into endurance, and the endurance grew into suffering, and the suffering grew into agony until, all tests completed except the emergency stop, my despair reached boiling point.

Weaving through the market traders into Naseby Square at five to noon, aware of absolutely nothing except the need to find a loo, willing to mortgage every scrap of all my futures for two minutes in a porcelain heaven, I found myself bearing down on a line of old gentleman in blue gowns with fur collars, a beadle in front, the Mayor, Dr Amberley, Sir Madison Moffat M.P. and Marcho in the rear.

In desperation, I stamped on the brake. After which – and I remember it distinctly – *after* which, a rolled-up newspaper hit the dashboard and I heard a voice cry, "Stop!"

Funny that, I thought momentarily.

Still in extremis, however, my brain abruptly switched back to wild notions of throwing in the towel. Making a run for it. Darting into The King's Head and hoping I could make it to the bogs in time.

And then, it happened. As he passed, Marcho gave me a wink and glanced upwards. My eyes followed, until they too came to rest on the effigy of His Gracious Majesty, Charles Stuart, King & Martyr, serene in all the safety and splendour of bronze.

A most timely reminder! Always remember the stoicism of great ones. Lifting my fingers as if for a toast, I bowed in gratitude. Right, Bryant! Triumph des Willens.

Despite the pain, I forced myself to go through the motions. On with the handbrake. Foot on the clutch. Press the starter. Off with the handbrake. Accelerate gently. And a salute – why not? – to the constable so politely holding back the vast wake of parents, Colonel Featherland and other lay governors, Watson, Carve, Tiny and the rest of Common Room who were goggling in my direction.

Nor did my luck end there. Coming to rest in the Abbey Lane yard, I glanced ruefully at Mr Swanage. Stalling like that? In the middle of Naseby amongst the cream of the county? Could there be the slightest jot of hope? Or tittle?

"Terribly sorry," he grimaced, patting my shoulder. "But I'm afraid I've run out of pad. D'you mind hanging on a moment while I pop upstairs for a new one?"

Did I mind? Within ten seconds I was out of that blasted car, round to a back wall, and hosing my soul out into a convenient drain. Earth hath not anything to feel more fair – as steam rises from that hard, bright arc of piss. Better than sex, better than booze, better than winning the pools a thousand times over!

Returning, Swanage plumped himself down beside me with a reassuring smile. "Just the Highway Code," he said. "Then it's all over."

As if it isn't already, I thought – but gave a confident thumbs up. Why lose face on top of total disaster?

"Suppose you were somewhere like Gloucester?" he began. "Say Sheep Street by the swimming pool."

"What, near the station?"

"Exactly. And, next to a pair of gates, you saw a sign with a red circle round an engine puffing smoke, what would you expect to encounter?"

I pretended to think. "A level crossing?"

"Congratulations, Mr Bryant. Your knowledge of the Code seems as exemplary as your driving."

Recounting it all to James on the morrow, I was somewhat perplexed by his response. The infantile Code test elicited a mild guffaw, the rolled-up newspaper an almighty one.

"Sorry," he spluttered, "but Paul, that's what they do. Hit the dashboard with a book or paper or something. Just in case you're hard of hearing."

"But that's not the point. He hit it after I'd stopped."

"Long after?"

"A second maybe."

"Then that's fine – all quite plausible."

"But it was *after*…"

"So what was the poor sod supposed to do? I mean, you go and stall like that in full view of the press and half the town – how else was he to avoid failing you?"

"Avoid? But why should he…?

"Paul, you are a ruddy dimwit at times. Just go down your form list for me."

"Why?"

"Just do it, starting at Macdonald."

"Why Macdonald?"

"If you say 'why' once more, you'll get a sodding dart through your left eye. Right now – Macdonald…"

"Marsden, Prescott, Ransom, Ruby, Standaloft, Swanage, Trebella …"

"Speak up there, old bean! Sewage, was that?"

"Don't be daft – you know perfectly well it's Swan… Oh, right! Point taken, sort of. But surely…"

However, since this discussion had begun in The Fox, and since the ale sparkled with that special vigour reserved for celebration, I didn't take all that long to convince. Hence, the most valuable lesson a youngster fresh from the cloister can learn: that corruption, at least in its more amiable forms, is by no means confined to Chicago, or dark alleyways or the boardrooms of the bloated. Look around and you'll find its blossoms everywhere, gilding life with their tempting veneer.

And since the poet enjoins us to do as the Romans do – nonchalantly, my fingers too strayed to my shirt and undid a button. "Now," I said, "about this race of ours…"

5: *Here Today and Gone Tomorrow*

With December came the first snows and all the excitement and disruption which accompanied them. Trying to cross the quad through a snowball fight was one hazard, attempting to avoid pneumonia whilst supervising touch rugger in a North wind was another. Nor, either, was there much possibility of mental solace: basking in Italy with Keats for instance, or Xanadu with STC.

Frankly, lessons became a nightmare. It might be mid-morning before the buses struggled through from the valleys, or Hereford and points yonder, so that classes were an ever shifting phenomenon – dayboys coming late and leaving early, and boarders exploiting the chaos wherever they could, with the customary cheerful nihilism of the teenage mind.

Correction: so-called mind!

On top of this, the impending end of term brought with it its own peculiar strains and stresses. The setting and marking of exams, for instance, together with the unfathomable intricacies of mark scaling in those days before computers, Ormulak's attempts to explain which merely doubled the confusion and left me a nervous wreck.

Report writing presented even more problems. Though Trewes and I relished dishing out vengeance in elegant prose, the more semantically-challenged of our colleagues, especially the scientists, found themselves altogether more at sea. And what was the surest (not to mention easiest!) way of checking a spelling or querying a comma? Ask the English Department!

Had that been all, however, one might have taken it on the chin. One might have grinned, sympathised and obliged, confining one's irritation to vandalising a Gestetner when no-one was looking, or just punching one's pillow at night. The trouble was, they wanted their errors, their obvious and pathetic solecisms, not just corrected but *explained*!

OK, you try elucidating to a fifty five year old Housemaster with a DFC and a 3rd in Forestry exactly what's wrong with his prize dangling participle! Or why it's permissible to omit the central e in judgment, but not in enlargement.

Ten days or so of this, and I was absolutely desperate for the vac to start, even if that meant a month entombed in Ombre Close. After all, there was Toby's party to look forward to, and at last I had a few pounds to spare. Eastward look – the land was, if not exactly bright, at least palatable.

With all this going on, plus carol services, House Christmas dinners and the like, you'll understand how easy it was for some of one's problems, the less pressing ones, to kind of retreat. Stow themselves away in some dark corner of the memory awaiting, like aconites, a more favourable climate. Thus it came about that late one Saturday afternoon, with all the cakes eaten and Renée busily stacking saucers, I found myself utterly unprepared for a bolt from the proverbial blue.

"Paul, my lad," called Tom Fairfield, sticking his head round the annexe door, "it's for you. Gauleiter Kent. Sounds in a right old bait."

Which proved a by no means unapt reading of that shrill voice. What right had I to invite visitors round and not be there to meet them? Did I suppose she had nothing else to do all day but entertain my guests while I swanned around up at Dr Amberley's? Or would I prefer it if she let all and sundry into my room? And would I take responsibility for it when they ran off with all the valuables I owned?

Valuables? Get real, darling! Permitting myself a hollow laugh at such gross hyperbole, I inquired, when at last she paused for breath, who 'all and sundry' might actually be.

"And what sort of a question's that?" she continued with her formidable asperity. "Is it my place to go asking the name of every foreigner just because he knocks at my door?"

Ergo: singular, male, overseas! "So sorry you've been bothered Mrs Kent," I retorted, my deductive powers taking a well-deserved bow. That curious phone call before half term, the one that had never been repeated – could there be a connexion? And exactly who was this stalking me? Mario perhaps, or Edoc or Lukas – no, Lukas had been ruled out, hadn't he? Still, why speculate? A moment or two, and all would be revealed. "I wonder if you'd be kind enough to put him on."

"I daresay that might be possible" – the iciest of tones, as though she fully expected this brigand to wrench her instrument from the wall, and make off with it to some thieves' kitchen in darkest Marrakesh.

The ensuing delay provided a welcome respite in which to get my mind in order. The guy's identity – sure, that was one problem. But how about other issues? More menacing ones? Like, for instance – though it was shattering to even so much as contemplate – the crime which dare not speak its name: bl*ckm**l!

Remember, we're talking of times well before the 1967 Act when to be found in the sack with another bloke meant Armageddon. Exposure in the press, professional ruin and, in all probability, a hefty sentence, breaking stones on Dartmoor. A sentence, moreover, which would expose one to short shrift from the criminal brutes who rule such places, and who feel entitled to confirm their 'normality' by beating hell out of anyone of a different kidney.

Dire vistas indeed, and boiling to a frenzy, when all at once came a metallic whisper: "Paulo? Is that you?"

"Alex," I cried, "Amazing! I mean, after all this time! But, what – I mean, how…?"

"Forgive me for not writing," he replied, obviously under some strain. "No, pardon me – for not having written. But last time, you recollect where that caused."

"My fault."

"Nobody at fault. It is just better that explaining is face to face, yes?"

"Sure, of course."

"Over – how was it you used to say? A jar?"

"Exactly!" I agreed, recalling with a smile his delightfully stilted manner of speech. Like dialogue from some pre-war spy movie set in Budapest. Not quite real.

But capable, as now became only too clear, of devastating!

"Paul, I cannot tell you what it will mean to me. My new self. To bring to you, reveal to you. All the changes there have been."

"Amazing," I said wryly, wondering if he'd lost a leg or something. Gone bald, had all his teeth pulled! "Can't you give me a clue? I'm all agog."

"Agog? What is agog?"

"Forget it. Look it'll be good to see you, but…"

"Good? No, my friend. Brilliant! For now we can be together, yes?"

"Great," I said cautiously.

"Now I have found freedom like yours. Thrown off the church like you. Its phobias and petty hatreds. Its barriers. Its denial of mankind's diversity which is so obvious to me now. Men suited to women, men suited to men…"

"Alex, mate," I interposed, trying to cope. "Look, wait a moment. It's like…"

"I must come to you at once. Immediately. Is best to take taxi?"

Of his urgency there was no doubt, but what was this turning into? A queer's convention? My smile began to wane. So too my elation. Were Commissar Kent bent at the keyhole, what price my career and reputation! Worse still – should any of the neighbours happen to be browsing her party line, who'd be first on the doorstep? The Daily Express or the Flying Squad? Probably both, and in about two minutes flat!

"Taxi?" I retorted, gathering my wits as best I could. "Well, it's quickest maybe, but bloody expensive. No, see here. I'll come to you. Just stay where you are, OK? Don't budge. I'll be round as quick as I can."

"You are pleased, yes?"

"Of course."

"Excited, yes?"

"Over the moon. Now, you'd better put Mrs Kent back on for a moment."

Best to face the music straightaway. Confront her at once, the old cow. If she'd overheard anything, even a morsel of this so toothsome exchange, there's no way she'd be able to keep it out of her voice.

"Mr Bryant?"

"Hullo again – look, Alex is an old, er…associate of mine. Could you sort of make him comfortable? I'll be back in two ticks."

"Tea, I suppose you mean. Or is it coffee in their parts?"

"Why not ask him?"

"I could do that," she conceded. "I must say, he seems quite civilised."

Quite civilised? Talk about damning with faint praise. Though what could she know of hidalgos and their world, of everything there was to surrender? So what! All that mattered was this: she clearly suspected zilch.

Moreover, it was good to hear that Alex was still his smart former self. That in the two years since we last met, he had, unlike his brother students, stayed safe from drugs and all that goes with them: dishevelment and stuff, that weird distancing of mind from moderation. My spirits began a sort of qualified mini-revival. Blue horizons and a new day could just conceivably, fingers crossed, be born. Or at anyrate, a bloody crisp hour or two!

Rushing back to the billiard room, I shoved the books I'd been marking into my pigeonhole and made for the door. But who, alas, should come bustling through in the opposite direction but Marcho, triumphant and flourishing one of the weekly papers.

"Just the ticket," he cried. "Thirty pounds for a quick sale. You couldn't do better. Drive you over, shall I? Clementine can spare me till supper."

"Hang on," I replied, pausing, recalling a day or two previously when, in a fit of madness, I'd enlisted his help in searching for wheels. Not too pricey, I'd insisted, but as pedigree as possible. After all, it would be my first car. In that situation, don't we all fancy ourselves outdoing Toad? Sweeping through the marches in some fabulous marque with pink leather seats, a loud radio, and an even louder horn.

Paradise!

"Look," I continued, images of limos and Alex, and Alex in limos twisting in my mind like barley sugar. "I mean – first things first…".

"My dear boy – a bargain like this? You'll have to get your skates on."

"OK, but make – Jag? Bentley?"

"For thirty quid? In your dreams!"

"Right, so it's base, common and popular."

"That," twinkled the old eyes, "is truly remarkable. You've got it in one."

"Really?"

"A Ford Popular."

"No way," I cried. "To such depths I will not descend. Not on your life! Never, never, never."

Sorry to do a Lear, but after all… If a car reflects its owner's personality, who wants to be seen owning worse than a Trabbie?

"Calm down, calm down," he grinned. "I've ringed one or two others. How about a Lanchester?"

"Too funereal."

"Or this: 'Wolseley 10, late 1938, 2,500 miles, one careful owner'.

"*Two* thousand, five hundred? Sounds more like one dead owner!"

"'Needs a good home. £40 o.n.o'"

"O.n.what?"

"Or near offer, of course."

"Look Roy, I'm in a terrible rush. I've got this guy waiting up at Abercorn, and so on. Could you possibly ring up and find out how near is near?"

"And get first refusal?"

"I'll be in contact, OK? Thanks a bundle! 'Bye." And off I rushed, grabbing the first bike in the rack that came to hand.

If my haste seems excessive, that's because of an instinctive notion that en route home I must shop. Be prepared, sort of. After all, what lay ahead could hardly be described as plain sailing, could it? Alex might even be OK to stop the night. In which case, what about breakfast? He could hardly be presented in Mrs Kent's parlour, so that meant stocking up. Bread of course, and so on. Other stuff. Like, whatever goes with bread...

I fussed back and forth along the lighted windows, finally settling on plum jam and a slice of pork pie – all I could think of, given my lack of kitchen facilities. Oh, and making a sudden raid into Woolworths to furnish myself with a bread knife.

Quick thinking, huh? No point in offering your stallion bread without a bread knife, OK?

Not that, maybe, stallion was all that apt a term. Sure Alex had that sort of MGM phiz which stirred the bits & pieces of every male who encountered him, but he'd always seemed to inhabit a plane about fifty miles higher than the fuck simple – or even, for that matter, the fuck fugue. Our encounters that summer away, for instance, had actually proceeded no further than glances and the odd embrace, a couple of them shirtless. What, in short, some manual he'd picked up termed fringe tantric. A kind of blissful blend of the chaste and tender, with Lizst on my old portable, and our only contact with Mordor the hourly train down by the river on its way to Limpley Stoke.

Now it seemed he wanted more. How much more? And, let's face it, after answering none of my letters that first year while I'd tried to scrape up the air fare to Spain. How callous can you get? Nothing. No response until the final throws of the dice. My telegram – his card.

It was the first time in my life I'd ever begged, and it's proved to be the last. If these annals of Tolverton suggest yours truly to be, as far as shag life's concerned, something of a chancer, a fixer, here today & gone tomorrow, just remember this. Each of us has his Rosebud. Mine was a square of pasteboard with a crest in the corner and twenty two words – yes I counted them – penned in blue. Not biro, nor hasty looking nor smudged. I could have understood that. Borne that.

But not this composure. This formality. The sense that here was a message considered and collected and quite, quite final.

Or so, till now, I'd assumed.

I suppose my bazaaring must have taken longer than I thought, for, encountering Mrs Kent in the hall, I found she'd already sent Alex upstairs. "And there's a message I'm afraid from Reverend Marchpane. Please will you call him as soon as possible." She opened the door to her lounge with one of those Kentish looks which brook no delay.

With a glance at the ceiling – what does he look like, what's he thinking? – I rapidly dialled Buggleskkely.

"Ah Paul – sorry to be a pest but it does sound good. Chap by the name of Pearman just outside Stroud. The two and a half thousand's genuine it seems, and he's prepared to take thirty five for cash. But others are biting, he warns – seriously, you'll have to get a move on."

"Typical!"

"Fancy a drive over? Joe's taking Matins, so I'm free after the eight thirty."

"Tomorrow?" Another glance at the ceiling as thoughts started to juggle fast as a foxtrot.

Roy must have sensed some sort of panic in either my voice or my silence. After a second or two, in contrast with his earlier enthusiasm, he said mildly, "Look there'll be other bargains. It's a long way for what might prove a pig in a poke. Why not…?"

He broke off at my giggle. Pigs, pokes. Why poke a pig? A peck of pickled piglets Peter Piper poked!

"Sorry, Roy. Not myself, OK? Look – thanks a lot. You know, for all your trouble and stuff." I took a deep breath. "Let's do it. Why miss out on a good deal?"

"Excellent, excellent. I'll get Clemmie to bake us some scones – oh, and I must ring my broker to extend temporary cover. In case."

One of those guys that think of everything!

"When can you be ready?"

Again I glanced at the ceiling with a mental shrug. How did I know? I'd never before entertained a shag who'd, like, stayed the whole night. Protocol, expectations – the whole boiling was Greek to me.

"Nine?" I ventured.

"Make it half past. Gives me time to get out of my God kit. We don't want Stroud thinking it's Dracula descending on them, eh?"

Dracula? At least he never had to face a night sharing his coffin! Or did I mean day? A thought which lingered a moment as I paused at the foot of the stairs – before leaping aloft with, of course, boundless enthusiasm!

"Alex!"

Crouched over a book, he sprang up, his eyes alight. Same hair, same skin, still a boy. Even the same crisp lilac shirt I remembered of old. In a moment we were in each other's arms, sharing I suppose a mutual relief. So far, so good. After which, presumably – though here's where the textbooks end – softly, softly, catchee monkey!

In fact, it was only when Mrs K was heard heading for her boudoir – that heavy matronly tread which bespoke cocoa in one hand, Dick Francis in the other – that we embarked on anything intimate.

Until that point it had just been shirtless, like those times on the terrace – but more poignant like updates generally are, reminding us that our own coral and crystal lives are potentially just as drab as everybody else's. And pointless. And, in so many ways, corny.

What had he had to reveal? Nothing special so far – bog standard, really. Stuff Hollywood peddles year in year out. For starters, of course, military service, horrendous for someone as sensitive as Alex. And on top of that, the hapless girlfriend, bull of a father, rows, threats, suicide – whether actually attempted or almost, I wasn't clear. And everything spiced up and smoking with slugs of good raw Catholic guilt. All weirdly entertaining in a Tennessee Williams sort of way, especially the flight to Pamplona with agents hot on his tail. But none of it anything much to do with me – until, that is, we got round to the postcard. The fatal postcard.

Though it had hit the flames long ago, its memory was clear in my mind. Branded there, you might say, slave-style. Especially that opening, that first phrase.

The rest? I'd hardly glanced at it. Well, who would? A slap in the face is a slap in the face!

Fortunately, it was Alex who opened up the topic. "That last wire, your reply to my little joke – how could you write such words?"

"What joke! End of relationship? Curtain down? Finito?"

"No…"

"Some joke! I nearly split my sides laughing!"

"No, you misunderstand…"

"Misunderstand? 'Cannot see you any more' – what two ways could there be about that?"

He shook his head. "Believe me, what I meant was…"

"Look," I shrugged. "It's water under the bridge. Why rake over things? There's no point." It was beginning to dawn on me that my heavy investment – plum jam, remember, and that bread knife – might have been somewhat premature. Reviving past pain like this only serves to remind one how it's that very anguish that's helped one move on. But to what end?

"There is," he said gravely, "every point. Paul, I was simply replying to your previous letter, yes? Or actually, the photo you enclosed. Your college garden? You by that deplorable statue, the Hepworth, your hair in your eyes? Your long hair?"

"I still don't get…"

"Literally, I could not see your face. Not see you any more, understand? A simple joke, that's all. No agenda for future times, nothing momentous."

"Pull the other one!"

"Pull the…?"

"Like, you seriously expect me to believe all that?"

"How can you ask!"

Intrigued, not entirely appeased, I reached for my shirt. "OK then – so why didn't you get in touch? Explain and stuff? Christ Almighty, what a mess!" Though at the time this had been the worst crisis of my life, hearing it parsed that way, seemed somehow to trivialise it. Trivialise everything for the time being. What was the point of trying if the Gods could intervene that easily and decisively?

He was biting his lip and nodding. "Yes, yes. You are so right. My only defence is – what you call it? Sod Law?"

In spite of my resentment, I couldn't help a grin. "Sod's Law, you mean. The certainty that if a fuck up's available, it will happen."

"Exactly. It did. Your telegram arrived on the very morning Marsha's father found out about she and I. That his perfect daughter was no longer, how shall I say, a girl. That we were living together. That, as I told him, there was nothing he could do about it."

"Tough shit!" I murmured involuntarily.

"From then on his one obsession was to – prove me wrong. His one terrible obsession! You understand?"

"Look, Alex…" I began.

"I was in no mood to write letters, my friend. Even to you. My loyalty had to be to them. Marsha and the child inside her. My own Xavier. My…"

And as a single slight tear glinted in his eye, what could I do? One second passed, two, maybe three – then it was shirt flung back on the floor, my arm quickly round him, and bed calling us to its dark cocoon. Not for sex or anything, both of us were too fragile for that. No, it was a kind of mutual benison which moved quickly, as far as he was concerned, into a fitful sleep. By contrast, I lay there pondering

See – it's now, as he rests, one can begin to recall what first drew one to him. His gentleness, of course, but beyond that – the brown curves of his neck and shoulders, the first light scree of hair defining his chest, the long loins, the hands with their raised veins and smart nails. And of course – funny how one forgets such momentous detail – his smell.

His highly individual smell, not at all rank or unseemly, but complex and old. As if his body had lain dozens of ages in the drawer of some second-hand bookshop, faintly and fragrantly assuming the glue and the dust and the coin and the crumbling pages. It always reminds me of those clubs in Madrid where old men dream of Franco over choice cigars, the odour of leather and stained silk making the most perfect of matches with silence and the curtained twilight.

OK, not to everyone's taste but it turns me on. Grabs me so much more than all the standard stuff, the Sitges swagger, or touching up hopefuls in the surf off Mykonos.

But so what? I prop myself up on one elbow to watch his sleeping form. Let's cut out the crap, I tell myself. What chance is there? What realistic chance of a future together? The guy's into girls, isn't he? Maybe willing to experiment every now and then, but basically straight. All that talk of sexual freedom – was it anything more than hot air? A way of breaking the ice between us? Is there really any prospect of his settling down to night by night life in the sack with a male partner?

But then a sigh floats from his lips. And, it occurs to me, maybe, just maybe this experience of straights and their jungle ways has changed him. Maybe when the dust settles we can patch something up. Find enough mutual ground to start things over again. Especially if he's sincere over having got Popes and stuff off his back. And as I begin to picture us naked on some island beach, hands clasped in the evening sun, sand on his bum and in his hair, sleep comes my way too, borne by his warmth, the rhythm of his breath.

In the cold light of morning – well, can you imagine any spectacle more depressing than a slab of pork pie on a cold white plate? Still, it was quick to prepare and pretty quick to eat. Brushing away the last crumbs, I shook my head. "Stroud?" I replied. "As the crow flies? No, not far."

"Astute bird," he smiled. "But I think I stay here and read anyhow. Thomas Mann, have you? Or Proust?"

"Afraid I'm a bit thin on Proust. Still…" – waving a proprietorial hand at my two shelves of Penguins and Oxford Standard Authors – "there's plenty of choice. How about J.B. Priestley? He's pretty deep."

"Post-Joyce existentialism?"

"Uh, well – depends how you look at it. Anyhow, help yourself and I'll be back by lunch, Okey-doke?"

"Okey-doke."

"Late lunch, naturally. I gather the Rainbow does two for one on Sundays. Or there's a place at Feyhill. The roast beef of Olde England, as they say. Sounds good?"

"Sounds good." But the glance he shot me was quizzical. "Is quiet, I think? So we can discuss?"

"Discuss?"

"As one might say, future things. Our future. Away from the bourgeoisie."

"Right-ho," I said cheerfully, that image of the sandy atoll floating before me even more seductively. So what if, ten to one, it could never be more than a pipe dream? We're all allowed refuge in fantasy now and then, aren't we? Just a dollop or two.

"Yes," he continued mistily, "far, far away – like Schweitzer."

"Right-ho," I said less cheerfully, hoping he wouldn't detect caution in my voice, "whatever." This was starting to sound daunting. I knew all about Lambarene, of course – the lepers and stuff. It had all been dinned into us at Bran's in social awareness lectures. Undeniably worthy and all that, but not totally in accord with my vision of white sand, with a stylish taverna nearby and my en-suite shower room five minutes away.

"Shall I bring maps?"

Quelling a sort of nervous giggle, I nodded. "Why not?"

"Paul…"

"Won't be long. See you."

He simply raised a hand in salute as I backed out of the door. I can't honestly say that I felt anything special, any premonition that this was the last time I'd ever see him, for instance – which of course it wasn't. My parting glimpse was just of this thin youngster, his shirt of faded lilac, his hair not yet combed, his eyes softly and lustrously gazing not exactly at me, nor anywhere real on this or any other planet. And if I detected something forlorn in his expression, well that was his problem.

A mental shrug as I began to bike downhill through the melting slush. What more could he expect? Springing stuff on me like that. Still, I'd get a smile back on his face somehow. No damage done – nothing a good long stint in The Fox or The Rainbow wouldn't cure. After all, a Double Diamond works wonders, works wonders, works wonders. No problem - if, that is, I'd any dosh left after buying this fabulous Wolseley.

The March was still chatting to Joe Jephson when I arrived, his hand on the old man's shoulder. The old man's very old shoulder. Dear Joe. With his white hair askance in the breeze, and that weathered skin which had, before theological college, known all too well the darkness of the mine, he looked about a hundred and fifty. Still, he could preach a good yarn. Unlike so many younger masters, he had the measure of the boys and they of him, and isn't that all you need?

"Greetings," he waved. "I gather you're missing me on St Ailbe."

"Sorry about that," I said, trying to look chastened as I shoved the bike back in the rack, hoping no-one had missed her. "Tell you what, I'll catch it next year."

"Listen to the scallywag," cried Joe, winking at his boss. "Next year, indeed! Let me tell you, I've never repeated a sermon in my life."

"No more you have," nodded Roy, consulting his AA book. "You're an inspiration to us all. Unlike some young idlers we could name, eh?"

I grinned, but a bit uneasily given the last few hours. I mean, what would they think, these priests, these paragons, if, by virtue of some celestial Bolex, they could witness a clip from last night? Me dreaming, for instance. The sweaty shoulders, the tight butts, the hairy legs clenched round each other, kicking off the sheets?

Gloucester was reached in record time and by mid morning we were partaking of coffee in one of the greasy spoons just outside our destination. Partaking, I emphasise, rather than enjoying. The brew was bright grey, livid as a pool of polonium, and I found myself yearning for Roy's awful Camp as I half-listened to the old boy's doubtless excellent advice.

"Secondly," he emphasised, slicing a scone in half, "insist on starting her up from cold. See how easily she fires, how quickly she settles down. Test the kingpins, check for even tyre wear. On the test drive, loosen your grip for a moment to see if she veers either to left or right. Oh, and don't forget the clutch. Slam her from fourth into third and note how much kick she gives."

"Third?"

"Gear."

"Right."

"Above all, take everything this Pearman says with a pinch of salt, eh? He may be kosher but, when it comes to selling cars, you never know. Don't be fooled by the 'we're all chums together' ploy. One has to be a bit ruthless. Pass the marge, there's a good chap."

"Trust me," I nodded with an inward smile at the idea of Marcho in ruthless mode, though, of course, there had been that signboard at Ilfracombe...

Any suspicions that had been instilled in me were, however, negated as soon as Pearman opened the door of his cottage. At that time of year it didn't exactly have roses round it but nevertheless the charm of the place struck you from the start. It was utterly pervasive, like scent from a herberwe. Here reigned serenity, here reigned fair play. And from whom could such comfort stem but Pearman himself? Plus his son, a close copy of senior but about six inches taller and rather more bald. Both seemed, with their cheeks and paunches, for all the world like very senior and reliable cricket umpires who'd never stolen a bus ride or sworn in front of their grans. Within a minute, I was putty in their hands.

The limo, snug in its tiny garage, looked perfect. I was able to walk round three sides of it, enthusing over its jet black sparkle and shine, noting how little its tyres had worn, and genuinely awed by the attractiveness of its interior. Seats in smooth tan leather, trim in a kind of light ginger carriage cloth, with lights and fittings in that art deco style you used to find in Southdown buses. And no signs of wear.

She was a gem.

Out on the road too, she handled much better than her quarter century might have suggested. A little play in the steering perhaps, a touch sluggish in acceleration – but with all this solid metal around us, what (as Pearman pointed out) could one expect?

I was hooked, and as I brought her to rest on the gravel, I was already reckoning how vulgar it would be to haggle.

"Say again?" I replied, raising my voice against the engine noise.

"Back her into the garage, if you would."

Not quite seeing why, since I was about to drive her home, I nevertheless complied. It was still his car, wasn't it? But not for long, I bethought myself, noticing how clear the area seemed of oil drips or pools. This car was clearly one in a million.

Following his hand signals and reversing her into the spot she'd just left – the garage was too narrow to permit clearance on both sides – I scrambled over the gearstick, and followed Pearman into his cottage where his son and Marcho were happily engaged swapping stories of Biggen Hill.

Financial arrangements were soon completed over a glass of sherry, and the keys surrendered, but not before a slightly tentative look came into our host's eyes. "Here's the logbook then," he said, pulling out a document from his bureau. "Tell you what, to save trouble, why don't you fill it in here and now, and I'll post it for you tomorrow?"

The March looked up cautiously but I was too elated to take much notice. 'Paul Bryant,' I wrote rapidly and boldly in the space for the new owner, 'Rhodes House, Tolverton'. Well, Docherty would be moving soon so it was best to think long term.

Within a minute or two, I was nosing cautiously down the drive with the Rover already positioned in the road outside. But just as I paused to juggle with first, there came a tap at the window.

Pearman, a touch red-faced, breathless from running down the drive. "Second thoughts," he muttered, thrusting a five pound note at me. "You're a good lad, and fair's only fair." Extraordinary – but before I could quiz him, away he rushed making even better time uphill than he had down.

A tad disconcerted, and most gingerly, I set my bargain in motion. No problem though. The engine hummed, the gears changed sweetly, the horn worked, the wipers worked, and the trafficators, unlike their Rover counterparts, not only flicked out but, without assistance, flicked in. All was right with the world. A mood further enhanced when I noticed a dial on the dashboard which glowed pink when switched on, swamping the car with – fantastic – the Billy Cotton Band Show!

'No-one here can know or understand me,' crooned Alan Breeze. 'Oh, what hard luck stories they all hand me!' I ask you – who on this earth could resist singing along?

And maybe that, my grandad's favourite song, is where it all started. For the trouble with long drives is, they give you time to think, and this began to prove the case as the minutes passed. Through Gloucester, past Newent, the twisting road ahead marked only by the Rover's brake lights flashing as some tight turn got tighter – so much time to pick things over. Assess, sort of, now euphoria was back in its bottle, exactly what I'd got myself into.

OK, so I'd joined the ranks. I owned a car. But how about what went with it? Insurance, road tax, service, not to mention petrol. And it would have to be greased, and polished, wouldn't it? And its tyres checked. And its battery topped up. And its anti-freeze replenished. Great Scott! The list was endless, like the road ahead. Why hadn't I thought this all through? Here was I acting like the Cardinal Archbishop of Salzburg or whatever, when the real me was a schoolmaster on seventy quid a month! How on earth could I afford it all? It was like – taking on a sodding wife or something.

Or a boyfriend!

Which is where the real panic set in. Considered squarely, so too it would be with Alex. Wouldn't his tyres need changing, his tank need filling, his universal joint need oiling and service?

An awesome prospect. And how about when he was ill or skint or suicidal? Who was it who'd have to drop everything in order to tend him, keep up his spirits, bale him out?

Me? Get real! Me, just out of college, a fucked up queer, who needed baling out myself? What on earth had I been thinking of!

And now there was this new dimension he'd landed on me. All this talk of going abroad and working with the hopeless – assuming it wasn't just a passing whim. Some prospect! Cutting oneself off from everything familiar and comfortable!

Sure there'd be compensations. Lots of them. Like, for instance, someone next to you at night in bed – but was that, what with farts and snores and stuff, anything more than a mixed blessing? A very mixed blessing!

Or someone to pass time with – but what spare time would there be in the jungle, warding off gorillas and vampire bats?

Or someone, then, to grow old and moulder away with – yeah, but I felt about a thousand already!

Dilemmas, dilemmas! All of which swirled round unabated even as we emerged from the woods into Over Tolver, with the traffic lights of the by-pass way below. Boy, had I got myself into a state!

Earlier we'd arranged that I should, on a temporary basis, leave the machine at Buggleskkely. Abercorn was too narrow to permit parking whilst Docherty, of course, had not yet vacated his slot on the quad. Fortunately, Marcho's garage was just wide enough for two cars and I took care to position mine well over to leave room for the Rover.

Scrambling past gearsticks is by no means the most comfortable of gymnastics especially when one's mind is in bleak mode. "Thanks a million," I nodded with what I hoped was not too obvious a frown. "Sorry it's taken so long."

"Glad to assist," smiled Roy. "Pleased with her, are we?"

"Chuffed!"

As usual he noticed – or appeared to notice – nothing, no reserve, no hesitancy of voice. It was to be hoped Alex would be just as easily fooled. But therein lay the problem. Get pissed off with a car, no way can metal protest. Get pissed off with a lover, two ticks and his bags are packed.

And so, as I headed over the rec towards the short-cut for Abercorn, do what I could, my blues got bluer. Like clouds cowling the sun. Like the dourest of Housman one turns to whenever things get out of hand. Or that slip of Wordsworth that had so excited me as a lad at Bran's.

Lucy!

You'll understand how it was that that particular scrap of Wordsworth tumbled into my head that particular moment. The old fraud at his most fatalistic and irrational. The way, as he nears his place of nooky – some rustic cottage, naturally – moon in the sky, what else? – he's shattered by the fear that his girlfriend might just have popped her clogs.

Not that I actually imagined Alex dead. Since when are parallels ever exact? Besides, I'm no poet, thank God!

Nor was it – and believe me I still cringe at the recollection – nor was it fear, exactly, that seized me.

Pausing for breath, I found myself picturing my room, with the tousled bed, and the plates piled up on my Spenser. I could see *Let the People Sing* tossed contemptuously on the floor. And I could see – I could see Alex not there!

Get my point? Not dead, but not there. Gone. Vanished whence he came, Pamplona or whatever. If, that is, he'd ever come.

No, the emotion that held me now in sudden thrall wasn't fear. Not by a long chalk. To make a clean breast of it, my overriding feeling was – hope. A sudden instinctive flare of hope that it would be so.

How much more of a bastard can one get? A guy flies all the way from Spain, strips his soul naked, sleeps in my arms, and I...?

Of course I fought it, sort of. Told myself sternly over and over again that no way did I want him gone. That of course I needed marriage, or as close to it as a queer can get. That of course I desired it all: union, the security that instinctive love brings, sharing a bed, sharing a bread knife. That no way would I baulk at the stocks and the mire: all the contumely majorities feel obliged to fling at their betters. Nor would I even resist Africa. If that's how it had to be.

But, deep down, I knew. Deep down I understood it for what it was, this actor's mote, this deception, this pathetic attempt at self-justification.

And thus at length, feeling mentally flayed, desiring nothing more than to have been born one of those solitary beasts content in their solitary lairs, I pushed on and came to a halt a door or two from my lodgings. The house stood there, dim and quiet. Nothing surprising about that. La Kent would be out, doing her usual stint at the cemetery while Alex – I pursed my lips at the thought – Alex would be hunched monk-like in a chair, engrossed in some past age or place, in some supernal dilemma. Monteriano maybe or with Miss La Trobe, poring over her Parlophones. All my stuff – Alex sharing all my stuff.

Pressing on, I entered the hall. How extraordinary, the stillness of the place. So? He must be asleep. Siesta time maybe – one of those peculiar Latin customs I was going to have to get used to!

As I mounted the stairs I began to turn over in my mind what to say. What titbits from my day to fling him. The way you do when one of you's been out and the other's stayed at home. A choice morsel or two to compensate. Roy's expression, for instance, as butter dripped down his cuff at that Stroud pull-in. Or his imitation of a Spitfire landing in fog. Or perhaps that peculiar look in old Pearman's eyes as he'd thrust that grubby fiver at me through the window?

I needn't have bothered.

Softly, so as not to disturb him, I turned the knob and slowly squeezed open the door. Just ajar – nothing dramatic. For a second or two I listened. No sound save the hiss of the gas fire. No stirring from the bed to show he'd woken. I nodded ruefully. Lucky man, to sleep so soundly! Taking a deep breath, I walked in – only to start back in – and I kid you not – wonderment.

Not there. Of course! Of fucking course!

Not in my room, not in the loo or bath, not even – after a ludicrous check – in the garden shed!

Nothing left of him but a pair of brown leather gloves, with monogram, which had dropped down by the bookcase. Oh, and that book, left on the sofa. An edition of Mallarmé with an old postcard tucked in to mark his place.

I flung myself into a chair, shaking slightly. What the hell was I worrying about? He'd gone for a walk or something. Exactly what I'd have done in the same situation. Taken advantage of a pleasant afternoon to get some fresh air and suss out the streets and shops of his new home.

Pull yourself together, Bryant, you tossbag! In an hour or so the light'll begin to fail and he'll be back.

And thus it gan unfold, the inexorable – sure the light failed, but Alex was not back. Butting my head against the low splash of grey and red in the west, I sprinted furiously down the hill and past Common Room. Apart from thumbing (and somehow I sensed that Alex was not a guy to thumb) there was, as I knew well, only one way out of Tolverton on a Sunday. The last bus left at four and there it was, engine already idling, waiting placidly in the slush at its stand.

No Alex of course. That would have been too much to expect. However, the ticket office was still open, the Brunhilde in charge making up her sparse takings for the day.

"Sorry to be a pest, but – I'm just checking something out. A passenger, like. Remember a sort of foreign looking guy, by any chance? He'd have booked right through to Gloucester."

"On which? The twelve or two?"

"Could have been either – probably the twelve, though." Why twelve? Why not two? My mind was in total chaos and words just shot out of their own volition.

"Foreign, you say? Anything else to go on?"

"Well…" I blustered. What did the woman want? Fingerprints? Identikit? Who was this bitch, an agent from Interpol? "He's sort of young, well dressed. No bag with him. No hat. Might have been unshaven."

"This week that departure was quite busy, I'm afraid. There were three or four customers who might fit that description. Hang on – was he carrying a tuba?"

A tuba! Alex with a tuba! I cold have wrung her fat neck

"No, just a double bass!" I retorted waspishly.

"In that case I can't help you. Why don't you ring Gloucester to see if they noticed anyone? They ought to have spotted a thing that size. Want the number?"

Ring Gloucester! A fat lot of good that would do. Why not ring Alice Springs, Auschwitz, Ultima Thule? Thanking her, I took the scrap of paper but crumpled it in my pocket. He was gone and that was that! I'd been given a chance and I'd blown it! I'd put owning a car before owning a human being, and now I must pay the price.

Pay the price?

It was only when seated in The King's Head, prodding a fork at some elderly Victoria sponge, that it all began to come home to me. I'd wanted him gone, hadn't I? I'd wanted to see the back of him, and everything that went with him, the stress, the shackles, the sheer responsibility. OK, very well – my prayers had been answered. What was there to moan about? Why feel this concerned, this sort of – lost?

Why keep telling myself I'd give anything to have him back, commandeering the bedclothes, using my toothbrush? Would I? Would I really?

In a mood of total confusion I wandered back to Abercorn, but not before calling in at Common Room and signing for a bottle of Famous Grouse at the bar. Astute bird. Who'd said that about something? But – and I yawned – let's face it. Three tots, a brace of aspirin, and all would be hunky dory for a few hours.

Or, at least, hunky dory-ish!

By the morning, all traces of snow had disappeared. I wish I could have said the same of this mood of mine, a kind of colada: one part failure, two parts relief, three parts remorse at relief! But there – since when did life come easy? And true I might no longer have a boyfriend, but wasn't there something else to fuss over instead? Something black and shiny and obedient which sang songs and would never sod off like some bloody self-indulgent will-o-the-wisp.

A short-lived optimism which took a sudden nose dive as, jumping downstairs, I observed Mrs Kent in wait, one of those looks on her face. Sort of screwed up as though she'd squeezed herself into a corset ten sizes too small.

"Mr Bryant," she began severely. "We need to have a word, you and I."

"'Morning Mrs K – will after breakfast do?"

"There are certain lapses, I'm afraid, which demand immediate action!"

"Lapses?"

"From decency – kindly follow me!" she thundered, turning into her office.

"No problem," I responded cheerily, despite my innards quailing. Was this it at last? The raven? Public disgrace, the strappado, headlines in the press! "What's on your mind exactly?"

"Noises! Is that exact enough for you? Noises that can be interpreted only one wa

"But surely..." Aghast, I ran my mind back over Saturday night. Sure her bedroom was close to mine, but still... Were the springs really that noisy? Could you really distinguish two people getting into bed from one? Were two lots of snoring discernible from one? In a panic my brain jumbled from this possibility to that. Had the old bitch actually crept out and keyholed, or something? "But surely," I repeated, "it's impossible to be absolutely..."

"Impossible?" she cried. "Didn't I hear it as clear as day? And without mounting more than a stair or two?"

"Mrs Kent, I assure you..."

"And I assure *you*, young man – I'm not the sort to toy with. There'll be no pulling the wool over these eyes, of that you can be certain."

"Of course, of course," I retorted hastily. "Trust me, as if I'd ever..." But was this the right tack? Wouldn't contrition be a better ploy? Throwing myself on her mercy, appealing to her soft motherly heart?

"Trust is it?" she barked, in the most astringent tones imaginable. "A fine time to be talking about trust. Like a thousand bees, it sounded. Most unsettling. I get back from church, ready for lunch, and what do I...?"

"Steady on," I said, suddenly puzzled. "Church? You mean yesterday?"

"The Sabbath was, I believe, yesterday, as usual," she replied, bridling even more, if that were possible. "Not that it alters anything. Deception is deception, any day of the week."

"Deception?"

"When you took rooms here, you assured me you shaved with a Gillette. Yesterday, to my utter disgust, I found to the contrary. Now all the world knows my tariff: that I charge my electrical gentlemen sixpence a week extra for the additional current. By my calculations that totals six shillings and sixpence since September. Well, Mr Bryant?"

"My most abject apologies, Mrs Kent," said I, almost crazy with relief. I could have hugged the old bag. So Alex had found my old Philishave, had he? What else, I wondered as I brought forth a fistful of silver, had he come across en route? "Three half crowns, there we are – pray don't bother with the change. Again my apologies. It's so difficult on a Sunday – when one runs out of blades, that is. I promise to be more organised in future. A thousand thanks for being so understanding!"

After which bowing and scraping, I needed a good hard run to restore my spirits. Gosh, it had been a close shave!

Shave? Close? Don't laugh too loud, will you?

Anyhow, arriving breathless at Common Room, I was a tad disappointed to find no James, and more than a little surprised to meet the March instead. Not of course in the wet & wishfuls, but with an expression on his face, all the same, as though he had indeed just endured the coldest shower known to humanity. Or taken lessons from Ma Kent.

"No chapel today?" I queried lightly, refusing to be fazed. Doubtless this, whatever it was, would prove to be just another red herring.

"Joe's standing in," he replied, rising from his armchair. "I wanted to show you something."

"Can't it wait? I've got my Monday test to chalk up before…"

"Before the troops get out? Precisely. Just what I was thinking."

"Roy?"

But without further protest I allowed myself to be led past chapel steps and the strains of the Benedicite. Past the 6th form block. Past the san to an obscure nook, it could hardly be called a quad, framed by the Art room on one side and the boilerhouse on the other. A small gateway led direct into a back lane and by this, to my astonishment, stood the Wolseley. And how spiffing she looked, the morning sky bright in her polish, her faultless chrome buffed to perfection.

"My God she's ace," I observed happily, worries dissolving, spirits soaring like a hawk.

"Think so?"

"But why bring her down here? Till the log book arrives, I can't insure her unless…"

"Paul – just come round here."

Obediently, pausing only to cuff away some bird shit on her boot, I followed him round to the right hand side. The side I'd never before seen. The side I now, all of a sudden, loathed and never desired to see again.

"Good God Almighty!"

"Thought you'd be interested."

For there across the front right mudguard gaped a huge and rusty hole. A crater almost. So vast that in a sense the mudguard could hardly be said to exist at all. So wide and jagged that there wasn't a cat's chance in hell of a repair. And as for a replacement? A whole new wing?

How many 1936 Wolseley 10s could there still be in existence, let alone available to be broken up for spares in the near future?

Well, one at anyrate. The thought had obviously crossed the Marcho mind too as I looked up in despair. Boys are notoriously cruel at times and it didn't take much nous to realise that this was the sort of thing a young master would never live down. To the end of my time at Tolverton I'd be known as Banger Bryant or something of that sort. The guy who bought a hole with a bit of car attached!

"Let's get her close to the wall," said Roy. "No-one will notice. Then we'll sort something out at lunchtime when they're all in the canteen."

So there it was. Thirty five quid down the drain. Half a month's salary. And what would she fetch for scrap? Four pounds? Five? My mind recoiled immediately at the thought. So trivial a sum – so ignoble an end. Not fitting, surely, for something which had brought me such elation, albeit short-lived. No, even temporary bliss deserved a better fate than that. It would be like seeing Alex trussed up and crushed into a metal cube three feet by three.

"So what do we do?" murmured Marcho, later that day, peeling a banana. "They'll be on their tapioca by now, you know." It was half past one and my mind more or less blank.

"Search me. I suppose I could drive her back to Stroud and…"

"Just so, but remember – you completed that logbook. As far as the law's concerned, you're the legal owner. She's your responsibility now."

"Responsibility?" Where had I come across that concept before!

"Afraid so. And you've about two minutes to make up your mind."

Various lurid thoughts began to swirl involving bonfires, cliffs and the like – or driving to Scotland and abandoning her amidst the bracken of some remote glen – when all at once a memory flashed into my mind. That lake in Emmet's Wood. Where once I'd nearly skinny-dipped with James, and might well do so in future. It was wide, wasn't it? And, like all ponds stemming from old mines, deep? Could there be a nobler end for a distinguished veteran? It would be like a liner going down.

Marcho was not the guy to jib at a spot of fly tipping, especially one as bizarre as this. As soon as lunch was over and the rugger buggers had got going, we lashed some old tarpaulin over the Wolseley's nose, and so her last journey began. She ahead, the Rover behind. One felt there should be mutes in front with their wands, lilies on top, retainers bowing, so dignified was her progress. On we glided through the back streets and over the two rivers.

Circling under the elms, we chose a shallow bank where she could enter the water gently. Opening the windows, leaving the key in her ignition, we eased her softly into motion. No band played her out with a Welsh hymn, no arm clad in white samite rose to greet her. She merely gurgled a while before turning on her side and sinking, like some old biddy, to her well-deserved rest.

And what did I feel next morning, the deed done, when it couldn't be reversed?

Regret at her passing? Anger at the Pearmans? Embarrassment at being taken in so easily?

Not really. I was starting to get used to this lark. The dice falling every whichway, but never my way. Why complain if that's one destiny?

No, what possessed me now was more a sense of being freed. Of about fifty brace of albatross slipping off my neck simultaneously. No more cars for yours truly. Henceforth it would be trains and taxis, or shank's pony as spring came to the hedgerows and by-ways.

And no more guys either? Well certainly – for the time being at anyrate. Toby's party, for instance – I'd give that a miss all right. Just now I could think of nothing worse than callow youngsters pratting around in togas and bay leaves, and thinking themselves the ultimate cat's whiskers.

And later, well we'd just have to see. Time would tell. Maybe, yes, like an ever rolling stream it does bear all its sons away. But then, maybe, like a never ending soap opera, it occasionally bears the odd one back. Till then, why not reach for the astute bird – and thank our lucky stars that the God we're landed with at least seems to have been blessed with a sense of humour?

6: *All Through the Night*

Ten days or so later, I was sitting in Evans's chair, white cloth over me, watching the punters drift past. It was market day, with throngs of drovers, ostlers and the like looking quite cute in their crude provincial way. Corduroy, trilbies and stuff. And a fair smattering verging on the young and fit, and, under the right circumstances, by no means averse to a romp.

You'll be glad, I'm sure, to thus note that December resolutions last no longer than New Year ones, and I was already feeling more myself, despite the odd pang whenever I caught sight of Xavier's gloves on my sideboard, monogram and all. Not that I'd shrugged off all notions of discipline. I had, for instance, eschewed that party though there the motives had been penury and reserve as much as self-denial. In any event there ensued a reward not long after, in the shape of a postcard from Julian.

His own handwriting? Actual and genuine? Quelle honeur!

In actual fact it was just a couple of lines, but it did express regret that I'd not been able to make 'Jugs's bash' at Keble, and did, moreover, and unequivocally, invite me to Banbury to see the old year out. Fireworks were promised – though with Julian one never knew. Irony could it be? Or actual boring gunpowder? Whichever might prove the case, maybe his returning that book to me had not been so significant after all.

Topics which, this morning, I was finding ample time to ponder. Since Evans was a one man band, having your hair cut there tended to be a bit of a marathon, despite the Trucolor interludes: Hogarthian customers demanding Hogarthian things. Cedric from The Fox had already dropped in for snuff, and Mrs Pyne, a most difficult woman at parent meetings, for cochineal, whilst for the last ten minutes or so Colonel Featherland had been choosing a rod and flies as a Christmas present for his young nephew.

Well, contrary to popular opinion, you can have too much of a good thing, and when once again the bell rang I looked round from the chair in mild but, as you'll appreciate, growing irritation.

Not that it lasted.

"Just the feller," grunted Featherland. "Good mornin', padre. What d'you think of this beauty?" Holding up a scrap of blue and orange, he rotated it to catch the light.

Marcho peered gravely. "Ought to give you fine sport right enough, Colonel."

"Me, sir? Fiddlesticks! Make my own beauties as you very well know. It's for the boy. Get him started. About time, don't you think?"

"I suppose it would be," nodded Roy. "What is he now, seventeen?"

"Comin' up. Very well, Evans. I'll take all four."

"Charterhouse, still?"

"Where else? Gown Boys, like his father."

"Excellent, excellent. Won't be long before he's at the altar, eh? Time and tide!"

"Time and tide!"

With a smile, I sank back into my reverie. The hours stand still when quality meets – I'd been long enough in Tolverton to understand at least that much, and I was therefore surprised to be awoken a few seconds later by a tap on my shoulder.

"Good-oh," came the familiar salutation, "wondered if we might run into each other. Tell me, how are you fixed for tomorrow? Up to anything?"

"Cards and stuff," I replied cautiously. "Presents…"

"Thought as much. Well then, why not shop in the valleys? Everything's cheaper in the valleys, look you! Cheap and good. Blaengwynfi lamb, for instance."

"Blaengwynfi?" I chuckled – his accent really was spot on – "there's no such place."

"Stone's throw, my lad, from Blaenrhondda?"

"Sure, sure – just follow the slag heaps!"

"I happen," twinkled the old voice, lapsing back into English, "to be serious. Consult the book if you don't believe me. Western Region, Table 142: Swansea, Neath, Aberavon and…"

"Remember me to Clementine, then," barked Featherland, sweeping past with his parcels. "Mornin' Marchpane. Much obliged, Evans."

A respite which suited me down to the ground. What had he been leading up to? Another jaunt like Ilfracombe? God forbid!

"Sobranies, reverend?" queried Evans, reaching under his counter. "I'm afraid the van didn't get through last week. That flood at Ross."

"Ah yes. Cracked main, wasn't it? Made a right mess, I hear."

"As a consequence I'm out of Blacks, see? Temporarily. Make do with Cocktails, will you?"

"Cocktails?" roared Roy in disgust.

"They're purported to taste exactly the same."

"Who cares how they taste! It's how they jolly well look!"

"Come, come, reverend. Who'd ever take you for a nancy boy?"

Despite the implied slur, I had to chuckle. The thought of Roy with green or pink in his ivory holder was indeed an image to treasure, and for a few seconds it took my mind off its new preoccupation. Namely, the undeniable signs that I was about to be dragged off screaming to another railway requiem.

Bored as I was with vac life in Tolverton, the idea held little attraction. Hours in that car, more hours on hard cushions getting grit in your eyes. And for what? So he could pick up another trophy for sale on the black market?

No way, José! This time, I must be firm.

"Maybe you've read about it in the paper?" observed Roy, making way for two more customers who'd just arrived arm in arm.

"What, the flood?"

"No, of course not. The closure – well, suspension officially. But they would say that, wouldn't they?"

"Would they?" No doubt about it – yet another grubby little branch line not yet plundered by scavengers. Much as I was fond of the old boy, much as I'd come to look upon him as an ally against the Myrmidons, this was too much! Much too much. Best to scotch it right away.

"In view of which, I rather wondered if you'd like one of our days out…"

"Look Roy," I began.

"…unless, of course, you have a phobia."

"Phobia?"

"About tunnels. A few of the lads are coming too, but in their case it doesn't apply – with you, of course, it would be different."

"Lads?" I inquired innocently. "Ones I know?"

"Carey and Jukes. Come to think of it, you teach them, don't you? Plus Foster."

"Mind them, might be more accurate!"

115

"Oh, and Marsden. You see Carey has an aunt in Treherbert who's seventy next week. They'll have tea with her while we explore."

Marsden – that rather reserved boy by the radiator with an air of Malvolio about him. And something of a mind. Maybe this trek wasn't such a bum rap after all. Would he wear white jeans?

"Explore?" I queried. "Let me get this straight. Explore some *tunnel*?"

"Not just *some*," came the haughty reply. "It's the longest one in Wales. Maybe Britain."

"Maybe the world?"

"Blaenrhondda to…"

"Blaengwynfi! Got it! And it's about to close?"

"End of the week. There've been falls from the roof. So after that, it'll be over to buses while they get it fixed."

"Oh, right."

"*If* they get it fixed!"

"You mean there's like, a question mark?"

"To say the least. British Railways, my boy – they're a devious lot. Best to grab our chance while we can. Just in case. There's a 2.32. Only takes ten minutes, you see. And nine back."

Now that interested me, that really was intriguing. What kind of Alice in Wonderland construction could it be where one direction was faster than the other? This needed delving into."

"So – are we on?"

Stuff to delve, white jeans as a possible bonus – what could I do but nod. "Why not?" I shrugged. "Sounds ace, like the Tunnel of Love. Remember, at fairs?"

And that other pierhead ride. Everyone's favourite. Wedged in three to a car. Rumble, rumble over the rough cast iron. Bar gripped tight. Lights, a shriek and here comes the first mask – Marsden. Hard swerve, swaying as we accelerate, lights, klaxon and the second mask – Marsden. Cobwebs now, wiping your face, a dull glow, hooters and the third mask – Marsden. Marsden in silver and orange flaring against the night, huge and menacing, like some bloody diabolical totem pole…

I sat up in bed sweating.

Who the hell was he, this Marsden? And why the Ghost Train? I hadn't been on one in years. Was this the Gods trying to warn me or something?

Shaking my head like a terrier, I tried to focus. Andrew, wasn't it? Andrew Marsden. Why him? Sure the looks were photogenic, the brain promising. But really, as a person I hardly knew him. In class his orations were rare, and as for that inscrutable expression, dire experience had taught me to beware of folk who bury their feelings that far underground. Besides, the guy couldn't be much over eighteen. Pursuit of Julian had sometimes felt like cradle snatching, but at least he was at college and his own master.

Eighteen? I sank back on the pillow, firmly resolved to put all such nonsense out of my mind. This was a mere blip – an aberration, nothing more. Having agreed to this Blaenwhatsit date, I could hardly back out at the last minute, but there'd be no sign of any interest in this Ganymede. No glances his way, no words addressed to him. Nothing to show I knew he existed except as one of a batch of 6th formers in my A level class. One tart in a mixed dozen!

How easy it is to head off danger when one's firm!

By eleven next morning, boys collected from their villages, our short sprint up the Heads of the Valleys accomplished, off we found ourselves turning from the main road, about to plunge down to Treherbert. It was a mild Saturday but gloomy, clouds stacked ominously in the west though no rain had yet fallen.

In the back all was quiet. After some initial jocularity and a horribly inexpert rendering of 'Maybe it's because I'm a Londoner' by Jukes on his harmonica, the Four Mesquiteers had lapsed into silence, especially after Carey's deft solution to the mudguard problem: a judicious use of chewing gum.

How easy it is to solve problems when one's resourceful!

By contrast, in the front things were hotting up. No sooner had the descent begun than Marcho started to fidget. Glances to the right, interspersed with little bounces in his seat. I found myself getting quite alarmed. He seemed particularly mesmerised by the valley, and the long dark loin of mountain far away across the river which formed a kind of Great Wall of China. Fine, no problem – if only there hadn't been quite so many hairpins straight ahead.

Straight, that is, so to speak – OK?

At last, after five sharp bends and narrowly missing a line of mean hovels, he braked hard and cried, "There! Quick everyone. See down there."

Far below, so far that it seemed like one of those toy landscapes on display in Hamley's at Christmas, a thread of single track could be plainly discerned parting the fields direct as ruled pencil until, for no apparent reason, it curved sharp left. Thence it headed straight for the mountain, as if intent on butting itself, brave but futile, against the merciless bulk of that indomitable grey.

Except – when you strained your eyes to the utmost, you could just make out a pinprick of black into which it evidently disappeared. No grandiose castellations and stonework for this line. No Byzantine portals. Just a dark hole, small as fairy's arse blotted against those high implacable swathes of barren rock.

For the first time, something of what the March felt about railways began to filter through. Began to impress me with its drama. And thence in time become, like with him, an imperative. As for now, there was just this impulse: I had to travel that line below. Who knows why? Nor, amidst any of my subsequent forays on last trains along lost routes, has it ever become any clearer. All I know is, I'm hooked, one of the tribe. And it was this Saturday, perched high above the Rhondda, that opened my eyes.

Sensible chap that he was, Roy had allowed ample time for an ample lunch at The Maesteg Arms, just beyond the level crossing. Though now demolished, it was at that time one of those homely Welsh hostelries happy to serve the weary traveller Cottage pie for next to nothing. Or Shepherd's pie. Or Fisherman's pie, as long as you didn't inquire too closely into which fish.

Excellent food for lads, nevertheless, and first rate for loosening tongues. When served, that is, with a modicum of the brown and foaming.

"Ale?" replied Marcho. "How should I know? I'm not a walking dictionary, my lad. Anyhow, there is no difference. I expect they're synonymatic." He beamed my way with a wink: the usual schoolmaster trick – perplex the buggers with long words.

Jukes, however, was determined. "So why's this called pale ale? Never pale beer?"

"Who cares tuppence?" groaned Carey, the youngest of the three. "It all tastes the same, idiot!"

"Idiot yourself!"

"That," intervened Marcho, "is because it is the same. Eh, Mr Bryant?"

"Afraid not."

Before I could utter a word in Roy's support, though in truth I knew nothing of the matter, out it drifted, an assertion so positive it could no way be gainsaid. Marsden, light glinting in his eyes.

I frowned.

Roy blinked. "What was that, Andrew?"

"Ale and beer, sir. They're totally different. It's a question of yeast."

"Yeast?" said Roy, reddening slightly.

"With one it ferments on the bottom, the other on the top."

"Yeah?" drawled Jukes dismissively. "So which is which?"

"Beer on the bottom, ale on the top, of course."

"Of course," joshed Roy gently, retrieving face a bit, or trying to. "Or the other way round!"

"No."

A tone which made it clear that whatever other talents young Marsden possessed, tact was not one of them. Nor was he wearing the white jeans on which I'd counted. Quelle washout!

Roy said nothing. Merely dug his fork deep into a lump of bream.

Maybe because it was his query which had started it, maybe simply because he was a nice guy, Oliver Carey seemed to feel it incumbent on him to break the ice. After a minute or two, he coughed and said, "This visit's really going to make Auntie's day. It's too far out, you see, for most folk, the buses and that. So thanks a lot, sir, for the driving and all."

Roy's fork saluted.

"Besides which, it's brilliant just to get away, right lads? Change of scene and, you know – perspective."

"You can say that again," agreed Foster. "First outing I've had since the summer."

"Me too." Reaching for more bread, Jukes looked my way this time. "I wonder why the school doesn't lay on more trips. Like this or abroad. I've got mates who board at Hereford CS and Monmouth and places. They seem to get all kinds laid on. Why not us?"

"Who knows?" I shrugged. "Different schools, different customs…"

"I mean," said Carey, "it's not like we're asking for the moon or anything."

Jukes nodded eagerly. "Olly's right. It's not a question of the USA or Thailand or…"

"Isn't there the Choir Weekend?" interposed Marcho rather curtly, pushing his plate away. "York one year, Lincoln the next?"

"If you've the voice."

"And Stratford? Mr Trewes' parties to Stratford?"

"If you do English."

"Well," said Roy, "at least you've lots of societies to amuse you. Mr Ormulak's bird watchers, for instance. Or Mr Docherty's film society."

"If you're a geek."

"A what?"

"From the Latin geekus, geeki," explained Jukes loftily, with a sly glance at Marsden, "meaning – a geek!"

"Talk about hard to please!" observed Marcho wryly, treading more carefully now. "How about all the rugger and so on. The annual tour. Anyone can join up for that, surely."

"Not quite anyone." Marsden loud and clear, that Torquemadan echo in his voice more evident than ever.

Again I frowned.

A pause before Marcho met his eye. "Do," said he, "by all means enlighten us, Andrew."

"Not quite anyone – sir. Only people, if you can call them people, who enjoy kicking hell out of one another. A better term might be brutes."

"Brutes or not," retorted Marcho, rising abruptly, signalling the waitress, "Mr Bryant and I have a train to catch. Now don't forget – back by a quarter to four. Not a minute later. Oh and Carey – remember me to your aunt, there's a good lad."

Typical Roy. Even when nettled, never forget the courtesies! And nettled he most certainly was, which puzzled me somewhat until I recalled Carver at The Fox one night, pouring scorn on the old man's Blue. How odd to think of him in shorts. Also, could one still be proud of such things at his age? His remarks my first Saturday rather suggested the opposite, but who could tell? And ought I anyway to say something emollient?

Before anything appropriate had come to mind, we were at the station and the opportunity lost. "Males!" he mused. "If only they could be born fifty. Present, er – company excepted, of course."

"I'm flattered!" I replied, whilst inwardly demurring. Would I prefer Marsden, for instance, to be fifty at this moment? Or forty? Or thirty? Despite his rudeness and nondescript slacks, I rather thought not. The vibes were there, and that was that. As a later Prime Minister would insist, You can't buck the market! It was, thus, only with considerable effort that I ignored my radar, and wrenched my thoughts back to here and now.

Not only was all quiet, but eerily so. A bit like some Welsh version of Keats's urn. Instead of a push and pull getting up steam, or a diesel making its usual hideous racket, there lay the bay, bleak and empty. No-one about. Nothing in the yard except a motorbike, a bus and a coal lorry, her tailgate down and sacks folded neatly in smart piles.

"Late up from Cardiff, maybe?" I queried as Roy looked at his watch.

"Doubtful – I mean, she's supposed to start here," he answered still not quite himself, sitting down on a bench and peering at its armrest. "I say, some of these rhymes are rather ripe."

Graffiti in the valleys can hardly be said to pull its punches, and we were happily occupied for the next couple of minutes until the clock ticked round to departure time. Shortly afterwards, a porter appeared from the lamp room.

"Neath?" he yawned, signalling to the bus which began to back out of its stand. "You'll be waiting a long time if you don't get a move on."

We gaped, understood, and made a run for it, waving madly at the driver.

Fortunately the conductor, glad of some company, was rather more helpful than his British Railways counterpart. "Since Wednesday, it would be," he said, tapping his knee with the ticket rack. "Wednesday last, see. It's these small falls there've been for a month now, pebble size, not much more. Then come Wednesday, Jones on the 7.52 reports cladding down. A right slab, mind, broke in two but still big enough to throw an engine off the rails. No exaggeration. I seen the photo, and Jones, he says, There'll be nothing more through here this side of Christmas. And sure enough, next day shut it, they did, Cardiff, like that!"

Which declaration, accompanied by an almighty snap of finger & thumb, prompted Roy's gathering dismay to increase still further.

"As a temporary measure, surely," he urged. "Just for a brief while."

"Brief, is it? And who's about to risk their necks for nothing? What's the point when the whole mountain's moving?"

Not that you'd have suspected any such thing, crawling as we were up the Adamantine grey of its flank. A steep lane, winding round hairpin bends tighter by far than those by which we'd descended. This side of the valley was even more barren than the other and hardly a landscape for which one could summon up much enthusiasm. Still, as journeys go, it would be brief. Nine minutes, hadn't Roy said? Funny to think that now I'd never find out why it was more one way than the other.

As you'll gather, logistics are not my strong point.

"Guess what!" muttered Roy, turning over a pamphlet filched from the conductor. "How long d' you suppose this takes to the other side?"

"Nine minutes," I retorted without thinking. "Oh, but…it must be a bit longer than the train I expect. At this speed, I mean. A quarter of an hour?"

"One hour and five bally minutes." He smiled a devious smile, tucking the leaflet away behind the strap of his camera case. "And presumably the same back."

"But the lads…?"

"Oh, they'll just wait at the station. They'll guess."

"Will they be safe?"

"For an hour or so?" he shrugged. "They're not fourteen. Nothing to fret over. We're the victims, that's for sure. It's just so frustrating, eh? All this way for nothing!"

No plaques, no signal arms, no trophies of any kind. Nothing to swell the coffers. I had to smile. Poor old sod. What a disappointment for him.

And that was that for the next hour. A rather long hour during which, however, my mood, bit by bit, began to assume the hue of the clouds we so nearly brushed.

Finally, after a ghastly descent, at roughly the time Carey & Co would be enduring goodbye kisses from auntie, we bumped drunkenly into the decrepit yard of Blaengwynfi station and came to a halt.

"All right to take a snap or two?" inquired Marcho as we hopped on to the broken tarmac.

"Take your time, boyo," retorted the conductor, totting up his tickets. "You've plenty enough of it. Us, we're off for our tea."

"Tea? But how about…?"

"It's all in there," observed the other wearily, indicating the leaflet stuffed behind the old Kodak. "Depart 5.20 – if the Neath gets in on time."

"Roy," I said wildly, drawing him aside, glancing up at the sky, now dim and sullen. "This is disastrous, OK? We can't expect them to wait three hours in the dark."

"What dark? There'll be a gas lamp or two. Besides, what do you suggest?"

"We'll have to have a taxi."

"From Blaengwynfi?" he retorted with a rueful chuckle. "Go ahead, take your pick." Waving an expansive hand around the empty muddy yard and the trickle of houses which stretched away down the shallow incline, he sat himself down on a luggage trolley and opened his knapsack in search of his cigarette holder.

"Roy, we've got to do something!"

"Have we?"

"Obviously. We can't just sit here. How about – phoning someone?"

"Who? And to what end?" More his usual self, he seemed to be enjoying the situation to an unwarranted degree – as though, somehow, he knew something I didn't. Which with Marcho, as I'd begun to learn, was par for the course.

"Well," I said rather plaintively, "I don't know about you, but I'm not too keen on scandal and the sack."

"Really?"

"Yes, really!" I was getting annoyed.

"In which case, you'd go to any lengths to avoid it?"

"Exactly."

"Well," he twinkled, lighting a bright pink Sobranie, "there might even be a way. Of getting back earlier, I mean. With a bit of luck we could do it by a quarter to five." Producing a flashlight from his knapsack, he added, "If we put our best foot forward."

I groaned in disbelief.

"Foot forward? You mean walk back? All the way over that blesséd mountain?"

"Not over." He flicked on his torch. "Through." Allowing its beam to float along the deserted platform and on to the tunnel, he paused at that coal black maw. That oval of nothing. Vast endless vacancy. No light, not even darkness visible.

"Surely you can't mean…?" My laugh was incredulous – and not a little uneasy as implications began to line themselves up.

"A mere three miles?" replied Roy. "Dead level? We can walk it in an hour."

"But the whole bloody thing's collapsing."

"Nonsense. Alarmist propaganda. If it's been there one century, it's clearly good for another."

"Roy, that is *so* illogical!"

"Faith believes nor questions how."

"OK, OK!" I retorted. How bloody irritating Christians can be at times. "But suppose, just suppose, the Flying Scot comes through?"

"It's closed – you heard the man. And look you there."

Sure enough, at the brink, clipped to each rail, two sets of tiny beacons winked their pert red warning.

"No-one but the District Superintendent himself could countermand those. Besides, every now and then there'll be a manhole – a recess into which linesmen used to retreat when a train came along. We'll be as safe as houses."

In the face of such assurance – especially from someone smoking a pink cigarette – what could I say? Was one's skull really more likely to be knapped today in that tunnel, than next week in some storm on the surface, with flying slates or falling trees?

Though it has to be added that the safety net of manholes proved something of a snare and delusion since most we encountered had already been commandeered as tips for rubble from the collapsing roof, and would have provided little protection had The Flying Scot indeed chosen to invade a tunnel in West Wales!

Within a minute or two we were heading into the black just as if it were a real-life pit. Just as if we were miners of old, though, I fear, minus the helmets and swagger. Not at all like Paul Robeson at the head of his men, belting out, 'Ar Hyd y Nos' - but rather, apprehensively, torch on the ballast, watching for rats.

As we rounded the first curve, Roy paused for a moment. "Losing my marbles," he said apologetically. "I've only gone and left my lighter on the seat. Won't be a minute. You go on"

"Look after your haversack, shall I?"

"No, I'll manage – catch you up in two ticks."

Have you ever tried trekking along railway track? Let me assure you – it's not the easy experience you might think. Apart from the obvious – the oil, the shit, the puddles – there's an even greater hazard. The sleepers, OK? Which aren't quite a pace apart. So you calibrate your step. Fine, no problem. All's well for a moment or two. Then it's board, board, trip, ballast, trip, board, trip, ballast, ballast, trip... Then you give up, and push on outside the rails where it's stumble, stumble all the way.

All of which, in sunshine, skirting meadows or crossing estuaries, might count as fun. But deep underground? With one feeble torch, and a million tons of granite about to send you to kingdom come? Let's say – I don't recommend it!

Nevertheless, Roy having joined me again, on we pressed, making good time, indeed sufficiently so for us to allow ourselves a brief rest about half past four. Given the tunnel's curvature, neither mouth could now be seen, the only evidence that this was not in reality Hades being a small semaphore and its red glow fifty yards or so to the north.

Presumably quite valuable at an auction of train memorabilia and suchlike. Which portion of it, I wondered, would Marcho have tried to snaffle if I weren't here? The arm? The oil lamp?

"Time for snap," observed my companion, perching himself on a rail, waving me to a pile of sprags opposite, and producing goodies from his knapsack. "Good old miners' term that, according to Joe. He'd have been in his element here, don't you think?"

"The lads too?" I ventured.

"Decidedly, if only we'd known. The adventure of a lifetime, as they say. That Jukes now. Thinking it over, one has to admit it. The boy has a point."

"Has he?" I replied through a mouthful of sandwich, feeling not especially well disposed. To mankind in general, and boys in particular.

"Not convinced, are we?"

"All I mean is, he's spoilt. What that generation needs is National Service – or a year or two at the coal face. Pick and shovel!"

"And dining on bread and water?"

"I'm serious."

"Well, perhaps you're right. It did no harm to Joe, after all. Going down the mine, I mean."

"Did no harm?" I retorted archly. "I expect it was the making of him!" But inwardly I shuddered at my hypocrisy, recalling Ormulak on Jephson – how the old priest had slaved down the pit from fifteen, year on long year, until he'd saved the few quid needed for college fees. Cramming by night, hacking away by day in dank filth such as this.

Hombre!

Looking my way curiously, Marcho nodded. "Fifty years ago, in west Wales, quite right. But this is the sixties. Government grants, men on the moon…"

"Pie in the sky!"

"My word!" he replied. "We are in a tizz, aren't we?"

"No way. It's just – they want it all, don't you reckon? The Marsdens of this world. And they can't wait."

"Marsden?"

"And Carey, et al," I added hastily. "Jukes, the whole crew."

"Even so, maybe life at Tolverton does seem dull to a teenager. Unrelenting, as it were. Lessons, prep, tests, exams – the predictable annual grind. Maybe there is a case for tarting the menu up a bit."

"Like, for instance?"

"More emphasis on the extra-curricular, I suppose. Archaeology, perhaps. Or Morris Dancing."

"Careful – mustn't get them too excited!"

"And trips. Think of the possibilities. Lourdes, even!"

He was getting quite agitated, the swiss roll in his hand unravelling and crumbling under the pressure.

"Whatever," I said rather vaguely, tiring of the topic. Naturally, part of me agreed with him. OK, most of me! But it was so hot down here. And claustrophobic. I just wanted out.

Neverthless common ground was at length established between us on one proposal at least for the new year: an art and architecture expedition to Vienna or Venice or somewhere, which we'd run together, the details to be hammered out with Chris back in Tolverton.

Assuming that is, we lived so long!

"Capital" cried Marcho, "just the ticket. Art and architecture. Can you imagine it, Jukes's face when we…?"

A loud clunk, as it jerked upright. The semaphore. Suddenly, decisively. All clear! Green now and brilliant.

For a moment there was silence. Then Marcho jumped to his feet, his face white. "Can't be," he said. "Can't possibly be."

An assertion with which I most heartily yearned to concur since I had no wish to breathe my last as mincemeat. There was none of the generous clearance here which you find on main lines. And no manholes with space enough to aid survival. If a train rounded yon bend at anything resembling speed, that would be that.

I too rose, but more slowly, kneading a leg which had succumbed to cramp. Its usual trick, but what a time to play up!

Fortunately, apart from the signal, there was nothing whatever to suggest disaster. The air was still and no sound of any description could be heard. Except our hearts.

Abruptly, Marcho dropped to his knees and placed one ear on a rail while I continued my frantic massage. A second or two and he looked up uneasily. Again he listened, this time longer. Then he jumped up, hands on hips.

"Apologies," he said, "but I simply can't be sure."

Had the stationmaster got it wrong about the line being closed? Or the clips been over-run? Or yon signal malfunctioned? Or had we somehow tripped a wire, and set it off ourselves?

Suddenly Marcho sprang into action. "Better make a run for it," he cried, grabbing up knapsack and camera, tossing me the torch. "Just to be on the safe side."

How we flew, spraying sludge left right and centre from our footfalls. Lord knows what leagues lay ahead of us, and no idea what, if anything, was on our tail, gaining ground, bent on our destruction.

No fox feeling fangs at his tail ever fled with such determination as Marcho and I. Over discarded rails, baulks, a mallet here and there – nothing hindered our headlong flight. Especially when, far behind us, sounded the first faint echo of a horn. One faint blast, no more, but chill to our very entrails as we sped.

On, on, round the never ending curves until – all at once, into the feeble torch beam it loomed. The cladding which Jones bach had had so laboriously to remove on Wednesday. Two jagged slabs of what resembled concrete, pushed precariously to the side of the line, so precariously they looked set to topple back at any moment.

A false impression, however, as quickly transpired. For as soon as we saw them, we glanced at each other. No words were needed. If Jones had pulled up in time, so could today's driver.

Hopefully.

Feverishly we set to work, levering the nearest slab away from the wall, back on the track. Boy, it took some doing! Easy work maybe for a couple of burly gangers, but for specimens such as Macho and myself – torment. Still, needs must when the Devil drives and, straining every muscle in our bodies, we sent the concrete crashing across the rails.

Another blast, nearer now.

The second slab proved more of an obstacle but, when eventually toppled – bonus of bonuses – it fell athwart its mate at such an angle that they formed a kind of mountain in miniature, easy to see and, we supposed, awkward to dislodge.

Panting with relief we resumed our flight, though with somewhat less urgency. A quarter to five said Roy's watch – how far away could the mouth of this bugger be?

What of course such novices as we failed to appreciate was that any inspection vehicle sent into so parlous an emergency would have to be not just adequate, but hyper-so. That day in the

Blaenrhondda tunnel it turned out that Cardiff had supplied none other than an old Glasgow and South Western snowplough, requisitioned from the north. Toughened roof, crane at the rear, and a nose at the front which would have demolished the White Cliffs of Dover had it been called upon to do so.

That puny rubble of ours it swept aside with no more than a tremor, and, with the mouth of the tunnel dark blue in the distance, we heard the roar of its diesel at our rear, the first rake of its cyclopean light already probing round the curve.

"What do we do now, then?"

"When plan A fails, time for plan B."

"Oh, yeah," I grunted, speeding on despite the pain. No time for plans now. Nothing but sheer brute sprint could save the day, OK!

But what was this? Why was Marcho no longer beside me and hurrying?

Glancing round I perceived that he'd evidently stumbled or something. Disaster! Back I hastened towards his kneeling form, but, before I could reach him, he'd got to his feet and turned my way with a wave. And was now picking his way over the sleepers, kind of strolling, with a smile on his face.

Strolling? With still over a hundred yards to go?

"For chrissake, Roy!" I yelled, pulling his sleeve.

"No need to worry," he beamed. "Plan B."

Get bloody real! I thought, panic increasing, turning back to the dregs of blue, such as they were, with all expedition – only the very next second to trip over a sprag.

Just as well, I told myself, pressing my body into wood and ballast deep as I could get, never mind the muck and stench. Terrified, on the verge of coma, able to see nothing, all I hearkened to was this appalling noise somewhere behind, reaching crescendo, about to shred me, consume me, send me packing to the punishment I so richly deserved. When –

"Upsa-daisy," said Roy cheerfully, helping me upright as the racket dwindled and stopped. "Nothing broken, I hope." Thrusting his free hand into a pocket, he turned to meet a figure approaching from the distant engine cab.

"Funny place for a prayer meeting, padre," chuckled an amiable voice. "Or was your friend just taking a nap?" He extended a hand. "Henderson, District Superintendent, Neath. You'll need a plaster on that, sonny."

"Marchpane," beamed the March, handing me his hankie. "Tolverton School."

"How rum! What a small world we live in, by George! You won't believe it, but I happen to be an OT myself."

"Well I never. Meet Bryant."

"One of your prefects I take it? How do. My gaol was Rhodes."

"Mine too," I nodded, shaking hands but seeing no need to disabuse him as to my age. When glory comes your way, why not bask a little?

Still wobbly, I allowed myself to be guided to a dynamometer car hitched at the rear where, plied with tea, I gradually came to my senses, marvelling how readily Macho adapted and took control of the situation. Doubtless the dog-collar helped but still – no grief from the officials, no question of reprimands. Just a kind of bemused toleration at the ways of railway freaks. And something shared.

What's more, they were only too keen to help. Their survey of the tunnel finished, they were heading back to Neath via Cardiff and the main line, and insisted on delivering us not simply to Blaenrhondda but all the way down to Treherbert. As for Marcho – that man was as happy as Croesus. Never in his wildest dreams had he expected to travel in the LNER dynamometer car with its polished panelling and brass. Nor to be able to discuss its finer points with an expert such as Henderson who, as we slowed, jolting past The Maesteg Arms, clapped Marcho round the shoulder, bosom pals already.

"Sorry, you couldn't have been with us from the start," he said. "After all, that might have been the final run through. All very historic."

"No hope of a reprieve?"

A shake of the head. "Very much doubt it. Too much lateral movement, I'm afraid. It'd cost a fortune to shore up, and with so few passengers…"

"They'll take it hard, the villagers."

"Not," said Henderson, giving the right away to his driver, "half as hard as we will. There's nothing so tragic as permanent way abandoned. Glad to have met you both."

"Take care!"

A roar as the wheels began to turn, with Marcho solemnly raising his cap and waving. It might for all the world have been a gun-carriage passing the Cenotaph!

"Blow me down – not the earlybirds!" quipped Carey, ghostlike under an eerie gas lamp. He tapped his watch.

"All right for some!" agreed Marsden, hands in pockets, shivering.

I shrugged. "Force majeure," I said dismissively, noting that the latter seemed to have spent the time having his hair cut. The result was to lend his face a leaner, harder look – but as to improvement? It was difficult to say.

"Enjoyed ourselves, have we lads?" Marcho in his most avuncular mood, hand on Carey's shoulder. "Sorry for the delay, but I expect you all had a good time."

"Not bad."

"Plenty of buns and lardy cake?"

"As ever."

"Your grandma well? I must send a card."

"Sort of," retorted Carey. "Except…"

"Yes?" smiled Roy encouragingly.

"Except that genius here believes everyone over seventy should be put down. Like dogs."

"What's that?" For once the old priest seemed nonplussed. "Surely not. Surely not, Andrew?"

"Well, what use are they?" Truculent and precise, the words might have been being spoken at Berchtesgaden. "Nothing but an unproductive burden. We don't get sentimental over redundant machines. Why make an exception for people?"

Understandably, this was greeted with silence – though what else could it be but a teenage pose? Surely.

"Good job," said I lightly, hoping to clear the air, "you didn't come out with anything like that over the PG Tips."

At which Carey simply raised his eyebrows while Roy consulted his watch at some length. From Marsden – not a blink!

Of Jukes and Foster, by contrast, there was no sign. They'd be round the back somewhere, having a smoke, having a wank – whatever genuine boys do! For me, despite Marsden's childish outburst, all I could really think of was our deliverance. Our stupidity, our second chance – or, perhaps, in the case of Marcho, third or thirty third. He was that sort of bloke!

Later that night, having dropped off our charges, we sat silently over a pint and a pizza in The Fox. No ginger beer for Roy this time, not on a Crispin Crispianus of this dimension. Over by the window, Tiny and the Carve were engaged in some pathetic quarrel, rugger tactics it sounded like, while Docherty played patience. Beyond them, the constellations.

"It makes you think," I said after a while. "Whether there really is a Hand that guides it all."

"Say again?" His mind had obviously been somewhere else, judging by the look on Roy's face. Unusually serious. Bleak almost.

"A God who intervenes? Is it likely?"

"My boy, what's brought this on?" Immediately his brow began to clear. "Thinking of entering the cloister, are we?"

I grinned. "Not quite."

"Prefect to Abbot in one day?"

"Yeah, yeah! It's just, I dunno – that train. If they'd been going any faster, we'd have ended up as Pedigree Chum, wouldn't we? Before they could stop. So answer me this – why brake when they did? There's no way they could have seen us in time."

"Sign from God? Divine intervention?" Marcho laughed, reaching into his haversack. "Or something more prosaic? Don't distress yourself, my dear chap." Opening his palm, he revealed a tiny clip of red and flashing beacons. "Just had time to fix it to a rail. Near thing I know, but all's well that ends well, eh?"

My skin blanched. "So that was it? Plan B? You mean if you hadn't…?"

"Picked it up at Blaengwynfi as a precaution?" he beamed, toying with his prize. "Who knows?"

Precaution, my foot! Like that station sign at Ilfracombe? But under the circumstances it would have been more than churlish to comment. I merely nodded with an appropriate air of relief, upon which he abruptly pushed the clip across the table. "Like a souvenir? A little something for posterity?"

"Posterity?"

"It'll have to be one between twenty, I'm afraid."

"Twenty what?" Still off balance, I picked up the trophy and peered at it.

"Your grandchildren, what else? Assuming you get round to having any." Chuckling at the accrescence of his own wit, he picked up my glass. "Another pint?" Then, swivelling round in his chair: "Carver, Tiny – one for the road?" Eyes goggled at this sudden and unexpected munificence. "David, room for a chaser in that, surely my boy."

So? Even priests push the boat out now and then!

And what of that trophy? That dodgy trophy to which Marcho and I probably owed our lives?

Well, queers don't have grandchildren, do they? More's the pity. So it's had to stick around with yours truly and, though long since dark and winkless, to this day it occupies a place of honour on a shelf by the barometer.

A useful reminder, I suppose, during one's periodic lapses into self-righteousness, that there really are times in this gewgaw life when crime turns out to be, let's face it, a blessing.

7: *The Battle of Weyburne Tump*

If, during that first term at Tolverton, the role of confessor in my life had been shouldered by Roy, it was Ormulak who'd filled the post of major domo, showing me the ropes, helping me negotiate my colleagues' foibles, and generally providing the kind of safety net which should have been the province of my Head of Department had said grandee not been too aloof and senior and idle to bother.

Now once more the little Pole came to the rescue. A chance encounter over coffee revealed that on New Years' eve he'd be driving up to some Katyn memorial function at Daventry, not a million miles away from some fun and fireworks at Julian's to which I'd been invited. A lift? Of course he'd be happy to oblige. Nay, delighted!

How to get back was a rather more thorny question, and one which, like most ravers extra,ordinaire, I was happy to leave to providence.

At about three, even so, on the Thursday afternoon I was perched on a sofa in Common Room, reading a Punch from 1917 one ear alert for the sound of Ormulak's Javelin, when who should come crashing backwards through the workroom door but Marcho clutching a huge consignment of votive candles.

"Have a peek at that," he cried, nodding at an envelope on top of the box. "Must dump these in the vestry. Back in half a mo."

It was close on a fortnight since our adventures in the Rhondda and, to tell the truth, I'd been so absorbed dodging the pain of Christmas that I'd quite forgotten Vienna and stuff, all those plans we'd discussed in the dark. Or aspirations I really ought to call them, expecting no more to come of them than that. And it was therefore a surprise, moreover quite a disturbing one, when the missive proved to consist of a brochure. For a hotel. And not in Vienna after all, but The Pensione alla Dorsoduro da CoCo, situated near the Academia bridge and convenient for all the tourist attraziones which Venezia could offer ze English milords.

Venice! A guy's dream till he gets there – a guy's obsession ever after.

At that time, of course, the city was known to me only through films – not, I hasten to add, the fabulous *Death in Venice* which wouldn't hit our screens for years yet, but black and white confections like *The Lost Moment* or even *Top Hat* – and each time those beams of bridge and spray gleamed at me, I vowed afresh to make them mine.

Hardly, though, with a bunch of schoolkids in tow! Jukes, Marsden & Co might be all very well in class, or even on a day trip across the hills. But a week of them, and in Venice? Beyond the call of duty, I fear. Way, way beyond.

Still, I had to let the old boy down lightly. It would hardly do to alienate one of the only two or three kindred spirits I'd found in the establishment. And anyhow I'd barely time to glance at the photos before he returned bearing sellotape and a tattered missal. "Interesting, eh?" he said, nodding at the brochure as he started to search a bureau.

"Out of this world, but…"

"Price is right and as for dates… Oh, drat! This really is too bad!"

"Roy?"

"Scissors!" he wailed as Ormulak's hooter began its summons. "Where are the confounded scissors? I've complained to Chris time and time again. Put 'em on a chain, I tell him…"

"Must dash. Look," I replied, bereft of anything approaching an excuse, "can I borrow this for a day or two?"

"Be my guest." Scratching his head, he began to rummage through the stationery drawer. "Chain 'em up I say, but does anyone listen? Barbarians!"

Julian's house lay some miles north of Banbury, in, or rather on the outskirts of, the township of Wartford Chase, a few dozen rows of raw terraced houses thrown up when the canal and mill arrived, now, like some ghost town in the Wild West, a place largely devoid of purpose. As so often in the Midlands, the drabness of the centre contrasted sharply with a scattering of spacious villas round the edge where the fat cats had thrived: bank managers, brewer, parsons, the usual crew. And, of course, the doctor.

Just the place for a young hopeful to put down roots, which Julian's granddad had duly done, his son in the course of time inheriting the property and continuing to live there though his own practice was some forty miles north in Latchfield. No matter that its outlook was about as attractive as a sewage farm, Corunna Lodge simply averted its eyes and lifted its nose, swathes of high dense box turning the paddock into a little kingdom all of its own, and protecting from prying eyes Corunna's drive, its casements, its lawns & verandah – and its gazebo.

Its very considerable gazebo! I gazed in awe at the floodlit mass. To be frank, it was more like a Crystal Palace in miniature, its domes and arches interlocking to form a vision in glass so dainty it might have been one of those ice extravaganzas you sometimes see in the food hall at Harrods. Weird, and quite out of keeping with the red brick and grey drainpipes of the Lodge itself.

One thing was clear: only substantial wealth could have built such a thing and, for that matter, heated it. Today, for instance – some boiler somewhere must be working flat out to defy the wintry air. Think of it, the sacks of coke it must get through! The sheer unabashed – and now it was as if I could hear my old dad talking – profligacy of it all.

Venturing through the open door – more waste! – whom should I find but Toby Copeland – or if you prefer it, Jugs, that oddly apt family soubriquet of his – scattering cushions on a series of jazzed-up palliasses arranged in a sprawling Druids' circle round the edge of what was clearly destined to become the dance floor. "Typical!" came his usual breezy greeting. "The early bird himself. Paul the Gaul!"

"What," quoth I, flattered, "always on time?"

"No way," he grinned, "always on heat! Or what Jules calls your homing instinct. If there's nooky on the menu, watch out for Bryant." He waved a proprietorial arm. "Behold, the Palais de Pleasure!"

"Guaranteed?" I inquired archly.

"Or your money back," he laughed. "I'll go find bro – probably still in the sack with Tina."

"Tina Ramb?"

Nodding in modified homage, he disappeared up the steps whilst I set my case down on the edge of an oblong dais presumably meant for the band. Already I'd begun to doubt my wisdom in coming, and mention of La Ramb, the kind of flash girl who floats into Oxford to hook herself a member of the affluent effluent, just about settled it. Why waste an evening watching other people get laid? Why waste a night in an unknown bed, even if by remotest chance Julian was available to share it – a deux, I mean! After all, there's nothing so comfortable as one's own pillow is there? Novel ready under the lamp. Chocolate creams, slippers, dressing gown – everything where it should be.

Nor had one's first glimpse of the arrangements been such as to encourage optimism. The buffet, already laid out under cellophane at the far end, seemed to consist of the usual college Ball stuff: paper plates, plastic glasses, a decorated salmon busy defrosting, coronation broiler, that hard kind of rice that gets between your teeth, and to cap it all puddings in pink cups masquerading as brulée.

Nor did the décor do much to offset the gloom. Clustered balloons in green and pink, some faded bunting, a vast awning striped like a butcher's apron, and one of those revolving mirror balls which give you a headache with their unremitting spangle, spangle, spangle.

It was all so predictable. The palliasses, for another thing. It didn't take much imagination to guess their function, nor, as I looked about me, to people this pavilion as it would look a few hours hence after the dancing. After the ties off, shirts off, all off!

Tanned hands stroking tanned legs, tanned torsos sprawled across rugs and mattresses. A rank melange of brown promiscuity, posing and preening, and eager to displayits youth to other youth without, as the Yankees say, mental reservation or purpose of evasion.

Salad days? Personally, I'd rather mix my mayo alone!

Suddenly, acting on pure impulse, grabbing my bag I raced up the steps two at a time. And not a moment too soon since in the far distance I could just make out a girl in hot pants driving a motor mower with Jules and Jugs in languid pursuit urging her to slow the fuck down!

Tina, Tina, Tina – aha oho little schemer!

To avoid which, wasn't anything preferable? Even a hard bench on Wartford Junction waiting for the York to Bournemoth (Fridays excepted)?

A very few days later, still downcast at my excoriating sexual inadequacy and forced into frequent inane bursts of glee to disguise it, I found myself sitting between James and Marcho at the start of term meeting, which began on a note of high fertility. Firstly, congratulations to Sue and James Frobisher on the birth of a son, Thomas Wilfred.

Polite applause.

Secondly, the announcement of Docherty's much delayed marriage.

Cheers and loud laughter.

Ignoring such ribaldry, shouts of 'Who aimed the shotgun, Dave?' and so forth, Amberley ploughed on with details of time and venue, giving me a moment not only to conjecture how Docherty's ghost of a body would cope with the marriage bed, but to reflect that, as a consequence, my life would soon be under the thumb, boorish and resolute, of Owen Murdoch. Scant time then for any plans I might have laid for a ration or two of hoi toi toi.

The next item, however, brought me down from the clouds with a veritable bump.

"It has been brought to my notice," said Eric with that inimical severity of his which, despite its surface amiability, made it plain that any deviance would be met with extreme disfavour, "that certain oddities of dress seem to have become current on the sports fields. At House finals last term, I myself noticed a member of the Rhodes squad wearing gloves. Gloves, gentlemen! At least we can be thankful, I suppose, that it wasn't a muff."

Loud laughter, though not from Owen whose face merely darkened to a more thunderous red.

"Let me stress," continued the Head, "that Games are, in my opinion, a vital part of the educational process and certainly not in any way a platform for fashion or any other kind of sartorial excess. In future, dress rules will be strictly enforced. I trust, gentlemen, I can count on your co-operation in this most crucial matter. May I also add, that while in previous years no dress code has been found to be necessary in respect of Common Room, I intend to introduce one, and to do so shortly. Those masters not yet in possession of a regulation tracksuit, would therefore be well advised to pay a visit to the school's outfitter at their earliest convenience!

"Now to happier matters. Mr Watson – a breakdown of the Oxbridge results so far, if you please."

"Thank you, Headmaster," said Watson reaching for his folder as he rose. "First let me…"

I felt a sudden dig in the back ribs. "See what you've done!" hissed Carver in my ear. "Idiot!"

Remembering his stetson, I just shrugged, and gently amused myself by conjecturing of what, were there absolutely no rules, his outfit of choice would consist. Ballet tights, maybe, with sequins? There was definitely something dodgy about the guy.

Even more amusing was the irony that this new rule made little or no difference to yours truly, at least for the time being. Like many schools, Tolverton operated a policy for games staff of one term off, two terms on, and this was to be my turn at fallow. Come summer I'd be probably be carded for cricket or tennis or similar, but which of us minds showing off in whites?

After that, well we'd just have to see. For now, the image of myself demonstrating the backhand to a group of adoring 5th formers served as welcome relief while Watson plodded through the list of the dozen and a half or so successful candidates in the November exams.

In those days, sixth-formers wishing to enter either of the ancient universities had to stay on a while extra, the so-called seventh term, to take the entrance papers set by the various colleges. For obvious reasons I myself had played no part in last term's preparation – it was considered far too important for a novice to be let loose on. Next year though would be different. Trewes had already indicated that he was willing to relinquish either Chaucer or Shakespeare to me, and it was a prospect I'd genuinely begun to relish. It all of course depended on whom the candidates were. Jukes would have been fun but he'd already been snaffled by Carver and his historians. As to others, I had so far no idea.

"Which totals fourteen," said Watson, looking up from his page. "Three schols, three exhibitions, eight places."

"Not a bad bag," nodded Eric. "Now to Any Other Business. Chaplain, you've something for us, I believe?"

"What's it this time?" whispered James. "Prayer book in Esperanto?"

I just shrugged though I had a shrewd idea what was coming. Since I let Roy know about my change of heart over Venice, I'd had several notes about flights, passports, hotels and so on. It sounded as though the notion was turning into reality.

"Well now," said Marcho, beaming at the assembled gowns, "to begin with, I have the pleasure to announce that our Lent visitor this year will be a junior research fellow from Royston Hall, Cambridge, the Reverend Beresford Dick-Whyte-Dick."

Suppressed guffaws from just behind – James and I merely exchanged a decorous grin.

"Now, for his stay he's been allotted rooms in Clive but before…"

"A wee correction, padre," interposed Murdoch. "It's actually Rhodes where he'll be staying. In ma coach house."

"Of course, precisely!" nodded Marcho imperturbably. "Slip of the tongue, many thanks Owen. Rooms in the Rhodes annexe – and very comfortable you'll make him too, I'm sure. But before coming into residence, he'll be paying us a visit for a preliminary look round. At which time, I trust he'll be welcomed by all and, er – sundry.

"Lastly, a more personal tit-bit. With the Head's blessing, I have been discussing with various members of staff the possibility of increasing the range of pastoral activities available to boarders. And, of course, town boys too. Culture, gentlemen, that's the thing. A tonic for the sixth-form. To broaden their minds and, as it were, equip them. Give them the wherewithal to face the ghastliness of the outside world.

"As a first step, I'm pleased to announce that the Head has agreed to the formation of a new society, the first meeting of which will take place on Friday at 4.30pm in the library. Tea will be served."

My eyebrows kind of rose slightly – wasn't this a peculiar way of announcing a school trip? But then, when did the March ever follow convention!

"I'd be most grateful if tutors could encourage seniors to sample the wares, as it were, and I need hardly…"

"Sample what, padre?" Tarn's voice boomed round the walls. "What sort of doo-dah is it? The Tolverton Tram Lovers' League? Black Magic for Beginners?"

Brushing aside the laughter, Roy nodded amiably. "Didn't I say, Ken? My apologies. It's a revival of the old Monarchist Society…"

"Which," hissed Carver softly, "last met in 1399!"

"...of which Mr Ormulak will act as Treasurer, with myself as Patron. The inaugural meeting will consist of a lecture on His Most August Majesty, King Idris of Libya – to be delivered by Mr Bryant who has also agreed to serve as President of the new club."

Not only did my eyebrows rise further, they positively hit the ceiling. King Whatsit of Where? What the bugger did I know about Libya? And as for being President of some monarchist outfit, well, frankly, I'd rather sport a beard and throw bombs! Dear old Roy was going to have some explaining to do!

For now all I could do was glower his way. The Head nodded amiably as Roy resumed his seat. "I'm sure," he said reaching for his mortarboard, "we all wish the Chaplain well in his new venture. Especially as some of us here served in Libya, eh Tom?" Gentle applause. "And have fond memories of the Emir's help and hospitality. Yes, I think I can say fond.

"Lastly gentlemen, foresight of a somewhat different kind. The replacement pool. You'll be glad to hear that not only has planning permission finally been granted, but the Fustians, God bless 'em, have agreed to foot the bill. Full funding, down to the last penny. Which means that construction will begin later this month, completion, DV, by the end of May."

This time a buzz of approval, during which the Head rose. "Thank you gentlemen – and I need hardly remind you about this evening. We meet at seven."

Although I made an immediate bee-line for Marcho, I was too late, Watson collaring both him and Ormulak and sweeping them off into his office. My irritation thus had plenty of time to brew, especially as it wasn't till halfway through the Head's party that I was able to get my béte noire into a corner.

Before that, the day had passed in a considerable blur, including a plea by Docherty, now he was moving off campus, for me to take over the 6th form Classical Music Appreciation Society (successful), and an attempt by Baxter to recruit me into either the Tolverton Ringers (unsuccessful) or the Common Room darts team (wildly unsuccessful). Fortunately no-one seemed to have noticed the mention of dinghy sailing on my curriculum vitae.

Of more interest was Trewes's pathetic manoeuvring to get my help with the school play – to which I was only prepared to agree providing I could also help in its choice! The result? A *Twelfth Night* doubtless destined to be horribly tame and safe with his finger in the pie, but who could tell? With any luck he might drop dead!

After all this, a deplorably long lunch with the gang ensued, during which James and I yet again confirmed our race date once the weather improved. Finally came a meeting with Murdoch in his rather spartan sitting room on the first floor of Rhodes. As I would not become his tutor until Saturday fortnight, this seemed a bit premature but I thought it best to keep mum.

"It's occurrit to me," he said, handing over a cup of extremely weak Typhoo, "that it'd be of assistance to you if I ootlined your duties & privileges once you become a member of ma hoose."

"Good idea," I replied – which proved to be the sum total of my contribution to the conversation over the next twenty minutes since without further ado he launched into what was clearly a well-rehearsed list: the handbell I'd ring on the boys' landing at 7.15 daily; the house prayers I'd take on Mondays, Wednesdays and Fridays; the study inspections I'd conduct on Tuesdays and Thurdays; the bedroom I'd have next to that of the prefects; the bathroom I'd share with Miss Frame, the study I'd occupy on the ground floor except, as he put it, "when I need it mysel' for a correction session" – on and on went the long dire briefing, prompting me to swear a silent oath that this association with Auschwitz would be as short as I could decently make it. One year max!

More, however, was still in store.

"Oh, and one other thing," he added, refilling his cup but not mine, "it's ma inflexible rule that all juniors take a shower before lights oot at nine. Youngsters have a natural aversion to lather, and I will not have ma hoose smelling like an Addis Ababa urinal, understand?"

I nodded, recalling the crudity from an earlier encounter somewhere.

"It'll be your job to supervise the bath area each evening and make sure they dinna get up to any, what one might call, horseplay. Get ma drift? Any transgressions – ye'll report them straight to me."

Then it's off to the gas chambers, I mused, or publicly hanged drawn and quartered – tick your box! Poor sods – just imagine it. You're in the middle of a spot of innocent hows-your-father when you look up, and there's that frightful Spitfire moustache bristling at you. Enough to put you off orgasm for life!

One year max, I repeated to myself – not a minute more!

Ironic really as decisions go, considering how things turned out. I mean the fact that I survived not much more than half my sentence. But, at the time – absolute determination.

All of which threw a not inconsiderable pall over tying my tie and polishing my pumps. Good job I'm no Trot, I thought to myself as I entered Eric's salon an hour later, or it's my own transgressions I'd probably be reporting! Mass murder of all garden gnomes and Scots gits! And losers who hide behind facial hair!

Old-fashioned, as in all things, the Amberleys gave but two large parties a year. Summer term in their garden, Easter term in here. As one might therefore expect, the venue proved quite a whopper – almost, to my way of thinking, a ballroom, and tonight there must have been well above a hundred punters already a-guzzling beneath its electroliers.

There was a political corner: Mayor, Deputy Lieutenant, local MP, Pretender to his seat, and Chairmen of both the Liberal and Tory associations. There was a church corner: Bishops of Monmouth and Latchfield, Rural Dean, Rector of St Tywyn's plus churchwardens and the Unitarian minister. There was a music corner, a hunting corner, a disgruntled corner, a matron's corner (where Irish was already halfway tipsy) and so on. Every tribe catered for, except – education corner?

No way!

Members of Common Room were clearly there for one reason and one reason only – to act as lackeys! Waiters to be precise, flitting round the various notables to tempt them with plates of crab & sausage dainties, and refill glasses. Which suited me perfectly. Equipped with a substantial decanter, I stationed myself next to, and just a smidgen behind, a large, folding screen, looking as though I was about to spring into action. Whereas, of course, I preferred merely to sip my glass and observe with growing cynicism the ways of this hypocritical world.

It had already begun to stir in my mind that one day I might write what you're reading now: a kind of 20th century cross, I flatter myself, between *Vanity Fair* and *Fanny Hill*. And what better starting point than the spectacle which lay before me. What you might call a fair field full of folk, though mediaeval angst was by no means the route I intended to ply.

But here they were, you see. In their best clothes, on their best behaviour, busy at the things they knew best: how to charm, how to disarm, and how to melt into the pack – which meant, of course, scotching whatever vesitigial memories remained of their youth. That halcyon time when they were hot with individuality, when their opinions were well to the left of Pravda, when they needed sex more frequently than trains on the Bakerloo line. In other words, when they had passion, compassion, and intimations of what lies radiant behind the radiance of the welkin…

Sorry to go on like that – still, you take my point. It would have been fun to blip a couple of hundred volts through the pathetic crew as they were now, to make them jump a bit – and remember what being alive was like.

"Come along, come along!" said Roy, doing a Watson. "Can't have you youngsters standing here idle."

"Ho, ho, very witty!" I replied, grabbing him by the sleeve. "Just the man – come along yourself." Shoving his empty salver on the radiator, I pulled him nearer the screen.

"My dear," he twinkled, "what will people think?"

"Bugger all, I expect, since they're brain-dead anyway. OK, let's have it. Spill the beans."

He looked at me quizzically. "My word, you do keep your ear to the ground. Though I'm afraid I know little more than you do. They say it'll probably be tomorrow."

"What will?"

"D-Day," he retorted, nodding towards our MP. "When Sir Madison applies for the Chiltern Hundreds, poor man."

"Big deal," said I, revealing my complete political naivety, "I hope he gets them. But what I'm referring to is Idris When I'm Dry. This dude I'm supposed to be lecturing on."

"Oh, that's your problem. Really, don't worry about a thing. I've an article from the Braganza Society which you can read out more or less verbatim. Just put in a few buts and therefores."

"Roy," I interrupted severely, "since when did I agree to be Patron of a bunch of weirdo monarchists?"

"President," he corrected me amiably. "I myself…"

"Roy! I am not joking."

Chastened somewhat, he assumed a look of penitence which was at least halfway sincere. "I'm afraid it was all rather spur of the moment," he confessed ruefully. "See, I'd forgotten to clear it with you earlier, and I thought – well. He's a good chap. Won't mind a bit. And after all it is a sort of quid pro quo, isn't it?"

"Is it?"

"Well, Venice, remember? As I'm doing all the footwork on Italy, I thought you might like to help out with Libya."

Put like which, and with that crestfallen look in those blue eyes, what could I do but calm down and accept my destiny.

A destiny which, by twenty five past four on Friday, despite the bloater sandwiches and mugs of cocoa, was looking bleaker than I could possibly have imagined. With the curtain about to go up, apart from Roy and myself, those present numbered exactly half a dozen. Castleton, Jukes, Marsden, a farmer's son from my 5th form set whose name eluded me, Mrs Jarrow busy with some shapeless knitting, and Tom Fairfield.

"Roy," I hissed as he arranged papers on our table. "How can I possibly read this stuff out to an audience of six and keep a straight face?"

"Seven," he whispered as in wandered Macdonald eating an ice lolly, "but I see what you mean. Leave it to me." Upon which he disappeared, only to return less than three minutes later, as if the Pied Piper, at the head of a motley band of 6th and Lower Sixth formers. At least a baker's dozen, and all intensely enthusiastic.

A sight which so perked up my confidence that I declaimed the Braganza tosh, more than twenty minutes of it, for all the world as though it were the Gettysburg Address or Hal's poncification at Harfleur.

Quelle triumph! Quelle spectacular debut, ensuring the Monarchists would clearly become one of those 'in' societies which everyone clamours to join. All very well except that Marcho and I were now faced with the problem of devising a topic for the next session which would sustain, or preferably increase, this unexpected momentum. "Thinking cap time," he announced at length, closing the shiny new minutes book. "Not that there's any hurry – we've got three weeks."

"Thank God for that," I sighed. "Oh, by the way, tell me – exactly how did you manage it, that stunt? Drumming up the cohorts so quickly?"

In vain did he try fobbing me off with his usual tap of the nose. Next day, it was all the talk in The Fox, with guess-who leading the critics, his spite a wonder to behold.

"Ken saw the whole thing, I tell you!"

"Senior detention?" I expostulated. "Never – Roy wouldn't have the nerve."

"That man," sneered Carver, "has the gall of a Ghandi. I tell you he simply marched in, dismissed the prefect, and told them he'd halve their time if they came along to hear you."

"All in a good cause," smiled James, giving me an affectionate nudge.

"Good cause be blowed!" bellowed the Carve. "What is this place coming to! It's about time Eric started to get a grip. Slack, slack, slack – it makes my blood boil! Macho needs to be taught a lesson."

Well bored with vituperation, it was not long before I made my excuses and shoved off. As time was short till my move, I'd decided to devote this afternoon to grinding out change of address cards. Always a chastening experience – nothing brings home more clearly how few people you really care for – but this time it seemed worse. The obvious ones, no problem. But when it came to the question marks, from then on my fingers kind of froze.

Julian and Jugs, suppose so (just about). Alexis – well yes, but where to? Mario, but was there any point after more than a year?

Nevertheless, I selected a blank card and began to write.

But before I'd managed even a word, there was a loud, insistent hooting below my window. Marcho on his running board, beckoning me down!

"Thank God it's Old Mother Kent's afternoon at the pictures," said I breathless, emerging on to the step, "or you'd have been for it."

"In you get," he replied, ramming the trafficator home with his elbow. "I've something to show you."

"Oh yes?"

"The answer to our prayers. Well – mine anyway."

Glad of the respite, I jumped in, and off we roared in the direction of Hereford. In those days this part of the border was still well forested and it was a steady climb of six or seven minutes before we emerged into open heathland, turning off the tarmac and following a rough track which looked rarely used and which, still climbing, finally petered out at a ruin.

We stopped.

"Weyburne Heath," announced the March, almost proprietorially, looking round him with barely-concealed delight. Ahead the ground sloped gently away towards a church and hamlet perhaps a mile distant which I recognised as Gifford Farrar. To our right, less far off, some scrub, a brace of rowans, and the amorphous bulk of Weyburne Tump with its cute little obelisk and stone circle. As for the rest – nothing. No cottages, no people, and the motor road barely visible in its defile.

"Idyllic!"

"Well idyllic," I agreed nonchalantly.

"So peaceful! You'd never guess it was once a battlefield and the scene of mass slaughter."

"Really?" I said, perking up at the thought of a spot of gore.

"Carnage, dear boy. Utter carnage." Beaming with satisfaction, he lit a purple cigarette.

"Romans versus a local tribe?" I ventured, my ancient history a bit hazy.

"Not at all. Doesn't it ring a bell – the Battle of Weyburne Tump?"

"Never heard of it."

"The most glorious engagement of the war? Roundheads slain by the thousand!"

Now I was on stronger ground. "You mean, the Civil War? *Children of the New Forest* and all that?"

"What else?"

"But Roy – sorry to be a pest, but aren't you barking up the wrong tree? I mean, none of those battles ever crossed the border as far as I know. Worcester would have been the nearest, and you can hardly call…"

"Dear boy, I know it, you know it – but how about a dozen credulous 6th formers?" He puffed contentedly. "Eager young Monarchists?"

I goggled. "You're not proposing to fake a battle?"

"More a battle*ground*," he replied sagely. "What better for our second meeting than a field trip? Fresh air, new horizons. And why trek all the way to Naseby or Cropredy Bridge when we've this on our doorstep?"

"But no ruddy battle ever took place here!"

"Oh, a very minor difficulty." He waved an airy hand. "A scrap of tunic here, a buckle there…"

"You're actually proposing to salt it?" Now he really had got me worried. "Roy, that could be a criminal offence. How about the landowner?"

"Ministry of Works," he answered blithely. "And there's no warden. Besides, who will ever know? We come over at lunchtime, scatter some scrips and scraps, bring the boys out for the meeting, clear up afterwards. Six hours at the most. Don't you fret yourself – safe as houses!"

Where had I heard that before?

"One more question then," I said. "Just suppose it were possible – to sort of assemble something halfway plausible. How about the de-briefing? I mean, you'd have to come clean at some stage. You couldn't have 6th formers going up to Cambridge believing there really was a Battle of Weyburne Tump."

"But don't you see – that will be the really fun part." His cigarette holder soared enthusiastically. "As they come across each artefact, they'll get more and more suspicious. You know what lads are. Finally they'll round on us, I'll admit the joke, and we'll all end up having a jolly good laugh. Might even, if things go well, stand them a half in, you know…" – he lowered his voice as if about to reveal the last secret of Fatima – "…the pub!"

Whether it was that – the prospect of Marsden & Co in mufti, in a bar – or a sort of last resurgence of undergraduate spunk, who knows? But eventually I found myself agreeing to the whole caboodle. The whole disastrous caboodle! I could just see it, my standing on Eric's carpet trying vainly to justify what would of course, in the cold light of day, appear totally unjustifiable, but, as options go, even that seemed a picnic compared to turning Roy down.

Hence began a most bizarre couple of weeks while the pair of us collected items for the scam just like jackdaws building a nest. Some of the stuff was pretty simple: a small ballbearing scuffed and scarred, marinated in a mixture of oil and mud, a wisp of red felt, a pheasant leg with some scraps of meat baked black and left under a patio stone for a week..

Much more taxing, though, were things like maps and remnants of signs, the ageing of which required use of the Forbidden City – that is, Mrs Kent's kitchen. Burning a sheet of paper over a sink is child's play. However, burning part, say just the corners, is a process of titanic sensitivity, especially when it's taken several hours to draw and colour the map in question which just needs charring a bit. Four out of my half dozen masterpieces survived their ordeal, one though going up in a crumble of sparks and hot carbon, the other whisked from the windowsill by a sudden gust of breeze and deposited on the most moist corner of the compost heap – where, I might add, it stayed!

Most of Common Room were of course, preoccupied with a horse of a vastly different colour, namely the forthcoming end of Docherty's virginity. Though the marriage ceremony itself was to take place in the bride's parish of Cragfield, over whose tiny Saxon church old Joe Jephson still presided, there was to be a blessing afterwards in school chapel followed by a grand buffet lunch.

In other words, one of those neat, efficient not-too-emotional occasions which the British do so well. Except – well, there were one or two straws in the wind. Nothing certain, mind you, but sufficient to cause me concern. A concern whose epicentre lay at the feet of one man in particular.

Carver!

Given his barely-concealed scorn for the groom, plus his unwavering contempt for all those to whom jock straps were anathema, I was more than surprised to hear that he'd volunteered to take charge of Dave's stag night.

"So?" I queried. "What's the scheming blighter up to, then?"

James hugged me round the shoulder. "Worryguts!" he chuckled. "It'll be fine. They're experts, Tiny and the Carve. They did me proud at my funeral, I can tell you. Ten pints and a chaser. Hangover lasted the whole weekend."

"Congratulations, but Docherty's probably a bit more vulnerable than you."

"In which case it'll last a week rather than a weekend. So what? Lucky man!"

Nor were my misgivings lessened when, early next day, I witnessed Roy bearded by Heckle and Jeckle as he locked up after matins.

"Buddies again, are we?" I queried, looking up from my semolina as he hurried in towards the end of lunch.

"Sorry I'm late – Staggers on the phone!" he said, a bit flustered. "Now what was that?"

"Oh, nothing much. Just that I saw you in conflab. You know, after chapel, with Carver and Tiny. Not your most usual of bedfellows."

"Well," he grimaced, "someone's got to love the dears, I suppose."

"Getting spliced or something, are they?"

"Got it in one. Westminster Abbey and a honeymoon in Cannes."

"Good for them. I expect it's legal over there!"

He laughed. "As a matter of fact, they're planning a trip at half term, if you must know. Fishing, somewhere up north."

"North?" All at once I pricked up my ears.

"So they said. Taking the Carmarthen-Aberdeen night sleeper. Via Cardiff, of course, not Lampeter. They were asking if I knew what time it called at Leominster."

"And did you?"

Pausing with a sprout halfway to his lips, he gave me the loftiest look he could muster. "Can you doubt it?"

An apparently innocuous scrap of conversation, and yet one which stuck in my head for the rest of the day. Why a night train, for God's sake? Indeed, why go by train at all? Carver's MGB was fast and new, and many a time I'd seen Tiny and their rods packed in beside him, off to snaffle a few unsuspecting salmon. True, if their destination was a fair way off, what with wear and tear, and petrol at the price it was, a thrifty man might well decide the train was more sensible. But since when could the Heck & Jeck be called thrifty?

No, the whole thing was most decidedly – and no apologies for this one – fishy! Thus it was still very much on my mind, when about nine that evening la dragon herself ushered up to my room the most unexpected of callers.

"Why, Dave!" I exclaimed, tossing the drivel I'd been marking on to the bed. "What a surprise. Come in and park yourself."

"Will you be wanting anything, gentlemen? A drop of coffee, maybe?" inquired Mrs K, all sweetness and light these days, since I'd given notice.

"Not for me," whispered Docherty, pale and nervous.

"Perhaps later," I said, "thank you, Mrs Kent," as she kind of bobbed backwards out of the door.

"Look here," said the emaciated form. "Is this convenient, Bryant? I mean, if not it can easily wait…" And he half rose from the chair he'd only just chosen.

"No problem," I replied, waving him down again. "What on earth's up? You look all in."

"Hardly surprising," he moaned drably. "I'm getting wed, aren't I!"

I nodded sympathetically. "Having second thoughts, perhaps?" was my subtle query, the plots of fifty movies running simultaneously through my head.

"Not quite that."

"Well – anything I can help with?"

Meeting my eyes at last, he ventured the ghost of a smile. "Possibly," he replied. "That is, you're part of this younger generation that seems to find these things so easy. And you're the only chap in this hell-hole who doesn't laugh his head off at a fellow's – difficulties."

"Kind of you," I said, crossing my fingers that this wasn't going to decline into tears. "But…"

"Not at all. And you're the only one I can trust not to blab if I confess this bit of a problem. Unlike you, I've got to survive in bloody Tolverton the rest of my career. Oh, yes. You see, I've only got…" He seemed to struggle with his words for an instant. "I've only got a 2i."

Was this the confession? The towering inferno he must heave off his chest? I almost let out a guffaw. What wouldn't I give to possess a 2i! Even from Nottingham or Leicester or wherever he'd been nurtured.

"Look, David…" I began.

He silenced me with a wave of his hand. "No, let me come straight to the point. If I don't do it now, I'll never – pluck up courage." He took a deep breath and sat straight upright. "You see, I'm over thirty and I've, well, never had a woman. Had, that is, in the sense of – had."

Feigning the surprise he obviously expected, I fought hard to keep a straight face. What a hoot! Was he really about to seek my advice? Did he really think I could function as an instruction manual on the female anatomy? Talk about the blind leading the blind!

Oblivious, however, on he forged. "You're amazed, I can see that. Quite right but – better late than never, as they say. So, I've done my preparation, right? Read a recommended manual, quite assiduously actually. The drawings are a great help, don't you think?"

"Oh, invaluable."

"But they don't tell you everything."

"No?" I said cautiously.

"No, no. There are some points on which they're, well, rather kind of *limp*."

At this I really did have to stride to the window and use my handkerchief. Not that he noticed.

"Vague, is what I mean. Too discreet. They tend to beat about the bush when it comes to points of etiquette, you understand."

"Any one in particular," I asked, turning round, muffling a sniff.

"Just one, but crucial. It concerns these, er… You must have come across them. Condominiums, I believe they're called ?"

"I gather," said I gravely, "the word's usually shortened somewhat."

"Seriously?" he replied, brightening a little. "Thank you for that. I knew you were the right person to approach. Now, I've read the instructions and understand the principle, but what nothing tells you is when."

"When what?"

"To put the device on. How's clear enough – but when, that's a mystery. In my manual, at figure 4 not a sign of it. By 5, there it is, fully, um – installed. Now, the order of things is quite clear up to, and including, the rotatory stroking of the inner thigh…"

"Dave…" I said hastily, nausea on the horizon.

"But what then? Do you don it before proceeding to the labial phase or…?"

"To be frank," I intervened firmly, "what you need, Dave, is specialist advice, OK? From a married man. A guy who's used to a real live wife. Not someone like me who survives on sort of, one night stands."

"Ah," he said wistfully, "one night stands! You've had so much sex, haven't you? So much experience? Still, better late…"

"Than never. Quite. That's why you need the horse's mouth. The info only a married man can supply. Girlfriends and wives, you see: they're totally different things."

"Really?" Eyes shining, he was now hot for anything. "In what way?"

"You'll find out!" I reached for a pen. "The guy you need…" and as it occurred to me, I simply couldn't resist it "… is Roy Marchpane. Let me give you his number."

"That old priest?" There was genuine horror in his voice. "Oh no, Bryant. Really, I couldn't."

"Nothing to be shy about, honestly. He's very approachable. Tell you what, let me ring for you."

And so there ensued one of the most bizarre phone calls of my life, with Mrs Kent all ears, and the hapless Docherty framed in her doorway.

"Oh Roy, sorry to disturb you. Sermon going well? Really, the Ammonites? Well, that should hit the spot all right. Can't wait! No, no, it was something else. To do with Dr. Docherty, you know, one of the biologists. The one you're marrying next week. That's right – well, look here. It seems he's in need of advice. Yes, quite urgent. No, I shouldn't think she's Catholic." A shake of the head from Docherty. "Nor deceased wife's sister?" Vigorous shake of the head from Docherty. "No, not that either. Hang on a bit – look Roy, you're on the wrong tack altogether. It's nothing to do with religion, OK? More a question of what you might call – condominiums."

Frowning a little at my whisper, Mrs Kent craned closer.

"Quite, but I can't say more on the phone. The thing is, can I send him round right now? Yes, yes. Roy, you're a brick!" Replacing the receiver, I turned around. "Voila – Buggleskkely awaits you. It's the large house by the Hereford roundabout. Can't miss it."

Back in my armchair, I gazed at the ceiling, my mind racing as I tried to conjecture what heights of Lewis Carroll would soon be being reached in that unsuspecting mansion. A curiosity which, moreover, was destined to remain unsatisfied till lunch the next day. This time it was I who was late, having been held up by a prolonged altercation with Carve and his sidekick outside the Livingstone dayroom. Indeed so prolonged, there was bugger all left in the canteen except dodgy offal and chips as curled-up as a Sultan's slipper.

"Are we still on for half past five?" I inquired, brushing an assortment of crumbs and sugar off the table.

"Half past...?" Roy smiled at me blankly.

"Our progress meeting. You know, about Weyburne. We've still some details to thrash out."

"Of course, of course. Five thirty in the vestry?"

"I'll be there. That is," I added, prodding my plate gingerly, "if I survive. This liver looks trés odd."

"You think so?" He regarded me quizzically. "Not nearly so odd, though, as your friend there." He gave a quick nod across in the direction of Docherty who was intensely and furtively peeling a banana as if doing it homage.

"Oh right," I chuckled. "I've been meaning to ask how you got on."

"As I say – very oddly. I'd laid out all the brochures – the almshouses, you know – assuming he was after lodgings for his mamma or some old aunt. But all he wanted to talk about was sex. Poor Clemmie had to leave the room, it was that embarrassing."

"Oh well, weddings!" I grinned, looking across once more at the trembling fingers, and feeling just a twinge of remorse. "I suppose everyone gets a bit excited."

OK, it had seemed a good joke at the time, but maybe I'd taken advantage where I shouldn't. Like most loners, deep down I harboured a genuine concern for the rare and odd, into which category young Docherty certainly fell. A concern which had by no means been abated by this recent skirmish of mine outside Livingstone.

After allowing myself to be berated once more on the issue of games kit, it had been my turn. To go on the offensive, I mean. I'd heard nothing further about Docherty's stag night and saw no reason not to inquire further. What time it would be, where they were holding it – that sort of stuff. You can imagine my astonishment when I was roundly rebuffed, told it was a party for colleagues of long standing only, not dopes fresh out of diapers, who weren't satisfied unless queering everybody else's pitch – and generally given to understand that the matter was not one I would be wise to poke my nose into.

Fair enough. After all it's true I was new on the team, and, except for the condominiums, had hardly spoken a dozen words to Dave. Yet somehow my brain wouldn't let go. It was like – in the same way some frail little wildflower would be no match for Carver's boot, neither would he. In which case, how could I stand aside and do nothing? That the terrible twins were up to something was as clear as day. But what? All I had to go on was this tiny, tiny sliver of instinct: that somehow it was connected with that conflab of theirs with Marcho. The fishing trip they'd said they were planning. Hang on though – what sense did that make? A stag night spent angling? And in February? No way did it all gel. Unless, of course, they meant to drown the guy...

Get real Bryant!

Besides, as the days went by, both Weyburne and the Gauleiter of Rhodes looming ever nearer, there was quite enough for my feeble mind to manage, without worrying about Docherty.

By the Thursday morning, my room resembled nothing so much as the Lost Property office at Baker Street. Stacked on one side were suitcases, boxes of books, a couple of pictures and my wireless – all ready for my move after the wedding. On the other, two bins of assorted artefacts, scrolls, signs and other highly convincing memorabilia which looked set to keep alive the fame of Weyburne Tump for at least five minutes!

It had been arranged that, on the day before zero, Roy and I would nip up to the heath and discreetly adorn the site with the various bric-a-brac we'd collected. Accordingly, about half one on Thursday we set off from Abercorn, in the front Roy and I, in the back the two bins and – Jukes.

Yes, Jukes. As the brightest of the boys, we'd decided to let him in on the whole thing lest he realise the joke too quickly and spoil the fun. Besides, he'd be good with the waverers, cajoling them on. What lad of eighteen would suspect one of his own to be a quisling?

Moreover, bursting with all the nimbleness of youth, he might well prove useful if any tree needed to be climbed or swamp forded!

And so it turned out. Three pairs of hands made light work of it all, and by a quarter to four we were heading home through the gathering rain, barely suppressing our glee at the high jinks to come.

In common with many schools at the time, there were no early evening lessons on winter Fridays, which suited our proposed schedule down to the ground. To start with, a little hors d'oeuvre of a briefing: the Civil War and its battles (Library, 2pm). Then excavations (Weyburne Heath, 3pm until dark). Finally an intense academic plenary session (The Cat & Fiddle, Cragfield, 5.30 onwards)

In all of which Jukes, it has to be admitted, came up trumps. Firstly at question time after the briefing, where a masterly query, as to how far the Tump's slopes would have assisted or hindered Prince Rupert's customary tactics, really set the ball rolling. Even Marsden was seen to open his eyes.

Even more so, however, at the heath itself where he seemed to take on a kind of roving commission, steering folk towards promising sites, deciphering maps, and above all verifying finds as each preposterous discovery was made. Marcho and myself had little to do but lean back on our shooting sticks and savour the fun.

Perhaps his finest moment came when Rudgewick in rapturous mood rushed up flourishing a sodden lash of what looked like black felt – and was in fact an oblong cut from a pair of Mrs Kent's old & voluminous knickers which I'd rescued from the dustbin. And not, as I recall, washed!

"No doubt about it," cried Jukes, inspecting the cloth. "Blindfold, executions for the use of!" He pointed to the pair of trees way over to the right. "That's where they'd have hanged them, see? No time to take prisoners. Let me demonstrate." And without more ado, Rudgewick was seized by the shoulders while Mrs K's unmentionables were folded, wrapped round his eyes and knotted at the back. Cries of awe from the spectators.

Roy and I exchanged smiles. With Jukes on board, Venice was clearly going to be a ball. Indeed several of these lads hunting through the scrub had already signed up and paid their deposits, only Marsden proving intransigent. As one might have expected.

Andy Pandy – oddball extraordinaire!

Aloof in the classroom, aloof out of it, it was difficult to fathom what made the guy tick. Strange that a male with such agreeable looks should be saddled with so unyielding a personality, but of the latter there was, I'm afraid, no doubt. In the Cat, for instance: where the rest of the gang divided into pairs and bought rounds, he stood alone, having ordered his solitary half, to pay for which he brought out a handful of small change.

"Lookee here," cried Jukes exultantly, plucking a small black coin from the other's fist. "Treasure Trove!"

"Bastard – give that back!"

"All finds have to be reported to the Rev, old son," grinned the other, dodging his lunge and flicking the coin to Carey.

"Oliver?" commanded Marcho with outstretched hand, and, as he slipped the object into his fob pocket, a nod to me as if to say Well Done. For it was only afterwards that we realised that each of us assumed said relic to be the other's handiwork, whereas... But more of that later.

Marsden's subsequent grim face proving a considerable damper on the proceedings, it was not all that long before the boys were clambering into the old 28 seater Bedford which served as school transport in those days before minibuses. And just as well since, way over on the other side of the car park, I had just spotted the arrival of a smart MG out of which were climbing Tiny and the Carve with, secure between them, none other than Docherty.

And no fishing rods to be seen!

"Rum?" mused Roy back at school, locking up just as the prep bell began to toll. "Well, yes, maybe you could call it that. But nothing more. Nothing sinister. Why read doom and disaster into everything? He's safe enough with them. All colleagues together, eh?"

"But since when did Carver drink anywhere in Tolverton except The Fox?"

"Cragfield's a separate village."

"Just about. And anyhow, whoever heard of a stag party consisting of three?"

"Doubtless they'll be joined by others later."

"Who? Have you received an invitation?"

"Talk sense," he chuckled. "Dog collar to a stag do?"

"But neither have I. Nor Ormulak, nor Tom."

His eyebrows rose. "That is, er, also rum," he conceded. "Still…"

"We ought to go back," I insisted. "Find out what they're up to. You're not going to stand by and have the poor chap's wedding ruined, are you? Have a heart, Roy, for Chrissake!"

At which they began, the protestations. He must eat with Clemmie, he had his nuptial address to write, he must take communion out to Sir Madison. Only after much manoeuvering did I get him to agree to drive us back around closing time. Then, if everything was shipshape and Bristol fashion, we'd see Docherty on top of the moon surrounded by crowds of admirers – if not, we could do something. Make our presence known. Intervene.

Somehow…

Thus it was some three hours later that the Rover once more nosed its way into the car park which by now was, if anything, less full than when we'd left. And again, it seemed, we were just in time.

Very slowly and awkwardly two shadowy figures were frogmarching a third towards the sportster. Not only was Docherty very clearly legless, if indeed conscious at all, but the car, when it started, instead of heading into Over Tolver and town, turned north westwards on to the old Shrewsbury turnpike.

"Rummer and rummer," I mused. "What on earth do you make of that?"

"Perhaps they're off to dinner."

"Gone ten? With Docherty in that state? I hardly think so. Besides, there's no decent restaurant on that road this side of…"

"Yes?"

"Leominster!" I crowed, as the whole dastardly plot suddenly clicked into place. One of those brilliant intuitive leaps which the Bryant mind is prone to, especially in times of crisis. "The poor old bugger! Roy, that Leominster time you gave them. You know, for the Aberdeen sleeper."

"The 10.34? But surely you don't suppose…"

"Shut up for God's sake. Now, think. Presumably the previous stop is Hereford – so what time would it leave there?"

"The rascals! Of course, of course. Well, usually it's 10.19 but remember…"

"Hell's teeth, we'll never make it!" I cried wildly consulting my watch.

"No?" he smiled blithely, starting the motor. "Trust in Providence, my boy. The Lord will provide alway! That train runs five minutes later on a Friday."

How we made the twenty six miles to Hereford in twenty one minutes I shall never know, what with rough roads, and deer as stupid as pheasants. But make it we did. And found time to fine tune our plan.

"See you at Ludlow," I shouted, waving goodbye through the steam, as the wheels began to turn.

As I expect you've guessed, it had become blindingly obvious that Carver and Tiny were intending to drive poor Docherty to Leominster, and there shove him aboard the sleeper where he'd snore the night away till Scotland. And the far north thereof at that. From whence it would be totally impossible to get back to his nuptials on time. Consequence: collapse of what scraps of reputation he still had. Plus probable extension of virgin status into far infinity.

Heaps of fun! Just what a grey man deserves!

Just as obvious had been the fact that there was no point confronting the conspirators at Leominster. At that time of night there'd be no help from staff, and the dire duo were quite capable of riding roughshod over gentlemanly pleas and executing their manly plan anyway. No, our only hope was for one of us to board the express at a point somewhere before Leominster and, hopefully, decant poor Docherty from a point somewhere after.

Thus, while I was enjoying the lush facilities of British Railways (bar closed, toilet broken, heating off) Marcho would be haring off to Ludlow as fast as the lanes would allow. And the pheasants and deer and, by the feel of it, black ice!

Making my way to a rear compartment, I was well positioned to peep forth unobtrusively as we jerked to a halt a quarter of an hour later. Sure enough, there were Carver and Tiny heaving an inert form into a carriage, watched by the guard whose expression made plain that whether Dave was man or corpse mattered not a whit as long as he had a ticket!

As we chuntered into motion, they stood back from the steam with a look of triumph bloating their faces. I was just a tad slow dodging down from the window and I fancied Carver just caught my eye for a fraction of a second. Just a mere glimpse, but I'll never forget that startled look. That blend of astonishment and sheer malice.

Well, to cut a long story short, Marcho made it to Ludlow just as the Aberdeen pulled in, his radiator grille sporting a clutch of feathers as token of the skirmishes he'd survived. With considerable effort we lugged Docherty – whom during the journey I'd managed to slap into something resembling consciousness – on to the rear seat where he sprawled, singing a hugely obscene rugger song to the tune of Crimond. Obscene and interminable since it seemed to last most of the way back to Tolverton.

As you'll appreciate, the ceremony next day could hardly prove anything but an anti-climax. There was Dave making his vows, slightly red of face, but otherwise scrubbed and pomaded into relative respectability. There was Marcho beaming away, doubtless thinking more of his forthcoming pheasant pie than the liturgy he was dispensing. And there, amidst the ranks of Common Room were Tiny Jarvis and Carver, the latter of whom glanced my way thrice with a stare so baleful it still sometimes wakes me with a start after too much port or a late night curry.

And myself? As the service proceeded, where were my thoughts located? Like always, all over the place.

Partly in Oxford, enjoying my next session with Julian or whatever substitute the Gods in their wisdom would ordain. Partly in Venice, planning schemes to dump the lads in various art galleries while Marcho and I sipped hock in the shadow of Zanipolo.

But, conversely, partly on the evening to come, my first under the smutty thumb of Murdoch. And on the bloody bell I'd have to ring every morning, and the unfamiliar bed I'd have to sleep in, and the ghastly bathroom I'd have to share with Miss Frame and her oranges.

Up and down, up and down, goblin lead them up and down!

I mean, that's the hell of life, n'est ce pas? One minute spirits soaring like some upwards avalanche. The next, barathrum. Down in the shits. Razor at the throat. Outrage and oblivion about to descend on one's blameless head.

And fuck all one can do about it. Like now, for instance. The perfect reward for all my altruism! We're at the most solemn part of the service, when to move even a muscle would be de trop, and just as my mind begins a delicious fantasy of Jugs scoring in a Moroccan hammam, there an inch or two above my head, gigantic and fearsome, I spot, swinging on its glistening thread, the absolute worst of my boyhood nightmares.

Yes, you've got it!

Will it, won't it? Will it, won't it? And how shall I cope if the worst transpires?

Now in general, let's get this clear – je suis's no wimp, OK?

Sans doubt!

Make me do a fakir across white-hot coals, cast me off QE2 in mid-Atlantic, bury me up to the neck in excrement like poor old Edward the 2nd – any such I could (I fancy) bear with equanimity. But a spider, on my flesh, crawling, scuttling down the neck of my shirt…!

I look up. Are those fangs glittering in the candlelight? Or just eyes pondering the infinite variety and beauty of the cosmos.

8: *Live and Let Live*

To say that the Reverend Beresford Dick-Whyte-Dick exploded on the Tolverton scene is, perhaps, putting it a bit strongly. But a marked impression he most certainly made. I mean, it's not every day you see a dog collar sported by a guy who shaves at night, gigolo style, rather than respectably before his eggs and bacon – whose hair is tied back in a pig-tail (secured by a red rubber band!) and the scent of whose eau de cologne bears the strongest possible affinity to Cannabis Sativa, and would knock a battleship sideways

"Do call me Berry," he said intimately, shaking hands before loping off in search of Chris.

"Spotty, more like it," observed Carver with a snort.

"I must find out what soap he uses," mused Roy enthusiastically. "Such a refreshing scent."

"Ronks like a poof, if you ask me," was Tiny's eloquent comment. "What a tosser!"

"By no means." Marcho waved his cigarette holder expansively, even though, Lent being upon us, it was empty. "In fact, he's terribly well connected. He was born in Africa, you know. His aunt was none other than the late Miss Ephrasia Honoria Dick-Whyte-Dick of Kashashaland, the well-known Afrikaans theocrat."

"Theoprat, more like it." Another snort.

"Let me tell you," retorted Marcho bridling, "if women had been allowed ordination in her day, she'd have probably risen to be Archbishop of Canterbury."

"But since they weren't, aren't and never will be, tough luck!" Catching up his books, Carver turned to the door. "Coming Tine?"

Marcho and I exchanged glances. Since our adventures at Weyburne, the second of my three half-term exeats at Tolverton had come and gone, and had proved hardly more colourful than the first. As any of you who've ever experienced it will remember, there's nothing more desolate than a boarding house sans the boarders, and, quite unable to face a week of it, I'd hired a car. It was too soon to risk Julian again and thus I embarked on a tour of churches on the Lincolnshire coast, availing myself of one of those cheap offers which abound in the tabloid Sundays. Four days at The Excelsior Hotel, Gleethorpes for the price of two. Can't go wrong with that, I'd thought. En suite, four star, early morning tea included. And should the cultural thrills of a seaside town in late February prove insufficient to occupy me, there'd always be a waiter to talk to. And maybe pick up. And add to my list of one night conquests.

Some hope! Only one was under fifty, and he looked like George Formby!

Rain, wind, lichen, loneliness. Some mixture – and thus my return to Tolverton and its folk was almost welcome, even if it meant putting up with the vacuity and contumely of Carver, Murdoch and the rest of that tribe. Wasn't there da Coco on the horizon to buck one up? And Roy, of course, whose urbanity served as a highly necessary antidote to the general madness of the place, spleen served up daily under the guise of discipline.

Like the previous morning, for instance, absolutely typical! I'd been summoned from my bed at six to assist in one of the Fuhrer's periodic study snoops. And what was the bee in his bonnet this time? Fags! The tobacco kind, not little boys warming their hero's loo seat! A single butt found next to the coke chute had convinced him that every senior was on at least twenty a day, an outbreak of heinous criminality which must be summarily and ruthlessly rooted out. Thus was I enjoined to search the upper studies, he the lower.

Though this enabled me to do a sort of Scarlet Pimpernel by destroying what pathetic bits of evidence I found, and thus saving at least a few folk from the tumbrils, it was also potentially highly embarrassing – as for instance when, halfway through ransacking chez Marsden, who should wander in, clad only in pyjama bottoms, but the victim himself.

Open-mouthed, I looked guiltily up but – no hassle. He merely shrugged, placed a thumb in his waistband, and leant back against the door.

"Surprise, surprise," I ventured lamely.

"Be my guest."

"Look, it's like – orders is orders. Understand? Not that that's any excuse really…"

"Forget it."

"Sorry."

OK, agreed, as apologies go not all that much cop. In fact, craven shit! But what's a bloke to do? Not only had I been caught in the act but there, almost within touching distance, was this turn up for the book! This toned, muscular apparition, a thin chain and cross of white gold enhancing the contours of its upper body. Andrew Marsden! Who'd have thought his daytime blazer and tie concealed anything so spectacular.

"Relax," he yawned laconically, his gaze shifting to my hand in the drawer. Nothing much there except the usual boy things. A packet of Wrigley's, a couple of 45s, some letters in a folder (how Murdoch would have jerked off on those!), a miniature torch in the shape of a mermaid, that sort of stuff.

Then, returning my stare with one of those thin smiles of his, the kind you see in etchings of the Inquisition, he reached over to his bookshelf. "Is this," he muttered, plucking forth a magazine, "what you're looking for, by any chance?"

I might have known! I might have known by the way it had been carefully hidden under a pile of Trewes's notes. 'Health & Efficiency', the latest edition, and in my hand before I could say Jack Robinson!

There was no time for thinking. Either I called up Murdoch that instant and denounced the guy, or…? Or what? Options, consequences? In that flash my mind could seize on nothing but instinct. Loathing of one, wariness of the other. Dislike versus doubt?

Eether, either, Neether, neither, Let's call the whole thing off!

Suddenly I'd slipped the publication into an inside pocket. "Just this once," I said in my most schoolmasterly tones. "Got it?"

No nod of assent or anything. No gratitude. Just that grim smile. And a murmur. "Don't forget, will you?"

"What?" I'd snapped, half turning.

"To return it, *OK* – Paul."

Disturbed, distracted, on another planet, somehow I got through my lessons, aided by the fact that tomorrow's outing – more of which later – would bring the opportunity of a heart to heart with Marcho. Though I have to confess it was with a somewhat bowdlerised version of Murdoch's study raid that I regaled him as we headed for Gloucester early on Friday, ten 5th formers and Beri-beri asleep behind us in the Bedford.

"Against the law?" replied Roy. "I doubt it. Against what used to be called honour, certainly. Against decency, mutual respect, humanity, by all means. But the law? Very doubtful. Trouble is, the old brute happens to be in loco parentis – which gives him, as he sees it, carte blanche over their lives."

"As *he* sees it, maybe!"

"All the same, if junior's suspected of stashing away contraband, he regards himself as having the same right as a father to put a stop to it."

I shook my head vigorously. "Firstly, what father would ever go behind his children's back like that?"

"Oh quite!" he twinkled.

"Secondly, a packet of Players hardly counts as contraband, does it?"

"Well, they're a disgusting smoke, but a lad has to start somewhere."

"Roy!" I expostulated. "Can't we be serious for once?"

He grinned. "My dear boy, calm yourself. Reflect a moment. Is it actually housemasters and their wicked ways that's bugging you?"

"Of course."

"Come off it. Isn't it really your loss of face in front of a pupil? Or, rather, presumed loss of face? The worry that he thinks of you on the same level as Murdoch?" A quizzical look my way. "Let me reassure you. He's a better judge of character than that. At Marsden's age, a chap can sum one up in an instant."

"OK," I replied, a touch dismally. If this was reassurance, I might as well pack my bags immediately! Thank God I hadn't told the old boy about H & E and the ensuing dialogue. That 'Paul' I mean, and the tone in which it had been said.

"If you want proof positive, how about our doo-dah? You know, Venice? Would he be joining us if he couldn't stand the sight of you?"

Appalled, I turned in my seat. "But I thought he hadn't paid."

"He hadn't till yesterday. Then along he comes at lunchtime waving a cheque. And for the full amount, not just the deposit. Good news?"

"Brilliant!" I retorted dismally.

So there it was. Yet more storm clouds. Thanks a bundle, Roy – why the heck couldn't you have waited till the evening to tell me? Now even the few specks of pleasure I'd expected from today's expedition looked set to vanish. Who'd be a schoolmaster? I mused, turning to look at the dozing bodies.

The onset of March might signify many things in many places – the Boat Race, the Grand National, Fair Day at Oswestry – but at Tolverton it means Inspection. The annual visitation of the CCF to ensure its tactics are as up to scratch as its Boer War rifles. Oh and the excuse for a gargantuan lunch to demonstrate to parents that all's right with the world. As long as you can afford the fees!

Since, from the 5th form onwards, membership of the contingent was voluntary, it was the custom to have dissenters entertained for the day in groups well away from the campus. Thus Roy and I had volunteered to host a visit to the national railway museum at York that Friday, driving as far as Gloucester, taking a local to Birmingham, and there changing on to the morning Scotch express. Why Dick-Whyte-Dick had expressed a desire to join us was not quite clear. After all he could have been assisting Baxter's group at the lake, scraping down dinghy hulls, or Ormulak's at St Tywyn, oiling gudgeons in the bell tower, or Murdoch's, off to pull weeds in Joe's graveyard at Cragfield.

Or perhaps, like us, he just adored trains.

Be that as it may, it didn't occur to either of us – and in retrospect it was, I agree, a howler of monumental proportions – that he constituted anything more than a supernumerary, and no way to be included in the high jinks we'd so carefully planned. For ourselves, that is, not the boys. The junket, the real raison d'être of the expedition. To wit, a couple of sessions of pure Parson Woodforde.

For both going and returning, in those days the main-line trains carried restaurant cars, and what had we promised ourselves but breakfast down (i.e. up) to York, and dinner up (i.e. back) to Birmingham? Lashings of hot coffee with the former, but, with the latter, joy of joys, a couple of the best bottles Bordeaux could provide.

Or Burgundy – we weren't fussy.

As long as the vintage was prime, we'd quaff it reverently. In those days, the cellar British Railways had inherited from the old companies was still the best thing about that hapless organisation and, as good citizens, and staunch supporters of nationalisation, wasn't it our responsibility to make good use of it?

How we licked our lips as the road whizzed under us. The lads and Beri-beri, well, we had no qualms about them. Their plump plastic food bags would provide them with crisps and chocolate and cornish pasties to their hearts' content, while Roy and I, stout warriors that we were, must perforce put up with – who could tell? Sweetbreads in marsala? Confit of barbary duck with nectarines? Pigeon stuffed with widgeon?

Dream on, buster! But at least of steak and chips there was a fifty fifty chance which, at eighty miles an hour through the Black Country, would be well epic. And which, unobtrusively, had already begun to shoulder all that Marsden angst to the back of my mind.

On wore the morning, our luck holding good at Gloucester and, eventually, Birmingham, as into our platform at New Street, and exactly on time, steamed a lusty Riddles 4-6-2, No. 70045, 'Rupert D'Oyly Carte'.

Getting pretty expert, huh?

She was a sight to behold all right, but even more so the nine unusually smart coaches snaked behind her, including a gleaming buffet car, presided over by a gleaming steward.

No kidding! His hair was brilliantined into a beach of little blonde waves set close to his skull whilst his cheeks shone so intensely that they might have been rubbed and fubbed to perfection with a bit of spit and jeweller's rouge.

"Welcome aboard, gents," quoth he, polishing his counter with the most pristine of glasscloths. "Top of the morning to ye. And what might be your pleasure this fine Spring Friday?"

"Well, now," replied Marcho, entering into the spirit of the thing, "how about that noblest of dishes, the English breakfast? Good yeoman fare, to keep the wolf from the door – if it's not too much trouble."

"No trouble at all, your reverence. And, if I may say so, an excellent choice. Accompanied by the bean? Or the leaf?"

"Oh, the leaf, the leaf. Always the leaf."

"And as for viands?"

"Tempt us."

"Very well then – you could try eggs fried, scrambled, poached or Benedict. Black pudding, white pudding or no pudding. Sausages, of course. Baked bacon, baked beans, or bubble and squeak. On the other hand, perhaps you'd prefer our cold sideboard. Pork pie, Game pie, ham on the bone, off the bone or marylebone. Alas we have no bananas, and as for fish we sold the last kipper at Cardiff."

"No kippers?" moaned Marcho, a vast desolation appearing to spread over his features.

"No kippers."

"Then we'll just have to do the best we can. What do you think, Paul? Everything else?"

"And," I retorted, "two boiled eggs!"

Sorry – couldn't resist that. But as we were rapidly becoming more Marx than the Brothers, I now discreetly took matters in hand, reducing the order to a modest fry-up for two, and shepherding my errant mentor off to a secluded table where we could giggle without causing offence.

"It's times like this, Paul," pronounced Roy, spearing the last fragment of fried bread as we crossed the broad ribbon of the Trent, "that one really appreciates what England means, don't you think?"

"Eggs and bacon?" I grinned.

"Did you notice the name of the engine?"

"I did."

"Well then." At which he launched into song: "*For he might have been a Roosian...*"

At which I countered: "*A French or Turk or Proosian...*"

At which our Steward countered: "*Or perhaps Itali-an...*"

At which we soared in triple unison: *"Or perhaps Itali-an, But in spite of all temptations..."*

And thus, kings of the world, on we swept on to York, confident of our shores, confident of ourselves, confident that no incoming hordes could ever besmirch it, this jewel set in the silver sea, this *"Blest isle with matchless, With matchless beauty bound..."*

"Noisy train that," said Beri-beri as we queued for tickets at the museum an hour later. "Must have been football louts. No thought for others."

"Well reprehensible," I agreed cautiously.

"Who do they think they are? How on earth can one read Duns Scotus with that racket going on?"

"Come, come," beamed Marcho, putting a hand on each of our shoulders. "Live and let live!"

A sentiment which he would have good reason to regret in the very near future!

With boys in museums, you never can tell, and this was especially true with our lot. To Roy's encomiums on the yellow Stroudley or the Stirling single-wheeler, they remained obdurately impervious, only brightening up when they came across the Royal coach. Or to be more precise, Queen Victoria's lavatory, left exactly as the last day she'd plucked the last sheet of paper from the royal loo roll. Though, taking a peek myself, yes, I had to admit it – the red plush on the imperial throne was breathtaking!

Similarly with the Minster. The Heart of Yorkshire's breathtaking tracery, the Five Sisters, the great East window, all these splendours left them cold. But the nearby crypt, scene of the 1205 Jewish massacre – well, that had them leaping about, indignant that neither Marcho nor I could supply information on the exact mechanics of garrotting, nor enlighten them as to how long it would take to boil a sixteen year old virgin to death.

Surprisingly, young Beresford proved a tower of strength throughout the afternoon. Despite his weird appearance and louche odour, he seemed to have the knack of handling boys. Like an amiable sheepdog, he harried them hither and thither, organising the stragglers, answering queries, coping with Johnson's nosebleed as if to the manner born.

It was almost as if the wheel had turned, and Marcho and I were now the supernumeraries. Not that we cared. Our minds were firmly fixed on the welkin – to wit, those steaks speeding so inexorably towards us. At about ten to five, the lads just starting to mill on to the platform, Roy glanced at his watch. "Should be just through Alne," he murmured. "Not long now."

Sure enough, a very few minutes later, edging round the curve, brakes screeching, came Bridget's pater, steam fluffed out like Victorian whiskers.

"Strange it should be the same engine."

"Strange," replied Roy, eyebrows a touch puckered, "it should be the same train."

And indeed the same steward. The same fine fellow. If ever there was a descendant of Harry Bailey, this was he. Who more fit to serve us smoking cuts of topside, succulent roast potatoes, tender broad beans tossed in melted Normandy butter, and, of course, the tempting fragrance of Chateau Obelard-Theirn 1938?

"Hungry, mon Brave?" quoth our rosy-cheeked savant.

"Famished," confessed Roy. "Been slaving away over the stove, I trow?"

"Can you doubt it?"

"Then" – closing those old blue eyes – "let's hear what you have in store for us."

"Certainly gentleman. On this fine March evening, fare fit for a King! You might try: eggs fried, scrambled, poached or Benedict. Black pudding, white pudding, or…"

"…no pudding?" roared Roy.

"Sausages, of course. Baked…"

"Hang on, hang on. Are you trying to tell us it's the same menu as this morning?"

Managing the tricky job of looking simultaneously both encouraging and crestfallen, the steward nodded.

"Well," I ventured brightly, "what goes up must come down."

Both glared at me.

"Still," said Roy turning back to mine host, "it is a bit thick. I mean, eggs and bacon for dinner!"

"Sir, I could not agree more. Just a few years since, when this was LMS, why it'd have been silver service with my helping you to capons and turbot, apple charlotte with double cream and cinnamon, stilton bathed in port, and all washed down with claret by the riddle!"

"Don't rub it in!" Roy's groan was heartfelt.

"Now even this" – a deprecating gesture at his menu – "is threatened. Oh yes, Euston considers it decadence, to say the least. Soon we'll be down to cheese rolls – and Nesquik in paper mugs!"

"Never!"

"God forgive them, for they know not what they do."

"But tell me, tell me…" By now Roy was barely this side of dementia. "You mentioned claret, yes? Surely they haven't abolished that. Surely you can still let us have…"

"Chateau Bellephon? Or a nice Loire? Rest assured, my dear sir. Into those realms the barbarians have not dared venture – yet."

"Thank goodness for that." Roy seemed to breathe more easily. "But what on earth do we drink it with?"

The steward leant over the counter confidentially. "Tell you what. I'd time to do a spot of shopping in Carlisle – for myself and mother, see. Something tasty for the weekend. There's more than enough to share. What would you say to a little gallimaufry by way of – offal!"

"Good-oh," said Roy, his eyes brightening. "But wait a moment – we couldn't possibly deprive yourself and…"

"You don't know mamma. The thought of quality on my train – why she'd be thrilled!"

"Well, in that case…"

"Why don't I whip up a red wine sauce, nothing special, just shallots, asparagus, lardons and a touch of nutmeg. Then braise some kidneys in butter, and serve them on fried bread with a salad garnish?"

"Why not indeed!"

"Will that suffice?"

"My dear, I could hug you," cried Roy, tears in his eyes.

"Mind you – mum's the word. It's more than my job's worth to give passengers what they want." And with that the little man whisked off into his pantry from which began to emanate heavenly odours plus *Here's to the rollicking bun*, from 'The Sorcerer'.

Just as heavenly was our second bottle of Chateau Bellephon, though a mere 1947, which we sat finishing fifty minutes or so later at the same obscure table we'd had on the way out. Which explains why Beri-beri failed to see us until he'd bought his can of Lucozade and turned to retrace his steps.

"Hi – there." Between those two syllables, what Saharan leagues suddenly stretched forth their aridity, more desolate than Shelley's low and level sands. Or you might say, camaraderie to chagrin in one tenth of a second. "I wondered where you'd vanished to."

And equally rapidly we got the message. While he'd been wrestling with Travers's headache, Challenor's mislaid keyring, and the general stress of coping with ten tired, fractious teenagers, here we'd apparently been, gorging ourselves on the fat of the land. And not just apparently – and with no consideration that he might like a glass too.

Well, there it was. Remorse comes ever too late and too little, and he brushed aside our offers of a drink with barely concealed disdain. And maybe with a shrewd perception that we'd have probably welcomed an excuse for a third bottle.

Nor did the next day produce any perceptible thaw, nor the next week, his penultimate one at Tolverton. Except, and at the time it struck me as odd, the fact that his hostility seemed mainly directed at Roy. Myself he treated with a kind of wary reserve, though behind it could be sensed remnants of our initial rapport, such as it had been. It was as though he saw me now as Roy's puppet and wasn't absolutely sure how loyal my bonds with Svengali were.

Moreover, l'incidente del vino seemed to provide a turning point in his relationship with the school in general. It was as if his eyes had been opened to the true nature of the place, resulting in a pretty intense disenchantment.

Surprise, surprise?

Little was henceforth seen of him in Common Room whilst rumours began to circulate of cartoons he was starting to execute for the lads: members of staff, no less, in unseemly circumstances. Nothing obscene, but still pretty devastating for school morale. All very awkward, and it was not long before matters came to a head.

By tradition, the peak of the Lent visitor's programme was a sermon always delivered on Ash Wednesday, reviewing the Lenten experience this year, and making vows in respect of next. It so happened that I ducked out of that particular delight, having somewhat over-indulged with James the night before, and needing all the kip I could get.

Come period two, my Chaucer set seemed unusually demure. It so happened that we'd arrived at the point where Damian, lurking in the tree, finally gets his wicked way with Emily. *And in he throng* has provided generations of schoolboys with their first personal bond with literature, and I bustled through the couplets in confident expectation of the glee to come.

Not a flaming dicky-bird!

Just one or two yawns, Marsden looking amused, a kind of tension in the air. And Jukes cupping his hand to his ear. "What was that, sir? In he gong?"

"You've the text in front of you," I snapped, a bit perplexed. "Or maybe you've caught something off Januarie, eh Jukes?"

No reply, no giggles, just that vague sense of expectation and some shuffling of feet.

Until, all at once, Macdonald lounged back in his chair. "So, what did you think of chapel, sir? Father Berry and stuff?"

"Father Beresford, if you don't mind. And what stuff exactly? You know how dodgy my alarm clock…"

"Stuff he's told us to give up next year. Deprive ourselves of."

"Ah, excellent. Whatever it is, make sure you follow his recommendations. To the letter, mind. There's nothing so invigorating as self-control."

"No jiggy-jiggy during Lent? You must be joking." Marsden's voice pierced the ether like an arrow.

"What?" I retorted sharply.

A genial smile from Jukes: "Pay no attention to him, sir. What Father actually referred to was excessive masturbation. The stress on excessive."

"I'm glad to hear it."

"Some people just have dirty minds."

"You don't say!" Drawing my gown around me tighter, I peered at the book. "Now shall we…"

"What would you call excessive, sir?"

"Twice a year," I said acidly. "How about you?"

Before Jukes could answer, a hand shot up from the back row. "Sir, sir. I've got a serious question."

"Thank goodness for that," I retorted. "OK, Beecham – fire away."

"Sir, I'm a bit hazy – could you possibly define it?"

"Define what?"

"That word, sir – masturbation."

Thumping my desk to restore order, I stood up. "OK, OK – look, this is getting out of hand. Not, er – hand! I mean, out of control…"

A wave of laughter no teacher on earth could subdue. Thank God Eric was away at the infirmary and not on one of his patrols.

Nevertheless, by his return that evening, news of Dick-Whyte-Dick's indiscretion had scurried even to the fastness of the headmagisterial study. Or should I say indiscretions? For, as so often happens in schools, it takes a major catastrophe to bring to light straws in the wind which might have both presaged and prevented it. Anyhow, be that as it may, by nine that night Roy had been summoned to the Amberley presence for an interview which proved short and sweet.

Immediately afterwards Roy convened a sort of disloyal jurga, not so much to lick wounds as to head off further squalls. He, I and Ormulak assembled in Joe's parlour at Cragfield, in front of a roaring fire (despite the mild spring weather) and with a glass of cowslip wine in our hands.

"My late father's," smiled the old priest, in response to my admiring a replica of a Davy lamp in solid silver which held pride of place on his dresser. "To mark, look you, his fifty five years down Pontlottyn Main. They was made of stern stuff in those days."

"Sure thing – we shan't see their like again."

"Indeed we shall not!"

Marcho merely nodded silently, as well he might, having just regaled us with the list of Beri-beri iniquities which Eric, in an uncharacteristically irritable mood, had thrown at him earlier, and which Ormulak was still scribbling down on a notepad. Most of them seemed, in my opinion, pretty trivial – stuff like being observed (and several times!) at the Durex counter in Boots. Or displaying a Labour poster in his window for the forthcoming by-election. Or signing up a certain 6th former of feeble mind as a member of CND, or insisting CU members call him Berry instead of Father.

Oh, and of course his way of provoking lads out of their accustomed somnolence. Not just the Ash Wednesday example, mind you. Evidently a few days earlier he'd started a group session by asking everyone to write down on a sheet of paper their most prized possession – and pretending surprise when to a man they listed the same portion of their adolescent anatomies.

"I'm sorry Marchpane," Eric had proclaimed with icy finality, "but the feller goes too far. You'll have to curb him, understand? Before I start getting parents on my back. I'm loath to boot him out and ruin his Cambridge career but I warn you – my patience is wearing thin. Pretty thin. He's primarily your responsibility – very well, if you want the scandal avoided, better get weaving!"

"To which each boy answered," muttered Ormulak, intoning as he wrote, "his manhood." Relinquishing his pen, he looked up. "I have not here written penis, you understand. Never should one be vulgar."

"Vulgar?" chuckled Joe. "You should have heard the pithead baths in the old days, boyo. By comparison, that's poetry."

"I daresay." Abruptly Roy stood up and paced to the window, peering out at the rain starting to fall. "But if we get on to semantics we'll be here all night. The question is, what's to be done."

"How about nothing?"

The others stared at me in amazement.

"I mean, all that stuff about rubbers. So what if he's dating someone? How Victorian can you get? It's all just a storm in a teacup."

"Most vehemently I disagree," pronounced Ormulak, putting down his pen. "In his own interests our colleague must be warned."

"Even though he's only here for another week?" I queried. "Is he likely to do much more damage in a week?"

"It's not you who has to take the risk, though, my friend," said Joe, albeit not unkindly. "And a heck of a risk it is with the boss in his present mood."

"Which will improve as soon as he gets over his in-growing toenail or whatever malady's bugging him."

"I wonder who?" murmured Marcho, absently, turning round. For a few moments he'd been silent. Now he stood there stroking his chin, like some old chieftain about to be delivered of some devastating and decisive battle plan.

"Roy?"

"This girl Dick-Whyte-Dick must be dating. I wonder who it is?"

"Does it matter?"

"Well, ask yourself. I mean, Ormulak's quite correct. The twerp must be spoken to. He's clearly a loose cannon that has to be made to back off. Somehow. In which case, who better to get through to him than his girlfriend? If only we knew her identity."

Ormulak propped his notebook against a fern. "It out of him," he pronounced, "one of us must winkle. Yes? One of us must be chosen as emissary."

With a wan expression Roy resumed his seat. "Easier said than done," he shrugged. "As a fellow priest, I could hardly break his confidence, even supposing I gained it. You'll have to rule me out. I'm simply not eligible."

"Nor me," said Joe.

"Nor me." Ormulak shook his head emphatically. "An emigré with white hairs talking of the boudoir – he'd merely, as Watson would say, chortle."

Three pairs of eyes turned slowly my way.

"Youth," said Joe.

"Integrity," said Roy.

"And a kind heart," said Ormulak, "which is the best of all. Ever ready to lend the helping hands."

So there I was – hooked as usual, and on the basis of qualities to which my title was, to say the least, shaky. And yes, that included youth. As I headed across the lawn to the coach house close on midnight, I could see myself as Beri-beri would see me. A young fogey. Indeed, a young fart in the pay of old farts. What a predicament!

His lodging lay at the end of Murdoch's garden in an annexe once used to house servants on the upper floor, with room for, presumably, some sort of landau below. The building had long since been converted into two floors of day boy studies, with a flat above for whichever unfortunate member of Common Room came lowest in the pecking order. An eerie place at night, with narrow unlit stairs round a central well, its walls unrendered, its balustrade shaky.

Loitering on the top landing a moment to give my umbrella a shake (one must always beware rust!) I was surprised when the door swung open and out peered my quarry. "Thought I heard something," he smiled. "Wondered if it might be the Scots git at my keyhole. Foul night, isn't it! Come on in. Like a Laphroaig?"

"Why not?"

"Glad to find there's another nightbird on campus. Soda?"

"As it comes."

Looking around me, I was more than a little surprised at the drabness of his quarters. I mean, mine could hardly have been described as princely, but, compared to this, they were Versailles for God's sake! Illumination, for instance, was horribly minimal – a small fanlight and smaller casement by day, a single unshaded bulb by night – though this was perhaps just as well since the walls hadn't been repapered since Mafeking, and the furniture, what there was of it, seemed to have been gleaned from the rejects of some docklands doss house. Only a series of posters brought a modicum of life and colour to the place: Coriolanus (with sword) in an astonishingly short tunic, Rita Hayworth in profile, a Hockney fantasia, plus four or five similar exercises in equivocation.

So what were they? Part of a come-on technique, or something? A suggestion that, here in this parlour, this faux-Illyria, anything goes? A bid for contact on the level of kinship, friendship, any ship as long as it passed in the night? Or maybe sheer, devil-may-care bravado?

I was soon to be left in no doubt.

"Guess my favourite?" Noticing my stare, he handed me a glass and pointed at a repro – that Sabine study by David which always reminds me of Kipling. How does the couplet go? *The uniform he wore was nothing much before/And rather less than half of that behind.* Not that these models had much in common with Gunga Din, judging by the muscles of their arms and thighs.

"Yuh," I replied tentatively, sinking on to a threadbare chez longue, hooking my umbrella over its arm rest. "Excellent draughtsmanship and stuff."

"If only the old boy had painted female flesh that free. Like, oozing sex. That'd really have brightened the place up," he said, glancing round. "Jesus, it's a dump."

"What d' you expect?" My wits at their sharpest, I smiled duplicitously. "A dump in a dump. Most appropriate."

He laughed, starting to relax. "Tolverton? Well, it's no Winchester, that's for sure."

"Understatement of the century!"

"So, why stay? If you feel like that, why not bugger off?"

"Dunno really." At last I was starting to enjoy my Orphan in a Storm act. "Like, boarding schools – they have their compensations, don't you think?"

He nodded thoughtfully, twirling his glass in his hand and fiddling with his hair band. "Actually," he said, "I've been meaning to ask you up for some time. But you know – things get in the way. Sermons, seminars, they suck up your time like a bloody vacuum cleaner."

"Tell me another," I smiled ruefully. Time for a touch on the tiller. "Death to any chance of, you know, relationships."

"My God yes. Especially when…" He paused for a moment, glancing my way as if making some sort of assessment. "Tell me, does git man allow you a lock on your door. Bedroom, I mean?"

"No way."

"Me neither. Not that it signifies."

"Really? Nothing doing? I mean, on the fuck front?"

"On the contrary. Bird with large house – and hubby away all day and most evenings."

"Sounds ideal. What is the guy, a doctor or something?"

"Or something. Rather less plutocratic than a bloody doctor."

At which a blip of dread, just the faintest blip, started to resonate somewhere deep in my skull, and one by no means lessened as he perched himself next to me.

"You too?" he said. "Seeing someone are you?"

"Maybe."

"Married or single is she?"

"Personally," I replied with a touch of swagger, "I never bother to ask."

"That's the stuff," he cried, putting an arm round me. "Treat 'em rough, like the bitches deserve. Local, is she?"

I nodded. "Though, unlike your Doris, there's no mansion on tap. Which presents a problem."

"Murdoch, I take it?"

"Precisely. All ears, and on the prowl all hours. On the rare nights I do smuggle her in, just the thought puts me off my stride!"

"Tragic!" he grinned, but all the same casting a wary look at a slight rattle of draught in the door lock. "Anyhow it's the same with me. Prying eyes. She's got an au pair, you see. Resident. To look after the kid."

That instinctive dread again bubbling up, I nodded.

"There's a motel we go to," he continued. "Out near Weyburne. Perfectly discreet as long as your cheques don't bounce. And only a quarter of an hour away. Though mind you she drives like the clappers. Typical. Why do women always drive like the clappers?"

"What else can you do in a Ferrari?" I forced myself to jest, though I could hear it coming now, the avalanche, feel the first few specks of sleet.

"If only. Hers is just a jalopy, actually. A cute old museum-piece Singer. Smells of gear oil and held together with string. You into cars?"

And thus dread turned into actual, churning turmoil. From now to daybreak and way beyond – nothing would make the dilemma retreat one iota or for one instant. So this lout in priest's garb was knocking off none other than my best friend's wife behind my best friend's back. Susie Frobisher humped by this moron! Or could there be two 1934 Le Mans surviving in the marches?

And thus not only was my errand effectively stymied, but now I had to decide. Spill the beans or embark on a sea of obfuscation. With James, with Marcho, Ormulak and Joe. With half the universe eventually, knowing my luck. And still the Eric versus Beri-beri impasse would remain unresolved. What a mess! What a howling mess!

And, since we're on quagmires, what price the one I was up to my neck in right now? For as he plied the bottle once more, he shot me an inquisitive glance. "Sorry," he said. "Prattling on as usual. Why does a guy never learn? What can I do for you?"

"Do?"

"Or is this just a social call?"

"Oh, right. Of course. Thanks for reminding me. Well..." Outrageous, playing for time like this, but I could hardly confess that my seedy little errand had already been accomplished. What now? What possible topic could bring me charging up to this bloke's room at midnight? Not that he seemed to notice the hiatus. Well on in whisky, he just sat there waiting.

Ablur with Challenor's key-ring and red rubber bands, my mind simply refused to focus. "It's like this…" I began hesitantly. And then I noticed it. The window!

"Sounds serious," he smiled.

"It all depends," I replied, my wits gathering momentum. "But I thought I'd better warn you. Nobody else will."

"Warn me?"

"That poster." I nodded at his casement where the trim oblong, backlit by scuds of moon, glowed its fitful red against the grubby glass. "D' you realise how much controversy it's caused?"

He laughed.

"Or maybe that's what you intended."

"Stirring the pot?"

"Upsetting the apple cart, more like," I retorted.

"Isn't that what a Lent Visitor's supposed to do?"

"In a mild way, OK, I suppose so. But d' you call that mild?"

"What would you call it – vindaloo?"

"Given Carver, Murdoch and all the other fascist bastards? Pure suicide, if you ask me."

Yeah, yeah, I know. Given his betrayal of James, where was the sense in warning the bugger about anything? But as an excuse it seemed cast-iron, too neat to miss. And let's face it – now I'd uncovered it all, the Reverend Dick-Whyte-Dick was history, OK? For him there was no tomorrow, except a swift and discreet exit from Tolverton. No way could Roy turn a blind eye once the story was out, nor conjure up much in the way of mitigation. The guy was finished, unless of course I changed tack again and held my tongue – which, as that would constitute an even worse betrayal of James, was hardly an option.

James! What on earth was this going to do to him? How would he face it? And more importantly – given his kid was but a few weeks old – how would he cope?

Preoccupations which so blitzed my mind as I felt my way down that eerie staircase that I hardly noticed the wind in the eaves, or the chance scuffs of moon on the lower walls like shadows, hooded wraiths, fleeing fitfully before me – or recalled, until standing on the threshold with the storm in my face, that I'd left my blasted umbrella hooked behind that blasted sofa.

Wet hair or another dose of Beri-beri? No brainer! And I could always retrieve old faithful next day while the guy was in chapel – or whenever I remembered.

Break began as arranged in the Vestry. Four cups of Roy's ghastly coffee on the sideboard, three pairs of inquisitive eyes fixed on me as I hurried in breathlessly. "Sorry about this," I said, dumping my tape recorder on a chair. "That pest Jukes wouldn't stop talking. Bloody 6th formers. Think they know it all."

"So, your bulletin?" Trust Ormulak to dispense with preambles, though maybe he guessed something from my manner - volubility, relish, whatever. It was the first time in my life I'd ever executed a man publicly, and though the elation disgusted me, it was a fact which I couldn't hide."

"OK," I replied. "I'm afraid it's not pretty, and not quite what we expected. There is a girlfriend – mistress, I suppose would be more accurate. Do people ever use that term any more?"

Roy lit a Sobranie.

"Anyhow," I continued, " the sting in the tail is – she's someone you know or know of and... I just wish to God we'd never started this."

Less than a minute sufficed to reveal all. Every last detail as though we were characters in a scene from *Dixon of Dock Green*, in on the doom of some dude in the room. Except he wasn't here, of course, nor we, really – as tales go, it resembled some vast improbable intrusion which had dived into our lives like the rankest of wasps, beyond our power to smash.

With a grim look, Ormulak rose, shrugged helplessly and bustled out.

Joe followed suit – but with finesse, squeezing my shoulder as he passed.

A minute or two's silence, then Roy looked up at me shattered, before turning away. Abruptly he pulled the phone towards him and began to dial Eric's number. Just as I'd expected. Solemnly, precisely, the special access between Chaplain and Headmaster, confessional style. Until... Until he came to the very last digit, when the old forefinger paused. Withdrew. Pressed firmly down on the receiver rest.

"Live and let live?" I murmured.

"Not exactly. But..." Reaching for his cigarette, he took a long draw. "Could you break up a marriage? Could you?"

"It might break up anyway."

"It might not."

I stayed with him till the bell – indeed in spirit for the rest of the day. In no mood for The Fox, I'd agreed to go up to Buggleskkely for drinks at half past five – not only to avoid gibes from Tiny and the Carve but also to return a couple of theological books Marcho had lent me. A nice sedate prospect which, however, had to be cancelled when Chris caught me after the last lesson with a summons from the boss. And not the usual sort either, but immediate. Three line. Major.

Well, my stomach turned over – wouldn't yours? Panic barely under control, I scooted forth, taking the short cut behind Livingstone where the steel and glass of the new pool had already begun to rise, brash and weedlike against the Victorian red around it. Ahead lay Eric's drive and as I darted into it, I found myself having to step back for the town taxi, a trunk strapped to its roof, and – not perhaps to my enormous surprise – Beri-beri ensconced in the back. Beri-beri ashen and comatose. Not so comatose though that he couldn't muster enough energy to rise up like a cobra at the sight of me and flick an acid V sign my way.

So someone had talked after all. But who?

It was one of those heavy humid afternoons you sometimes get in the borders even in spring, brooding and dour, the sky like a blanket about to drop down and smother you. Nor did the rhododendrons help. Still flowerless, tall, overflowing their borders, they made grim sentinels all right, appropriate to the thoughts racing through my head.

Could it have been Ormulak, so apparently compassionate, so imbued with that mid-European acceptance of force majeure? Could it have been Joe, similarly au fait with life's hardship? Neither seemed likely but then – was a change of heart on Marcho's part any more probable?

Even more disturbing, however, was a growing sense of personal resentment. Like, anyone's bitter when they get the push, but why blame me? That look on Berry's face, that gesture. I'd made an enemy there all right – to the grave!

My thoughts still awry, I was ushered by Elsie into Amberley's study just as he was swallowing some concoction from a tiny medicine glass. Looking a little less pale than in recent days, he waved me to a seat and peered down at his notes.

"Sorry to track you down at such short notice," he began, "but matters of import have to take priority. Concerning what, I assume, there's no need for me to specify."

I nodded.

"Just so. Well, that being the case, there's no need to beat about the bush. I've had no alternative…"

"Thanks, sir – I think I know already."

"Indeed?" He seemed surprised.

"His cab, it just passed me. It was pretty obvious he wasn't going away for the weekend."

"Oh," he nodded, "you mean our charming Lent Visitor? No, no. A mere bagatelle – open and shut case that, dealt with in five minutes. Two phone calls and a note to his Bishop. I doubt he'll ever grace a pulpit again. No – it's a more difficult matter I need your help over. And that of any, shall we say, confidantes you might have had."

"Sir?"

"Let me tell you about the first really difficult decision I ever had to make. As a Headmaster that is. I'm talking about more than twenty years ago now. A place called Lexborough up in Westmoreland. Very remote, and closed long since. I suppose it's not surprising that some folk, especially young ones, get frustrated in a wilderness like that. So frustrated, that is, that they get up to tricks. The usual kind of thing."

"Tricks?"

"Sexual misconduct then, if you want it straight. Marital infidelity with all the trimmings. It came to my notice that a new young master, straight from Emma, had been amusing himself with some hanky-panky. His degree wasn't up to much, nor his physique. But for the war we wouldn't have looked at him twice. What he did possess, however, was looks. A bit like yours, perhaps."

I was horrified to find myself blushing.

"Touch of the Hollywoods, you might say. The sort of appeal a silly woman might risk her husband and family for, given the right circumstances. Well, need I say more? My Head of Greek, a slightly unworldly chap named Sykes, happened to have married such an incubus – or is it incuba – anyhow, one not only stupid, but indiscreet with it. She and young Hopkins were observed by a parent one Sunday morning, emerging with their luggage from a hotel not fifteen miles away. I ask you! The husband had been absent in Oxford for a Gaudy and the pair had jumped at the chance like rabbits. So there it was, the case as it fell on my desk, ready for judgment."

He paused for a moment to adjust his blotter – then gazed my way shrewdly.

"What would you have done, Paul?"

"Really, Dr Amberley," I blustered. "How can I possibly…?"

"Come, come. As one professional to another. After all, one day you too may find yourself cast as Solomon. Tell me – how would you have handled it?"

In retrospect, it seems so simple. All I had to do was give it to him straight. Point out the obvious fact that, where sex is concerned, the world gets by on a mixture of hypocrisy and myopia. That the difference between what's OK and what's banned is arbitrary. That for the elect (of which this Hopkins may or may not have been one) fucking aint just a sideshow or diversion, but a fundamental sine qua non which not only transcends the boundaries of standard morality, but seeks to demolish them. That there's a brave new world coming when love will leap from the closet and brush new colour into the drabness of lives now withering under their mulch of greed and conformity and downright resignation…

Quite the little Forster, huh?

Well, all that's what I would have said, had I had a million in the bank. As it was, I looked at my feet and mumbled, not very graciously: "I suppose he had to go. Be sacked, I mean."

"Which one?"

"Hopkins, of course."

"And what about Dr Sykes?"

"I don't know. Counselling maybe. Support. Did the wife depart with her lover?"

"She did."

"Leaving the children with her husband?"

"Correct."

"Well then, he'd have needed all the help he could get."

"Undoubtedly."

"So, what did you do?"

"What I had to." Looking his age, the old man levered himself out of his chair and strolled to the window. "Dismissed him too."

"You're joking. Turfed out both of them? Victim and culprit?"

"Of course. And so would you have done in my shoes."

Just managing to keep my silence, I stood there frowning. Why the hell was he telling me all this? Was it a prelude to firing me as well? Ending my career simply because I'd kept quiet about something when maybe – and only maybe – I shouldn't have? For Chrissake! This can't be for real!

After a few seconds, he turned to face me. "Time, I think, for me to come to the point. Mr Watson tells me you're a close friend of James Frobisher. Is that the case?"

"Yes, I suppose so. I mean – of course!"

"In which case, in his interests and the school's, I'm sure you'll be glad to keep things as quiet as possible. Refrain from comment. Ignore rumours. Let speculation die down as quickly as possible. In my experience, it doesn't take long."

Puzzled by this apparent change of tack, I nodded. "I think I can promise that."

"Very well. Now your friend will be here in a few moments, accompanied by the Second Master. As you'll be aware, the staff contract here requires that a friend or lawyer also be present at a disciplinary, er – hearing. Not something I had to bother with in the case of Hopkins."

"Or Sykes," I said slowly, the mischief, the indignity, indeed the iniquity about to be unleashed beginning to dawn on me. "But surely… Look here, Headmaster. May I point something out?"

"If you must."

"James Frobisher, he's well – the salt of the earth. You can't really be contemplating, I mean…"

"Doing a Sykes?"

"Use any damned words you choose. It's totally unfair. The guy's done nothing wrong. You can't ruin his career."

"Can't, Mr Bryant?"

"Look sir," I said furiously, "I don't mean any disrespect, but if you go ahead with this, you'll have more on your hands than you bargain for. Aren't you aware how popular he is? Incredibly popular? You'll have representations from Common Room on your doorstep before you can snap your fingers."

A wan smile. "From Common Room? I think not. Remember, I've been dealing with teachers longer than you've been alive."

"The boys then. Or parents. Petitions and stuff."

"Clearly your view of humanity is somewhat less jaundiced than mine. Shall we leave it at that? Oh and – I'm minded, by the way, to overlook your personal transgressions in the matter. Rather grave transgressions a tribunal might think. Failure, for instance, to report serious professional misconduct direct to me as soon as it came to your notice. Collusion with others, as yet unnamed, to pervert the course of justice…"

"Now wait a minute…" I began.

"Pray don't alarm yourself," he smiled resuming his seat. "I merely illustrate that the musket has powder – if needed. In fact, my view's this. That your actions amounted to no more than a youthful lapse – which is extremely unlikely to be repeated. But there's your problem. If, based on what I deem best for the school, I've a right to make that judgment, I have an equal right to make others. How I dealt with Dick-Whyte-Dick, for instance. Or how I propose to deal with Frobisher. It's pure logic, d' you see? You accept all or reject all – there's no halfway house. So which is it to be?"

A silence broken after a second or two by a knock.

"Ah, do I hear Watson? Come in, come in, my dear fellow."

Chris looking diffident. "He's safe in the waiting room, Headmaster."

"Young Frobisher? Just so. Perhaps you'd like to sit by the davenport. Mr Bryant's here to assist us, as you see. In fact we were just having a difference of opinion when you knocked. An interesting point, eh Paul?

"Whatever…"

"Perhaps, as a classic, Mr Watson can give us a ruling, a definitive ruling, eh? Incubus, that's the problem. If the scourge in question is female, does the noun become feminine? That is, assuming it counts as second declension in the first place rather than that wretched fourth. I'm a trifle rusty on nouns these days..."

And, amazingly, thus it went on. Not the solemn Old Bailey tenour I'd anticipated but more like a kind of charade, all civil and urbane. James, obviously apprised beforehand by Chris of his wife's conduct, played an absolutely straight bat. Betraying no emotion whatsoever, he let the proceedings run their course to a conclusion which, clearly, he regarded as inevitable, just like Amberley. All of it simply washed over him, all the detail: the explanation which would be given to Common Room, compensation in lieu of notice, wording of references for his next school, if any – none of it seemed to faze him, any more than Philip's fireships or Napoleon had long ago, presumably, fazed his ancestors. It was, I can tell you, an astonishing insight for me into the ways and wherefores of noblesse oblige.

Not that Marcho displayed all that much astonishment either when I sat with him that evening as he cleaned and varnished some croquet mallets. At each shift in the story, he just nodded or tapped off his ash. At length, when I'd been silent for a while, he put down his brush.

"God moves in mysterious ways," he said.

"Really?" I retorted, perhaps a bit abruptly. "Not much God about it, if you ask me. There was a tip-off, OK? Nothing mystic, nothing celestial. Someone went to Amberley and blew the gaffe."

"And you're keen to find out who."

"Naturally."

"Even though it might wreck your relationship with Joe or..."

"Leon, yes. I mean, not exactly wreck but..."

"And what if you never know?"

"Then I'll remain," I retorted, glancing at him, yet again trying to decide, "in a state of perpetual anticipation, won't I?"

It was a fine night as I walked back down to school, with the moon full over the valley, blurred by none of yesterday's wind and rain. Not that I was in any mood for views. Constantly my mind roved over the field. Ormulak? Surely not. Joe? Impossible. Roy himself? But hadn't he begun to phone, then stopped…

People change their minds, a voice inside me said. And what about that dodgy side of his? Purloining station signs and so on. The kind of petty thieving you expect from a barrow boy, not a public school chaplain.

And so it went on, query stacked on query, and no solution any the nearer. By the time I got back to Rhodes, it must have been well past eleven, and suddenly, while searching for my key, I remembered it. That wayward umbrella of mine.

A slight blaze of anger, as Beri-beri's cab jumped into my mind. It would have been just in keeping with his V sign for the guy to have snaffled such a trophy, right? In revenge, to make a bonfire of it, or cast it into the sea from some cliff. Imbued with righteous indignation, I hurried across to the coach house and up the stairs, throwing open the unlocked door.

But there it was. Amidst the chaos of hurried packing, discarded tubs, circulars, wrappers – and moreover propped neatly against the sofa, with a label round its neck. How thoughtful of him. Maybe I'd misjudged the guy – until, I read it. 'J*d*s'. Just that. No need of Bletchley Park to work that one out! Bitterly I tore it off and strode out on to the landing.

None of yesterday's eeriness now. As I stood there wanting to lash out, the moon presented it all to me in a new and sharp clarity. The walls and the loose iron and the worn steps, everything in clear relief. No shadows now. No intimation as yesterday of shifting shadows, some hooded wraith fleeing down the steps before me.

Why the hell couldn't I get a similar clarity into my head? A dose of the old straight thinking to sort it all out – this corrosive jumble of black and blacker. Sobranies and stuff. Those old eyes, deceptive in their apparent frankness – and a rather darker shade of blue now than what seemed the half century since first we met.

Marcho as a scab? Was it possible?

Twinkle, twinkle little bat – how I wonder what you're at!

9: *Just one Picasso*

In those last few days of term, it was well weird. Not once but several times I caught Murdoch with a broad smile on his face for no accountable reason. Like a cat fed on cream - or, more appropriately, a jackal fed on some poor bastard of a springbok. Clearly he was about to add yet another notch to his holster although, as his deputy, I'd be the last to know who or what was to bleed.

So what? Venice was imminent and nothing, not the unexpected loss of Vale of Tolver to the idiot Tories, not doubts over Marcho, not residual unease about Marsden and his agenda, if any – not even, I fear, the absence of James – could dent my spirits.

It had occurred to me that Eric might recall my brief association with the OU Sailing Club in seeking to fill James's minor posts, but no problem. This mantle passed inexplicably to Trewes who henceforth, from time to time, could be seen dindling through Common Room with a rudder under his arm. Fine by me – it was the Lion of the Seas that grabbed my imagination, not Newent reservoir.

Eric had agreed to let us leave three days early, and had, moreover, come out in the dark of this nippy March morning to see us off. And what an odd group we must have seemed, clustered round the Bedford, its door open and lights blazing.

Not quite as numerous as a Tabard pilgrimage – though, I daresay, equally devout! – our final tally had come to total a very respectable fifteen. As well as myself, seven U6[th] formers from my English set; a couple of 5th formers from Rhodes and a pal of theirs, Charlie Peckham from Clive; a brace of L6[th] scientists; plus Chris Watson and, of course, the March himself, resplendent in his best suit, PSV licence polished and gleaming on its lapel, chatting away to the Head   - about precisely what, I preferred, under the circumstances, not to think.

In point of fact, only the previous evening, one of the two boffins had had to drop out, having fallen victim to a particularly vicious hockey tackle. How convenient – a place free! Within minutes I was on the phone to Corunna Lodge. The Oxford term had just ended and there was a fair chance Toby might be at a loose end – unless, of course, disaster had swooped at prelims and he was faced with a retake. Still it was worth a try. A week sharing with young Jugs was not to be sniffed at, and I found my finger twitching as it dialled the number.

"Hi," I said brightly, "could I possibly speak to…?"

"Paul, you tosser! Going deaf in your old age, are you?"

Copeland tones all right, you could have picked them out in the Tower of Babel, but not, alas, those of Toby.

"Julian! Glad I've caught you in. Er, great… All by yourself, are you?"

"Sounds fascinating. Why so secretive? About to recruit me into M15 or something?"

"Just asking…"

"Mum's out at bridge, Dad's in Latchfield dishing out pills, Toby's abroad in Venice …"

"Jammy devil!"

"… and Argos's here with me. So, in answer to your question, no I'm not by myself. Argos, say hullo to Paul."

"Woof, woof," I replied. "So how long's he likely to be away?"

"Jugs? Another ten days or so I gather. Why?"

"Well, don't laugh, but I was just about to ask you out on a trip there myself."

"Straight up?"

"Absolutely, and," I continued through his chuckles, "that means you, capisce? By yourself. Not you and Tina or Daphne or Kirsty or whatever current female flesh you're pulling."

"Moi? On the wagon, mate, this one, no kidding. Thank God I found out in time."

"Position ridiculous, expense damnable?"

"For starters."

"Welcome back to the fold!"

And thus it was, after a little more similarly amiable salesmanship, that our numbers were replenished at a cost of forty four pounds – that is, the original price minus Turnbull's deposit which was *not*, as Roy had had to reiterate several times over the phone, returnable. Picking Jules up at home, however, would have entailed a considerable deviation from the direct route to Gatwick, so a rendezvous was agreed on in Abingdon where he had relatives. Nevertheless, still a slight deviation, hence this early start.

As we pulled away, I found myself on the step, holding the rail with one hand, waving with the other. To Mrs Amberley, Matron, Murdoch and the other Housemasters, Tiny who'd just puffed up in a tracksuit, very red-faced – and above all to Eric, standing a little apart from the others, hatless, looking slightly shrunk in his tweed overcoat. I couldn't help thinking of the recent newsreel shots of the King these days, at Sandringham or Ascot.

It was just on twenty to nine as we shuddered to a halt in the forecourt of Abingdon station. Jules was perched on a trolley reading the Empire News and looked up with a smile as I approached.

Having an excuse to give him a greeting, hug him in public, was a delight in itself – for me at least, though he seemed not unenthusiastic as well! – until a blast from the horn reminded us we were in Oxfordshire not San Francisco, and in full view of a phalanx of prying eyes. The onset of daylight seemed to have brought our tribe back to life, a process further enhanced a few moments later as they stocked up with chocolate, crisps, gum and the like at the kiosk.

After which, it was inevitable, I suppose, that glee should break out, and in the time-honoured public school way. But this time, not exactly rugger songs. For with a flourish, Jukes – it had to be Jukes! – produced an ice cream cone and immediately launched into:

Just one Cornetto

to which the rest of the coach immediately responded:

Give it to me

Delicious ice cream

From Italy

Well, it was only to be expected, the popularity of Radio Lux in those days being what it was. And yet, the cheesy Walls jingle, with its backdrop of canals and palaces, though profoundly meretricious, provided a cute enough prelude to our adventure – sufficiently so for Chris to permit half a dozen reprises before clapping his hands loudly with: "Now then, boys. Enough's enough. Let's have a nice round of 'Onward Christian Soldiers' shall we?"

A suggestion met, as the wise old bird had expected, with total silence – at anyrate until Chris had taken the wheel and he'd nodded off to sleep. Then some whispering, a snigger or two, before the refrain began again, very softly and in a different voice:

Just one gig-olo

Give him to me

Delicious boyfriend

On toast for tea!

Whose voice? Marsden's? It was difficult to tell. And anyhow, why make a thing out of it? Boys will be – piranhas! Julian and I glanced at one another with a sort of fond complacency. What did their feeble jibes matter to us? From now on it was full steam ahead to San Marco and Shylock's Rialto and nooky under the stars. Nothing could derail us now. Renaissance, here we come!

In fact, as things turned out, half steam might have been a better description. Travel abroad all those years ago was even more of a lottery than travel at home, and readers won't be surprised to learn of our two hour delay at Gatwick. Nor of our diversion to Treviso because of congestion at Marco Polo. Nor of the lightning railway strike that afternoon which meant that our final leg had to be by the most idiosyncratic of rural buses – one which seemed to wander over half the Veneto before making up its mind where to lay down its rusty head.

And thus we arrived at Piazzale Roma just four hours and fifty minutes late, and in dire danger of missing dinner at the hotel.

OK, a chapter of woes – but isn't there always some bonus on offer if you take a long cool look? And in this case, how long was long?

None of the party, you see, had visited the city before – oh, except Watson, that is, who'd been stationed in Trieste at the end of the war, and had popped across now and then for American fags and nylons. So, for the rest of us, there began one of the great experiences of life. Our first trip down the Grand Canal by slow vaporetto, and not, as would have been the case had we been on time, at some anodyne mid hour of the day – but at sunset! Glorious sunset. A deep Technicolor gold glowing on the walls of each palazzo as we passed, flaming in the casements, burning in the ripples ahead as though luring us inexorably to some delicious Homeric fate.

Even the lads were entranced. At first busy with their Kodaks, by now they were just gazing, hooked on that incomparable spectacle as it unfurled on all sides. Marsden seemed especially rapt. He'd managed to secure a choice seat in the stern (of course!) and I was amused, and I suppose rather relieved, to observe the degree of his absorption.

Perhaps he was just an ordinary kid after all. Perhaps, in the stress of term, I'd read into stuff meanings which weren't really there. OK, no real harm done – but if his innocence did establish itself over the next day or two, well, fair's fair. I'd have to find a way of making it up to him. A drink maybe. Or vecchia á deux in some congenial bar.

My fears about dinner, I'm glad to say, proved totally unfounded. Coco himself, a balding German of about sixty, stern of mien but affable underneath, awaited us with all the imperturbability vital to one of his calling, collecting passports, herding us into the giardino where glasses of Punt e Mes were already poured and, ultimately presiding, with his son Vittorio, over tureens of steaming macaroni and meat sauce. Followed by cold roast veal and salad. Followed by some sticky Bavarian confection whose name I never did manage to master. Altogether, a meal to remember and in quite a different league to Mrs Todd's efforts at Tolverton.

Afterwards came room allocation. Plain sailing on the whole: obviously Roy with Chris, and so too the lads in pairs though this, of course, threw up a couple of potential problems.

Odd numbers in both the U6th and 5th form contingents meant that one from each must share with the other. Usually, school hierarchies being what they are, this would have caused considerable ruction. Not so today. The 5th formers had drawn lots – most civilised! – which meant Johnson and Peckham teaming up, leaving Guy Travers up for grabs. You'll remember him – the megafit redhead I'd met on my first Saturday. I was just about to suggest the U6th formers settle things the same way when, all of a sudden, surprise, surprise, who should volunteer but Marsden?

You could have knocked me over with a gondola! So the great loner had a human side after all. Good for him! And what a charming coincidence that now the two most photogenic guys in the group would be bunking up together. A choice little frisson for my artistic sensibilities to play with!

Just as simple was sorting out the vacuum left by Turnbull and his poor old shin. Pete Daines was, for reasons not hard to divine, heartily relieved to be promoted to my single – airless little cupboard though it was – leaving Julian and I to share a rather quaint room on the second floor, with a prime view across to the Redentore. More to the point, it boasted a prime bed too: a King sized double, soft and sumptuous, and sufficiently new to avoid – subject of course to final testing! – that fatal problem with hotel beds. Creaky springs.

A bonus, yes, but how much more inviting had it been Toby about to share it with me. Still, Jules was a long-term mate and, despite my timidity that ghastly night at Corunna, it would be better to have his body next to me than be alone – wouldn't it?

"All present and correct? Come along, come along, Foster! We don't have all night. Comic down, Castleton. Time to pay attention, my boy."

Unpacking over, we were now assembled in Coco's salone, a room of hard seats and dusty mirrors, ready to be briefed on the delights before us.

"The step, Daines, you'll have to sit on the step. Really, you'd be late for your own funeral! Very well, gentlemen. Now in the blue folder, if you'd turn to section C, page 4…"

Chris was one of those guys prone to taking their status with them wherever they went, like a crab its shell. Whether Tolverton or Timbuctoo, no matter, he was still the Second Master, and would remain so even were we abducted by aliens and forced to spend the rest of eternity on the sixth moon of Saturn. For instance, his schedule.

Neither Macho nor I had given much thought to such matters beyond drawing up a vague list of things to sample. The Doges's palace, the Frari, S. Giorgio – all the usual tourist titbits, but not in any particular order. By contrast, Chris had applied himself to his Baedeker and settled on fifteen absolute musts: three per day, allowing for travel each end and Sunday off.

And, after a fashion, it worked. Bright and early, the whole contingent would set out dutifully for whatever treat was scheduled. After coffee, attendance would be rather thinner. After siesta, we'd be down to a rump of the three 5th formers for whom participation was mandatory, plus Daines, whose mind played happily in a world of sparks & quarks, and who was quite content to be led past Titians and Tintorettos by the score, none of which, apparently, he so much as noticed.

Not that Chris and Roy were in any way deterred by this attrition. Let's face it, seniors were seniors, and had to be given latitude. After all, the horses had been taken to water – let the drinking be left to them. A duty which, like all students in all generations, they'd doubtless discharge with quite remarkable assiduity!

Gaudeamus igitur!

As for Julian and I, on the pretext of tracking down Toby we too on occasions saw no harm in absenting ourselves from the third session. Since we always returned well in time for dinner at seven, neither of our leaders seemed at all put out by this, and so the bulk of the tour slid by in a blur of beauty and what the chic of this world call chilling out.

Then came Sunday.

The first time we'd disembarked at the Academia, we'd noticed a huge banner slung across the face of the bridge by ropes. A crude garish affair in red block letters, embellished with the usual silhouette of Ché, it appeared to consist of some exhortation or other by the local Communistas. Maybe announcing a rally, maybe just making a political point. None of us had Italian sufficient to make head or tail of it, and when we inquired of Coco he simply shook his head, said "Phfff" loudly, and refused to discuss it further.

That the local Reds were a force to be reckoned with had already, of course, been made clear to us not only by the Treviso strike, but by a two hour stoppage on the vaporetti that Friday which had forced us to walk back to lunch from the Riva Schiavoni. It seemed a pity to have that angry swathe of canvas glaring at us every time we came home, but what could we do? We were mere guests – it was their city.

At least that was the adults' point of view which just goes to prove, I suppose, the superior virility of the public school teenager.

About half past midnight on Sunday, Julian and I, as you might guess, were in mellow mode. Our steamer was nearing the Academia landing stage when suddenly he smote me on the knee and pointed. "Unbelievable!" he said. "D' you see what I see?"

It had been a long, unusually hot day at the Lido and I was sleepy. Conscientiously we'd looked for Toby during Mass, during lunch, on the beach, in an ice cream parlour, and at a waterfront bar while waiting for the ferry back. After dinner we'd resumed our search in S Stefano and various hostelries between there and the Campanile with the result that, if not precisely stonkered, we were certainly well oiled. Sufficiently thus, on my part at any rate, to pay zero attention to anything except where the next drink was coming from. Even so, I forced myself to peer up at the structure looming towards us.

"That bloody canvas. It's gone! See?"

It had indeed gone, that canvas, bloody in more ways than one. But as I opened my mouth to reply – well, the wittiest riposte ever devised by homo sapiens would have frozen on my lips that moment. For there, at the top of the bridge – though in shadow since he was leant over the rail with a lamp directly above him – whom did I spy but…?

No, not whom you're thinking. Not young Copeland, but, of all people, Alex. El elusivo! Xavier Mell, my Alex! Unshaven, it's true, but otherwise smart in a lilac shirt and loose white waistcoat. Though I couldn't exactly see his face, I mean in detail, there wasn't a shred of doubt about it.

Did I wave? Did I shout? Of course, like a loony, in the second or two before the bridge blotted him out..

Did he see me? That, I'm afraid, was a question not destined for an answer you've yet any chance of understanding – for by the time we'd docked and I'd dashed up the steps, the bridge was, of course, empty. Just space. What De La Mare terms so poignantly 'vast vacancy'.

Nor was there anything to be done. The boy had certainly not descended this side, and as to the other? S. Stefano, as I knew only too well, has more exits than one of those baths in a textbook of Victorian sums. Pursuit would be futile, even more so than at Tolverton. No, all I had to console me was the usual old wives' tale, pathetic refuge of the born loser: that encounters, like Routemasters, always come in threes.

Which in a sense would turn out to be true. But later, and weirdly.

As for now, totally pissed off, I stumbled back down to Julian, though what help could he be? Since the first rule of bed life is never try disclosing one shag, actual or potential, to another, I could hardly explain how matters stood. On the other hand, I was too exhausted to fib. So we walked off in a kind of wordless limbo, our senses overhelmed by that mixture of bad drains and boundless regret which constitutes Italian night.

By the time we reached our pension, Coco had pushed off to bed and the bar was shut. Not only did the salone seem suspiciously quiet, but the first floor too. None of the usual late-night noise of running water, or footsteps and laughter as bodies prepared themselves for bed – moreover, both the lads' doors were open but no-one in evidence.

It was then we heard it. A faint noise from upstairs, what one might call subdued commotion. Julian and I looked askance at each other. No music, so it could hardly be a party. No thumping of floorboards, so it could hardly be a fight. Nor were Castleton and Foster sufficiently clued up in culture to be holding a literary soirée or anything of that sort. In which case – QED! It must be an orgy!

We raced upstairs, threw open the door and gasped in utter astonishment. For there stretched full length and face down over the bed, dresser and two chairs was that huge revolting canvas from the Academia bridge. Poised over it, a figure, tiny can in one hand, a sort of broad knife in the other. Clustered round about, in various stages of undress, adoring spectators in the shape of our whole tribe of lads, except Marsden and his Travers. Moreover, the whole room swam with that kind of giggly mood which suggests earlier imbibation of something rather stronger than Lucozade.

The figure looked up from its work. Jukes, of course, smudges of paint on his neck and ear – fender paint, the sort that never comes off. "Nearly finished," he said brightly, scraping his knife round the can. "Just gotta cross the..."

"What the ruddy hell is going on here?" I inquired aghast, visions erupting of his being hunted down side canals by crack units from the Kremlin. And me. And all of us!

"Sir?"

"What on earth are you playing at?"

He grinned. "Nothing much," he exclaimed, turning back to finish the last stroke. "Just flying the flag."

"Stop that!" I yelled. "You complete idiots. Don't you realise who you're dealing with? Partisans! Lethal brutes! Whose knives, let me tell you, aren't designed to paint pictures. For God's sake! D' you seriously want to spend the next year in hospital? While they fit you with artificial legs?"

"Just a joke, sir," piped up Carey.

"Anyway," joined in Tim Foster, "how would they know it was us? My dad says Eyties are virtual cretins."

"That so?" I gestured at the slogan. FLOREAT TOLVERTONIA. "You don't think even a cretin might work that one out?" I grabbed the knife. "OK, OK, so now we put matters right. Score right through every single letter."

"No paint left."

"That so? Well it goes back anyway. We'll put it up as it was, the original stuff face out. And just hope no-one investigates until we've left. Where are the ropes?"

"But it's not dry yet." Jukes dismayed, surveying his handiwork.

"All the better – we can smudge it a bit. After all, who's going to notice? A few wood lice, maybe? The odd rat? Oh, and by the way. Exactly where did you get that paint?"

By half past one we were back on the bridge. It had of course been impossible to roll the thing up for fear of harming the original slogan, so it had been carried lengthwise by all ten of us, looking like some monstrous tapeworm, or one of those dragon things they have at Chinese festivities. Fortunately, by this time the streets were deserted – so too the canal except for the odd barge or private launch to the Casino.

With the numbers involved, it was easy enough, despite its bulk, to haul the monstrosity into position so that once again Ché glared his baleful gaze down to the Salute. Easy too to fix the first rope. Not so easy, however, to make the final adjustments before fixing the second.

By then most of our helpers had let go their grip, and were looking around, yawning and thinking of bed. So it was that when I fumbled with the final knot, and it unravelled and slipped through my fingers, too few folk were left to hold the weight. Down it swung, one end in the water, one end tied to the bridge rail above.

Or rather, sort of tied. Tied temporarily. Tied by Jukes in a spectacularly elaborate knot of his own devising, and one which boasted this most sublime of characteristics – immediate and complete disintegration as soon as the slightest tension was applied thereto.

And so, gracefully and proudly, like a liner at launching, that banner slid its full length into the Grand Canal and floated slowly away, as if to the strains of 'Nearer my God to Thee', with Ché grimacing fiercely at the heavens.

"Christ," said Julian ruefully. "That's torn it. What do we do now?"

"Get it back," I replied. "Shoes off quick. The two of us should be able to drag it in easily enough."

"What?" he protested, glancing down at the black surface. "Dive into that? It's filthy. You want us to catch cholera or something? Lockjaw or worse?"

"Local boys do it every day." I must have sounded pretty scornful. "Do they catch cholera, for God's sake? Now come on, don't let's waste more…"

But by now an engine could clearly be heard. An empty motoscafi, saloon dark, heading home to its mooring beyond Treporti. We rushed to the approach side, waving them to steer nearer the bank – but all in vain. It was as if a robot was at the helm. Fair and square the boat surged on in the middle channel. Back over we rushed, just in time to see her prow pluck up our banner. Catch it sweet as a shawl, and proceed onwards with its ends floating out each side like some vast untrimmed version of Murdoch's moustache.

"Now what?" said Julian with a grin.

"Bed?"

"Bed!"

After all, what do they say? Everything comes to him who sleeps? No doubt about it on this occasion. At a little past six, I suddenly sat bolt upright, rubbed my eyes, and pinched Julian's nostrils together.

"Whurra, aasaf, uh, uh?" he opined, wildly brushing my arm away. "Hey man. What the fuck?"

"Get dressed pronto. I've got it. That banner."

"What?" Dubiously. "So where?"

"Don't be daft – I mean I've had an idea."

"Oh yeah?" Even more dubiously.

"Vittorio, right? Why on earth didn't we think of him last night?"

OK, OK, technically speaking a man can't be an idea. But he can be the kernel of an idea, or rather stratagem, which is precisely what had come into my head five minutes ago. By now, the first faint streaks of grey were threading the east. In half an hour it would be dawn, in an hour full daylight and too late. We had to act quickly. Somewhere along that ruddy canal, that ruddy banner was washed up on steps, or wrapped round a mooring post or something. The fate didn't matter. The fact did. That as soon as its absence from the Academia was noted, a search would be started – it would be found, its attackers identified, and we'd be for it. Sadly, our plane didn't leave for two more days. It was impossible, given that length of time, for us to expect to escape reprisals.

But Vittorio owned a boat, didn't he? A sleek motor launch with white leather seats, the sort of thing in which Veneto man flaunts his squeeze around the waterways. Might he not be willing to flaunt us around for half an hour? To save Da Coco's reputation?

I mean, who'd want to stay at a hotel where fifteen patrons had just been murdered mysteriously in their beds?

As expected, the boy was already up and in the kitchen, sorting out the bread baskets whilst his mother gutted fish. It took a moment to explain our plight, another to grab keys from behind the Madonna, and away we swept in a great cream surge, under the bridge, towards the Rialto.

Even in this half light, canvas that long would surely be, we assumed, pretty visible. All three of us had powerful torches and with their assistance, plus Julian's binoculars, we swept every inch of the canal as our wash smote the ancient piles. Cats ran, rats ran, students bunched up on the station steps in their sleeping bags peered hazily forth. But nowhere, nowhere could we spot our quarry.

OK, if at first you don't succeed, etc, etc... We tried the Zattere, we tried the Lido, we tried the islets towards Burano. All to no avail. By ten to seven the light was becoming critical and we decided on one last throw of the dice. A sweep back down the Grand Canal whence we'd come.

No need for torches now. Half blue was in the sky and folk beginning to stir. The first vaporetti backing out from their stakes, the first waiters starting to set tables at the canal side.

As we motored slowly down, our hopes too dwindled. Nothing was said but all three of us instinctively understood. We'd lost! Whatever the consequences, we'd lost. Most likely the banner had already been found, and was at this very moment being sliced up into shrouds – to encase certain bodies after their throats were cut!

Throttled back, the boat dindled along past Harry's Bar, past the quays of S. Marco, past SS Chusan moored for the night opposite S, Georgio, none of us willing to make that conclusive decision to swing her about and head for home. Until, at the Arsenale arch, Vittorio spat suddenly into the bilge. "Finito!" he announced, spinning the wheel hard round.

It was then we saw it. Julian first, obviously, but soon it was perfectly clear to the naked eye. That canvas, half in the water, half out, like some hapless corpse of a wino. Somehow or other it had made its way round the lagoon, and into the Arsenale before stranding itself on one of those wooden slipways that tourists love to snap.

How we danced – at least, sort of danced, as far as is possible in a twelve foot cruiser. Within half an hour we were seated at a celebratory breakfast – Coco had whipped up some scrambled eggs with mushrooms and pancetta – our trophy stowed in the giardino shed, safe if well soggy.

Oh God, thine arm was here!

Needless to say, none of this was revealed to Chris, and neither therefore to Marcho. Apart from their look of surprise when they descended at nine, breakfast usually consisting of simply rolls and jam, everything sailed on as normal, and soon the two of them were rounding folk up for our morning cruise to Torcello – an hour or so across the lagoon, then free time to look round the basilica or, if you were energetic, climb the tower. Young Travers would doubtless be scrambling skywards like a monkey – would his playmate, I wondered in an idle moment, be following suit? At the moment they seemed happy enough, sharing a packet of Maltesers.

After our sunrise tribulations, it took Julian and I a fair while to relax. Fortunately, the steamer was one of those large Lido specimens, its bar well stocked with the necessary. A sip or two of campari soda, cool and scented, and we were lounging back in our seats, enjoying the wind in our hair and the dull haze of sun on our arms and shoulders.

"Never noticed that before," queried Julian, flicking a mole low down on my torso.

"Quelle surprise! After all your opportunities, pervert!"

"Salacious bastard!"

"Love you too," I smiled lazily. For once the Gods had come up trumps, and no mistake! Like, whatever Toby's merits as a travelling companion might have been, Julian's were now a proven fact. What more could a guy want? He was laid back, responsive, hygienic, and didn't snore. He stood his round without delay, but without that alacrity which so marks out the insecure. And above all, during sex his mind was fully on the job, you could sense it, not like some punters who seem to be solving cube roots by the long method while slaking your frenum.

Has she no faults, then, Envy says, sir? Well, sort of. Sure, there had to be something of a blemish – what's more tedious than perfection? But at least his was venial. It was just that, every now and then, he'd come out with a statement of the obvious, and usually when it was something one was trying to forget. Like now.

Halfway through his glass, he sniffed and heaved himself more upright. "That banner," he said reflectively. "It's fucking big."

"No problem," I murmured, eyes closed.

"What the hell are we gonna do?"

"Sort it, OK?"

"Tomorrow's our last full day. We can't leave Cokey in the lurch. Or Vittorio."

"Perish the thought."

"It's fucking big."

"It's also," I retorted, opening my eyes, "fucking hot. Do we have to discuss this now?"

"Sorry."

"No, no," I said penitently, cuffing his shoulder, "mea culpa. It's the sun. Like, I sort of heat up and revert to lizard. You're quite right. Time's short and we ought to decide. Got a pen?"

And so we began a list of our options, half an hour or so of intense thought and debate – at the end of which, guess what? Not a line, not a word. That page remained absolutely virgin! After all, what does one do with a huge hunk of thick canvas? It can't be burnt, given its regulation coating of alum. It can't be buried or stuffed down a well without the locals noticing. In other words, one's up the proverbial gum tree!

"Roy?" queried Julian resignedly.

"Roy it is," I nodded, fuming inwardly. I'd have given a million to come up with a solution on my tod, but there it was. When the chips were down, his experience was needed – no more to be said.

At least we chose our time well, that post-lunch calm of heat and cicadas when nothing jars. He was perched on a step in the shade, enjoying a quiet smoke while Watson fussed way off in the background, chivvying the 5th formers round an exhibition of dusty ampullae.

"Roy," I said squatting down beside him, "the truth is, we've had a spot of bother."

The old eyes twinkled. "You don't say."

"It's like this…" And in a couple of minutes I filled him in on the whole story. Not a hint of surprise crossed his face. Not once did he look anything but mildly amused and when I'd finished, he simply nodded and said, "What a wheeze! Beats Rider Haggard any day. You know, I rather fancy a coffee. How about you and Julian?"

"Later maybe. At this moment…"

"Your dilemma? Oh quite! Not to worry. Chris and I'll come up with something. Some ruse from Caesar, or there's always the Old Testament. Just leave it with me."

And leave it with him we did – all day, and the next – while we enjoyed our lees to the full. Early morning at the Rialto, cakes at E Rosa Salvatore, a matinee at the Fenice, and, finally – Parnassus! On our knees at the Scuola S. Rocco and Europe's finest painting, the great Tintoretto Crucifixion.

Our farewell dinner at the Dorsoduro had been fixed for half an hour earlier than usual, ostensibly to allow time for packing, and, round about six thirty, clad only in a towel, I was making my way back from the shower when I heard a distinct cry from Marsden's lair. Not pain exactly, but not quite pleasure either. Soon there was another.

Looking back on things, I suppose this marked the real start of my enslavement. A sensible bloke would have shrugged and walked on. As it was, intrigued as much as concerned, I knocked on the door and entered.

Shirtless, shoeless, clad only in jeans, the two of them appeared to be locked in some kind of wrestling hold on the bed – a large double at that, as my appalling mind couldn't help noticing! Though the older boy was on top and had Guy pinned down by the shoulders, it was clear that their bodies were pretty evenly matched. Travers, well-muscled but smaller of frame and more agile – Marsden, heavier and with powerful arms. Also a knack of anticipating every wrench and feint of his victim as he strove.

"Guy," I said. "You OK?"

Both froze and looked my way.

"Are you OK?"

As the boy nodded, Marsden released his hold, slid off the bed and approached me, hands on hips. "Just a friendly match," he panted.

"So I see – dare I ask who's winning?"

"Both of us – neither," he shrugged. "It's just fun." Then quieter, hardly more than a murmur. "*OK*, Paul? All your yesterdays. Remember?"

His body was close to mine now, so close I couldn't help noticing the fragrance of his sweat, or the way his chest was heaving after exertion. Lightly haired, like mine. Slightly browned after yesterday's sun, like mine. I swallowed hard. This was no boy, but a man. Like me.

"How would you know?" I answered lamely, but without turning away.

Suddenly it was weird. A kind of weird consciousness burst in my brain. Not of my nakedness exactly – or not just that – but my sort of hopeless vulnerability. His eyes seemed to be basting me, as though in response to mine. It was like we were two opponents in some gladiatorial ring, skin to skin, about to lock into a battle which only one would survive. My lips were dry, his slightly open.

For a moment, stasis. Before his hand flexes, flips the towel from my loins. Before I reach for my net & trident, he for his sword, and damned be him who first cries, Hold – enough!

'Cos that's how I saw it, honest! That's how it seemed. Rawest Cinemascope! Stench, strength, maddened brawn against brawn, until – last reel. Myself on the sand bloodbound, his foot on my throat, both of us awaiting the thumbs down from on high. The inevitable thumbs down.

Inevitable?

Not if I can help it! piped up a voice in my grey matter. Strange how, even as the jaws clamp, something makes us resist. Dart aside. Spear the eye. Anything so we survive. Don't lose the light. Persist.

"Travers," I said abruptly, placing my right hand behind my neck, "put your shirt on for God's sake. And this room's a disgrace. Both of you, get it smartened up before you come down! Marsden, you're the senior. I'm holding you responsible. Understand?"

At which he smiled, and brought forth from his pocket that cute chain of his with its cross. He held it up provocatively. "Fasten it at the back for me, could you, sir?" he asked.

"Fasten it yourself." My reply was as curt as I could make it under the circumstances, but again he smiled and was still smiling each of the three times I glanced his way during dinner.

Not that I was unduly fazed. The moment had passed safely, hadn't it? What could either boy actually say? And now – the even keel. Here I was in jacket and tie, the exemplary young schoolmaster, my mind apparently on Smollett, the letters of Gray, and the thirty sixth line of Wordsworth's *Elegiac Stanzas Suggested by* a *Picture of Peel Castle in* a *Storm, Painted by Sir George Beaumont*. Which perhaps it would have been, had that other little problem, the curse of the canvas, not remained still, as far as I knew, unresolved.

Dessert finished, I looked inquiringly across at Julian who just shrugged.

"Roy," I began, turning his way, "any ideas as…?"

"Never fear," he said. "That little difficulty has spent all day in the bakehouse. With the flues shut. Should be dry as a bone by now."

"Fine and dandy, Roy, but tell me – like, its disposal. Have you come up with anything? A solution?"

"Oh ye of little faith."

"Roy…"

"Calm down, dear boy. In that ghastly Yankee parlance you affect, 'no problem'. Eh Chris?" Watson nodded. "Or as they say in Tennessee, I think we can cut it."

"Quite so, quite so," confirmed the other with a chuckle. "And aptly put, as always. Which reminds me." Every inch a Caesar, he rose, tapped his glass with a knife, and peered severely over his spectacles. "Now boys, time to pack. Deadline eight fifteen. By then, every case must be on its bed, open, bathrobe on top, ready for inspection. Anyone who fails will be excluded from this evening's treat. Fact, I assure you. Absolute fact. No exceptions whatever."

A slight buzz of voices, from which arose that of Jukes: "This treat, sir? What is it? Punch or Judy?"

"I'll Judy you, Jukes, if you're not careful!" retorted Watson.

"But what treat, sir? Tell us, sir. Tell us." Various voices in insistent babble.

"Well then, if you must know," chuckled Watson, "Marilyn Monroe! On film, of course. Not in the flesh – your parents might object."

"Not my dad, sir."

"Like father, like son, eh Macdonald?" Brief laughter. "Well, be that as it may, I've reserved seats at S. Stae, the open-air cinema, for 'Some Like It Hot'. But only for those ready. So off you go. Get cracking now."

He turned back to us. "Come along, come along. That should keep the coast clear for half an hour or so. Vittorio awaits us in the salone. Did he find them?"

"I gather so."

"Find what?" I queried innocently.

"Shame on you, Bryant," cried Watson. "With your brains, I marvel they saw fit to award you a degree at all!" And off he marched, with Roy and Julian in tow, the latter hardly able to contain his mirth.

Vittorio was indeed waiting, the banner spread out over three tables beside him. Very woebegone it looked now, dry and cracked, all its smoothness vanished, its bold red script so smudged it resembled nothing so much as an abstract masterpiece from the Tate Modern

Flourishing a carrier bag, the boy waved us into position. "Each at a corner," he said, "and pull tight. Tight as you can. That's it. Now do not slacken as" – from his bag he pulled an ancient pair of garden shears – "I cut her."

Horrified, I watched as he sliced that banner lengthways into two. Now we were really for it! What the hell was going on?

In a few moments, our late monster had been reduced to twelve neat oblongs, each double folded and laid in a row.

"So far so good," pronounced Watson. "Now, I'll conduct the inspection and carry the lads off to S. Stae. Chaplain, over to you."

"Don't look so shattered," beamed Roy. "In my experience, customs rarely bother a church party. We simply tuck an oblong inside each bathrobe pocket, close each case, and stand it outside the door ready for locking. Back in Britain, we collect up the evidence and bob's your uncle."

"But what if customs do intervene?" Julian looked concerned.

"Very unlikely Anyway, how much duty would there be payable on a few inches of disreputable canvas? Now we have to toss for it."

"For what?" I asked wearily.

"Twelve squares, eleven boys. One of us must take the risk too. Paul, you call first."

"No way." I shook my head decisively. "With my luck, I'm bound to turn out the fall guy. So why bother with a contest? Hand it over. My God, what a mess!"

And indeed, like the guy at the Garrick, it could hardly be called handsome, this ragged scrap, red blotches on one side, black loops and shafts on the other. I fingered it with some disdain, wondering wildly, for a moment, if it would flush down the loo. As you'd expect though, more cautious counsel prevailed and it was finally found a home inserted between the boards and dust cover of a volume of Veronese which I'd borrowed from Ken's library.

Macho's judgment over Customs proved perfectly correct. Wearing his dog collar he presided over his flock with a beaming smile. One by one, each case was chalked without scrutiny – until they came to mine!

"This one, sir. Open up, if you please."

"Really?"

"It won't take a minute. Now if you'll have a look at this list…"

If ever a suitcase was toothcombed, mine was that excruciating day. Each item of clothing was brought out and fondled. Each item of footwear and toiletry. It was only when my pink shower cap saw daylight that some giggles close by betrayed the presence of the boys and Julian. Unable to resist the prospect, while Roy and Chris had tooled off to bag a cup of tea and retrieve the Bedford, they'd stayed to watch my torment – doubtless hoping I'd a large bottle of illicit moonshine stashed away somewhere in my knicker bag, or some porno postcards or whatever.

Eventually, the officer got to Veronese, squinting at it aloft and extracting the canvas cautiously as though it was impregnated with LSD or TNT.

"And what have we here, sir?"

Utterly unprepared for such a question, at first I simply gawped in embarrassment. "Er…"

"Odd place for a painting."

"You think so?"

"This is, I take it, an item belonging to you?"

"Oh quite," I replied thinking hard. "Yes indeed. Italy, you see. Just the ticket for inspiration. That's one of my daubs. Rather successful, don't you think? I call it, um… 'Migraine'."

"Which way round, sir?" he said, inspecting it under the lamp. "This" – reversing it with a swirl like a matador's cape – "or that?"

"Ah…" Bereft of words, again I just stared.

"Or shall we just say it's the world's first ever double-sided oil painting?" Handing it back, he chalked my case with a broad smile, leaving me to creep over, red-faced, to where my loyal acolytes seemed, amidst much giggling, to be putting their heads together.

"Jukes!" I said fiercely. "If any of you ever breathe a word of this…"

"A word, sir?"

"I'm warning you."

"As if we would." At which, he turned to face the serried ranks, holding his hands out in the manner of Karajan or Flash Harry. Instinctively, I knew what was coming. Knew almost word for word as the unison began:

Just one Pic-asso

Give it to me

Delicious migraine

At half past three.

"Really, Bryant," cried Watson, striding through the swing doors. "Choir rehearsal at this time of day? And in the customs shed! What can you be thinking of? Now, lads. At the double. You'll find the coach outside in bay D. Come along, come along. Bryant, do come along, for goodness sake!"

10: *In the Twi-Twi-Twilight*

"Tell us, sir. You must. It's only fair."

"Chuffley," said I sternly, "put a sock in it, OK? Otherwise I might mark your prep and then where ould you be?"

"In detention?" suggested his friend helpfully.

"Quite right, Gilchrist. Alongside you!"

"But I'm not a moron, sir. Why me?"

"For speaking out of turn. Now – how about you all belt up!"

"But we only want to know, sir."

"Know, eh? Well, I'll tell you about know. Its noun form is knowledge, OK? Which is what your parents pay for, poor misguided souls, and what you might just get a glimpse of if you shut up and turn to poem number 17 in your Betjeman."

"Larkin, sir, don't you mean Larkin?"

"Of course Larkin – now just get on with it."

Never easy to restrain at the best of times, today 5C was a veritable pack of monkeys following their stint in morning chapel. Or, to be more precise, Marcho's indiscretion at their stint in morning chapel.

"Page 17, sir?" inquired Chuffley.

"Who needs a hearing-aid?" I beamed caustically. "*Poem* 17, idiot."

But Jukes Jr. was there already. "*On Being Twenty Six*! Oh, sir! What a tease!"

At which Rudgewick, every inch the farmer's son and thicker even than Chuffley, raised his hand. "Blease, sir," he intoned deliberately. "Be that a clue?" The torrent of laughter and repeated requests of "Tell us, sir" which followed were now quelled only by the ultimate sanction: my pulling a cane from a drawer and laying it across the desk. Twenty obedient heads now bent to their books and for a while all was quiet.

Marcho! How that man could put his foot in it! One of his more singular little tricks was, every Monday, to read out a list in chapel of those whose birthdays fell in the coming week, so that cards could be sent or prezzies or whatever. Rather endearing I'd always thought – until I realised that the custom also extended to staff unless they requested anonymity. Since all did, the first I knew of this technicality had been half an hour ago when "Mr Paul Bryant, Rhodes House" had floated down the aisle at my unsuspecting ears. Hence 5C's sudden inquisitiveness over my age, and my pretty clumsy attempt to deflect their interest. The last thing I wanted was for it to get round the school at large that I was just about three years older than the oldest pupil in the 6th form. That way does not, decidedly not, lie discipline!

One by one as they finished the poem, puzzled faces gazed up at me, though it was left to Jukes – who else? – to articulate their quandary. "You are joking, sir, aren't you?" he said.

"About what?"

"Being twenty six, sir. That can't be right."

"No?" said I brazenly, but with a feeling of dread in my entrails. Was this the moment of truth? Was I on the brink of being outed? Being revealed as little more than a teenager like them?

Well, nothing for it but to make the best of a bad job. No point in dissembling – schoolboys always find you out in the end. "So," I continued, "if you're such a clever dick, how old am I?"

Scrutinising me intensely, Jukes cocked his head to one side. "My guess is – forty. No, forty two."

"Fifty!" countered Chuffley authoritatively.

"Moron!" snorted Gilchrist, "he's still got his hair. Most of it. Forty two, sir, isn't that right?"

The brief cacophony which ensued – numbers from thirty five to fifty five gaily sailing to and fro – prompted me to recall a remark Ormulak had once made: that schoolboys invariably have a deep need to believe their teachers well into, or at least verging on, decrepitude. Why so? I wondered, grabbing the cane and whacking it down hard on my copy of The Illustrated London News.

"Why so?" I quizzed James Frobisher that evening, as we sat in the garden of The Pony and Trap out at Feyhill, a not particularly stylish pub, given its proximity to the town's council estate, but far enough out for James to be safe from accidents – the embarrassment of meeting Murdoch or other similar of his former colleagues.

"Who knows?" he replied, nonchalant as ever. "It's the sort of question that keeps a million psychiatrists off the dole, though. Or do I mean psychologists?"

"Search me."

"Anyhow, they're all crap merchants. Charge you fifty guineas and end up stating the obvious."

"Which, in this case, is?"

"Oh sex, I expect. As usual. And understandable since teenagers think of bugger all else."

"Exactly like us, you mean – so what?"

"Well, one thing junior can't stand is the thought of his parents actually at it. It'd be like admitting he was made by a fuck."

"Which he was."

"Yuh, but at fifteen it's a bogey most of them can't face. So they construct this myth or whatever: that poor old mum and dad are past it, and have been all their lives. It kinda minimises the threat."

"So I'm a threat, and the lads minimise it by deeming me to have one foot in the grave?"

"Summat like that."

"I'm highly flattered! Tell me – how do you want your fee? Cash or will a cheque do?"

"Cash by all means." He grinned. "As long as it's in roubles!"

Summer term well established, but the exam season not yet unleashed, I'd been bidden here for a drink by James on his return from Somerset. Since falling from grace, he'd been licking his wounds on his parents' estate at Hallatrow, and had now returned briefly in order to sell his house before moving to a new job in June. Or new career, to be more accurate. With teaching closed to him, it was obvious he had to seek new pastures, but... Well, it seemed an odd choice to me. Surely he could have done better.

Anyhow, it was ace to be with him here, sharing a laugh – since returning from Venice I'd had scarcely any time to myself and not a single evening out. Just as well perhaps since there'd been no word from either Wartford or the dreaming spires – let alone Alexis – whilst Marsden seemed intent on keeping a low profile, sitting in his usual desk, every now and then looking up with that infuriatingly demure expression of his, every now and then flicking that lock of hair into temporary submission.

Just as well there was no time to brood. No opportunity to make futile plans. Only the odd hour like this to remind one how adults are supposed to live.

"Good to see you back on form," I ventured.

"Why not? Look, who's that bloke in Dickens with the chain? Coils and coils of it?"

"What, Marley?"

"Well, the way I feel, it's like every last bloody link has done a bunk all of a sudden, like that!"

He snapped his fingers and I blinked. "You really that glad?" I retorted. " To be shot of the place, I mean?"

"Tolverton?" He picked up his glass. "Shot of more than that, I'm glad to say. Haven't you heard? About Sue giving me the push?"

"You're not serious."

"Susie the floosie! Take my word for it, bloody women – more trouble than they're worth."

Watching him drink, I tried to make up my mind. Was this just bravado or what? La Dame sans Merci - was he genuinely glad to be rid of her, or was it some kind of cri de coeur, a prelude to his reaching for the shotgun?

"What I don't understand, though…" Turning his glass upside down over a wasp, he gazed reflectively at its antics. "I mean, a guy like him! A loser, an absolute wimp of nothingness! What's he got that I haven't?"

"Who knows? A bigger dick, maybe?"

A sudden punch in the air. "Bingo!" he retorted. "How the deuce is it I knew you'd say that? Exactly that?"

"Great dicks think alike?"

"In which case, how come mine's so miniscule compared to his?"

"Is it? How would I know? Since I've not – had the privilege, as they say."

Just in time I stopped myself from interpolating a 'yet', though I suspect he sensed the omission.

One of those Frobisher smiles. "Enough about me," he said. "How about you? What is this methuselahn age you're keeping from the lads, for instance?"

"No big deal," I replied. "Same as you I expect, roughly."

"And the great day is…?"

"Tomorrow, thank God. The sooner it's over the better. Why do people make such a fuss?"

"Tomorrow," he nodded thoughtfully. "Weather forecast good. Stars auspicious. Maybe we ought to go for it."

"Sounds intriguing. Go for…?"

"Our wager? That pool up in the woods?"

"Oh, right!" Abrupt excitement down entrails way: I was wide-eyed.

"Except, I've a better idea. How about a canoe down the Tolver? It widens out below where Crawshaw's mill used to be –

plenty of room for diving and racing. And well secluded. No roads anywhere near. How does that grab you?"

Grab me? It absolutely pinioned me, suddenly, delightfully, and right where a man's most vulnerable! Moreover, to cap it all, this was the third birthday invitation I'd received in the past twenty four hours. You go for years and years marking each May 15th on your tod with a bottle of scotch, and now – incredible! An embarrassment des riches, as the Frogs say. If things went on like this, I'd have to do a Bob Hope and take ugly pills!

"James," quoth I, "that would be fantastic! Problem is, I'm already booked by Ormulak. To see his yaffle or something." There was no point in mentioning my date with Marcho as well. Too much popularity might sound bumptious or boastful or even worse – shooting a line.

"See his yaffle? Sounds faintly disgusting!"

"Well, it's a first for me. That's for sure."

"I should damn well hope so! What on earth is it? Any clues?"

"Not a sausage."

"Could be one of those stringy thingies Lonnie Donegan plays."

"Idiot – that's a skiffle!"

"Or something out of Alice – one of those monsters dreamed up by that paedo chap."

"Lewis Carroll?" I smiled mischievously. "Actually it'll probably turn out something dead boring – like, to do with those ghastly bells he and Baxter dote on. Anyhow, it's his idea of a treat – so I'm stymied!"

Whether it was my rueful expression or the absurd idea of Ormulak reading dodgy prose that amused him I've no idea but he clipped me round the head with his late edition of the *Argus*. "No problem," he grinned. "How about making it really late? Say midnight? Ever swum in the dark have you?"

In a trice, I admitted that I hadn't, and thus was the whole escapade fixed up. What I failed to admit was that for years such a pleasure had been one of my fondest fantasies – and now the Gods were handing it to me on a plate. Wow! And who knows, maybe something else?

Thus it was that my twenty third birthday dawned bright and sunny, ideal yaffle weather, according to Ormulak. Presumably, ideal weather too for whatever Marcho had planned for later in the evening. Even more mysterious than the Pole, no hint whatever had slipped his lips as to the nature of this second soirée. For all I knew it might be fireworks in his garden or a trip aloft in a hot air balloon. Or maybe fireworks aloft in a very hot air balloon.

That in all probability it was something appalling, that he'd found half a mile of abandoned railway in a wood near New Radnor and that my treat was to stumble along its sleepers, ruining my shoes and getting stung by brambles, had not escaped me. At anyrate, it would give me a sound excuse for some good solid fortification in The Fox before setting out. But when, exactly? So set had he been on keeping everything secret that I'd not even been given a departure time. Nor was he anywhere to be found that Wednesday morning, in Common Room, chapel or elsewhere.

Not till after lunch did I finally run him to ground, in his element – where else but on the greensward?

It being a half day and the sun showing no signs of abating, the campus now resembled nothing so much as one of those TV adverts for Butlins. Eric, his linen jacket blowing loosely in the breeze, chatting to cadets busy caulking a tatty whaler. Lads in white shorts heading for the tennis courts, lads in bathing shorts heading for the pool, lads with bats over their shoulders heading for the nets or field. And most vivid spectacle of all, croquet on the cloisters lawn, all reds and yellows and stuff, and the players decked out in house colours

A match had just started, Stanley versus Rhodes, and who should be umpiring but Marcho, from the safety of an enormous striped sunshade. Beside him stretched a long bench at the far end of which sat four disconsolate souls, each clutching a mallet, presumably substitutes or something of that ilk.

"Like to try your hand sometime?" he said gaily.

I shrugged. "Looks a bit expert for me," I replied, perching myself beside him, and peering intently at the spectacle of balls positioned by hoops, balls positioned by other balls, and mallets being plied with savage ferocity.

Since Venice, relations between us, as by now you've probably surmised, had undergone something of a repair, despite yesterday's faux pas in chapel. And it wasn't just a question, by the way, of his having saved our bacon over the banner. Though I still resented his perfidy regards James, I had to admit that his rapport with the boys was outstanding, and could be the product of nothing but a genuinely liberated spirit. Besides, there was the tank á la Glycol. Under severe interrogation, old Joe had finally cracked and told me all he knew. Which was not much, but sufficient. That Marcho's ordination had (as I suspected) come after the war. That earlier he had (as I suspected) flown Hurricanes out of Chalgrove. That he'd been awarded the DFC, and that the subject was never to be talked about. How very English!

As English indeed as the contest being fought out before me. Except for one unfortunate, whose ball had been twice hammered halfway to London, all were now clustered round the second hoop. Though the niceties escaped me, there was certainly something awesome about the ardency with which the participants approached their business: they way they measured angles, stretched out on the ground to peer backwards through the hoop, practised test swings and so on. All very expert – and impressive too, except to a bloke like myself to whom competitiveness is the anathema of anathemas!

I rose to take my leave.

"Going already?"

"I only popped over to ask about time. You know, this evening?"

"Of course, of course. Oh, by the way, many happy returns, dear boy. All we need now is what one might term dusk plus."

"Dusk plus?"

"By far the best time for flight. Indeed so. Now, assuming about twenty miles to the field – or is it forty? – we ought to leave about, um... Let's say, rendezvous here at half past seven. How's that?"

"Cool," I replied, breathing an inward sigh of relief. Plenty of time to fit him in before James. "See you then."

"And by the way," he called after me, "make sure you wear something warm."

Flying helmet and goggles? One of those fleecy RAF windcheaters? So it really was to be a hot air balloon – or worse! Gliding, maybe? Or parachuting! My stomach turned over at the thought. And how sad that paradox is, that it's so often other people's attempts to be kind that cause one the most distress.

All afternoon it stayed with me, this sense of unease, together with a sort of descant – a niggling perplexity as to how, having kept his secret so long, the old boy had accidentally let drop so obvious a clue at the eleventh hour.

I mean, what else could it be but accidental? Like, flight means flight means flight, doesn't it? What else?

So thus it was with my head full, not of yaffles, but the Hindenburg and Amy Johnson and the Bermuda Triangle, that I approached Ormulak's place on a well-oiled and very matronly Raleigh borrowed from Murdoch's wife.

It was nearing half past three, with the sun still a brazen blur in the sky, when my perturbation was more than a little increased as I rounded a sharp bend only to encounter – yes, a sentinel. A billy-goat with vast notched horns solemnly guarding what appeared to be the only gate. Ormulak's home stood well back from the lane on a kind of mound, his whole demesne being surrounded by stout wooden fencing, with no other way in but this.

Confession: goats and I do not, I'm afraid, get on. They smell, they make these gross sounds, they produce yucky milk, whilst the males not only look baleful but are capable of an unpremeditated savagery which even the stoutest stick finds difficult to ward off.

And all I had was my bicycle pump!

As it turned out, there was nothing to worry about. Like everything else on planet Ormulak, that goat was overfed and amiable and, at the sound of my wheels, galloped dutifully off, thereby, by means of a cord attached to his collar, opening the gate to admit me.

Still a little unnerved, still suspecting I'd been lured into the Serengeti or something, I pedalled hastily up the drive, keeping a sharp lookout for ocelots, crocodiles and the like. No signs of exotic life materialised at all, however, except for Ormulak waving madly at me from his verandah.

Like a number of the post-war Common Room intake, the maestro had built his own house on the outskirts of town, in his case a kind of large chalet of the style beloved by East Europeans for their weekend retreats. For all the world, this might have been a dacha in some forest anywhere between Moscow and the Danube – except here it was the Tolver that wound round and round below, and, way beyond, the spire of Cragfield.

Indeed it soon became apparent that the whole place had been designed as a kind of little Poland, pending the time when the family could return to their homeland. That this was clearly a pipe dream, that the Iron Curtain once down would never rise again, I hadn't of course the heart to suggest, instead lavishing praise on each little touch of their heritage as it was presented to me: the miniature shrine to General Sikorsky which graced the conservatory, the traditional peasant dress in which their plump daughter, Marie, was clad, the bookshelves laden with Norwid, Krasinski, Reymont and the like – and, of course, Chopin playing discreetly in the background.

All very touching. Absolute heartstring stuff – even so, I couldn't resist a sly glance at my watch every few minutes. How about these yaffles, OK? If this adulation stunt went on much longer, I could say goodbye to my pre-Marcho session in The Fox with Tiny and the Carve.

Fortunately, the scrapbook of his boyhood in Warsaw, the lanes and parks of Zoliborz, seemed to be the final item in my initiation. Throwing it down beside the spinning wheel, Ormulak gestured at the garden beyond the open patio doors. "Now," he cried, "for our expedition. While my Gilda prepares the smalec, my friend, and the nozki and the glazed paczki, we will track him down, yes? The yaffle!"

Dazed rather than glazed, I nodded haplessly and, my head swimming with syllables, off we set down the slope, equipped with a ladder (carried by me) and what looked like a fishing rod case (carried by him), eventually entering a small spinney which appeared to mark the rear boundary of his property. Knowing even less about trees than I did yaffles, I'd no idea what species they were through which we toiled. All I could see was that some were ailing, most not – and it seemed dead weird that it was the former which claimed the little man's attention. Every now and then, he'd stop at a trunk, put his ear to it and give it a sharp rap. Then off he'd trot again.

After this had been repeated half a dozen times or so, he patted the bark of his latest victim and announced contentedly, "Yaffle!" Starting to unzip his rod case, he broke into sudden birdsong, so shrill and demonic that at first I thought he'd had a fit.

Then I remembered. The guy's other obsession besides his bells. Bird-watching, God help us! Every weekend he'd lead a troop of youngsters down to the river to watch waders, or over into Hadley wood. Or when you were with him on campus, he'd suddenly clutch your sleeve, point at the heavens and cry, "Red-winged wagtail! Stupendous! Observe, observe." And now, it appeared, here I was enrolled – one of the fraternity, expected to waste tedious hours admiring an egg in a nest, when I could have been down at The Fox getting fit!

In fact, I was worrying unnecessarily. Ormulak was an old hand and the whole operation took less than fifteen minutes, including time spent in lodging our ladder against the tree, and fixing a bulb to one end of the rod and a mirror to the other.

Yaffle, it transpired, was the local name for the green woodpecker, Picidae Picidalis, a bird so well camouflaged that your only hope of spotting it is when it's inside its hollow tree, putting its feet up after slug and chips.

And yes, I actually saw one – or at least something – thereby becoming, I suppose, a confirmed yaffler. In fact, the whole process was dead easy. You poke the rod down inside the tree, press a button so the bulb lights, then peer in the mirror. Upon which you spy a bird, frozen still, gazing up at you in stark terror.

It doesn't move – it doesn't sing & dance or put on some show like, say, laying an egg or devouring a reluctant ant. It just stares at you.

Modified rapture – though come to think of it, if it was the other way round, and you were sitting there watching Coronation Street when suddenly an enormous eye, six feet high, appeared at your window, I suppose you'd die of fright too!

Anyhow, I said how splendid it all was, my host threw a handful of earthworms down the trunk, and off we set, back up the hill.

Smalec, had he said? Nozki? OK, but there must have been at least a dozen other dishes making up the feast which graced that tea table – and (thank Heavens!) not a sign of a samovar, nor the rancid butter with which Slavs are said to beef up their PG Tips. Instead, at the centre stood an ominously large bottle of what looked like brilliantine, which Ormulak proudly introduced as orzechowka, a green walnut vodka.

"Cheers," he cried. "Or as we toast at home, Podbrodek Podbrodka!"

"Podbrodek Podbrodka!"

Well, I'll tell you about that there bottle. If you ever had, by mistake, poured its contents over your hair, you'd have ended up not only bald and scalpless, but with a two foot smoking hole in your head! Indeed, as I wobbled back into town, it felt as though my brain had been taken over by an impi of Zulus, stamping their war dance to the tune of the Trish Trash Polka!

"What's it to be, boyo?" inquired Tiny.

"Make it a duffle orchofski, off you please," I confided, holding on to a pillar.

"Pint of Lucozade, Cedric!" Turning my way, he gave me a quizzical look. "All right are we, then?"

"Podbrodek Podvodka!" I retorted, gazing at my lovely, lonely roll under its plastic case, and wondering why the cheese was slowly kaleidoscoping into technicolor.

I must say Tiny did turn up trumps, tolerating my very bad jokes about Poland and, in due course, helping me back to the quad where treat number two was waiting.

Fortunately, having also invited along the Blaengwynfi boys and a friend or two from Venice, Roy had brought out the Bedford, and I was able to get half an hour's kip in the back. After that, though hardly my normal self, I felt confident of being able to pull open a parachute ring if called upon to do so.

What I didn't quite understand though was why, if we were about to soar into the heavens either by helicopter or magic carpet, Marcho had stacked a dozen or so very large nets on the back seat. Nets? 'Goe and catch a falling star', I quoted to myself happily, and floated back to sleep again, pondering how to fix such a celestial object into one's photograph album without melting it.

It must have been just past sunset when I was finally awoken by a tap on the knee. Marsden, in flat cap and check shirt.

"Andy?" I said vaguely, wondering why he was standing over me like that, silhouetted against the glory, and furthermore why this time he wasn't in silver.

"We've arrived," he said. "Thought you might be interested. Want a hand?"

Noting (more cogently now) that there was no nonsense about 'Paul', though no 'sir' either, I allowed him to help me out on to terra firma. He might be way too inscrutable for his own good, but at least he could keep up a front when it mattered. No-one would have guessed this was the same lad who'd thought he had me over a barrel that last night in Venice.

We appeared to have stopped at the end of a long oblong field with trees on either side. Light was still stabbing up from the western horizon in broad orange streaks of extraordinary beauty, though the darkness behind us was also lit, but more tamely. Faint pinpricks here and there, and all white, like those tiny bulbs which pepper the branches of Christmas trees. And, moreover, glittering on such levels as to indicate that some sort of gorge or monstrous ha-ha lay between us and them. The air was moist and scented, and possessed of a cloying warmth which made you want to slip off your shirt and enjoy your skin like a hottentot. My sleep had done the trick, and, as I yawned and stretched my arms, I felt like a boxer coming up to the mark. Risks? Danger? Marcho, do your worst!

"So, where is it?" I inquired, looking round, adjusting to the twilight. No balloon as far as I could see. No auto-gyro with its slender blades, no dinky little microlight with its engine chattering. Nothing really, except the long long avenue stretching up from darkness like a promiscuous tongue.

"Them, you mean," retorted Roy cheerfully, handing out nets. "It'd be a funny sort of bat hunt with twelve of us and one of them!"

"Hunt?" Something inside me began to bridle

"Nice surprise, eh? Just the right time of year. We ought to get some good sport tonight."

Confession: huntsmen and I do not, I'm afraid, get on. They trample one's tulips, corrupt children and bray like they own the universe – all the while guzzling Pimm's and dooming stags & foxes to unimaginable agony in the name of conservation. Hypocrisy drips from every one of their in-bred jaws, and I now found myself blinking at Marcho, hoping against hope that I'd got hold of the wrong end of the stick.

"Here's the first," he murmured. "Watch closely, lads."

And, sure enough, out of the east stormed a tiny black figure, flying low and dead straight, like a doodlebug of yore: mindless power intent on nothing but its target. Wholly admirable, not something to be trapped and killed and broken and rubbished – bats, of course I mean, not doodlebugs. Don't get me wrong or anything. Heil Hitler, or anything.

"Gosh!" breathed Daines in awe, as a second and third followed in quick succession.

"Quite a spectacle, don't you think?" Net over shoulder, bum on shooting stick, Roy was clearly in his element, relishing the air, the night, the bustle of nature – but also some element yet to become manifest. Some primality. It was as though I could hear its raw tenuto. Some lust that males are supposed to share. Are supposed to be built to share.

"Swift little beggars," he added. "Swift and sure."

I nodded vaguely, my mind fanning open once again to what's actually its earliest memory: of my mother and neighbours at our gate, twilight like this, summer, ears cocked at the drone above, alert for cut-out.

"Perfect flying machines," he continued. "Aerodynamics, huge power, total radar, they've the whole bag of tricks these chappies." He looked round at me. "Want first go?"

"Go?"

"At catching one. After all it's your treat, my dear fellow."

"Let me, sir. May I have a try?" Foster, holding his net in front of him like a sten gun, his fair hair and enthusiasm making him seem for all the world like a member of the swastika youth. No wonder Trewes had allotted him the part of Sebastian in the summer play. A more complete contrast with the homespun Carey as Antonio could hardly be imagined.

"Tim, just calm down," admonished Marcho. "Where are your manners, my boy? Mr Bryant first."

"Look, thanks a million, padre, but, like… I'd rather take a raincheck on this if it's all the same…"

"Nonsense. Nothing's more fun once you get started."

"For whom?" I queried icily. "Those poor creatures? I think not. One minute free as a – well, one minute free, the next wrapped up in nylon mesh ready to be… Who knows what?"

"Released?" twinkled Marcho, lighting a Sobranie. "Will that do? We don't kill them or encage them, you know. They're not exactly edible. It's a mere question of trapping them – then setting them loose. They enjoy it. Come round for more. Have a whale of a time. Just like trout on the hook."

"Are you serious?"

"Honest injun. We make their day for them – as it were!"

"So what's the point?" I frowned. "Why bother?"

"The sport. The fun. The challenge of pulling off something that can only just be pulled off, and then not without bags of luck and spot-on judgment! Understand?"

"Not really," I said loftily, thinking it all sounded rather juvenile. "Trap one of those in one of these?" I inspected my net. "It can't be hard."

"Think so?"

"In fact, easy as falling off a log!"

"Please, sir," moaned Foster. "Couldn't I just…?"

"In a minute," said Marcho, brushing the boy aside. "I'm about to give Mr Bryant his demonstration first."

"But, sir. I've done this before. I don't need a lesson."

"Neither," I announced firmly, "do I." Losing patience with the whole thing, all I wanted to do was make a token attempt to join in before having some more kip and dreaming of James. After all, wasn't that to be my real treat? Tonight, just the two of us, jousting!

"Look here old chap, I really must insist…"

"Relax! It's all perfectly obvious, OK? They'll soon be wishing they'd stayed in the belfry!"

So saying, I strolled out into the middle of the green, holding my net in both hands, and feeling (though for me it was unaccustomed) the adrenalin rush. The surge as your senses wake up to the fact that this here, this now, is Centre Court with all the world watching.

After a few seconds, some brash young chancer curved confidently into the far end of the alley and began his run towards me. Like one of those Wimbledon dudes I held my ground, bouncing from foot to foot, ready for a last minute leap to one side or the other as necessary. Not that either was likely. My adversary was keeping a course straight as a plumbline. A very little, little let us do, and all is done!

Adjusting my position slightly to the south west, I raised my net, moved it somewhat backwards to give myself room for a thrust – oh how childish all this is, I sighed to myself! – then brought it suddenly forwards in a slight arc…

And missed – my adversary bustling on into the sunset unfazed.

Well, I expect you can guess – it took half a dozen repetitions of the same humiliation before I threw in the towel and allowed Roy his little triumph. His tedious little satisfaction of demonstrating how, in order to dodge the bat's radar, you ply the net not from the front but behind, accelerating it as the animal passes, and knocking it to the ground if you're fast enough.

"And brute enough," I found myself complaining to James a couple of hours later. "No kidding, it felt like taking a hammer to a Swiss watch!"

"Which would not," he agreed, driving his paddle deep, "improve its timekeeping."

"Quite," I replied lamely, watching him as he sat at the stern, the lantern glistening on his muscles as he kept course, thrusting first on this side, then the other. The vessel was not one of your modern fibreglass kayaks, but an old-fashioned Hiawatha design, cumbersome as an elephant and necessitating considerable strength to keep in motion. Well, that was a commodity young Frobisher seemed to possess in plenty – and have no objections to displaying!

On reflection – how feeble they must have sounded, my strictures on bat baiting. I mean, talk about brutality – what's more brutal than a rugger match, the game at which Jimbo excelled? Or rather – my mind began wandering down its favourite path – one of the games. The other, whose pitch was five foot wide and highly sprung, would doubtless find him in similar mode, fast, fierce, his whole body one honed, furious unity as it plunged and pierced its way to what – the big O? Satisfaction?

Satisfaction! What a delusion! Since when did it ever last longer than ten minutes and then – back again on heat. Back again, yearning for more. Like a robin doomed to spend every waking minute in pursuit of food. No rest. Never any respite. Thirst, slake. Thirst, slake. Thirst, slake. Like the hammer of the slavemaster, beating out time in a galley. Or rowers' hearts as Chiswick Eyot recedes. The rhythm of ultimate desire, both inenarrable and, tragically, inescapable.

OK, Bryant. Enough of that! You're here aren't you? By choice? Let's shove pretentiousness in the locker and enjoy what you came for.

In the moonlight, Tolverworld is bewitching. The constant interplay of black and moonglow intoxicates the eye, ordinary things like stiles and stanchions taking on a theatrical beauty as though we're steering through the Warner backlot yonks ago, before the Hitler war, about to meet James Cagney in his donkey's head. Nor did Shakespeare ever write anything truer: earthlier happy *is* the rose distilled.

He's earthly, he's happy, isn't he, James? My James, that is. Using the power of that fabulous body. What does it matter to him, stuff like famine, overpopulation, malaria, nuclear proliferation, the consensus among anyone with an IQ bigger than a hedgehog that mankind's got about 50 years left? If only I could learn the same detachment, the same landed gentry trick: how to peel off the angst, item by item, bung it on a saucer, torch it, and warm my hands in its flame. How to be content with the brevity that has no ending.

Anyhow, well curious is my first discovery of the night, that we're not the only ones out on the river. You'd naturally assume that all good souls would be tucked up safe by now, dreaming of the National Lottery or next week in Benidorm. Not a bit of it. We've already passed an inflatable and a couple of skiffs, one of which is towing a li-lo on which reclines a plump girl. She's propped up on one elbow, intent on her origami and doesn't return our wave. Here and there in the woods we catch glimpses of candles or torches or stuff, with people chanting – whilst a couple of hundred yards beyond Trefoil bridge a group of lads has made a bonfire on the bank. They're toasting sausages and wave us over, but James speeds on. What's his problem? I wonder – disapproval of naked youth? Or perhaps he just doesn't like snorkers!

Or maybe – he simply wants us to be á deux. Completely á deux. Which, of course, despite the distractions of bums and bonfires, is what I want too. After a while, after some meadowland and a further wood, things become quieter, and, by the time we reach Crawshaw's ruin, a thick stillness has fallen. We might be all there is in all there is, the moon trickling down on us alone, and nought besides.

Lashing the painter to a stump, James jumps ashore, taking a deep breath of the night air. "Isn't this fab?" he says. "We must do it again on my birthday."

"Mid-December, I suppose?"

"Getting warm," he replies nonchalantly. "October, if you want to know."

"Warm, did you say?"

"Wimp!" he laughs as I scramble ashore.

We strip off and for a moment confront one another like two prizefighters. Each of us glances down at the other as though acknowledging the symbiosis of our manhoods. Then we turn and leap into the treacle-dark stream, yelling and splashing in true schoolboy style.

At this point the Tolver has been deepened and widened, presumably as a kind of bathing hole for the former mill hands, and, after a few minutes more of commotion, we line up on the far bank ready for our mini-Olympiad.

"How many lengths?" queries James. "Half a dozen, Tarzan? Or is that too much of a good thing?"

"Suits me." I'm enjoying this warm black tent of night. What does the bloody race matter to me, who wins, who loses? All I'm concerned about is the sex afterwards when at long last my hands hit their target. And so on. I mean, there can't be any mistake about it, can there? Surely, all the signs point one way. Like, you don't go skinny-dipping at night, somewhere this remote, without expecting to get your rocks off, do you?

Besides, no wife around – no wife around for weeks! He must be desperate for it, OK?

"My count." Abruptly, we drop into that tense swimmers' crouch. "One, two, three…"

In a crash of black spray we're off, surging through the water in a fast crawl, side by side, equally matched. This is the culmination of a long year's lust – on my part at anyrate – and it's as though some spirit of the night has taken over. Waved sal volatile over and over against my nostrils, forcing out of me every last ounce of power and speed. By the last lap, tiring, our muscles raw with lactic acid, we're still abreast. Above the harshness of my own breath, I can hear his, and once, for a second, in the moon, through the foam, I catch a glimpse of his face – eyes closed, desperate, his handsomeness now a grotesque parody as though all along it was nothing but a rubber mask which circumstance might twist and spoil at will.

And despite the pain, I suddenly realise how things are. He's male in a way which I'm not. Now, at this moment, he must win. Victory, that's all that matters. God can be in his heaven or out of it – what does Frobisher care? All that's real and vital and meaningful is that his should be the arm that first touches that muddy rat-ridden bank of roots and slime ahead.

So I slow my stroke. Not too obviously. Just like I would were I at the end of my resources. I slow my body through the last few yards. Enjoy his triumph as his hands punch the sky. Tread water next to him as our guts heave for air, the blood pounding in our brains.

But we're young. Not much more than puppies really and it doesn't take long for our lungs and veins to return to normal. And we're still next to one another in the water, James still grinning idiotically as though he's broken a world record and will be headlines in the News Chronicle the next day. I move a little closer, brushing some droplets from his neck, and then the most extraordinary thing happens.

Placing a hand each side of my neck, hard round my collarbone, he ducks me! And not just your schoolmate kind of ducking, but long and brutal as though he wants me dead. Really dead – like Antinous in the Nile.

As I come up spluttering, and with this curious kind of déjà vu sort of feeling, he's laughing his head off and stuff – and I think I get the point. The guy must need it rough. Maybe that's how straight life is, not the cadence of two souls astride the same bliss, but Guy dominating Goil, tearing through her iron gates, the more blood the better.

Oh well, I think – new horizons and all that! Smiling too, I wade towards him, only this time to have my shoulders grabbed and my whole body pulled towards him on to his raised knee – not savagely or anything, but enough to make me gasp in pained delight. What the hell is this? The weirdest foreplay since the Marquis de Sade? Ought I now to reciprocate by getting him in a scrotum lock?

But there's no time for that or anything. Thrusting me away, he blinds me with some violent splashing, then dives to one side and, before I can regain any kind of proper balance or equilibrium, has swept my feet from under me and pulled my body deep below the surface where I writhe, retching for air, his knee on my back.

And at last I really do get it. At last the penny really does drop. It's like a re-run of Marsden in Venice, spelling it out to Travers who's the herd leader. Who's the boss of the outfit.

So, there's to be no hoi toi toi, no passion – that was all a pipe dream on my part. Instead, just this. A consolation prize, if you can even call it that. Male bonding on the Tolver with James as both referee and victor. Half an hour of being splashed and slapped and near-asphyxiated, on the assumption that guys like me enjoy taking it from guys like him.

At last I'm released and push my way to the surface in a riot of bubbles, groping for the bank, levering myself upwards – only to be pulled back once again, and corkscrewed down into a bed of reeds. Even when I do eventually reach dry land I'm no safer. Fed up with the whole thing, still gasping for air, I give in, lie on my back with him kneeling athwart me, pinning my arms down, grinning. And there, a foot from my face, sways his member. His pride and joy to which, half an hour ago, I'd have given a King's ransom to pay homage.

Now it's just a slack brown tube, a bit hapless. Nothing of interest. Just the appendage of a rather dim male, sans mystery and metaphor, who uses it to forge the next generation in much the same way as any workman uses any tool.

I yawn and wonder how long it'll be before his vanity is satisfied. Obediently I allow myself to be rolled over down the slight slope and back into the water, this time taking care to fill my lungs maximum. Now he grabs me round the thighs in rugger tackle, his free hand searching for my throat.

And as he does so, that sense of déjà vu, having taken its time like these things do, gradually coalesces into memory…

"Good birthday, was it?" cried Watson, striding through the next morning. "That's the ticket. Only once a year so enjoy it while you can. Baxter! Where's Baxter? Has anybody seen Baxter?"

Confession: birthdays and I do not, I'm afraid, get on. They remind you of what you'd rather forget, they raise false hopes, and they invariably get you so pissed that half your liver turns to cardboard.

And why that particular anniversary? What's so special about being born? Why not the when-I-first-realised-I-was-gay-day? Or the on-first-discovering-all-straight-males-are-turds-day?

Or (perhaps most importantly of all) the on-finally-conceding-that-daydreams-should-be-left-firmly-corked-in-their-genie's-bottle-day? And never ever let out, even on probation!

Or, let's be realistic – is that last an insight at which one honestly ever arrives this side of the Jordan?

11: *What You Will*

Death took Eric Amberley at just past four on the morning of Commem. There was no great fuss. At one moment he was alive, the next not, his old alarm clock dashed to the floor beside him. No last words (that we know of), nothing much in the way of histrionics though his wife – who was, as usual, sleeping in the dower room – thought it odd that his last action seems to have been to reach for Wisden. The 1928 edition. Which was found on his counterpane, his hand clutching the Oundle/Stamford match for that year.

But then how little the average wife knows of that Bible, what it lists and what it infers.

By the time he was found, it was of course far too late to postpone the events of the day and Eric, whatever his present playground, was thus able to savour the fun of causing maximum inconvenience to the maximum number of people. That is, of course, assuming a soul can savour anything. Or have fun.

Most of the Fustians had chosen to break their journey from London overnight at The Green Dragon, Hereford, and for the next two hours or so the phone lines between there and Tolverton crackled with the mixture of elegy and conspiracy which such disasters invariably elicit. By coffee time, Mr Christmas Watson B.A. had been installed as Acting Headmaster, with Mr Leyland Trewes M.A., B.Phil. as his deputy. Both of course on the quiet. So as not to mar the festivities, Eric's absence was explained away as a minor heart attack from which recovery was certain, the fact of his death not being revealed to a shocked community until next morning's papers.

One or two of us had, in fact, guessed something was up from the demeanour of the clergy. Roy made the better fist of it, carrying himself well despite a rather chalky pallor, but dear old Joe was a different story. Hunched, on the verge of tears, it was all he could do to get through the Bidding Prayer without breaking down.

I don't think I'd ever fully appreciated how profoundly revered Eric had been, except of course by the Carve who was incapable of revering anything but himself. Only the school's third Headmaster that century, Amberley had been confidently expected to see the place through to Halley's comet – well, perhaps not quite that far, but you know what I mean – and the chasm which now opened so unexpectedly before us brought with it a sense of foreboding that even this sunny spell which had held sway for the last month couldn't altogether rout.

"I'm afraid it's going to be a traumatic few weeks for us all," sighed Trewes, more Bunthorne than ever. "Alas, alas!"

I'd been summoned before pool duty on the Saturday after Commem, and found him standing on a chair in his new study, adjusting some frame on the wall. It was only when he stepped down that I realised it was his degree certificate, posted there for all to see like the accreditation of some bloody pharmacist or optician. Was this the new order then? Everything to be worn on the sleeve – nothing to be tolerated unless it could be graded and rated? No room for the pagan leap?

"Yes," he continued, seating himself limply. "I'm afraid it's all hands to the pump for the time being. Cesario and Sebastian, for instance, the tiresome twins. And Feste, God bless him. My new duties will, I fear, leave little time for them. Still, I expect you know the play well enough by now to cope on your own."

Well enough? *Twelfth Night*? Of all the poisonous insults! Wasn't it one of those sublime texts constantly in my thoughts, waking and sleeping? Wasn't its hidden agenda the very lodestone of my life? So far my rehearsal duties had been largely confined to checking lines as the actors moved sullenly through the scenes he'd so incompetently blocked. Now I'd have the chance to add some fire to the proceedings. Bring out the manifesto – bring out the sex.

My elation was, however, short-lived. By the end of the interview, not only had I been saddled with the school play, but the kitchen sink as well! School magazine, 6th form debating, and all

Oxbridge teaching except Swinburne. Trewes rather liked Swinburne.

Ruefully I recalled that long-ago warning of Ormulak's about over-commitment. But how does one say no? I mean, under circumstances like these? Crisis changes priorities – fact! And there's no way one can avert one's gaze. It's less a question of being a Good Samaritan than not being a total bastard!

Anyhow, I reflected, stepping out into the sunshine, it's only for the rest of term. By September they'll have appointed a new Head, and Trewes' degree certificate will be back in the downstairs loo or coal shed or wherever it came from. And OK, shyster that he is, he may well resist taking back the Tolvertonian et al, but just let him try! What a battle royal that'll be! I rubbed my hands in anticipation as I pushed through the wicket which led to the old pool and its lawn.

And its denizens.

Fifteen, twenty, maybe more Sixth-formers, stretched out on the grass, keen on developing the sort of tan which dazzles tarts as they swarm in Ibiza, Benidorm and similar aspects of paradise! A few weeks ago, I'd have been eager to find myself a deckchair and bask for hours surveying the scene. Now it held just about as much interest for me as a tray of tomatoes. And for why?

Not so much my recent disaster at Crawshaw's – though my libido had taken a battering that night which would manifest itself in strange ways for a long time yet – nor any sudden Pauline conversion from sinner into saint. No, it was something altogether more prosaic and trite.

Murdoch!

That guy's insistence on my supervising junior showers every day had, I'm glad to say, rather jaded my palate. Not that thirteen year olds, as nature made them, had ever held the minutest scrap of attraction for me anyway, but as soon as word got around that I was fairly lax about things, the odd senior would begin to drop in so as to shower with a younger "friend". On some days there might be as many as four or five of them, and usually in a state of at least semi-enthusiasm.

Ace, you might think? Far from it, I fear. In the same way the fiftieth approach to Calais hardly holds the same allure as the first, so repeated sightings of Beecham or Kim Turnbull, however magnificent their credentials, had come to count as, rather than pleasure, mere routine. Though not without its dangers. Even something as innocent as sharing a towel with your buddy probably contravened one of Murdoch's ten thousand rules, and would have rendered me, as moral guardian of bathtime, open to his wrath.

At least here by the pool the bodies were clothed, though virtually all the swim slips managed their usual trick: enhancing rather than hiding the bargains on offer! Still, what's fashion for? If it's OK for les femmes to flaunt it – all those bikinis and stuff – why not their victims too?

Having acknowledged some waves of greeting, I exchanged a word or two with old Dobson, the school's porter who doubled as lifeguard, as usual deep in his Daily Herald. At well over sixty, quite how he'd cope with an emergency was far from clear. But his wages came cheap, and he was most assiduous over his major task. Applying the daily bucket of chemicals which kept the water acceptable.

With nothing much to do, I looked around me, hands on hips. An agreeable scene, with grass on all four sides of the water, fringed with a variety of tall cottage garden plants – hollyhocks, lupins and the like – its rustic vista marred only by the gross concrete bulk of the new pool which had risen opposite Livingstone

Though it had been officially opened at Commem, so far I'd not inspected the place. Now seemed a good opportunity and I strolled over, wondering how so ugly a building had gained sanction from the planning authorities.

While the open-air version remained in use (until the end of term) it had been decreed that its successor should be available only for water polo during PE time, and thus I wasn't surprised to find the entrance bolted. Even so, and though the double doors beyond were frosted, I found myself revelling in those lanes that must stretch there, long cool and inviting. Absolutely demanding to be swum in.

It was a hot, muggy day and I swear, had some sorcerer come along with a key, I'd have paid a king's ransom for just half an hour in that clear blue. Not even, maybe, swimming. Just water lounging – lazing around. You know how it is.

There was of course a time allotted at the old pool for staff – and wives! – ghastly prospect. All that adipose! And, worse still, all that bonhomie. Not my style at all. Once I strip off, I want the world my way. No distractions. Free rein for my thoughts, not having not to look at whorls of female flab as I'm invited to supper on Tuesday week, 7 for 7.30, quite informal, don't bother with a tie, park in the road not the drive if you don't mind, do you eat meat?

Anything but that! Dear God, anything but that! But as I was, consequently, forced to face the prospect of a summer without swimming, my mind began its usual trick of picking over possibilities. Why not use the new pool discreetly when no-one else is around? Like at night? Answer: because it's locked up before prep, chump! Why not force a window? Answer: and risk there being burglar alarms in operation, twit? Why not just get hold of the key, and do what James Bond would do – have a copy made? Answer: because I'm not bloody James Bond, how would I get hold of it, and where the hell could I…?

Suddenly, one of those heady moments when all obstacles vanish simultaneously! Mostyn's had a key cutting service, didn't they? Dobson would be busy saving lives till five, wouldn't he? Thus Mrs Dobson, Renee of the tea trays, an altogether softer touch, would be in charge of the lodge, wouldn't she? So all I needed was an excuse to borrow the keys for half an hour, and bob's your uncle!

And, miracle of miracles, even that suddenly materialised. An excuse so copper-bottomed, so plausible, that even Murdoch would have fallen for it.

As soon as Baxter relieved me at half past three, I dashed over to Rhodes, dug out my old camera and sprinted back to the lodge. "Afternoon, Mrs D," I said amiably. "Mind if I borrow the pool keys for a few minutes? The new pool, I mean."

"A few minutes?" she queried suspiciously.

"Photos for the school magazine – official publicity, n'est ce pas?"

Doubtless impressed by my French, if not my battered Agfa which hadn't seen a film since I was seventeen, she handed over the bunch without further demur and in no time at all I was pushing my way through the chaos of barbed wire, pipework, curtain rails and tiling which constituted Mostyn's stock. Fascinated as always by the shop's antiquated Lamson system – a network of overhead wires along which shot cash canisters from assistant to counting house and back again – I found myself lingering a bit before resuming my errand.

Right at the back, lit by a single unshaded Osram, the key counter awaited me bristling and glittering with banks of chrome and bronze blanks – all presided over by an attendant in brown overalls, who, as he looked up from his vice, file in hand, turned out to be – most untowardly and improbably – none other than Andrew Marsden of all people!

"Paul?" he intoned with that soubrette smile of his, amused by my evident discomposure.

OK, nowadays, every kid of fifteen and over has his or her weekend job to buy their booze & hash, and fund their mobiles, but half a century ago things were different. The school week extended into Saturdays and Sundays and that was that. Even for a dayboy, paid employment during term time was out of the question, and Marsden was a boarder. And not just any old boarder, but a member of the Murdoch chain gang. How on earth had he managed to escape the vigilance of that malign eye?

"Good heavens…" I began, caught momentarily on the hop.

"Hey, relax." His tone was cool and intimate, as though he hadn't the slightest doubt I was safe to confide in. "Frankie covers for me if you-know-who's on the snoop. No problem, honest."

"Let's hope you're right." Thawing a little, I deposited my key ring on the counter. "Tell me, how long's this been going on?"

"Getting on for a year," he replied. "Since my…"

"Quite!" I interposed hurriedly, but not unkindly, recalling all of a sudden some bits and pieces I'd extracted from Marcho since the bat hunt. That the lad was a scholarship boy, that his father had died suddenly abroad, that the family was, despite a remarriage, in straitened circumstances. All stuff to elicit sympathy – and explain away some part of his strange ways. And yes, though I still found this air of familiarity daunting, and though there was something about our encounters which invariably flagged up Caution with a big C, I have to confess I found myself tempted to regard him in a new light.

OK, OK – of course it would prove to be short-lived, but at that instant a guy who could run rings round the Gauleiter of Rhodes seemed to deserve at least a modicum of respect. "Quite!" I repeated. "So I suppose you're having to save a bit – I mean for college next term."

He nodded. "Every little helps" – thus using what would become a national catchphrase years later when, doubtless, some prick he'd slept with had risen to senior partner in a major advertising agency. For now he merely pushed that lock of hair out of his eyes. "But how about you?" he inquired, parking his file on the bench. "I wouldn't have classed you as, like, the DIY type. Or am I being dense? Could I possibly be being honoured with a social call?"

"Absolutely. I thought we might down some Dom Perignon at The Fox maybe. Then fly to Paris for the weekend."

"I think I'd prefer our old favourite, wouldn't you?"

"Favourite?"

"Bella Venezia?"

Fancy bringing that up! For God's sake, had the guy no finesse? I felt my stomach muscles tighten once again. Drop your guard for a moment, and peril swoops. How could I have been so stupid as to warm to someone like this even for a second?

"All our yesterdays?" he queried, his eyes sparkling with mischief. "Remember?" Another customer, however, hoving within earshot and on the hunt for bathroom joinery, Marsden reverted to more professional tones and switched on his lathe. "Will you wait, sir, or call back later?"

But before I could reply, he'd held up the bunch to the light and frowned. "For Chrissake! D' you want them all cut?"

What a mutt, I was! Of course I should have asked Mrs D to point out which one opened the front door. As it was, there must have been eight or nine mortices, all looking identical. This was going to cost a fortune! Then I noticed the odd man out: a single Yale, shiny and virgin, probably the key to some lowly side door or something, maybe the boiler room or chlorine plant. Ten to one there'd be a way through to the pool itself. And anyhow, it would be more discreet than prancing up the front steps in full view of any passer-by, wouldn't it?

"Just the Yale for now," I replied with an attempt at nonchalance, pulling out my purse. "So what's the damage then?"

"Call it five bob," he shrugged as the interloper retreated. "Ten and six to anybody else, but old Mostyn can afford to forego his profit for once. What's this then? Key to Murdoch's booze cellar?"

"Fort Knox, actually."

He nodded but shot me a quizzical look. "Don't the contractors usually do duplicates?"

"Contractors?"

"Well, this master looks brand new."

"Does it? See you at rehearsal."

Again he looked at me quizzically as though we were comrades in some huge, internecine conspiracy, select and immanent. Which is how, looking back on things now, over these long years, I can see it not only seemed to him but perhaps was.

Not that I was in any state to recognise the fact. How could I have been? Time was pressing: keys to be returned to the lodge, yet another stab at *Twelfth Night* less than half an hour away, and Evensong immediately after. The usual bazazz of boarding school life!

And indeed it was only while hurrying home, my prize stowed safely away in a back pocket, that the irony of the situation struck me. OK, I was now possessed of the key to bliss – but when on earth would I ever have leisure enough to use it?

By the time I reached the Glade – a slope next to the Burn, a tributary of the Tolver, where the school's open-air theatre had been built by Victorians clearly impervious to damp and gales – my cast, doubtless with an eye to getting off early, had already coasted through most of Act 2, and greeted me with barely-concealed hauteur.

Not surprising, really. Tolverton was no RADA and, in a cultural limbo like ours, the lads were bound to regard rehearsals as one big yawn – except, that is, for the ones on Saturday. These they positively detested, presumably being only too well aware of what their less fortunate contemporaries who attend day schools were getting up to. In winter one could just get by – in summer, when the air was hot and the klaxon of the ice cream van sounded brazenly through the trees, the scowls from a dozen hostile faces were apt to make one reach for the bottle.

Suppressing a desire to call the whole thing off and head for Jamaica, I nodded at Sebastian. "OK, Tim," I said. "The exit's stage left. Antonio – 'The gentleness of all the gods…'"

"'Go with thee,'" began Oliver, his voice a distant muzak as I settled myself, arranging my notes on the table, unwrapping my Mars bar, noting that the little grebe in the reeds seemed unusually active this avo.

"'But come what may, I do admire thee so, That danger shall seem sport…'"

"Hang on," I interposed, pointing an accusing biro. "No distortions, if you don't mind. The punters come to hear Shakespeare, OK? Not the works of Carey."

"Sir?"

"Admire, right? Where did that come from? My edition gives the line as 'I do adore thee so.'"

"Oh, Mr Trewes changed that."

"Mr Trewes did what?"

My exasperation must have been pretty obvious as Pete Macdonald, normally the most taciturn of blokes, turned round from his chair in front. "Sir, he's right. Doggo did alter that. See?" And he pointed to his scruffy copy where the amendment was clearly marked in pencil.

"OK, but why?"

"Doesn't it sound better, sir?" ventured Carey almost plaintively.

"Not at all. It sounds pathetic."

"But sir…"

Carey's protestations were cut short by Jukes lounging in from the wings, lute strung across his shoulder. "Sir, the idea was to avoid confusion. Right lads?" He looked round as the others nodded.

"What confusion? What the hell are you talking about? Adore – I mean, its sense is clear enough, isn't it?"

"Only too clear. Grown men don't normally 'adore' young men, do they, sir? Mr Trewes didn't want people getting the idea there was anything dodgy going on."

"Between Antonio and Sebastian," added Foster helpfully. "After all, I have to marry Olivia in a couple of acts, don't I?"

"Oh I see and it doesn't help to muddy the waters!" I shook my head, bemused for the thousandth time at the naivety of the teenage mind. And the minds of all B Phils who nail their pathetic degrees to the church door. "Well chaps, I've news for you. From today, we revert to Shakespeare, confusion or no confusion. And not just in this case. Any other Bowdlerisations inserted by Mr Trewes are hereby revoked. Understand?"

"Doggo won't like it."

"Mr Trewes, if you please."

"He may throw a wobbly."

"We'll face that if and when it happens. OK, Antonio…"

"But sir," persisted Jukes, "Mr T says the play's about love…"

"How very perceptive of him!"

"So how can you have love between two men?"

"What do you want – diagrams?"

"Yuh, but surely that's just lust – not the 'make me a willow cabin at her gate' sort."

"Lust, is it? Thanks for the expert opinion," I snapped, reflecting that intelligence is all very well but that its practitioners can sometimes be an utter pain in the arse. "So how come Jonathan and David? Or Oscar and Bosie? Mightn't they have had something to say on that point, maybe?" Thank God this wasn't one of Malvolio's scenes. How Marsden would have relished seeing me at bay – and joining the hunt with both barrels.

Completely unfazed, Jukes perched himself on a bench, ready for round two. "Yeah," he drawled, "but it's changed, society, nowadays, hasn't it? Since your time. Swept away all that misogynistic crap. Conceded that girls are just as…"

"Look!" Again my biro stabbed the air. "The word is 'adore', like it or lump it. And if the latter, go take a running jump into the nearest radical-chic midden you can find! Tim, we'll go from 'My bosom is full of kindness' unless, of course, Mr Trewes has baulked at bosoms too!"

"Oh no, sir – they're wholesome."

If ever, I reflected, hunched in my pew an hour later, if ever the term curate's egg could be applied to a day, this had been it. Triumph at Mostyn's all right, slim and shiny, still in its tissue paper – on the other hand, that bugger of a rehearsal. And there were still half a dozen hours to go! What might the whirligig still have in store?

Roy had seemed somewhat flustered throughout the service and now, though the anthem turned out to be a piece of fruity Victoriana by Ouseley, very much to the Marcho taste, there he was in his stall, shuffling notes, still fidgeting around, opening and closing his spectacles, and rubbing his forehead. Moreover a forest of eyebrows shot up when the offertory hymn, no. 607, was announced as 67, and on that hot sultry summer's evening we dutifully chirped our way through 'In the bleak midwinter…'

"Is always thus," whispered Ormulak, leaning over from the next pew. "Whenever Confirmation draws near. Bishop, Fustians, mothers in silly hats. Such stress. All too much for the poor fellow."

I nodded wryly. Not too much for someone else though, I reflected, since the same weekend would witness my own particular stressfest. My comedia del farte, in the shape of the most chaotic dress rehearsal ever seen on a public stage! Still, since when did junior teachers elicit sympathy from anyone? Roll on the vac! A good stiff dose of Jugs or Julian would soon put me right. Or pastures new, maybe. Maybe I needed a total change.

As it happened, intimations that I might soon get one, and hardly the sort I'd envisaged, were not long in manifesting themselves. Around the middle of the following week, as I strolled out of lunch, who should take me by the arm and steer me into the Head's garden but Chris Watson, all dolled up and dandy in a new suit and Aberystwyth tie.

"You're looking smart," I grinned, thumb and finger testing his lapel. "Trés natty indeed."

"Stuff and nonsense," said he going slightly pink. "Off the peg at the FST. Ever use them, do you? Good value, the FST. Fact is, we've some candidates here today. Preliminary view."

"For Head beak?"

"Precisely. Head, as you put it, beak. So apple-pie order, that's the thing. No litter, no slackness. Everything shipshape and Bristol fashion." He straightened his faded but newly-ironed tie.

"That explains one or two bods I've seen floating around. Bald guy, for instance, broken nose."

"Ah, J.J. Elwes that would be. London Welsh and a Blue from Cambridge."

"Aren't we honoured?" I replied, doubting he'd cotton on to the irony. "But how about that specimen with weird hair and odd socks? Looks like Igor from that Frankenstein film? What on earth did he get his Blue for?"

"In his case, it's a double first. Maths and English, plus a stint at Harvard researching the plays of Marmion, Sir Walter of that ilk, with whom you're doubtless conversant."

"An intellectual Headmaster?" quoth I, unable that instant to work out whether Chris had just delivered the world's most feeble jest or just plain ignorance. "I'll believe it when I see it! But tell me – how does it feel to interview your own executioner?"

"A piece of cake, actually – unlike certain other duties."

"Chris?"

"Well, now, for instance. This minute."

"What," I retorted, still unheeding, "having to hobnob with a junior member of staff?"

"Not quite," he said briskly, his spectacles glinting as he peered round as if for eavesdroppers. "Having, as a matter of fact, to admonish one."

"Admonish?" I was thunderstruck.

"With regret, of course. And sympathy." He glanced at me sort of sideways with all the headmagisterial rancour his nature could manage.

My mind was racing. What precisely had crawled out from under the carpet? My history with Julian? That dalliance with Alex at Ma Kent's? Sharing a bed at Corunna? Or maybe my humiliation at Crawshaw's mill?

Had someone observed it through binoculars? Or worse still, filmed it on his Bolex!

"The problem is," he continued, "you're your own worst enemy. Indeed you are. I'd have thought it pretty obvious after what – three terms? – that you're not in England now. These are tribal lands, boyo! Not Park Lane or the Albany."

I looked at him blankly.

"You simply don't tangle with a man like Gruffydd Carey – not if you're set on a future in Tolverton, you don't. Quite apart from being on the governing body, he has the largest and most lucrative haulage business in the area, owns the Radnor Arms, sits on the council and chairs the Eisteddfod committee. Etcetera and you name it."

"So? I've no need of a lorry and I don't wander around in bedsheets declaiming bogus Welsh poetry. I've never met the bloke, Chris."

"No, but you teach his son. And, more to the point, you're directing said young hopeful in *Twelfth Night*."

"Right," I murmured, two and two starting to make four. "Antonio, I see."

"Who, according to my information – a letter from his father, no less, and handwritten, mark you – is being forced to recite lines of a debased and corruptive moral…"

"Hang on, hang on…"

"Debased and immoral character which your departmental boss had earlier struck out. I must say, it sounds very much open and shut to me, open and…"

"Shut – I've got the point."

"On a prima facie basis, you understand."

"Did he actually quote the 'lines' in question?"

"Not exactly."

"Then pardon me, but I will. Hope you like Shakespeare."

"I adore Shakespeare as you very well know, you young rascal."

"Adore? What a coincidence! We're halfway there already. Now here's the problem…"

And briefly I outlined the semantic dilemma which had managed to reduce poor Doggo Trewes to craven servility. Watson's face remained impassive throughout until, as I finished, he gave a sort of snort. "Storm in a teacup!" he barked. "Never heard such nonsense in all my life. I'm afraid Leyland always was an old woman. Married a Land Girl who'd been billeted at his uncle's, you know. Fact, I assure you. Absolute fact. Sports a moustache these days – girl, not the uncle – so she's hardly allowed out in daylight. Now don't you fret. I'll take care of him. Gruffydd too if that becomes necessary. We share a locker up at Feyhill. Bit of a spiv, of course, bore of the clubhouse, but keep in with 'em, hey? Keep in with 'em! One day he'll be an honorary Fustian!"

Surprised to find him so solidly on my side, I assured him I would indeed try, at which he clasped me round the shoulder. "But next time," he chuckled, "why not warn me first – all right? Tip me the wink, eh?"

Elated, I left on cloud nine. Fairness was something I'd come to expect from Chris, but support of this magnitude…? I was, as they say, dead chuffed.

As it happened, I'd been invited by Marcho to partake of the dreaded post-lunch digestif that day, and what more natural under the circumstances than for the conversation to turn to Headmasters: Thring, E.F. Bonhote and others of the great unremembered. Of what a paragon Eric had been, of what a paragon Chris would be, were he ever to have the chance.

"We're told," said Roy, raiding the biscuit tin for the third time, "in 2 Corinthians, chapter Lord knows what, that there's such a thing as too much tolerance. Don't you believe it. As a virtue, it oozed from Eric, bless his cotton socks. And believe me, it's what made him a great Headmaster. Indeed one of the greatest."

I nodded, pushing thoughts of James and the other sackings to the back of my mind. Sometimes it's more politic to go with the flow.

"All of us," continued the March blithely, "every single one of us would do well to follow his example. And Christ's. Wandering round the lake, doing good. Setting an example to his disciples. Always rejecting earthly snares and lures."

Again I nodded, pushing thoughts of all those stolen artefacts and stuff to the back of my mind. Sometimes it's more politic not to cast the first stone!

"What does that old hymn say?" He rose, finger to lip, balancing his cigarette holder on a copy of Bunyan. "'Let holy Charity, Mine outward vesture be' – or is it Thine? Upon my word, that'll just do for Confirmation. Thank goodness I haven't printed the service sheets yet."

"You print them yourself?" I ventured, keen to get well clear from all this gospel stuff.

"Why not? Didn't you know about my Adana? I've this offset litho down in the crypt – neat little job. Avoids printers' errors and saves money."

"Not time though."

He gave a dismissive shrug. "What's the hurry? There's a couple of weeks yet. So tell me. Where are your play programmes done? Worrall's of Kington, I expect."

"Who knows? I leave all that to Trewes."

"Pure extravagance. I could give you a better price."

"I'll mention it."

"Do. After all, you'd have more cash to spend on scenery then, wouldn't you?"

"Scenery?" I grinned, my mind flitting to the half dozen paint-clogged, mice-gnawn flats which had encased every Tolverton production since the year dot. "Is that what you call it?"

"Well then – costumes, make-up."

I pulled out my diary. "Which reminds me," I said. "There's a make-up lesson in the offing, and the cupboard's bare. Yes, Monday week. Any idea where the nearest Leichner stockist would be?"

"Oh, dear. Nothing nearer than Birmingham, I suspect. Couldn't you make do with rouge and burnt cork?"

"Thanks – I'll certainly consider it!"

"My boy, I'd drive you in myself but for the retreat. Pre-confirmation, you understand."

"No problem. Hope it all goes OK. Anywhere well known?"

"Llanthony," he said with a twinkle as though that single word would open up profound corridors of meaning. I complied with a convincing nod, and that was the last I saw of him for several days.

Not that he was by any means out of my thoughts. That curious blend of the sage and the dodger, the miser and the benefactor, the optimist and the pragmatist, was quite sufficient and intriguing to engage my thoughts whenever the going got tough in the classroom or rehearsal hall. Or on the games field, for that matter. Who was this guy Marchpane? What reality lay behind the tweeds and Sobranie? For example was his fixation with railways just a pose to amuse colleagues & boys, or the reflection of some deep love of order to which at present I had but fledgling access?

One thing was for sure – and it was a development over which I had mixed feelings yet questionable control – I found myself feeling as though, slowly but inexorably, I was growing more and more his man, almost maybe dependent on him, even maybe imitative of him. Not in any outward obvious way, like that summer at Cromer when I'd been soundly smacked by Aunt May for doing a Groucho Marx round the pier. Well, twice round the pier actually, and past the Punch and Judy.

No, this was decidedly inner, an inward affinity, tracking his thinking and feeling, noting his wake this side and that through the rapids. And yes, you're right, perhaps it would have looked insidious had anyone noticed. But so what? Think back to school – that dreariest of places, the physics lab. When a magnet collects those flakes of iron filing, whose fault is it? The magnet's or the iron's? And is it a fault at all – or just two natures fulfilling the destiny allotted to them at birth?

Which made our next encounter, Roy and I, all the more surprising and bitter and – what's the word? Excoriating?

Each man, the Ballad tells us, kills the thing he loves. Yes, well, pinch of salt as usual with Victorian floridity. But substitute wounds for kills, and you've got something. Something, I might add, potentially far worse. Death can be quick but wounds linger – and some never heal.

I had, I must confess, been feeling somewhat below par as the day of the make-up demonstration approached. Not that there was any problem over either the Leichner – Clewbury's in Hereford turning out to have ample stocks including two identical wigs for the twins – or, more importantly, my own expertise. After all, I'd been taught well for my one and only West End appearance, hadn't I?

No. It was mainly the time of year. Exam supervision is hardly the most riveting way to pass a day, and when one's evenings are completely dominated by report writing or play rehearsals or both, it's hardly surprising that one's daydreams get stuffed with sagas of wild escape. Winning the pools, meeting John Ford in The Fox who'd immediately cast me in his remake of Stagecoach, or, more mundanely, just cutting my wrists – not terminally, of course!

Additionally, as the time drew near, a new worry began to assail me. A species of what you might call anticipatory dread! I could feel in my bones what that day was going to bring, how the runes were going to fall. If you deliver a lesson on 5 and 9 to a group of apprentice actors, what – apart from the ruddy make-up itself, of course – is the one thing you need? The one indispensable thing?

A model.

And guess who would, sans doubt, volunteer? And be so fast off the mark, hand up, volunteering, that no-one else would get a look in? So fast indeed that for me to select any other candidate would look so queer and suspicious that the news would be round the dorms in half an hour. Not to mention The Fox and over at Belsen!

You've got it! Leaning against the mantelpiece, brushing a lock of hair out of his eyes, looking sort of relaxed and in command – even more so than at Mostyn's – none other than Malvolio himself. Nodding as I jabbed a reluctant finger his way. Pulling off his shirt as he approached the chair.

"What's this?" I protested, but not vehemently. "You're at a make-up session, not on a Paris catwalk, my lad."

"Mr Trewes doesn't like greasepaint on the ruffs, sir." His eyes glinted with what – thespian ardour? "He always makes us up like this."

"That's right," said Jukes yawning. "Quite correct."

"And bloody cold it is too at Christmas I can tell you." Pete Macdonald, doubtless daring me to draw the line.

"For the revue, he means, sir." Jukes again, in helpful mode!

"Well it's not Christmas now," I countered, trying not to gaze down at the torso below me. "So you can just put up with it. OK, gather round everyone. Step one: bold crosses of number 5" (I held up a fresh stick of ivory) "and 9" (a rather gungy attenuated stick of brick red) "all over the neck, face and forehead in the proportion of four to one."

"Mr Bryant zur, them crayons there. Which way round?" queried Rudgewick, the perfect Sir Toby, not a scrap of padding needed. "Four of that liddle 'un, is it? To a dab of that whoite?"

"Absolutely," I cried above the torrent of laughter. "If you want to look like a Cherokee in a Wild West Show!"

Face bleak, Jukes flung a protective arm round the unfortunate Rudgewick. "Very funny," he said throwing an accusing glance my way. "But you hardly made it plain, did you – Mr Bryant?"

"Didn't I?" Suppressing a last chuckle, I placed a hand on Marsden's head. "Then let me show you. Thick crosses thus, here and here and here, like so. Other side too. Head over, Marsden, that's the ticket. Thus and thus – until you've got total cover. Then you blend the two colours into one, smoothing them evenly into the pores of the skin. Watch closely."

His facial skin was rougher than I'd expected. My fingers lingered a bit on its surface. Rougher though closely shaved, iconically male, perdurably bewitching.

It may be, as the poet avers, that when we're young it's the face, the visual, which sparks off the whole shooting match. But what's equally true is that it's touch which seals it. Or if not exactly seals, at least advances empathy between two skins to a point where a relationship – awful, formal, bloodless term! – can, if the wind sets fair, begin its long, long voyage. To bliss or perdition, as the fates decree.

As I stood there, thumbing grease across his cheeks and into his eyelids, and as I felt the touch of his leg against mine (inadvertent?) it was as though some warning started to bleep. That this might be the first step towards checkmate. All right, long and protracted as games go, but shades of the one way road all the same. Stepping into that hooded carriage. Hurtling up to that stone fastness. No way out. No way back.

With considerable effort, I pulled myself together. Stepping aside, I reached for my orange stick. "Now for the detail," I said. "The thing here is to observe the contours, OK? The moulding of the..."

Suddenly one eye flicked open. Like a mummy revived, like all the ages sprung to life. Gleaning, horrible. You see, I'd never before deigned to notice the detail of flecks and discs which give that organ its character. Its colour and blaze. And as it forced itself on my attention, again the vortex started its spin...

Even so, I fought, managing to turn again to my audience. "Moulding of the face," I repeated, "and of course lips. A mixture of Lake and 9 for the lines, Carmine for the lips. The lips of a young bloke, that is. Crimson for a wrinklie. Now Shakespeare doesn't..."

"How about a woman, sir?"

"Look, Chuffley – just relax. I'll get to you in a tick. Never fear, Olivia and Viola shall not be forgotten!."

"And Maria!"

"Thank you, Travers. And, of course, Maria. Plus Uncle Tom Cobleigh and all! Now, as I was saying, Shakespeare never clarifies exactly how old Malvolio's meant to be, but given what we know about life expectancy in Elizabethan England, we can safely assume..."

"Sir," interposed Jukes with his usual innocence, "isn't the play set in Illyria?"

"Well?"

"Not England."

"Nominally yes," I retorted just about keeping my exasperation in check. "But a steward's a steward whether it's Bombay or Bournemouth, OK? Now can we get on? As I was saying, the guy's age can safely be reckoned somewhere in his thirties. Therefore, from liners like these, we select…"

And again reality gan flux. For now it was the lips' turn. Almost imperceptibly, they began to part. Like they were spotlit. Like it was that Busby Berkeley scene, Broadway in black and white.

Monochrome lips, parting slightly but definitively. And seductively. Pursed to receive the benison of benisons. Not a cheap gasper like in the film. But something of more allure, more…

Get control, Bryant! Carmine, that's all. Carmine, that's the ticket. They're begging for Carmine! No way could anything else be on their mind.

Could it? Not that lips have a mind. Nor, ergo, can they have, can they possibly have, anything approaching, remotely approaching, an – agenda…

But gradually the camera drifts in, and me with it. Closer and closer, focus shifting as we move, each second slower than the last…

Outside here, this inch of limelight, all creation gladly surrenders form, morphing into some sepia mush, tangible only in the way phlogiston's tangible – so nothing's real except this putative welcome, this beckoning, this crescent of dark grey bloom, its promise neural and nascent and terrible.

And about as negotiable as madness itself…

"Mr Bryant!" called a voice somewhere in the fog.

Ignore it, I thought – just a goblin trying to muck things up, deny vox.

"Mr Bryant! Could you spare me a moment?" Followed by a tap on the shoulder, so peremptory this could be no illusion, no rabbit in the hat.

I turned round to find Roy Marchpane right behind me, sort of simmering, sort of indignant in a half-amused way, his PSV licence still clipped to his lapel.

"Pardon me?"

"Could we have a word in the Vestry, please. Right away if you don't mind."

"Hang on, mon brave. We're just at a crucial…"

"Apologies, but I must insist!"

"And apologies, but I must decline!"

"My dear Bryant…"

By now the cast, all agog, were more avid and tense than Cardiff Arms at the last kick of a Five Nations – I took Roy by the elbow.

"No need for an audience, OK?" I said, propelling him through the door, still shaken by the abruptness of this intrusion, my decisiveness, such as it was, a kind of autopilot kicking in. "Now, whatever it is, surely it can wait half an hour. I'll be with you as soon as I've finished this demonstration. Fair enough?" No response. "Roy, fair enough?"

Still no answer. No verbal one, that is. With a wince as though he'd just trodden on a drawing pin, he turned on his heel and made off towards his eyrie.

At least this interlude had served one good purpose: to rescue me from my previous trance, reverie, whatever. Once again a schoolmaster, I returned to my task resolute, if not exactly calm. "Sorry about that lads – now where were we?"

"Lips," said Jukes all innocence. "Andy's to be precise."

"Oh yes?" I began. "And any more lip from you, Jukes…"

The universal groan with which schoolboys greet the corny got the session well back on course, and it was barely twenty minutes before I found myself at Marcho's domain, poking my head round the door, a penitent look on my face.

Not that it worked. The old guy was sitting with his back halfway to me, examining what looked like some sort of tablet through a magnifying glass. It wasn't till much later, not only after this crisis but the one that followed, that I was informed it belonged to a Manson apparatus, and at that from the Cambrian, and at that from a long, long redundant halt – Abermule!

Sorry to digress yet again, though anything which helps us into a guy's state of mind can be deemed, I suppose, sort of relevant.

I cleared my throat. I shut the door. I coughed. Only then did he turn slowly round and acknowledge my presence with a glare.

"Put the kettle on then, shall I?" With an attempt at congeniality, I smiled my warmest smile.

"Suit yourself," came the reply – and then, bitterly, "As per normal."

I chose, of course, not to rise to this, but it was perfectly clear that the interval, far from cooling him down, had given whatever was bugging him ample opportunity to fret and fester. In the green room he'd seemed irritated and on edge – now it was more like a volcano about to burst its cone. For the moment, however, he was holding himself in check, while I grew steadily more tense.

For a minute or two we sat there in silence, until I could stand it no longer. "For goodness sake Roy," I blurted clumsily, "what the hell's up? Has someone been pissing you about? Is that it?"

From his inner pocket, he pulled a sheet of blue foolscap, placing it on the table and adjusting it back and forth until it lay absolutely and perfectly parallel to the edge. "As if," he replied with deadly calm, "you didn't know."

"Roy?"

"Et tu Brute!"

"Sorry, I'm completely in the dark…"

"Oh yes," he retorted, a kind of bleak quippy humour still restraining the resentment in his voice. "That's what they all say, don't they? The neater the ambush, the more innocent the face. I see it all now."

See what? I wondered without comment – despite the old man's evident distress, there was something artificial about the situation. Something weirdly vicarious. Like he was enacting a scene from a Clemence Dane potboiler he'd last seen at Wyndham's thirty years before.

"Everything scuppered!" he went on. "All my arrangements. The whole thing ruined. Yet again, my head on the block!"

A parade of self-pity which might have been more effective had it not been for the self-mockery which seemed to accompany it.

Added to which, I was, I'm afraid, starting to lose my cool and quite markedly so. It had been a tiresome afternoon, supervising the last of the term's O levels in an exceptionally stuffy library, and now here I was, expected not only to herd a large cast through the final straight, but, into the bargain, placate a fifty year old toddler in a tizz. Fray one's nerves? It was enough to fry them!

Under normal circumstances I'd have sat Roy down, poured him a drink, and found out in due course, and told in his own eccentric way, exactly what it was nagging his pride. Instead, a kind of jet of anger suddenly lit inside me.

Why couldn't he come to the point? Why all this shadow boxing? Things were difficult enough without playing power games on a hot evening when the very air seemed to coat your throat. I'd not crossed him in any way, had I? Not as far as I could remember. So how was it any concern of mine, this latest bee in his bonnet? Why should I worry about whatever imagined slights he'd bunched up into some mental cat o' nine tails with which to thrash himself?

Yet I tried. For old times' sake I tried, just about keeping myself in check. "Scuppered! Sounds well serious. D' you want me to call round later and…?"

"And what? Temporise? Try to talk me round? Think again, my lad. Regrets won't wash. We'll have it out here and now."

"I'd be quite ready and willing," I replied in slow, deliberate, controlled tones, though my brain was fast whizzing to crescendo, "to express regret if I only knew, Roy, concerning bloody what!"

"As usual. Go on. Play the giddy goat – the usual Bryant cop out."

"From what, Roy? From what?"

"For a start, how about this?" At which he flourished the document in front of him, clearly, as I now realised, ripped from a noticeboard. "Those are, I imagine, your initials at the bottom?"

"Let's see," I frowned. "Yes, but so?" I mean, what could be contentious about a piece of typescript like that? Had it been a Dick-Whyte-Dick lampoon I could have understood the Marcho ire. As it was, how could a routine notice to my play cast possibly upset the old boy to this extent?

"Nothing much." Laced with asperity, still his tone was tempered by that slight smile, that kind of Max Wall impishness. "Except that I've no intention of conceding. Not one inch. I'll appeal to the Head. I'll appeal to the Bishop. You won't get away with it – never in a month of Sundays. I'll take it to the Fustians, if need be."

"Take it," I shrugged icily – nothing gets me more nettled than some prat pulling rank this way – "to the ruddy Hague if you want. Talk about obsession. You're making about as much sense as the proverbial stuffed bloody parrot!"

"So it's sneers and scorn now, is it? Persiflage! The last refuge of the scoundrel!"

"Wrong again!"

"Wrong?" he glowered.

"Not persiflage. You mean, patriotism. Shout the ruddy house down if you must, but at least get your quotes right. Patriotism, OK? Dr Johnson!"

By now his mood was darkening rapidly. "Oh, cheers," he retorted. "Clever aren't we? Very clever – with our 3rd class Honours!" Bristling his PSV disc as though it were a wartime decoration, he took a step closer. "But never forget this – some of us actually fought for King and Country!"

"Bully for you!" I countered. Well, if he could attack me like that, where it still stung, why worry about his feelings? "Three cheers for the hero!"

"What a – what a very horrid remark!" He seemed dazed, genuinely taken aback.

"All that rah-rah stuff, OK?" I barked, really losing my rag now. "Save it for the Cenotaph. It doesn't wash round here, old love. No more than that ghastly cigarette holder of yours. Now if you don't mind…"

"Cigarette…?" He seemed to choke. "How dare you! I'm shattered, you absolute lout."

"Takes one to know one!"

His face reddened still further. "May I remind you," he bristled, "who's the senior here!"

"For Godssake!" I cried. "Look, I've no time to play games, OK? I've way too much on my fucking plate!"

"You'll soon have a great deal more. Especially with language like that!"

"Roy…?"

"Don't Roy me, you, you cad!"

"Cad? Good God!" An abrupt peal of laughter, his archaic slang hitting my funny bone. "Is that the best you can do, old darling?"

"Very well, then," he stormed, delving back into some dark recess of old battles. "Judas, if you want it straight! Smart Alec! Coming in here, upsetting the apple cart. Treading on toes as if you owned the place."

"Judas?" I retorted, my umbrella in that wreck of an attic shouldering suddenly into my memory – along with his perfidy over James. "Talk about glass houses…"

"Ruddy upstart!" he choked, his voice even more shrill.

"For God's sake stop shouting! D' you want the boys to hear everything?"

"Why not?" Frenzy unabated, he turned to the door. "At least then they'll know what kind of guttersnipe they've got masquerading as a teacher!"

"OK, OK, that does it!" I snapped, amazed at such an outburst. The guy had clearly lost his marbles, hadn't he? "Two can play at that game, Macho Man! Macho the March! That's it to a T. You and your ridiculous ego!"

"My what?"

"In plain language, bump of self esteem! Mr Warden of the pissing Almshouses! Rev Bev! King of the Camp!"

"Am I," he choked, " actually hearing this?"

"Sobranie Sam who never inhales," I jeered, fully into my stride. "Spiv boy with his pathetic relics for sale!"

"You utter, utter…"

"Macho Marzipan, DF fucking C! I know your sort of bravery, chum. Remember James? Smiles and favour to his face – but who stabbed him in the back? You appal me!"

"How dare you!" he sobbed wildly, reeling, raising his fist, almost in tears. "How dare you! How dare you! Of all – people! Just you wait. I'll teach you to monkey with me, mister. Take on the Church would you? Just remember, the Holy finger writes, and, having writ, moves on! Got that, eh? Understand that, eh?"

Brandishing my rehearsal schedule at me, he took a step closer. "You'll rue this day, you contemptible arse!"

"I doubt it!" I scoffed, making a sudden grab for the blue, but, of course, missing.

"Oh no you don't! Evidence! This'll cook your goose, all right. You're for it, my lad, and no mistake!"

"I doubt it!" I repeated, but with a weird kind of frost at heart, a feeling that I'd passed a point of no return without meaning to, that the track ahead bid fair now to prove stony, lonely, and ultimately, with all its implications of futile sprawl, deltaic.

And now it flashed back at me, an image familiar and frequent since I first found out what turds men could be. An image of Gericault's raft on that vast implacable ocean. That fragile bundle of spars, its rags and skeletons and tattered sail, with mountainous seas all round. Myself at the edge, naked, next to be swallowed, counting the seconds, gazing up in awe as it crested, that mighty and welcoming wall of green love.

12: *Clash of the Titans*

Well enormous, and well gloomy too – though outside it was still light enough for a couple of boys to be ending a desultory croquet match – the marquee seemed to exude a shabby grandeur as I dodged under its flap and shone my torch around. The long tables were piled with plates and doilies and cutlery, as well as trays of food, the less perishable items. The scones, the Banburys, the jam tarts, and Mrs Todd's specials: bridge rolls stuffed with potted hoof and Primula, abetted by that ghastly farrago the English call salad cream. Very special! Bring out the Alka!

OK, things are different now that the public schools have been Americanised, what with their recruitment campaigns, alumni officers, centrally-heated buildings and all – plus the outrageous fees which must be the corollary of such vanity – but in those days treats were simpler. Schools gave you tea. No champagne and sherry and beluga on rye. Whatever the occasion, you got tea. Hence the marquee. This week there would be no fewer than three grand events to tax Mrs Todd's urns. Tomorrow, a memorial service for Eric, mourners there to bow before him, gathered in from every place. On Thursday, Confirmation, beaming parents making their first visit to a place of worship in a dozen years (and pretty certainly their last!). And finally on Saturday, the End of Term after the second performance of *Twelfth Night* – this would be the grandest tea of all, with tinned pineapple and three kinds of ice cream raising the menu to the dizzy heights of VE day!

A crowded programme indeed, not only for the kitchens, but everybody else on campus – and herein, though quite unwittingly, had arisen the seeds of conflict between Marcho and myself. Or at least the more obvious ones.

Dousing my torch, I perched myself on one of the canvas chairs. Not particularly comfortable, but at least the place had the merit of solitude – space to collect my thoughts. And patch up the carapace which I was wont, like all of us, to present as myself to the world. OK, it might be rather battered in my case, but one still had to function.

The weekend over, Roy had, as threatened, taken his grievance to Chris, with the result that a joint meeting had been arranged for Tuesday evening. This had just concluded, having turned into even more of a stitch-up than I'd expected. Which just proves what old Public School hands tell you: keep your head down, accept what fate doles out, and never challenge, or try to improve on, mediocrity.

Invited to state his case – and remember, the whole wretched issue was still Greek to me – the old boy had, surprise, surprise, invoked history. Since time immemorial, he averred, Confirmation had been held on the last Thursday of term, with choir rehearsal on the evening before. This year was no exception. At which point he'd flourished a Roll & Calendar. There it was in black and white. Wednesday July 2nd Choir rehearsal, Chapel, 7.30pm.

"But how about prep?" had asked Chris irritably.

"Three days before the end of term?" Roy had folded his arms. "Come off it, Chris. The Housemasters are glad for the chaps to have something to occupy them."

"I suppose so. Well then, come along, come along!"

"Next, on the same page, as you can see, are the arrangements for Thursday. Confirmation, The Bishop of Brecon, Chapel, 5pm. School play dress rehearsal, Glade Theatre…"

"I see, I see. Conflict of interests. Well, we can sort that out without much trouble. Hey, gentlemen? Let's see. Bryant, your play will just have to go later."

"According to the Calendar," said Roy pointing to the entry, "it *is* later." So sure was he of his case, that his voice purred sheer reason and armistice. "See there, 6.30."

"Then how come all the fuss? Really, Chaplain, I've no time to waste on senseless squabbles..."

"With respect, *Headmaster*," replied Roy, placing in front of him that oblong of blue bond, "you need to see this. Our friend here has seen fit to ignore the published programme, the programme agreed to by the Calendar committee a term ago, the pattern as established for as long as anyone can remember, and has scheduled" – here he paused, to draw breath for his climax – "his dress rehearsal a day earlier. 6.30 on Wednesday, at exactly the same time as my choir rehearsal!"

"But surely, you're in Chapel, he in the Glade?"

"Indeed, but there seems to be an overlap of personnel."

"Ah, so that's it. Many?"

"Just one."

With a snort, Watson leant back in his chair. "One boy and the walls of Jericho collapse! Really, gentlemen! After all, what are we quibbling over? Mere rehearsals. Can't he simply miss one and muddle through?"

"Never!" Our unison was sharp and impressive.

"Besides," added Roy suavely, "the lad in question happens to be Oliver Carey."

"Gruffydd's boy?" Watson reached for his propelling pencil. "Oh!"

"My soloist in *Low we Bow before*..."

"And," I interposed abruptly, conscious that yours truly had been silent far too long, "my Antonio in *Twelfth Night*."

Chris was tapping pencil on blotter, a smile irradiating his face. "*Low we bow.* Well, I never. Haven't sung that old tripe since the Coronation service at Bangor. Swotch, isn't it? With a baritone part like John Peel, eh? To waken the Dead!"

"Especially when performed by Carey."

"Indeed, indeed. Now how does it go? *Paraclete whom all revere...*"

"*Lo, we bow,*" joined in the March lustily, "*before thy bier, Lo be-fore thy bier.*"

"Well, now, I look forward to that. My aunt Megan was married to a Swotch, by the bye. Parson over Craven Arms way. Don't rightly recall whether it was the same family or not, but she was musical too: grandfather Precentor of St Woolos, mother a noted..."

My cough at this point I trust was subtle. It was certainly necessary. Now don't get me wrong. I'm as fond of a spot of church music as the next man. Parry, Jackson, Sumsion, you name it. But bring two old farts of the stave together and they'll jaw till the crows come home. "Olly's Antonio," I said, "seems to be developing nicely. Should prove quite a star turn, as long as the dress goes well tomorrow!"

"Not tomorrow!" A renewed flare of the Marcho anger. Sudden, passionate. "How often do I have to tell you!"

"Now, now," cried Watson, fist striking his desk. "I will not have staff brawling like this. Control yourselves, gentlemen. Quiet, calm deliberation will unravel every knot, eh? Which reminds me, padre – isn't it about time we did that again?"

"*Princess Ida*? No, no!" Shaking his head. "Beg pardon, I'm all of a dither. *The Gondoliers*, of course! Well there's a thought. With yourself as Plaza Toro, needless to say."

"If you insist."

"Capital idea! Why not? Perhaps outdoors this time. In the Glade. Real gondolas on the Tolver! Now there's a thought!"

Another of my little coughs. This was getting far too cosy for my liking. Next thing, I'd be roped in as Head Carpenter, fashioning a flotilla out of old boxes!

"Yes, well," said Chris with a start, peering closer at my schedule, "we can discuss all that later. Now Bryant, I see your first performance isn't till Friday. Very well then. The whole thing's simple. Why not revert to Leyland's timing? Have your dress rehearsal on the evening before? As in the Calendar. It is supposed to be sacrosanct, you know."

"Best practice, Head," I replied. "Simple as that. Don't forget I trained with the Putney and District Youth Theatre, so I know what I'm talking about."

"We're all grateful for expertise of such an order. But…"

"After a dress, actors, especially schoolboy actors, are totally shagged, OK? Er, apologies, I mean totally exhausted. They need a day to sort of recharge, get it together, gird their loins for the battle ahead."

"Yes, in an ideal world maybe, my boy…"

"That way you've a chance of really ace performances. The kind of thing that makes all the weeks of work worthwhile. An experience the participants never forget. A triumph that stays with them all their lives." I paused Ronald Colman style. "Surely you can't deny them that?"

Well – if the March could play to the tear ducts, so could I!

Whether it was remembrance of their own past glories, or, more likely, embarrassment at my admittedly gauche theatricals, I've no idea – but both men were silent for a few seconds. Nor did either move.

Finally, Watson turned to Roy. "Carey really is crucial, padre?"

"Been practising for weeks. No-one else knows the part."

"And the play?" Now the same almost pleading stare was directed my way. "Crucial to you as well, I suppose?"

"Been practising all year. No-one else knows the part."

"Then there's only one solution as far as I can see. Tomorrow, we'll have to squeeze in both rehearsals. Bryant, you an hour later. Chaplain, you an hour earlier. I can square that with the Housemasters. And now everyone's satisfied."

"Except," remarked Roy sweetly, "that puts my rehearsal at the same time as Eric's memorial. Bang in the middle. Not likely to be very popular, I think, since that's in Chapel too."

"Besides which," I added in support, "two rehearsals in one evening? The boy would be totally shagged. Sorry – exhausted. I mean…"

"If I may say so…" began Watson severely.

"Apologies, but it's out of the question!"

"Totally!" I agreed.

"This time a decision has to be made, Chris – no room for compromise. The choice is clear. Eucharist or – entertainment!" Preening with confidence, Roy's voice seemed to transform the little office into a soaring nave. "One or the other!"

"Or," exploded Watson, rising from his chair, "neither!" As abrupt as it was unexpected, his irritation cowed us both. "I've had quite enough of this," he went on. "Intransigence on both sides plus, I suspect, a fair measure of personal pique. Look at yourselves. You should feel ashamed. How can Common Room expect to inspire boys if it can't sort out a minor glitch like this? Very well – here's my ruling. Since you can't agree, Oliver Carey will perform for neither of you."

"But Chris," wailed Roy in dismay. "How about Swotch?"

"I shall sing the solo part myself. Indeed I shall."

"But" – the voice now thoroughly crestfallen – "the lad also acts as my head thurifer."

"And," retorted Chris blanching but swallowing hard, "so shall I. Kindly spare me your thanks. Oh, and let my secretary have the score pronto."

"How about Antonio?" I queried, amused at his discomfiture. "Are you going to play him too?"

"No – you are. With a book if necessary. No protests. That's final." He pressed a button. "Elsie, I'll see Carver now. Not arrived yet? Who's next? Docherty? God help us! Send him in then, send him in."

And that had been, most definitively, that. For an hour or two, the prospect had thrashed around in my mind, a bit like bad beef in the gut. For Chrissake, as a con I'd always been hopeless, ergo my abandoning theatre as a career. Lines simply would not stick, not in the right order anyhow, and no way can you garble Shakespeare without disaster. It would have to be, as he'd said, with book, and all the concomitant humiliation that would entail. Thanks a million, Chris! Thanks a million, million, ye Gods!

In fact it had occured to me, after lunch, to make a desperate phone call to the Lodge. Julian had once played Poins, hadn't he? That meant he was au fait with verse speaking, and anyway Antonio was a short part by comparison. The guy might just do me a favour for old times' sake. It was at least worth a try.

But he was out. In fact away till Sunday, somewhere Mrs Copeland thought, in the north.

How all occasions do frigging inform against one! As I sat in that gloomy tent, not for the first time did my mind run over ways out. Not Pago Pago or John Ford for once, but the darker prospect from which there's no return. Nothing messy. Just a discreet pill or something.

Don't they say that with cyanide just a whiff will do?

And if for the moment such impulses were hardly more than posturing, how long could a guy hold out? With my track record, what treats could I expect from the future? Sex, no. Respect, no. Promotion, no. And worst of all: Friends, none.

Marcho's look as we left Chris yesterday had made that quite plain. It could have frozen a Mammoth in its roar. Not just bleak – positively Carverian!

Which just shows – since, that very moment, unable to take the claustrophobia any more, I dodged back into the fresh air, only to find myself virtually in the arms of none other than said ray of sunshine himself. On his way to a late jar at The Fox with Tiny.

"Been stealing the tarts, boyo, have we?" joshed the latter amiably. "Naughty, naughty. Sticky pickies!"

Carver managed half a sneer.

"Thought I saw a rat run in," lied I neatly, switching off my torch, "actually. But it must have been a trick of the light. A shadow or something."

"Obviously. What self-respecting rodent would be seen dead sampling that pit of – salmonella. Pardon the rhyme! Coming down?"

"Might give it a miss tonight."

"Give my love to Murdoch, boyo!" He walked on.

"Better uses for our time, have we?" hissed the Carve, lingering for a moment. "Like packing our bags, while the going's good!"

"Hang on a tick," I said, grabbing his arm. "What the hell are you getting at now?"

"You two!" called Tiny over his shoulder, not slackening his stride. "Daft to waste good drinking time. See you there."

"Why pack my bags, Mr Oracle?"

"Don't you worry," said Carver, patting my shoulder in mock sympathy. "Wattie's a good soul. He writes super references, so I'm told."

Despite my accustomed inner panic, the usual scores flitting past me like an identity parade, I more or less kept my head. "In other words, it's your usual bullshit. Sod off, Carver!"

He shrugged. "Have it your own way!" but as I brushed past towards Rhodes he called after me. "Find it interesting, yesterday, did you? The Special paper?"

Something in his voice made me turn back. "What, O level History? Fascinating – like all bloody invigilation. You took over from me – you should know!"

"I just wondered – whether you deigned to read the questions, that's all."

"Don't be stupid! Why should I waste time over crap like that?"

"Oh, I don't know. There was one on the back page, number 17 was it? 18? Anyhow, right up your street. The Civil War. One of your obsessions, so I'm informed."

"Which Civil War?" I said slowly – as if I didn't know! Once again the drums began to beat.

"Rather neatly worded, in my opinion. How did it go? 'In the conflict between King and Parliament, which of the early battles, 1642 to 1644, do you consider to have been the most significant?' A pity only one of my 5th formers saw fit to answer it."

I closed my eyes. "No need to tell me…"

"Blease sir, which come first, Henry the 8th or Henry the 7th?"

"You can't be serious."

"Dear dim Rudgewick, none other, who wrote a stunningly good account of the Battle of Weyburne Tump. So accomplished it would have won him a grade A or maybe a scholarship to Harvard, except for one small fact."

"Look here," I began.

"One small problem well known to yourself, and which will also be known by our dear Acting Head when I see him tomorrow at 9.15. Pack your bags, Bryant. You're finished. You and Macho Man."

When your back's against the wall, it's amazing how suddenly the brain zips into overdrive. "Maybe," I retorted with hardly a second's pause, "I won't be the only one, brawn brain!"

"Bravo!" he sneered. "Card up the proverbial sleeve, is it? I don't think so!"

"You mean, you don't think, period! How awesome. Double first – that towering intellect we're all so envious of. And you can't spot a chasm, even though it's a mile wide and floodlit!"

"Bollocks!"

"It's tragic! So near and yet so far! I mean, with Eric you might just have got away with it. But Chris, well he's still a practising teacher, right? Knows the Board's rules inside out. Keeps to them too, I imagine – unlike some people!"

"Good try!" he mocked, but I could see he was nettled. "Any other bombshells?"

"Suit yourself – see you in the dole queue!"

"The what?" he said, reddening slightly.

"Slipped our mind did it? That it's strictly forbidden for any invigilator to read a script before they're posted. Otherwise, who can tell? A phrase crossed out here, a comma added there, one or two spelling corrections, and B soars to A."

"What the hell are you implying?"

"Implying?" I produced my most sardonic laugh. "It's fact. You've just admitted as much."

"I've never tampered with a script in my life!" Seriously worried now, his face was a picture!

"Prove it. If you know what Rudgewick wrote, you must at least have been in a position, had you so wished, to – shall we say – edit."

"You bastard."

"Fine, OK – you go to Watson. Spill the beans. It'll be your funeral!"

It was good to see him outgunned for once – standing there pale, fuming, incapable for a moment or two of speech. Grinning, I took a step or two backwards, flicking him a V sign, savouring my triumph. "Off you go," I said. "Tiny's waiting. Good luck with the jolly old arrows!"

Slowly he raised his index finger. "Pleased with yourself, are you?" he said fretfully. "Reckon that's the end of it? Think again. It so happens I've already ordered an examiner's report on those O level papers. When that arrives, it's bound to spotlight something as glaring as a fictional battle. You're just postponing the inevitable! What a tasty scandal for the new Head to cut his teeth on! Very juicy! Two birds with one stone. Tell you what – I can't wait!"

At which he turned on his heel and rushed off towards town – in such haste one could almost smell the sulphur in his wake. Still buoyed up, still full of adrenalin, I followed him a short way, hoping to get another in another jibe or two. His point about October, when the reports arrived, was of course a valid one, but we could cross that bridge when we came to it. After all, Rudgewick would have left by then – he was hardly 6th form material – and the new regime might well prefer a first term without any dirty linen in evidence.

No new aphorism coming to mind, my pursuit of such feeble quarry was not worth prolonging, especially when I found myself in a certain passage to the side of Livingstone, looking up at our latest folie de grandeur.

The new pool.

Too excited for sleep, nothing would have suited me more than a twenty length thrash through the chaste blue, nothing would have provided a more sleek and satisfying crown to my triumph over the Carve. For a moment, I stood there, fingering my key ring, on the brink, on the very cusp of throwing caution to the winds and deferring to all the teenage instincts which, despite my cap and gown, still slurped around in my veins.

But no. It would be madness. Too many folk still out and about on errands, too many windows in Livingstone still lit. OK, this evening had already started hares enough – why risk starting more?

Yet a couple of hours later in Rhodes, rest still eluding me, there was I, creeping down the service stairs clad only in jeans and sweater. How different things seem at midnight, stars ghostly in the sky, what sounds there are, remote and feint. By now the private side was dark, just a solitary light still showing in study passage.

Coast clear! Crossing the lawn, keeping close thereafter to buildings and shrubberies, in no time at all I'd made it to the boiler room, and thence the pool itself, having been careful to lock the door behind me. I gazed rapt at the long, inviting sheen, all the more attractive now it was lit only from what stray beams filtered down from the high windows.

High Windows? Does one never escape Larkin? It would, of course, be half a dozen or more years until he penned those lines, or at least published them, but I don't think it's boastful to suggest that the same idea came into my head that night at Tolverton. Or a sliver of it at least, without any – sure, granted! – of the genius.

And as for 'forty years hence' – well, it's near on fifty now. How fares, I wonder, his vision of paradise?

Not something to tax my brain back then. All I knew was, it was finally mine: me time, ace time. No need to haste or worry – no need to acknowledge that anyone else existed in this joke of a universe. Delicious to slowly strip off, feel the air round my neck and shoulders and balls, allow my raison d'etre off the leash, poise at the water's edge, slide sideways into its warm chill, before taking a deep breath and plunging into a fast crawl the whole length of the lane. Delicious too, on reaching the end, to have no bloody James Frobisher trying to duck me or drown me, whatever, to satisfy his rampant ego!

Males, I thought, launching into a brief flirtation with the backstroke. Who needs them? Best to find an island somewhere – my Pago Pago dream again – with no other bugger to spoil my paradise. OK, it would mean pseudo sex, but one could live with that. Plus a diet of crabs and seaweed, but one could live with that. Plus incessant sun and quiet and time to write. One could most certainly live with that!

Treading water for a moment, looking round for a li-lo – if one was going to daydream, why not do it in comfort? – I was all at once appalled to hear a noise. Slight but distinct. Something like a hinge creaking. From precisely the direction I'd entered.

But hang on – that was impossible, wasn't it? I'd been ultra-careful about pushing that door to and checking the lock. Nor would any bastard of a maintenance man be around at this time of night, not on their pittance of a wage! Moreover, if it was a member of Common Room, would it seriously occur to him to enter any way other than the main entrance?

No, there were only two possibilities. One, that Altzheimers had at long last swooped, in which case I'd soon start seeing stuff, not just hearing it. The other – much more dire and daunting as it abruptly cohered and focused. Namely, that Mostyn's lathe was capable of cutting two Yales at the same time. And not only capable, but had actually done so. In which case, there was nothing for it but to relax and make the best of a bad job. Indeed, a disastrous job.

And sure enough, in a moment, there he was, my pet hex, brushing back that lock of hair, raising his hand in silent salute, before sauntering to the lower board, just where I'd stripped off not five minutes ago. Leaning on the rail with one hand, he picked up my boxers, inspected them, then calmly pressed them against his cheek.

Quelle weirdo! They must have been still warm. What kind of prevert was this guy?

Still, in that blue tracksuit of his, leg flexed like that, he made, it had to be admitted, one hell of a choice titbit. Neck, chest, bum – the whole confection was like it had been crafted by some Stradivarius of the human form. Perfect proportions in an incomparable posture.

Except, as a spectacle it would last all too briefly. Sans doubt! Any moment now it would play some trick or other. Cast my smalls into the briny. Or break into motion, fling off its own clothes, sear down the lanes towards me and – well, who knows what outrage he'd got in mind? The actual details were of no moment. Let's face it – he was still a member of the school for the next four days, wasn't he? Just his being here was quite sufficient to wreck my career once and for all.

A swim in the nude with one of your pupils, Mr Bryant? Is that what one would describe as professional conduct?

Almost motionless, paddling just enough to avoid drowning, I watched and waited for his next move. I'd not returned his salute, but he knew I'd seen it all right. I could almost imagine his relish at my embarrassment – and more than that. My perplexity as to what to do next. He'd figure that out with no trouble at all, the brash sod.

And duly, after a minute or two, break into motion he did. But not in the way I'd conjectured. Not in the way my febrile brain had imagined. Far from it. He simply levered himself on to the board, took out a packet of Woodbines and lit up!

Was this for real? Did the blighter want to ruin both our lives?

See, you have to remember that in those days smoking was just about the most heinous crime a pupil could commit. Senior or junior, it didn't matter. As offences go, it applied to everyone, including prefects and the gods of the 1st XV, and invariably invoked draconian punishment. Why, it was even worse than being caught down town without your cap on!

And woe betide any master on whose watch a transgression took place. Only last January Tom Fairfield of all people had received a final warning when Customs had found twenty Gauloise in one of his skiers' suitcases. And that had been a thousand miles away in the Tyrol, for Godssake!

Even so, Marsden being Marsden, what could I do? Rise from the waters like old Triton and harangue him in the nude? Hardly – even the prospect had a touch of farce about it, and one could just see him regaling Jukes et al with the joke of the century! Probably best to do nothing. He couldn't be seen from outside and the probability of anyone else coming in this late was virtually nil.

It was then a thought struck me and I looked at the roof. And launched myself into the fastest crawl I could manage.

"Don't panic," he laughed as I surfaced in front of him, shaking water from my head as I grabbed the bar. "There aren't any. I've checked."

"Pardon me?"

"Alarms. Every model I've ever seen has a little red stand-by light. Look for yourself."

And indeed the ceiling presented its usual blameless face, unmarred by lights of any colour.

"Quite an expert, aren't you?" I retorted, disconcerted as always by this ability of his to pre-empt one's mind. "Still, it might be best…"

"Relax! There are no fucking smoke detectors in this building, Paul!" he smiled emphatically. "Nor microphones, nor hidden cameras. Honest!" Then he bent over and extended his hand. "Coming out?" Cute and ironic, his expression lent the invitation about five hundred layers of meaning which I had no time to fathom or even to skim as, cursing myself, I shook my head and backed away a bit along the bar.

Well, what would you have done?

"Tell me, Paul," he said, his eyes fixing themselves on my shoulders, "what is it makes you so bloody nervous all the time?"

"You've really no idea?"

"Afraid of getting yourself into *The Daily Herald* or something?"

"It wouldn't just be me, don't forget."

"What a hoot! Think of the headlines!"

His gaze rose from where it had feasted and met my eyes. Both of us were acutely conscious that he only had to stretch forth his hand again, and that would be that. End of restraint. End of all restraint. And, truth to tell, at that moment, that's what I wanted. That's what I yearned for. To be taken hard. Yanked out of my fucking middle-class shell, turned into one of those flotsam characters who inhabit Eastern quays and die in the gutter – but first at least break the traces. At least, before death, taste the cup!

Grab my rocks, you bastard, get fucking on with it!

But instead, he took a drag on his fag, and handed me my towel. "Me," he grinned, "I'm a sucker for comfort. Why don't we go back to your place?"

It was enough. A mere dozen words, but it was enough. Yet again the spell was broken and I was safe. I'd expire under the quilt of some Cheltenham nursing home after all.

Or so it appeared.

"With Murdoch all ears?" I retorted, starting to dry my hair. "Tempting, but I don't think so."

Again that ironic sardonic look of his. "Christ, you're such a – tosser."

"You know the law, OK?"

"In a couple of days I'll be out of this dump!"

"But I won't."

"That's rather up to you," he grinned, his meaning unmistakeable.

"Look," I retorted breathlessly, "this encounter – it never happened, understand? Read me, do you?"

"You're the boss," he shrugged, but his tone was so weird. Not anything you'd have expected – disappointment, frustration, anything of that sort. No way. It was kind of triumphant, amused, disdainful, as if he'd somehow got exactly what he wanted. He saluted, gave me one of his Malvolio bows and turned towards the door, as he did so flicking the stub of his wretched gasper far away into the pool.

What a toad! No two ways about it, I'd have to thrash back after it. To leave the bugger floating there would be far too risky. Just imagine the scandal, the committees of inquiry, the Nurembergs there'd be if old Dobson came across it tomorrow.

Still, my second barter with the blue had at least the benefit of allowing me to get on to an even keel – emotionally, I mean. Undoubtedly, I'd done the right thing.

OK, the guy was desirable. OK, in a decent world, i.e. most other countries, I could have contemplated a future together with him. But British law, hoary resilient old monster that it is, precluded any such notions unless you were prepared to swap a peaceful life for the other – that precarious kind of existence where every knock on the door might be a harbinger. Disgrace in a Scotland Yard mac, handcuffs jingling in its pocket .

Nor would things (it seemed obvious then) change in my lifetime. There were too many bigwigs with boyfriends – judges, princes, playwrights – for them to allow the closet to be prised open, and all their jinks and junkets dusted off and brought to light.

No, I'd done the only thing I could, and thank heavens he'd taken it so easy. Or at least quite easy, in his own odd way. No fuss or tantrums, I mean. If things were different, I could have got bloody fond of him.

A feeling not substantially altered, when, half an hour or so later, I found a slip of paper on my pillow. A London number in blue biro, followed by: 'Mine in the vac – yours?'

With a grin at the divine lunacy of the young, albeit a reluctant grin, I reached for a match. Besides, for much of the holiday I'd be in Prince Regent land, wouldn't I? No time for distractions like London.

Nor did the next few days throw up any wobblies, term dying off in its appointed course like wisteria in autumn. Last reports had to be written, packing finished, and pocket money accounts submitted to, and scrutinised by, Murdoch, all agog for a missed sixpence! As for me, I was off to Ombre and its relative freedom on Saturday afternoon the minute Guests' Tea was over.

I must admit that I had hoped for some kind of thaw from Marcho, anything that would permit me to warn him about Weyburne, and Carver's threats, without loss of face. But, as the days passed, it became clear it was not on the cards. Had it just been the question of those wretched rehearsals, our contretemps would have in all probability been short lived: but no, it must have been that accusation of mine over James which had cut deep. Why on earth had I lost control like that?

Anyhow, whatever the case, not a single glance was cast my way during Confirmation, not even when Chris twice allowed the incense to go out. Also, the vestry door remained resolutely closed every lunch, whilst, to cap it all, he didn't even attend my first night.

Just as well, at any rate as far as Friday was concerned where, traditionally, the bulk of the audience is made up of pupils. No problems during the first act – everyone demure in their suits and school ties, a House Tutor at the end of each row. However, as soon as Foster and I jumped down from our papier-maché rocks to start Act 2, well – mayhem wasn't the word! I must admit, it didn't help that I dropped my book, and had to scrabble around in the birdseed for it, and then took half a minute to find my place again, having been vainly searching through *Cymbeline*. But boys can be savages can't they? All I can think is that it must have been my costume. The long droopy headgear in green wool that made me look like one of Snow White's dwarfs. Or the fact that my girth being considerably greater than Carey's placed immoderate strain on various buttons, one of which did, alas, pop at a rather inconvenient moment.

Anyhow, all was put right for Saturday. A peaked cap was borrowed from the naval section, plus a dark blue greatcoat and a pair of shiny trawlerman's leggings.

I quite looked the part!

This plus the fact that this second audience was largely composed of staff and parents calmed my nerves considerably, even to the extent of my permitting myself at make-up to sit next to Malvolio – the only place available (almost!)

Since the pool, there'd been no communication between us, not even a word. It seemed clear enough that my not responding to his note had irked him, under the circumstances a perfectly reasonable reaction. Besides which the play was developing into quite an obsession in his circle. Basking in the praise yesterday's performance had elicited, he was now attending to his face and hair like a young Gielgud in the making.

More than once I felt a qualm of regret at burning that number – burying it into some drawer would have done just as well – but it looked as though there was to be no turning back. Even when

I asked to borrow his spirit gum, it was passed my way without a glance.

It wasn't until just before the start that I eventually caught his eye. I'd been doing what all casts are strictly forbidden to do, taking a peep at the audience. In this case, given the absence of curtains, round the edge of a flat.

I know, I know! Just couldn't resist it, OK?

There was Watson dead centre in the first row, on his left the new Head, none other than that Igor figure in odd socks whom I'd met at his interview. On either side Fustians. Behind them a mixture of Old Tolvertonian ties, and parental faces, plus one or two odds and sods I hadn't expected. Colonel Featherland, for instance, and what I assume was his dame, heavily powdered, with lorgnettes at the ready. And Cedric wearing a deerstalker – how on earth was The Fox managing without him? And Mrs Amberley with that son of theirs, home for the summer from Douai – how grown up he seemed compared to September's shrimp. Dormitory life had clearly done him no harm!

For whom was I searching? Nobody in particular, maybe? Or maybe – Marcho, just hoping against hope that he'd somehow relent. Or maybe – even more subconsciously, so deep I could hardly admit it to myself, a face I could ascribe to Mrs Sylvester, Widow Marsden as was, the status of whose son in one's life seemed to be hovering between meteorite and comet.

At which, I'd let go the canvas only to spot him in the wings on the far side watching me. Three times his forefinger wagged to and fro in admonishment, but on his face – nothing. An actor's blank before he gets into gear, lets the adrenalin flow, primes himself to face his public with nothing but a first line in his head. Even so, as he backed away, I had this sudden impulse to dart round behind and what – beg his pardon? ask for his number again? fix up a date before or after my vac job? – when I found Elsie tapping my shoulder.

"Sorry, Paul," she said, "HMV as usual I fear. Chris wants you at Governors' Tea afterwards."

"In his garden?" I queried, aghast at such a titanic honour.

"'Fraid so. New Head wants to meet the talented director, so I'm told."

"Talented?" I laughed. "Be off with you, baggage!"

Just a few seconds, but enough to lose me my chance. How empty those wings seemed now, even though they'd filled with courtiers and maidens and the like. No time to brood, however – I'd obviously not heard the five, so off I rushed to find my props and stuff, and above all my book. My bloody book! Pray God, no 5th former's snaffled my book!

The actors' world is well gothic. Themselves one moment, some other dude the next. And night after night romping in two hours through emotions that in real life would take years to evolve. No wonder past ages derided them as strollers. Who but a charlatan could profess love in front of a packed dress circle, and come across as plausibly unspecious. But, let's face it, that's the whole trick. At the moment you say it, you have to mean it. Live the emotion in real space, real time.

Like tonight, as Foster, sleek in silver doublet and tights, waves me farewell, his auburn hair glowing under the lights, I actually feel it – the overwhelming passion an older man can conceive for a younger. Approaching the footlights, I look them all in the eye, the burghers of Tolverton who never stroked an illicit throat in all their lives, and I begin. The book's under my arm – at this juncture it's superfluous:

> *The gentleness of all the Gods go with thee!*
>
> *I have many enemies in Orsino's court,*
>
> *Else would I very shortly see thee there.*
>
> *But...*

One pace backwards, two.

> *...come what may...*

Count to three, turn to face the wings where Foster has just made his exit – and, what the fuck…!

Malvolio? What the fuck…?

But now his hand unclenches and he nods as out they stream from me, those most delicious of words:

…I do adore thee so

At which he turns a thumb to his breast, his forefinger at me, and kisses the back of his hand – my voice swelling suddenly and joyously in diapason

That danger shall seem sport, and I will go!

It's one of those peak moments in life you never forget – and, whatever their outcome, never regret.

Euphoria indeed – for about ten seconds, until I remembered that Governors' invitation. There'd be no chance of seeing the guy after the play, but how could I beard him before? In the interval, he'd be surrounded by family and friends – during the action, when not on stage his time would be taken up with costume change, the dreaded cross-garters, adjustment of make-up, and all the other stuff a busy production involves. No – all that was hopeless. Somehow I must make my time with the Fustians as brief as possible. Then spirit young Andy off somewhere, anywhere, just for ten minutes. Find out his plans, dovetail them with mine. Whatever sacrifice it involved, arrange a rendezvous before he had time to start college. Above all, get a new copy of his vac number. That was crucial, even if it meant a touch of grovel.

By four fifteen, the whirligig of time had wrought its revenge, and the tea tent was full to the brim with actors and audience shouting hard at each other over the general din. By contrast, tea in Eric's garden was an altogether more sedate affair. A sprinkling of senior staff, plus a couple of dozen elderly coves pretending enough knowledge to discuss what they'd just seen. No

Marcho, of course, but one or two other favourites of mine. Otto, for instance, busy with a choux bun, Ormulak, Harry, Joe.

Checking my watch – must get the hell out of here by half past at the latest! – I grabbed a plate and headed their way. Only to be intercepted by Watson with Igor in tow.

"Just a minute Paul," he called breezily. "I've someone here anxious to make your acquaintance. Do shake hands with a fan of yours, my boy. May I introduce Mr Parish Hunn, our new Headmaster. Headmaster, meet Paul Bryant, here only a year but already making his mark. A colleague who always rises to the occasion."

"So I see. And rather spectacularly, if I may say so. Mr Watson's filled me in on the production's – vicissitudes. Still, all's well that ends well, and I've been most impressed. The play too, of course. An invigorating afternoon in every way. Allow me to congratulate everyone concerned, and please do pass that on. As it happens, drama's always been a pet interest of mine. Not on your level, of course. Personally, I've not enough imagination to direct, but I love being directed."

"Don't we all!" I ventured.

He laughed. "Any plans yet for next year?"

"Nothing definite," I replied feeling my watch beat at my wrist. "It all depends on who comes back in September. I mean…"

"One possibility has been floated," interposed Watson, flicking a look in my direction, partly wink, partly frown. "One of our occasional stabs at G & S. There's been talk of *The Gondoliers*."

"Admirable, although" – the Igorian eyebrows turned back my way – "I imagine like all Heads of Drama you deplore anything so lightweight."

"Not really," I said, sort of flattered, "but I'm not exactly Head of Drama, by the way. In fact the school doesn't have such a thing."

He smiled encouragingly. "Who knows? Perhaps that's something we can rectify."

Which rather lit the tinderbox and no mistake! A Headmaster who preferred watching plays to sleeping through them – this was going to be a Ball! Moreover, it soon turned out that we shared a mutual interest in Ibsen, and that he'd played Squire Ulfhejm at St Bees. Soon I was waxing lyrical on the virtues of Meyer's translation against Archer's – until…

Five began its boom from the chapel tower.

Talk about Cinderella at the Ball! Regardless of damage to my career prospects, I extricated myself from that conversation like greased lightning – well, pretty quickly anyhow – not that Hunn seemed put out. He even managed a faint smile before wiping his brow with a handkerchief and turning to the other hopefuls hovering at his hem.

Short though the distance, and monumental my speed, I found myself, needless to say, just a tad too late. As I dodged through the car park arch, there he was climbing into an elderly Austin, its tailgate weighed down with his trunk and bike. Notwithstanding my waving with both arms, off it set, a cloud of blue streaming from its exhaust.

And then the miracle. One last despairing wave – and the saloon stopped! From the driver's side, an elderly woman alighted and took a few steps towards me before pausing, waiting for me to catch up. My impressions of her were all too vague – kindly face, hair an old-fashioned Celia Johnson style, coat a nondescript fawn, that sort of thing.

Truth is, I was more concerned with the figure emerging from the other side, leaning on the door as he stood upright, a sardonic grin on his face.

"Mr Bryant?" said his mother, extending her hand. "You must think us terribly rude rushing off like that without waiting."

"Not at all, Mrs Sylvester. It's brilliant to…"

"You've no idea how far it is," she continued in some world of her own. "To Cromer, I mean. And Andrew doesn't drive yet."

"Give him time."

"Do you detest driving in the dark too?"

"Oh, absolutely."

"Still, all his friends have passed. I do wish you'd use your influence and persuade him to take lessons."

Chance would be a fine thing! I thought to myself wanly – but just about managed a sympathetic nod.

"Of course next year, the mileage will be less. Just a little north, you know. And they've just built a new hall of residence. Isn't he lucky?"

"Isn't he," I agreed. "Just the ticket."

Why isn't the bugger coming any closer? What's he using that door as, a shield or something? Or a decoy? Of course, he's no way of knowing I've destroyed that note. Maybe he thinks I'm into games the way he is. Cat and bloody mouse!

"I can't tell you the difference you've made," her voice continued somewhere to my right. "Andrew really looks up to you. Talks of no-one else at home."

"Uh? Oh, most flattered…" I began.

"No-one else," she insisted, "I assure you. As far as results are concerned, well it's crossed fingers isn't it? But if he does succeed it's all down to you."

"Not at all. He's been a model pupil, actually."

"I'm so glad. Between you and me" – she gripped my wrist and drew nearer, as if confidentially – "he's been a model son."

Which put the kybosh on it, well and truly. After that, how could I intrude? Push my way to the car, and for what? He was her model son, the property of a family, entrenched in a social web to which I had no access. A web of love and support. He wouldn't miss me long. Whatever whim possessed him to write that daft note – well, it would be soon forgotten.

Let go Bryant. Get real. Push off East and find someone who punches at your own weight!

"So pleased, so pleased. If you're ever in Cromer..." Already Mrs Sylvester was retreating to her car, but as she swung herself in, at last Marsden stepped clear of his door. Again he pointed his forefinger my way and his thumb his. Then waved. Then jumped in the front and, amidst a burst of blue smoke, out of my life.

Too much! Altogether too much! So this was teaching was it? Emotional attachments like this, ending like this. A new protégé in each generation, outcome always the same. Model sons returning to the bosom of their model families, leaving me to my bachelor cell.

No, let's not dodge facts. My queer cell. My gay cell. My sodding cold, alone cell. Whatever Marsden had had in mind, it was not going to happen. Sure, technically I could phone his home in a day or two and request his vac number. But what excuse could I give? Why would a respectable schoolmaster want to contact some callow teenager, even if he was a model son. Fuck model sons, fuck model mothers, fuck the fabric of the whole fucking universe!

I hunched off to Rhodes where my suitcase awaited me in my study, ready packed and labelled. I glanced at my watch. If I got my skates on, there was just time to catch the quarter to six and get myself home that night.

It did occur to me that there was something to be said for sleeping over. Allowing rest to work that balm it seems to conjure up. Leaving town in the optimism of a fresh morning, rather than tail between my legs, a creature of the tag end.

But as I looked at those stairs, empty now, more than ever like a gaol, I bethought me of my ghastly bedroom, its austerity, the threadbare counterpane – not to mention the mockery of the six beds next door in the prefects' dorm, and the Fuhrer's double below. And I shuddered. It was as if I could see myself under that counterpane at sixty, clad in thick pyjamas and bedsocks.

Clutching my case and umbrella I fled. Nothing on earth could have persuaded me to sleep in that room that night. Out the back way I dodged, past the laundry baskets, past the dustbins, past the polish of Mrs Murdoch's two-seater.

Idiot that I was! Idiot, idiot, that I was! Why do I always succumb to impulses like that? If only I'd given myself time, thought the whole weird scenario through! Put myself in his shoes. Taken a minute or two to conjecture his movements from curtain to car.

Quelle twerp! Maybe I really had deserved my 3rd after all!

13: *Out of the Frying Pan*

It's often said that where vacations are concerned, schoolmasters fall into two categories. Those for whom term is a churlish interruption to the holidays, and those for whom the holidays are an unconscionable interruption to term.

In fact there's a third, of which I very rapidly realised I'd become a fully paid-up life member. These are the guys (and quite probably the majority) who in term time yearn for the vac, and in vac time yearn for term.

However brightly it had burned in my imagination that Saturday, Ombre's glow took about two days to revert to its usual cindery ash. Mum and Dad soon went back to their familiar routine of work in the week, bowls club and shopping at the weekend, paying of course polite attention to this stranger whom they'd understood less and less of as the years went by, but feeling, perhaps wisely, that it would be inappropriate to go too much out of their way or make any particular fuss.

Could I stand much more of this? Even if it did afford the opportunity to write up my jottings so that eventually all this stuff might see the light of day? True, there was pleasure of sorts ahead – mainly my August vac job in Brighton, but could I face the tedious time till then? The unflinching routine of knitting and snores, three-way Scrabble, Bruce Forsyth on the box, and Sunday treat of lunch at The Old Dove carvery?

The great rift, Bryant versus Holy Church, had put paid to our plans for a July tour of Welsh narrow gauge for start. Nor had alternative schemes met with any greater success. Vague talk of a trip to the Harz mountains with Julian had fizzled out with the onset of beach weather, whilst Toby was performing as a singing gondolier on Cherwell punts to eke out his grant, and couldn't be budged. Typical! And though one or two others had expressed interest – well, you know what folk are. Yes, great, fabulous! – till a better option turns up. Usually a freebie, or some prelude to serial nooky.

More than once I cursed myself for having burnt that phone number of Marsden's. By now he must have finished wondering why I hadn't made contact, must indeed have jumped to the obvious conclusion and be looking around for alternatives. Younger numbers, fitter numbers and way less uptight!

OK, maybe that did make my future less unstable, less insecure. Unfortunately it also made my present screamingly dull. Think of it – we might have been visiting tombs together, reading out bits of poetry to each other over supper, holding hands whilst listening to Bach. Instead of which – Ombre Close, zilch times zilch to the power of zilch!

Taken all in all, this July looked like turning out about as digestible as a plastic avocado! Nothing to do but apply myself to boning up the arid details of English grammar so as to at least get by in Brighton.

In fact, I needn't have bothered. Language schools, then as now, were little more than knocking shops to which teenagers flocked in the summer months as a refuge from home, and an opportunity to bonk as frequently and ubiquitously as possible. The last thing demanded of its teachers by the Seaview Tutorial College was expertise. As long as you turned up for classes roughly on time and not too obviously hung-over, as long as you used condoms, shaved occasionally, and had a stock of jokes to keep the Japs and Ities happy, you were made.

Moreover, as an added bonus, there was the town. Not of course Brighton of the abominable charabancs, that frowsty gew-gaw neverland whose cash registers ring red hot from ten till six. Still less the Brightons of Pinkie and his racetrack gang, or Prince Porkie and his effete sycophants.

No, the world I was after was that of the Lanes with its dark corners and discreet restaurants, or – even more intimate – those boxes at the Theatre Royal where you could sit back in the darkness with your boyfriend, sharing Quality Streets while Cicely C or The Crazy Gang strutted their stuff.

If, that is, you had a boyfriend to share QSs with!

To improve my chances of meeting which, I had, eschewing the offer of on-campus accommodation, booked myself into one of the boarding houses Seaview used as seasonal overflow – namely no. 812 West Skipton Street, a shabby Victorian villa in which they'd allotted me a room on the third floor.

"Small world," sniffed the landlord as I hung my mac and scarf up on the pegs inside the front door.

Mr Laceway's platitudes were eventually to prove more grating than anything Tolverton could offer, but these were early days. Gazing obediently, I followed his finger to a hatstand opposite, one of whose branches sported an identical scarf striped light blue, light yellow and, in the widest band, a magenta one could only call rabid. There was no mistaking it. No. 812 now housed not one but two scions of Arnos College, Oxford.

"Gosh," I said mildly, pretending an interest I didn't feel. Arnos was a large community, since the war swollen by tranches of National Servicemen, and the likelihood of my knowing this stranger was remote. I might just recognise the face, but so what? Jules wouldn't be back from Corfu till the end of the month and who else of the brotherhood did I care tuppence about?

"Funny thing is, he's on the same landing as you. Now what do you make of that?"

"God moves," I shrugged, wondering why this guy Laceway wore his trilby indoors, "in a mysterious way."

"You can say that again," he agreed dolefully. "Now here's your key. Lose it and you have to get a replacement from the Bursary. Electricity's shilling in the meter, though pre-war zlotys will do – which, by the way, I'm able to supply at two dozen a quid, but keep it quiet, and you have to be sparing. Bathroom on each landing, shared between the two rooms. Hot water six to eighty thirty in the morning – seven to nine at night. Provide your own towels. Provide your own loo paper. All clear?"

Only too clear, indeed echoes of Murdoch, but there it was – I needed a car and for that I needed cash. Despite its oddities, the Seaview paid well and was hardly the kind of place to make frequent or accurate tax returns. Given a bit of luck, September would see me returning to Rhodes in style with wheels. Decent ones this time. Not some rusty banger with half a million on the clock!

So delicious was the prospect that sleep that night came with unusual ease and rapidity. Such rapidity that I forgot to set my alarm clock and woke with a start a little past eight. Just time to shower and get to college for my first class. I'd planned to give myself more leeway, but what the hell! I still didn't have to shave more than a couple of mornings a week, and as for breakfast, I could always grab a croissant at break.

Wrapping a towel round me, I padded to the door and peered out. Coast clear. Grabbing my sponge bag, I headed for the bathroom – at precisely the same moment as a similarly-clad figure emerged from the door over the landing, presumably having overslept too, and clearly on the same errand. It was with mutual surprise that we came face to face, and in more ways than the obvious.

For, not to beat about the bush, I was totally unprepared for the confrontation which now glared at me so close, and so balefully. Reynolds! None other than Simon Reynolds, my most bête ot noires, the guy I'd dished over Julian in that historic skirmish at college.

A fact, as his expression made plain, he'd by no means forgotten.

Late as it was, no way was there time for both of us to shower. Given our past, no chance either of one of us giving way.

Impasse – and, at that, a wordless one, the scorn on his face equalling, I daresay, the contempt on mine.

And talk about surprise, nay shock – for the body confronting me might well, on someone other than Reynolds, have been counted attractive. Its skin was smooth and hairless, lightly tanned and with well-defined contours. Its towel was slung low on the hips, revealing a flat, hard stomach and suggesting that what lay below could well prove substantial. Even the long strong neck had its points, as too the features above – the prominent nose, the wide mouth, the deep-set eyes which betokened the kind of personality you cross at your peril.

Indeed, had this been anyone other than Mr Loathsome, by now I'd have been intent on dating, not hating.

As it was, we simply glowered at each other – until, somewhere on the floor above, a loud alarm clock broke the silence.

"Ten past," he said in that harsh voice of his, so bloody masculine, not gentle like most queers.

"Really?"

"No time for two showers."

"Really?"

"In which case, there's only one solution."

I nodded, wondering if he had the necessary coin to flip, I being equipped with no such thing. So you can imagine my surprise when his solution turned out rather different – by no means the standard one of Westerns and cheap fiction.

A moment and we're chest to chest, tight in the cabinet, water bouncing off the glass on to our shoulders, my left, his right.

Which prompts me to wonder, just for an instant, why all my clothes-off encounters are so weird. I mean, will some dude walk in here in a moment and make it a threesome? After which, what next? Four? Five? Or a deluge tumbling into Margaret Dumont's lap?

By now, being a decent sort of chap, I've long since closed my eyes, waiting for things to take their course. To be honest, there's no doubt what I'm hoping for. Like – it's strange but ineluctable this lust stuff: how a guy can be everything you despise yet still turn you on. How, though in the street you'd dodge down an alley to avoid meeting him, here, for a moment or two, you wouldn't say no.

But, and I stress this most sincerely, for a moment or two only.

I open my eyes to find him regarding me with that cross of his between smile and disdain, imbued with total self-absorption. Whereupon, to my disgust I realise that I'm hard but he's not.

Which was, whatever way you look at it, humiliation, though easy to avoid for the future. After all, why not take my shower at Seaview with the students? And thereby improve my language skills – tossing the soap bar round to one another, sharing gel, and picking up all the bathroom banter in Italian and Spanish and German and Russian and some lingo I never did learn the name of.

Why the omission? Well, let's say as knowledge goes, it would have been well superfluous. Its sole orator at Seaview was called Alvi, and Jesus was he *cursaz*! No need to talk to him – it was quite sufficient to look!

And so the hot days of August bled away, with me taking four showers a day and cruising bars at night – all quite pleasurable, but none of my problems resolved. Though it was a matter of some satisfaction to notice that Reynolds got no further with Alvi than I did!

Throughout all this time, Tolverton and its hang-ups seemed further away than Pluto – a truce, however, destined to expire towards the end of the month when the press began its poisonous annual game: namely, trying to predict how well or badly the nation's youth had done in the forthcoming exam results.

A-level Friday!

Since time immemorial, the publication of exam grades in late August has provided the excuse for a final gathering of the clans. Up on the baize go the grades – up on their toes press the hopefuls. Then the whoops of joy and cartwheels, or the chagrin and tears – but so what? Plenty of shoulders to leap on. Plenty of shoulders to weep on.

Remembering it all an eternity ago at Bran's, I managed to swing a couple of days off from Brighton to re-live the thrills again. OK, as a teacher they'd hardly be identical, but still – Jukes's A grade would be as much mine as his, as would Benson's C. Both, I might add, equally respectable grades in those days.

Naturally, none of my group, I fear, had the slightest chance of a Distinction – Jukes was the only one scheduled to return next term for Oxbridge, and that would be in Classics or History or something. Nevertheless I looked forward to meeting some radiant faces, and maybe sharing a beer or two with them now we were, on the face of it, equals. It was a pity Marsden's wouldn't be one of them, Cromer being too far away to hope for that – and anyhow did one really want to stir it all up afresh?

There was, nevertheless, still the problem of Marcho, but one couldn't go through the next twenty years dodging the old boy every hour of the day. Sooner or later we'd have to come face to face and it might as well be now, if thus the Gods judged apt.

Given the arduous nature of the journey, I'd hired some wheels, or to be precise a rather smart Sunbeam, and as I drove into the campus early on Thursday afternoon I was surprised to find, not the emptiness I'd expected but quite a little hive of activity. A Harlech pantechnicon plus two other outside broadcast vans, technicians unplugging lights and cables, a couple of ill-dressed males clearly from the artistic staff, and Murdoch taking his leave of a silver-haired charmer whose face seemed familiar from local TV programmes.

"Dinna tell me," observed the housemaster, strolling over and wiping a smear off my bonnet with his cuff. "You've won the pools I ken. So you'll not, I tek it, be back for the start of term."

"Got it in one – off to Monte Carlo next week!" I retorted casually. "So, what's all the excitement? I thought the results weren't out till tomorrow."

"Results?" he queried.

"A levels – I assume that lot are here because we've topped the league tables or something."

He roared with laughter. "Verra likely. League tables for numbskulls, and you might be talking! No, no. It's this find of Marcho's. You'll see all aboot it on the box this evening."

"What find?"

"It's all fuss about nothing. Some wee Roman coin he found out at Weyburne. You'll have to watch the news at six. I canna remember the details. So, you're looking braw enough."

"You too," I lied with a grin.

"I'm off to make some tea the noo. Fancy coming over?"

"Great," I replied, pulling out my holdall. "I'll just have a wash and brush up first if you don't mind."

Despite the heat outside, the corridor struck me as deathly chill and I couldn't suppress a shiver or two. Neither could I suppress a desire to take a brief look round the door of a certain study. What did I expect to find? Who knows! Some tiny relic maybe? Some keepsake of an affinity that might have blossomed?

But the walls were bare, his stool and chairs stacked in a corner, his carpet spotless, his worktop chaste and gleaming. The cleaners had done their work well. Not a trace of him was left, the room bland and neutral, ready to welcome its next tyro.

Again I shuddered – not from the cold this time, but the thought how everything's like this when you think about it. The books we own – for a while! The hands we hold – for a while! The hopes we entertain – for a while! The abominable impermanence we've no choice but to tolerate.

For a while!

Lighten up, Bryant! The sun's out over Brighton and you've still got a fortnight ahead of you. Who knows, maybe Alvi will turn out to be a millionaire's son, or a film star incognito. Maybe he'll spirit you off on his yacht. Portofino and all playgrounds south.

Still, loping up the familiar and gloomy staircase, it wasn't long before my thoughts retreated to Marcho and his Roman coin. Well, Marsden's actually. It was he who'd found the ruddy thing, wasn't it? – though Jukes who'd had to screw it out of him. But how typical of Roy to take all the credit. Doubtless the news clip would be brief, but it would be interesting to see if he could keep up a mask in front of the cameras. So often there's a hint of something in the eyes, isn't there? Or the way the hands tremble just slightly.

Time would tell – if, that is, the whole interview didn't end up on the cutting room floor!

In accordance with public school tradition, where members of Common Room come a bad last in everywhichway, the cleaners had not yet reached as far as my bedroom. Just as well. Its homely disorder was a great deal more welcoming than the Spartan sparkle below, and I was just about to fling myself on the bed when something caught my eye. A note on my pillow.

Didn't I know that paper? Know that hand?

Stunned, for a moment I stood there motionless, until – suddenly it gelled. Everything gelled. Of course! Tearing it open, I cursed long and loud and comprehensively as I drank in the signature.

No need to tell you whose!

So this was what had lain behind that gesture as the car departed. He must have slipped upstairs just before the performance and left it here. He must have assumed I'd read it that night. He couldn't have conceived that I'd bugger off so suddenly that it would remain unopened for more than a month.

Frantically I scanned the page, not that there was all that much to scan.

As words go, they were few and to the point. Typical Andy. More like a telegram than a letter: 'Paul – a posse ad esse? I'll be staying with Tim Foster for most of the summer. His number's RIV 4945. But it's up to you'.

Ad esse? Even I could work that one out. Trembling, I threw myself on the bed and tried to think.

But hang on – most of the summer? What the hell did that mean? It was mid August already. Had I missed it, this unexpected reprieve, this last chance at the brink? Hand shaking I lay there, obsessed with myself, hardly daring to think of it, that forlorn wait by the phone. The way he must have sat there, willing it to break silence. The frustration that must have coursed through him, the impotence all of us suffer as we stare at the dumb black hump which in a second, if it so deigns, can transform bleak house into great expectations.

Clearly I had to take a chance and ring. But after so long a time, what excuse could I make? The truth would seem a bit pathetic, but what else was there? What else could possibly convince? And suppose he wasn't there? Suppose he was already shacked up with some Alvi he himself had found? Or suppose my call was answered by some ghastly reincarnation of Mrs Danvers, namely Foster's mother or gran?

It was all I could do to rouse myself and join Murdoch on the private side as arranged. Phyllis being still out at the stables, we took tea in his study – white mugs and three dank digestives on a saucer. Not what you'd call an elegant soirée, but in a sense therapeutic by virtue of being entirely predictable. Stuff I could attend to with half my mind, leaving the other half to torment itself, playing that Rubek's cube of possibilities which never quite fit.

After twenty minutes or so of prefect appointments, laundry arrangements, and his brilliant new idea, compulsory press-ups for the 5th form at seven each morning, he reached for the last biscuit and said, "So, looking forward to term then, the noo?"

"Why not? I mean – of course."

"And you've good reason to, laddie. I gather the new man's quite taken with a certain dominie in his English department."

"You're joking, I presume?"

"Not at all. By all accounts, he thinks the sun shines oot of your fundamental orifice, no less."

"All accounts?"

"You can't get closer to the ear than Chris."

"Well, OK – that's very gratifying. But what of it? He's hardly going to double my salary, is he? Or build me a proper theatre?"

"Who knows? Consider this, ma friend. Hunn's clearly been appointed to put this place on the map. No more marking time, I'm glad to say. Could be he sees drama as an asset."

"Which nobody can deny. But what's that about marking time? I'm afraid I don't quite…"

"Let's not beat aboot the bush, Paul," he observed peremptorily, lounging back in his swivel chair. "Old Amberley was hardly the man to set the world alight, agreed? Hence his popularity in the county. A rather remote county, as I dinna need to point out. But there's a new world coming, laddie, and schools have to move with the times. Luckily, there's a few of us in Common Room who've seen the light. Ye'll make certain of siding with the right party, I'm sure."

Distressed at this, my mood darkening still further to hear Eric denigrated so basely, I made some non-commital comment, whereupon he regarded me even more shrewdly. "Speaking of which," he continued portentously, "a tip. If I were you, I'd distance yoursil more from Marchpane noo you're established. Some of us noticed the two of you last year. Och aye! Thick as thieves. Spending too much time together. It's a futile thing, tek my word for it, to wed yourself to yesterday's man."

What a tosser this guy was! Though, as you'll realise, it was hardly a warning I needed. Nor would I demean myself by pointing out that it was Roy's spivvy activities and betrayal of James that had cooled our relationship, rather than any question of Common Room politics. Why give turds like Murdoch their pleasure?

"Thanks for the warning," I nodded. "But let's hope tonight's broadcast helps raise his stock a bit."

To which there was no immediate reply except a frown, and a renewed stirring of tea with his biro. But as I rose to leave, he swivelled his chair sideways. "I've nobbut contempt, ye ken, for amateurs," he said archly, "and so called gentry. The war taught me that. A man's either up to his job or not. Dinna ever be fooled otherwise, Paul."

Which arid sentiment was still adding bile to the storm clouds when I drove through Gifford Farrar at a little before six, heading for the lake. I hadn't liked to watch the TV in Common Room, and those town pubs which ran to sets tended to have them switched permanently to channels over the border. Only in a large establishment like the White Rock country club which boasted a separate viewing lounge could I expect to be able to watch Marcho in peace.

I had to give it to the old boy – he was quite a performer! Though the piece totalled barely five minutes, he managed to do a Cleopatra all right. You know, make thirsty where most she satisfies.

First a potted history of the Romans in Wales. Then some stuff about Roverian, the Imperial warlord whose head graced the coin. Then the coin itself, black and misshapen against the silk of its cushion, the only specimen of its value and age, according to Cardiff, to have survived the centuries intact.

But what surprised me more than anything was that he didn't, after all, hog all the credit. I was mentioned briefly, and Jukes, but most of the limelight fell on Marsden (and they'd found a photo of him from The Tolvertonian!) whose acumen in spotting and rescuing the artefact was dwelt on at some length.

It was all too much, Andy albeit in black and white, those features, that cute lock of hair. Even under normal circumstances, I'd have found it hard enough to cope with, but given the past few weeks…

I betook myself to the bar and ordered. First of the few? Not on your life! Gin, our universal saviour, in copious quantities. Good oily Booths! So what if the Sunbeam ended up in a ditch and they took away my licence! Or hanged me!

Well, as is the way of things, I awoke next morning, unhanged, still the licensee of a brain and a prick – and to merciless daylight intent on haling me to the mark like a prizefighter, ready to be mangled in my next bout. I still hadn't rung London and it occurred to me that, if the results amounted to good news, that might be a neat way of breaking the conversational ice.

Good news? Understatement of the century! I could hardly believe it. No less than five of my set had achieved grades A, with both Jukes and Benson (joke of jokes!) earning Distinctions. I could just imagine the envy on Trewes's face at being thus upstaged, and I must confess it did my spirits a power of good. If Marcho had chanced by at that moment, I might even have shaken his clammy hand.

Andy's results? Creditable Bs in English and Economics, but a surprise Distinction in History. Excellent. I felt an almost proprietorial pride in the boy. Grades like that would stand him in good stead at North Staffs, and set him fair for whatever future he chose.

Which would be what? I wondered an hour or so later, as I jammed through the folding doors of the foyer phone booth at The King's Head. Teacher, solicitor, civil servant? Carefully, I unfolded my billet-doux, propping it up against the square of mirror in front of me. A London number obviously. It did cross my mind fleetingly, that the metropolis was an odd place for a teenager to pass the summer in. Wouldn't abroad have been more natural? Didn't clan Jukes, for instance, own some kind of gite near Roscoff? But, a moment, and all such preambles vanished.

"Andy, is that you?"

"Sir? Good timing – I was just on my way out."

"Oh, sorry – anything special?"

"Just a flick. Not important."

"So, how's everything? Enjoying life in the big smoke?"

"Chiswick, actually."

"Oh, right" – glancing at the number – "yes, I suppose it would be."

A pause.

"Look, I'm sorry it's been sort of – like, a long time. I mean too long. Far too long."

No response.

"I've obviously got some explaining to do," I confessed, my voice cracking a bit under the strain. "But maybe not over the phone. I mean, you know – it's too impersonal. Anyhow" – sensing that a touch of levity might not be amiss – "the bloody thing's probably been tapped by MI5!"

No response.

"Look," I continued, less in control now, "it's not how it seems, OK? Can we meet and talk?"

"Is there much point?"

"All I want is a chance to explain. That's not too much to ask, is it?"

"Depends." His voice sounded curiously thin and faint. A bad line probably – what else could it be?

"How about," I said, a little too eagerly, "tomorrow? Lunch or something. By the way, you'll have something to celebrate. We can make a party of it."

Sudden change of tone. "Grades, you mean? You've seen them?"

"Of course. You'll get the letter in the morning – assuming you told the office your vac address."

"Come on, no teasing. Just give it me straight."

"Do we have a date?"

"And no fucking blackmail, either. I'd have said yes anyway. Now, how about it?"

"Got a pencil, have you?"

"Bryant – you are the most exasperating cunt in the universe! All right? Any more delay and I'll cut your fucking balls off!"

From which I surmised that a) he was alone in the house, and that b) I wasn't, after all, too persona non gratia. "Chance," I retorted forcing a chuckle, "would be a fine thing." And in a sense the crude schoolboy slang did strike one as comic. But more significant than that was its exuberance. "Right, here goes," I said revelling in the reassurance I suddenly felt.

Quelle transformation! Bored to vivacious in sixty seconds flat. Or was I missing something? Anyhow, for the time being at anyrate here he was, back to his old self, in command, my transgressions apparently forgiven. A mood further enhanced by his exam triumph, after which we got down to the question of rendezvous. As to time, it seemed prudent to postpone things to the weekend – it was only a day away, and would avoid my having to make awkward excuses at Brighton.

As to place, though it's true my folk had already left Ombre Close for their annual fortnight in Margate, it was too out of the way and, besides, taking him home might smack of commitment. All I could think of on the spur was that crummy hotel in West Kensington which James had phoned from. OK, it would turn out to be a soulless sort of a dump, but funds had to be conserved and it'd doubtless be adequate as somewhere basic – just for a drink, snack and chat.

Regards anything else, my mind refused to go there.

Hang on, hang on – a cop out, is that what you're thinking? No way, maestro! At least not exactly. Like, if this were an encounter with a rent boy, things would be different – he'd have a professional interest in keeping his mouth shut. With Andy – there'd be a risk, not much of a one maybe, but a risk, the law still being what it was. On no account was I prepared to truss myself up for *The News of the World* as a second Lord Montague. The afternoon to come would be – exploratory. No harm in some innocent flirting if it came to that, but nothing which could end up in court.

It was only after I'd put the phone down and was in The Fox enduring what Cedric boasted of as coffee, that it sank in. Although the idea had been rejected, I'd actually been contemplating sex with a recent pupil.

In retrospect I'm constantly amazed how close to the wind I sailed in those days. It would be several years yet before bed between males would be legalised at all, and then only for guys over twenty one. To enjoy a nineteen year old meant decades in chokey, plus the sort of press exposure that would close off squarely and firmly all doors on professional life thereafter. I'd have to have a face-lift and flit to Uruguay – or worse!

How adept we are at deceiving ourselves! As I rattled up to Victoria on the Pullman the next morning, I hadn't a care in the world. My plans were so squeaky clean, they'd have passed muster with the Cheltenham W.I. Even so, I was about to lunch with a guy I liked and who liked me. "Getting to know you, getting to know all about you…" I almost sang the ruddy song out loud!

And OK, if my new resolve did have its dodgy side, if, way way deep in the grey matter, there did lurk an agenda, it was clearly accepted and understood that consummation, if any, would be years hence and far abroad.

Our rendezvous was to be under the clock on the Dorking side. A bit corny, I know, but as it turned out, highly appropriate. You've seen those weepies where girl waits for boy as the great gilt hands jerk remorselessly forward, knell by knell – ten minutes late, twenty, thirty – her joy turning to unease, consternation, despair. And how, just as she gives in and hails a taxi, hubby-to-be arrives breathless in his Aquascutum greatcoat and sweeps her off to married bliss in Surbiton. Well, that's how it was with me! Except I waited sixty minutes, not thirty, and still he didn't turn up!

Why didn't I take this as a warning? Why the buggeration didn't I simply stomp off to the Ebury, treat myself to a couple of courses and devils on horseback plus a good bottle, judging myself well rid of callow youngsters who can't keep dates?

Quelle conundrum! I suppose if any of us knew the answer, we'd write popular books on the subject and make a fortune. As it is, we suffer – and suffer with that peculiar mixture of doubt and chagrin that makes even a good claret taste bitter.

In my case, I hit on a compromise. It was just too shaming to hang around under that wretched clock any longer. One fifteen had shimmied into two fifteen, and any more protracted a wait might cause comment on the platform! Fortunately a nearby bar provided the most discreet of vantage points and there, for another forty minutes or so, I busied myself with a brace of bottled Guinness – jet black, just right for a wake – before flicking a V sign to the Gods and setting off for platform 19 and the three o' clock fast, back to my lair. At least I hadn't reserved at West Kensington, so wouldn't be much out of pocket.

Southern Region must have been short on rolling stock that day since the train that awaited me was composed of pre-war non-corridor compartments. Despite their shabbiness, this suited me perfectly: in my present mood, all I wanted was solitude. Space and time to brood, without interruption from the outside world.

Even so, at the whistle, something made me let down the strap to take a last look outside – and unbelievably, at the barrier, there he was. Andrew, his back to me. Letting out the loudest yell of my life, I waved wildly, and just as the train jerked into motion, he turned, waved back and broke into a mad run. Fortunately I'd esconced myself in the rear coach, and fortunately these were the days before automatic doors. Chancing dire warnings of £5 fines, I crammed open the latch and, just as we started to gather speed, reached out and scooped him in, saluting farewell to the officials who'd been puffing after him.

"Bit of a close call, cobber?"

"Eheu, eheu!" he retorted, chest heaving painfully. "You can bloody say that again!"

Nodding sagely, I sat back to let him recover in silence. Anyhow, it gave me time to register the changes a couple of months had wrought. Especially his close-cropped hair, a style known at the time as a crew cut. Especially the Festival of Britain duffle bag draped over his shoulder. And most significantly of all, hugging his left wrist, a bracelet of the chunkiest links of heavy silver I'd ever seen.

What was all this? Cocking a snook at his past? Throwing off the last vestiges of servitude? Or – and the thought made me bite my lip – had the lad already filled out his dance card? Found himself a substitute pére Tate & Lyle in my absence?

And it was only now that there dawned on me another peculiarity. Another deviation from the Marsden of yore. He was actually wearing rugger kit. Not, mind you, boots and stuff – instead he'd donned what my Scotsman perversely termed daps – but even so all the rest was there. Matching top and socks, the latter down round his ankles, plus faded blue shorts. Oh, and there was mud on his face.

Andrew Marsden in a jock strap? Fresh from the scrum? Bonded with guys he'd once, at that long-ago lunch at the Maesteg Arms, dismissed as brutes? No way could this be for real! Surely there must be an explanation.

Not that it bothered me long. It was more intoxicating to simply drink him in. Those legs, for instance. Sorry to sound like the Wife of Bath, but I'd simply never noticed how cute they were. Like one of those alabaster youths that get you going at the V & A. Muscular, but elegant and perfectly proportioned. And brown with it. Clearly he and Tim had been spending a lot of time on the lawn – in what state of déshabillé one could only (and delightfully) conjecture!

My original plan had been a taxi to the hotel, a long and boozy lunch, then some smoochy jazz up in the bedroom on Radio Lux. I'd even brought a couple of Brubeck 45s on the offchance my suite might boast some kind of player.

But what now? Tea in some Brighton café, all dimity and Victoria sponge? Was that the note I wanted to strike? Hardly, but what else is there to do in a seaside town at four in the afternoon? The pubs wouldn't open for another two hours, and Andy was hardly a guy to be thrilled by a walk on the pier!

Then just as my search for options looked like foundering, he began to stir, levering his body upright on the threadbare cushions.

"Sorry about that," he groaned. "Cock up of cock ups, but what could I do? There's nothing more unpredictable than a shoot. It ought to have been over by twelve, sod it!"

"Shoot?" I inquired blithely. True the Glorious 12th was past, but – grouse in West London?

"Yuh, I've made it into the media, sort of. A location job. Just off the Thames. Syon House mews."

"Ah," said I in Pooter mood. "If mewsic be the food of love…"

"Play on," he interposed glibly. "But Shakespeare, man, this ain't. Just Aunty Beebs. *Radio Times* publicity photos for some new serial they're planning. *The Barlowes of Beddington*. A sort of rehash of Goodbye Fish & Chips – of which I expect your generation were addicts."

"In the same way," I retorted, preferring to ignore the age gibe, "lawyers love courtroom plays, and boxers can't resist fight novels? Come off it!"

"Boxers don't read, do they?"

"Ditto most Tolvertonians. Who are also not particularly noted for their appearances in national magazines." I gave him a wry glance. "Confession time, my lad. Who was it?"

"Sorry, you've lost me."

"To get hired? Who did you have to sleep with?"

"Don't you mean whom, *sir*?" he grinned, kindling at the ravishingly subtle hint of salaciousness in my tone. "Afraid I can't remember – flocks and flocks, like the stars of heaven." Abruptly crossing over, he perched himself beside me. "Any objection?"

I was about to make the obvious query when all those resolutions of mine rang their jolly old fire alarm. With considerable effort I curbed myself and, easing slightly away, said brightly, "Joking aside though, how did you swing it?"

After which it all came out. An account of how Tim's father had seen the Harlech programme and offered him agency work – just pin money for now, but later who could say? Hopefully enough to defray a fair slice of his uni costs.

"Not that North Staff's likely to be hyper-expensive," he conceded, rotating his wrist chain as we swept through East Croydon. "But who wants to pinch and scrape?"

"No point in starving," I agreed cautiously.

"Anyhow, it's all in the air. Maybe I won't even bother."

"What, with college?"

"Well, it's hardly Oxford, is it? That would be different. But if people think I've got what it takes – that I'm photogenic – why waste my time at some provincial shit hole?"

"Oh yes? Said that, have they?"

"Not just them – Tabor too."

"Tabor? Who's he when he's at home?"

"They – happen to be a contractor, mainly for Harlech. They're considering me as anchorman on a one-off – even so it might lead to other things, and anyway the cash would help. Expenses at the very least. Consulted you on it, has he, the Rev?"

"Mr Marchpane?"

"Well, it's all to do with archaeology for schools. Apparently they wet their pants over that Weyburne clip and now they want more. I'd be a sort of David Attenborough – you know, showing off the site, interviewing the Rev, and experts like that bloke from Cardiff. I assumed they'd include you too."

I shrugged. "I expect there'll be a note waiting for me back at school. In fact, maybe back at Rhodes. In fact, maybe on my pillow?"

Raised eyebrows at the implied change of subject, together with an attitude of wariness – which, however, gradually relaxed as I ran through the summer's vicissitudes, and especially how and why I'd failed to make contact.

"So that was it," he nodded. "Just shows. I'd put it down to, whatever – pique or something? That you were fed up with my crap Malvolio or something. Playing tit for tat."

"On the contrary…"

"Still," he continued. "Who's fault was that? The miscasting, I mean. Why the hell didn't you give me Sebastian?"

"You serious? Sebastian? Compared to Malvolio he's nothing."

"Except the only real hunk in the play." He relaxed back into the seat, his hand dropping on to the tautness of his stomach.

"Maybe I didn't fit the bill? Was that it? Not attractive enough? Not sufficient allure to hook a punter like Antonio? Or anyone else for that matter?"

Well, it doesn't come more blatant than that, right? Summoning up my last reserves of restraint, I just managed to announce, "I know what we need", thereupon producing the packet of Passing Clouds with which I'd furnished myself earlier.

An appreciative nod. "Swish," he said, bringing out his lighter – more silver, clearly a lad of style – "in fact, well snazzy." And so we sped on through Three Bridges in a blue haze of uncertainty and, in my case, emphysema. This was only the third or fourth cigarette I'd ever smoked, a fact which I suspect he saw through and maybe appreciated.

My mind was, of course, already working on how to play things once we arrived. A first priority was clearly to get him into some respectable garb and have his make-up washed off. "Ben Nye is it they use now?" I queried as yet another signal box whizzed by in a green blur.

He grinned, passed a forefinger across the mud on his cheek, and presented it to my lips. An action which, in that blip of time, I can't say exactly registered as a presage of things to come, but what's that tag of Browning's? *A second and the angels alter that*! I took it into my mouth and savoured its substance – and, surprisingly, its taste.

"Chocolate spread?" I choked, almost beside myself as his nail traced my tongue. All those other flavours too. Caverns and kind of salty tar and pearl.

"As ever was," he nodded. "Camera prefers it, so they say."

And not just the camera, mon brave!

"Like some more?"

More, yes indeed, tons more – all you've got, and as soon as possible!

But as I lean over to lick his neck, I find myself pulled to my feet and stood against the door like a mummy in the Egyptian Room.

He starts to drag the seat cushions to the ground, but it's only as he shapes them into a bed that I get the idea. There's just time for one more attempt to avert disaster. "Andy, OK – shouldn't we talk this through just a...?"

Too late. He's slipped his shirt off – and as I note the rich dark red of his nips and scent his heathery man smell, I'm lost. So we career through Haywards Heath, half of me wondering if the signalman's alert enough to note this amazing thing. Two guys, shirtless, on their feet in a compartment, oblivious to the outside world. One reaching for the other's neck. His partner passive, head back and turning from side to side, as something's licked fiercely from his skin.

Mud? Blood? It'd be difficult to tell from that distance, wouldn't it? And at that speed. And with the whirl of dust and sparks from the rail!

14: *Into the Fire*

Heatwaves in England, genuine ones I mean, are so once in a lifetime they tend to bugger up – if you'll pardon the brilliance – the whole boiling! And thus, ironically, prove even more of a pain than fog or snow. Poor sods, how we struggle to cope! Unlike the continent where it's sixth sense: lower the awning, off with the togs, and pass the night cool and Emperor-clothed on the patio.

By contrast the English turn lobster red, continue to eat beef and dumplings, and assume that a knotted handherchief over the head is enough to ward off sunstroke.

Or at anyrate that's how it used to be – and indeed was in that far distant Brighton I'm recalling. And as August gave way to September, 812 West Skipton Street was, I can tell you, broiling with the best of them.

"I could put those in my fridge if you like," said my landlord, noticing a couple of milk bottles on the windowsill, placed there in a vain attempt to ward off curdling. "Shilling a week if you're interested. But none of them zlotys, mind. I've an eye like an eagle."

Jackal more like, thought I, declining his offer with an amiable wave of the hand. It was one of his rare forays into my domain with dustpan and brush, but I was in no mood to chat. Having started my exam marking, I was keen to get on with it, before wandering down to the pier to catch a breeze and read the paper. And I suppose see what talent the Saturday coaches had brought in, though these days this was little more than a routine.

"You ought to be out in the sun," sniffed Laceway, "a youngster like you. Not shut away here, working yourself to death." Adjusting his trilby, he leant on the broom. "Ever tried that bit of beach just beyond the crossover? You know," he purred confidentially, "that stretch between Volks and the sea where they're planning to let all them nancy boys take off their smalls. A right old riot that'll be and no mistake!"

I looked up from my script. "In which case, Sid, why should it interest me?"

"I was only saying…"

"Yes?"

"Keep your hair on, it's only a suggestion, like. For the moment anyway. I was just recommending it as being not so, you know, crowded. No offence."

"None taken. Especially as any crackpot scheme like that's a dead duck. This is Sussex, not St Tropez."

He nodded. "Expect you're right," he agreed, fishing in his pocket. "Family trade. Last thing we want is to frighten that away. Bite the hand that feeds us. Fancy a Polo?"

Pole instead of Polo and I might well have pricked up my ears. Or Estonian. Or Romanian. After all, which of us isn't partial to those high cheekbones and whisper waists! But as it was, I again waved him away – though I must admit I did take the trouble to extend my teatime stroll to that particular slice of shingle. After all, the council must have had some reason for selecting it for this naturist reserve of theirs.

317

Not that, as I've hinted, my interest was really anything more than desultory. Since that weird encounter on the train, I'd been experiencing what I can only describe as a kind of sexual torpor – or maybe inertia would be closer to the mark. Like nowadays with a computer when it sort of gets stuck, when the screen's on but, click and bang as you might, you can't get the bloody cursor to move an inch. So I too needed some kind of kick-start to get the gonads going again.

I mean, OK – sex to qualify as sex ought to leave you well shagged, no problem. But comatose? There are limits, and I tell you – by the time we'd reached Brighton that day, I'd been virtually a stretcher case, in dire need of oxygen, adrenalin, you name it! Tongue out, bereft of reason, my brain a whirl of innuendo – and all tinged with a species of instant nostalgia. The conviction that what I'd just experienced would prove a unique one-off.

Sans doubt!

That never again would it be our lot to scale such peaks, not on the Trans-Siberian, not on the Sunday stopper to Fort William, not nowhere!

But it was more than that. Somehow that mind-blowing rush had apparently satisfied something in me that wouldn't need satisfying again for yonks, if ever. Or, as the Yankees say, 'Been there, Done that'. I mean, an Englishman simply doesn't make love on the floor of a 3rd class carriage, right? In bed with his cocoa cooling – that's close enough to Eros for the bulldog breed.

What I thought I needed for the foreseeable future was a nice sedate slug of English blandness. Immersion, as it were, in the world of *Brief Encounter* where raw piratical devilment consists of drinking three pennorth of brandy outside opening hours!

Right, well, that's my story anyhow, make of it what you will. And if it seems to smack of camouflage, tough luck. All I told myself I knew was that whilst Jugs would have revelled in sex on the Southern, and its memory, Alex would not. So wasn't it obvious which camp was my real home, even if I couldn't, with any certainty, fathom why?

Which feelings were now compounded as I strolled over the rusty rails and towards the sprinkling of bodies spread out towards the sea. Bodies, of course still clad, albeit skimpily – it would be some years yet before the area became a German paradise!

I had, of course, taken the precaution of donning a bathing slip under my jeans just in case spotting Alvi or similar did the job and kicked my Puritanism into reverse – but no such luck. Most of the punters were old and evidently carved out of shoe leather, whilst the few under pension age were in pairs. Not that that stopped them eyeing me up in that ghastly predatory way confirmed queers have. As if like vampires they're intent on making you one of them.

OK, so technically speaking I was signed up already – but no way was I going hang a label round my neck. No way join the vacuum. Surely life held more promise than that. Resolving to have myself castrated at the earliest opportunity – could it, I wondered, be done on the NHS? – I looked around for the easiest retreat.

It was then I noticed him.

Reynolds!

Of all people, the dreaded Reynolds, and not in the mode one might have expected. Not feral, leg to leg with his latest prey, or glued to binoculars directed at number next. But alone, inert, hunched with his thermos in an empty patch right by the breakwater, a rather forlorn sight despite designer shorts and Sitges shoulder bag. Indeed, pathetic.

For a second, just a second, I paused. Something inside me glowed, a kind of affinity. Compassion almost for a fellow human gaffed on the same spike of queer desire, destined for the same solitary limbo as myself. Would it be so very difficult to squat down, say a word, make contact?

But no, this was Reynolds! Natural foe like Russians and black widow whatnots – and despite appearances, in all probability as alert as a pike and twice as dangerous. His sort, well it's common knowledge – they take any attempt to be kind or matey as a sign of weakness. Bugger him, and bugger all like him!

Self-preservation thus asserting itself, I was able to back away to the pier without his noticing me, and to console myself instead with a disgusting knickerbocker glory downstairs in Scantorini's. The same ice-cream we'd chosen at the station by coincidence. Andy and I, that is. After our marathon. Desperate to close the glucose gap!

Scooping up the cherry, I was reminded how we'd meticulously divided it between us that day, and the pert look the waitress had given us when we asked for two spoons. And how we'd lounged on the sand till dusk. And shared pizza. And tried to delude ourselves that there wasn't a mere twenty minutes left till the last train back...

Still, what's the point in mulling over stuff? It only becomes a yawn, like *Casablanca* on the 20th viewing. Or the 50th anyway! Best to bin it, look to the future, pretend there's a point to life.

I'd not heard from Andy since, nor did I expect to. Soon he'd be doing his Claribel at Keele, three leagues beyond man's life. And it wasn't only a question of distance. There he'd find guys of his own age to experiment with. Which is what a lad needs, aren't we told? Not someone like yours truly with all his ways and prejudices and hang-ups fully toasted and past revision.

Although, stirring my glass, I couldn't suppress a further chuckle. What on earth had the B.R. staff thought when they found the cushions spread on the floor like that? Or when they noticed the pristine and sparkling cleanliness of the mirror below the luggage rack? Not surprising since we'd had to wipe its grimy glass clean of about half a pint of a certain young scholar's – shall we say – vitality?

So for a while I enjoyed my ice cream and recollections – well, selected ones anyhow - before seeking solace with Dean Martin & Jerry Lewis in the local fleapit.

On my return I was surprised to find two letters propped against my door, their forwarding address in my mother's unmistakable Godolphin & Latymer hand. Even in those days there was no four o' clock post on a Saturday so I surmised Laceway had yet again been negligent over clearing the box. Lazy bastard, I said to myself, brandishing my penknife.

Neither proved the kind of harbinger I needed. The first was from James reminding me that I'd agreed to go over to Hallatrow for his birthday weekend. Great fun, I thought. To be half-drowned in the family swimming pool with mumsie and dad looking on adoringly at their big strong son! Some way or other I'd have to get out of that, though how, for the moment, eluded me.

The other was also an invitation though this time formal, an ivory oblong with gilt edges, its RSVP in extra bold and underlined. You know the sort of job. Mr & Mrs Parish Hunn At Home, 6pm, Wednesday September etc. etc… Not in itself unwelcome – free booze, free blinis – though what it signalled might give cause for concern. Clearly the new broom was going to sweep clean from the start. No putting up with Eric's time-honoured entertainment pattern – the Hunn must do it his way! What other customs, I wondered, were destined to fall beneath the flail?

That the new order might well – indeed almost certainly would – prove beneficial to myself hardly seemed to matter as I sat there on Laceway's old sofa ruminating. Of much more moment was the prospect of returning to Tolverton. Back to Murdoch, back to the mindless classroom banter, and above all back to the feuds with the pseuds, Marcho, Carver, Trewes – and this time without Andy there in the background as an earnest of any kind of respite.

Could I face it? No way, said my soul. No alternative, said my bank balance!

A division of opinion which remained largely unresolved during my last few days at Brighton, especially given the bore of packing and the excitement of exchanging my Seaview cheque for the neatest little Austin – its original grey resprayed bright yellow, the exact shade of school custard, with a black hood and flash wheel hubs. With less than 30,000 on the clock you could almost call her new, and, driving into Tolverton a couple of days before term, it felt like a virgin era was unfolding before my avid eyes. Sure there were problems to fix, especially that of Marcho, but now things were different. Any time life got too much, away I could speed and – farewell all my cares and woe!

OK, they'd still be there when I got back, but that's no obstacle to bother about when you're twenty three, your shades cool, your shirt unbuttoned, and who knows what on the horizon!

By contrast with the previous year, Common Room turned out to be almost empty, the younger members, I presumed, taking advantage of this rare Welsh sunshine to say goodbye to the old pool. Only Ormulak and Murdoch were in evidence, the former busy with bell strap and glue, the latter on his feet by the fireplace peering closely at yesterday's Argus.

His concessions to the weather? As you might imagine, disastrous. A string vest through the mesh of which wound chest hair as dense and matted as creeper. The usual khaki shorts, so baggy they could have accommodated two of him, and which had clearly not been pressed since El Alamein. And open-weave sandals which revealed toenails gone absolutely jungle, I jest not. Rims a shitty black and green.

Still, his greeting was amiable enough. "So ye've made it," he said. "Better late than nivver. I want a word with you in ma den."

"Anything interesting?" I queried looking over his shoulder.

"Ma wee surprise or the paper?"

"Well, either I suppose," I retorted stepping back a bit. "Sorry to snoop. It's just – that photo looked a bit familiar."

"Familiar?" His snort was contemptuous. "A travesty, no less. In ma book a complete travesty. Read it for yoursel' The termite should be strung up! Wilna be a minute." Thrusting the broadsheet into my hand, he picked up a Gestetner skin, turned on his heel and marched into the workroom.

I'd not been mistaken. The photo was indeed a familiar face, none other than, however improbable it may seem, the Reverend Beresford Dick-Whyte-Dick on the occasion of his induction as vicar of Llanammerty with Wishbrook and Stoke Mytton. Even more improbable was the sight of Roy Marchpane in the cluster of diocesan clergy lurking in the background, teacup in hand and smiling broadly.

"Well, blow me down!" I expostulated. "Have you seen this?"

Ormulak looked up from his repair. "So?" he shrugged. "The transgressor is to be forgiven. Is not in accordance with the Christian ethic?"

"In a sense – but I mean, look. Marcho all smiles and pally at the bunfight."

"Yes, yes, but some link there was, remember? His aunt. Hadn't Roy met her in Africa?"

"Search me. Though come to think of it, yes, she was mentioned."

"And admired, yes?"

"Perhaps."

"Then would not such an invitation be entirely natural?"

"No way!" I retorted firmly, uneasy at being driven into a corner like this. "On the contrary, I'd call it highly unnatural. For Chrissake, Leon – Dickhead? It was Marcho who shopped him to the Head."

"My boy, keep your voice down!" Somewhat flustered, Ormulak rose from his chair with a warning gesture.

"But why? If the cap fits, wear it – I mean, let it be worn."

"This a public place is, not private."

"So? What's there to be secretive about?"

"Only this. That you have no evidence the culprit was Roy, am I correct? Not a shred. Wherever did they come from, such ideas? You were there in the vestry. You were with him."

"But not all evening long. Maybe he changed his mind. How else did it all get to Eric?" Confused images were by now popping out at me from the rubble of the past: of midnight phone calls, dark stairs, shadows melting into vacuity.

"Take my word. Marcho knew the Headmaster and his ways like – how does your phrase go? Like the back of the hand. Never would he have endangered James Frobisher like that. Never in a month of Mondays."

"OK," I retorted, smiling. "Then if not Marcho, who?"

To this there was no reply – just hesitation, then a slow shift of his eyes to the workroom arch from which could be heard the faint clank of a Gestetner.

I followed his glance, but it was several seconds before I could put two and two together.

"You serious?" I frowned, turning back. "Get away! What possible motive could he have?"

"Morality? Vanity? Does it matter?" The little fat finger rapped the table. "Both are lethal, to victim and perpetrator alike."

"But Murdoch – are you sure about this? Totally sure?"

"Not totally but, as your judges say, beyond the reason of doubt. You see, after Guests' Tea the party went on in here for a while. Half a dozen or so of our colleagues. And not just tea, you understand."

"Podbrodek Podbrodka?"

"Just so," he nodded with pleasure. "And thus one thing led to another, fomented by that Carver and his acolyte."

"Tiny, you mean?"

"The pathetic Tiny. It was all their poisonous stab-in-the-back chatter until the subject changed. To that of their friend."

"Frobisher?"

"At which point it got worse."

"Sounds about right!"

"Never shall I forget Murdoch's glee as he recounted how he himself, sprung from nothing, had been instrumental in trampling such illustriousness in the dust. I didn't catch all, but enough. Sufficient to be convinced."

"Well," I mused, "that fits. That certainly fits. For Chrissake – mankind! Civilisation! It's all a delusion, isn't it? The whole bloody pack of cards. Change places and handy dandy!"

"Handy the…?"

"Just Shakespeare. Which is the justice, which the thief?"

"Ah so!"

"Where's it all gone, I wonder – certainty and quiet kind? The sort of thing your yaffles enjoy. Not that their solution's much cop. Not for a mere human anyway. One can hardly chill out in a blasted oak, up the bloody branches!"

"No, but all creatures have their haven. Even mere humans."

"For example?"

"The cloister, obviously. But also the stage, the lighthouse…"

"Great!" With a grin, I leant back against the table. "For all of which I am so eminently and overwhelmingly qualified?"

At which a finger touched my arm and I think he replied – though I can't be certain, so soft was his voice – I think his words were, "Don't distress yourself. Time may make you so."

Or come to think of it – did he say 'will' make? For that matter, did he say 'crime'?

Either way, the irony still bewilders me all these years after, though then there was no time to ponder or query. Neither of us had noticed the Gestetner stop, and suddenly here he was, Murdoch, standing next to me, his arms full of quarto in serried piles. "Help me carry these back, laddie," he commanded. "Then you and mysel' must get doon to brass tacks? Ye'll never guess it, the most extraordinary news since… "

"North, East, West, South," cried Watson striding in from the lobby, a cross-looking Baxter in tow, "all a shocking waste of time. Ah, Owen. Just the man! My office, if you please. These house fixtures won't wait a minute longer. Oh and Bryant – the Head's party this evening – could you kindly give the office a yea or nay?

They're waiting on numbers. RSVP? Remind me to translate it for you sometime. All that Oxford training! Come along, gentlemen. Fixtures, fixtures!"

Oxford training! Some help that is in life! OK, so I know the etymology of minx, how many cls there are in Marvell, and that *Wuthering Heights* was first published by Mills & Boon – apologies, wishful thinking! – but as to anything important? Forget it!

Like now, for instance. Clearly I've made a bloody fool of myself, jumping to conclusions like that about Marcho. After which admission, all begins to topple like a row of dominoes. That stupid row over rehearsals, for instance. What was that he'd called me? A giddy goat? Well, how appropriate. How absolutely spot on. A bull in a china shop, that was me. That was how I'd been acting all year. God, how callow I must have seemed to the men I worked with. Like a puppy bounding about, knocking vases over, getting its paws mucky, in short a right old pain up the proverbial! Mr Magoo to the life!

Nothing like remorse for putting its oar in, is there?

So, OK, analysis accepted. Regret, regret, regret! But what the hell does one do about it? How does one put things right? A fat lot of help Dominus Illuminatio is when it comes to those kinds of practicality. The truth is, that shouting match of ours had been pretty no-holds-barred. Is it really possible to rebuild bridges after such acridity?

Thoughts of which nature bugged me right through unpacking, and the sandwich lunch which I took at Trefoil Bridge, perched on the back seat of my saloon, throwing spam at the terns. What I needed was exit, but with dignity on both sides. Some kind of strategy which would mollify Roy but not involve me in too much loss of face. The sort of thing that must be rife in Trollope or the divine Jane, or the continentals. Proust, if only I'd read him, or Pushkin.

How our pigeons come home to roost! After an hour of this, my task not made easier by the sight of a couple in the grass getting on with life in the simple way only straights can do, I gave up. All I knew was that Paulo and the March must make contact as soon as possible. Maybe the words would come, maybe they wouldn't. But no way could I go on like this. At least if I got face to face with him, there was a chance he'd sense something. See contrition in my eyes or stuff.

Wild hopes, wild thrashings about in neverneverland, but at least they kept my mind busy through the lanes to the ring road, and thence Buggleskkely.

Still hot, still airless, it was one of those heavy afternoons, so silent that what scraps of noise there were seemed counterpoint to the overriding serenity of nature. There was the odd bark, the odd bird, but closer and sweeter, on the other side of Roy's wall, the sporadic whirr of a handmower.

Switching off the engine, I sat there listening. And envisaging. Though I'd never seen it, I could just imagine the long peerless sweep of the lawn, with the March bent studiously over his Qualcast, ensuring that the stripes were parallel to within a thousandth of an inch.

Sod off – no way will I translate that into metric!

As I was saying, I could just imagine it all, the emerald gleam, the chiselled borders, Clemmy knitting benignly, their dog at her feet. Pure A.G.Street!

I was just about to dash over to this paradise and trust to luck I wouldn't be unceremoniously thrown out when – bazooka! The whole image shattered, like a mirror dropped or a stone in the pond.

For, indeed, the mower once more struck up – but simultaneously out from the gates began to back that venerable Rover of theirs, Roy at the wheel and the boot pointing my way. With a grind of gears and flurry of smoke, the old warrior lurched forward a few feet, before coming to rest opposite the telephone kiosk, its motor still running.

All of this watched keenly in the mirror, of course, by yours truly!

What next?

Only, I suppose, what any student of 5th century Church history might expect. Gingerly, the ancient saloon began to back until it was parallel to mine, a few feet away on the opposite side of the road. Its driver stared straight ahead for a few seconds before winding down his window.

I did likewise.

Another few seconds and, very slowly, he screwed himself round in his seat, gazed my way – and smiled. Tentatively, but smiled!

I did likewise.

Then, as though enacting a ritual, both of us alighted in slow motion, pacing to the centre of the road where, for a moment, we regarded each other in silence. It was well weird, I can tell you – and exactly what it must have been like for Leo the 1st and Attila, though I daresay neither of them sported a cigarette holder with a glowing Sobranie.

Then upsadaisy – reserve burst, and we were laughing, shaking hands, pawing each other like two prep school boys after the Xmas hols. Nothing all that coherent, until at last I managed to blurt out: "So how did you spot it was me?"

"Mirror mirror on the wall..."

"Even so."

"A car that colour?"

"Watch it!"

"My dear, who else would drive round in a dribble of Monk & Glass?"

So great minds really do think alike! I conceded inwardly, before remembering Ormulak too and, in a wild Bryant moment, wondering if the Gods actually can intervene. But I pulled myself together. "Beware," I quoth. "You're talking of the woman I love!"

"Then get her a respray, my boy, get her a respray!"

We both laughed, then a brief silence before I put on a kind of sigh and looked down at my toes. "Look, Roy, about you know – that awful day…"

"Expunged, believe me, to the last tittle!"

"Yuh, but…"

"And beyond!"

"But some of that stuff I said…"

"That we both said, and neither meant – agreed?"

"Well, of course. But, surely, isn't all this too easy?"

"What," he twinkled, "would you prefer? Bullwhips at dawn? Or shall we both write out 'Sorry for being a daft ha'porth' five thousand times? That'd be a terrible waste of biro, you know."

"Sure. Like this whole summer's been a terrible waste. Of time, I mean."

"Then why not put it behind us? End of chapter one. Roll on chapter three."

I could feel a lump in my throat. "Has anyone ever told you," I muttered, "that you're the most preposterous guy in the universe?"

"Many times, in many places."

"And the most…"

"Exasperating? That too."

"Which isn't," I retorted forcing them back, "what I meant at all, not…"

"Quoting again," he grinned, clutching my shoulder. "Now who's being preposterous?"

I gave a shrug and rather damp blink. "Saves thinking I suppose."

"Really? I must give it a try."

Searching desperately for words which won't come, I have to accept defeat as a baker's van turns in from the main road. "So, like, where do we go from here?" I ask lamely.

"Oh, he replies, consulting his watch, "tea, don't you think? A little early but under the circumstances… And you never know, if we can tear Clemmie away from the shrubberies, there might even be scones."

And now with all the stateliness of a masque we return to our cars, stash them away in a drive overrun with hollyhocks, and enter the back kitchen, stamping the muck from our shoes. I've had plenty of time to think: to bless the Fates for this reconciliation and to find some kind of pedestal on which once more to stand my Marcho. Yet still there's the thought of all that pilfering. OK, he's urbane, kind and amusing. OK, he had nothing to do with the James affair. OK, he's untainted with the narrowness of soul which infects so many of my other colleagues. But still I can't quite get out of my mind, that reservation. Not quite as disturbing as Swift's over Stella and her bowels, but nevertheless pertinacious.

He steals!

Or purloins, if you want to make it sound more middle class.

Anyhow, as we pass through the lounge he's chattering on about Sunday, the first of the academic year when by tradition the sermon is delivered by the School Captain, but I don't pay much attention. I've only been here a couple of times before and there are so many photos and pictures for my mind to feast on, and books in huddles, that somehow words take a back seat.

By now Clem's busy in the front kitchen. Funny how wives have a sixth-sense when something's brewing, and I wonder if I'll ever be blessed with a partner like this. Acumenical, as one might say. She waves a greeting, and passes a tray to Marcho. "In or out?" she says.

"On a day like this? Out, and let the wasps do their worst! What do you say, Paul?"

"I'm game if you are." My previous visits have been in the winter and I'm curious to see this lawn of his, reputed to be the longest in the village.

Clem nods. "South or snug?" she inquires.

"Oh," replies her mate, eyeing me a bit quizzically as though not quite sure whether to lend me sixpence, "why not the snug? Indeed, why not? The sun's quite fierce and there's more shade there."

Again she nods, this time with a kittenish laugh. "You are honoured," she says, handing me some pots on a salver. "Will you bring the jam? One of them's greengage. I hope you don't mind."

After which (no possible reply occurring to me!) we proceed out into a small courtyard, myself in the rear, and thence on to the lawn. Which, by the bye, fully deserves its reputation, measuring twice the length of a croquet pitch and then some. By a sundial at the near end there's a table and a pile of canvas chairs, but we pass by, heading for a gap in the wall a little along on the right. A gap which proves to be guarded by a door, a very old door askew on its hinges, which Marcho is about to nudge open for Clementine to pass through.

When he pauses. Turns back, and regards me with a curious look, the like of which I can't remember seeing before. Difficult to describe but well lacking in his usual panache. Then he glances at the sky and says, "You know, I think we'll stay here. It's not as bright as it was. Paul, can you give a hand? The deckchairs there."

And so, still wondering about this sudden volte face, I start my struggle with wood and stripes, while Marcho unfolds the tablecloth.

Why the change of plan? What mysteries lie behind that bleached oak? A plantation of cannabis? A pet alligator? Nothing would surprise me, but why had he proposed going there in the first place?

"Butter or cream?" inquires Mrs March looking up from her tray.

"Beg pardon?" I gulp, my mind still running over what possible raund O of delights – thanks a million, Lord Foppington! – I was being denied.

"Your scone, my dear. Do you prefer butter or cream?"

I was still not quite myself a couple of hours later as I entered a very different kind of garden, its tables laden with a very different kind of fare. No jam here, no homely daisy cakes, but food to impress. Shrimps in aspic, patés varieux, a vast tongue folded and sliced, quiches, cooked birds in unnumbered flocks...

And people to be impressed. Not just, as I'd supposed, we Common Room hacks, here to do obeisance, but the cream of the county too. Though I wonder, on reflection, how dissimilar its own errand was! Carey, for instance, buttering up Frank Mostyn. Or Sir Madison, still alive though in a wheelchair, earnestly lecturing his successor, a sallow girl in blue perched on a stool beside him, showing, in my opinion, rather too much of a rather indifferent knee.

Remind me, by the way, to tell you about that by-election sometime. It certainly warrants a book in its own right!

Fustians, of course, abounded as did members of the third estate, plus Mayor and, this time round, Lord Lieutenant as well as his deputy. Plus the hunting crew, the Masonic crew, the Rotarians to a man – you know the sort of thing. The big trawl!

And, of course, presided over by Mr Parish Hunn and spouse – the latter in St John's Ambulance uniform esconced with Mrs Jarrow and Irish, doubtless discussing blisters - the former sidling from group to group, making a quip and moving on.

Yet another deviation, you'll appreciate, from Eric's time. At the Amberley soirées, the world came to him, not vice versa!

Oh, well. Plus ca change, I warned myself. What good does bemoaning the new order do, except turn one into a Pantaloon, and that's an image to be deferred as long as possible. Besides, there happened to be at least one innovation of which I could heartily approve. No longer were members of Common Room cast as waiters. That function had now devolved upon members of the 6th form – and indeed, as I soon found out, the few hopefuls of the U6th.

"Riesling, sir?" offered Jukes. "It's pretty dire!"

"Don't we look smart," I retorted, and so he did, clad, like his fellows, in black waistcoat and one of those long white aprons worn in the best bistros. "Pay you for this, do they?"

"Peanuts," he said cheerfully, "but we get the leftovers."

"Amazing, I'll have to apply at once!"

"Sorry, too old. You need stamina for this job."

"In which case," I grinned reaching for a glass, "I'd better start stoking up."

But he jerked his tray away. "Don't bother with this muck," he said, nodding towards the conservatory. "Over there – champagne on ice, reserved for the Fustians. But don't worry. The guy serving is Turnbull. He quite likes you."

"Glad somebody does," I retorted half-playfully, starting to thread my way towards the manna, but finding myself waylaid first by Miss Frame, desirous of altering our bathroom rota, then by Ormulak with a new protégé (potential yaffler?) in tow – one Jason Thornby, hired, apparently, as an assistant to the ailing Ken Tarn. After ten minutes I'd hardly covered half the distance when I was again arrested by a tap on the shoulder.

This time Igor, smiling his rictoid smile, and proffering me a glass of the nasty. "Without a drink at this time of the evening?" he said. "Really Mr Bryant, I seem to have misjudged you,"

"Oh, that's good of you, Head. Cheers!"

"Tell me what you think. It's a Riesling, from my own vines near Passau."

"Really?" – hoping to sound impressed. Which I suppose I was in a way. After all, how many academics, even pseud ones, can afford to run huge vineyards in Bavaria? It was only later I found out that his holding amounted to one row in a co-operative, and had resulted from a special offer in the Sunday Times! "Yuh," I said. "Yuh, most refreshing. I like that touch of, er - greengage on the palate."

"Exactly," he nodded vigorously. "Exactly right. Greengage. Not many people would have spotted that. I can see your discernment extends into many fields."

Which left me somewhat flummoxed. Young as I was, I had no illusions about the Igors of this world. Honeyed words means they're after something. Sans doubt! Fortunately he didn't seem to expect a response. "Talking of which," he continued, "expect a summons from me in the near future. Nothing to fret about, just a proposal I have in mind. All plain sailing, in, er – how shall I put it? More ways than one! But first I need to have a word with – what's that chap's name?"

"Trewes?" I ventured, hardly daring to hope this was happening.

"Just so – Leyland Trewes," he smiled, as if to indicate: we understand one another only too well, you and I.

Then he was off, buzzing round other nectar, some banker by the look of his suit, though which I couldn't tell as he had his back to me. Nor did I give a toss, being already brimful with this new turn of events. So it hadn't been an empty promise after all. Head of Drama, wow! Or would it be Director? And all the concomitant goodies. Vast new auditorium with revolving stage and professional lights. Vast new productions, Rogers & Hammerstein, Oh What A Lovely War with real trenches, Sinbad the Sailor! Plus the ancillary stuff. Reviews in the T.E.S., foreign tours, invitations to Stratford as guest producer, OBE, OM – for about two minutes the whole future of English theatre seemed to bask in my hands.

Emptying my glass on to an apprehensive camellia, I turned back towards the conservatory. A future as dazzling as this certainly warranted a stoup of bubbly, didn't it?

Except – always, always! What they give with one hand, they take away with the other. Learn that about the Gods and you might just avoid doing a Dicky Carstone!

Suddenly it collapsed. The whole thing. Not just my stage dream, but my entire future. Every blasted day from henceforth to the grave. One moment I was sailing across the lawn, tomorrow's man heading for sunrise – a minute later I'd been wrecked on the threshold, next stop crucifixion, dead and buried. Good as.

Think I'm exaggerating? Fine, understandable, but take a look through my eyes. What do you see behind the trestle? An amiable boffin with acne, all cringy and servile, bottle at the ready?

No way. It's a horse of a very different colour, isn't it? Red for danger? Deadly nightshade?

"Hi, Paul," it says blithely.

"Good God almighty!"

"Why look so surprised?"

"But, how on earth – I mean, I was expecting Turnbull, not..."

"Andy Pandy, pudding and pie? Sorry about that – Kim's just coping with a call of nature..."

"Bugger Turnbull!"

"Not my type, thanks very much. Like some fizz?"

"But I gathered... I was told all you waiters were Upper Sixth."

"Right."

"No, no. I mean present not ex."

"Right."

"Including you?"

"Hadn't you heard?"

"Heard what?"

"Oh nothing much – only that a certain young mastermind's been invited back to try Oxbridge."

"Then this is appalling," I whisper. "Absolutely appalling. Look, it just can't happen. We've got to talk."

"OK, midnight do? I'll bring the vino."

"You'll do no such thing. Now understand this..."

"Come along, come along," cried Watson, shepherding Colonel and Mrs Featherland through the French window. "I'll drink every drop there is, is, is, eh Colonel? Tommy Trinder – remember him?" Suddenly noticing my presence, he wagged a finger in mock severity. "What's this, Bryant, what's this? Not a Fustian yet, you know. Though from what I hear, it won't be long! One of our bright young men, Colonel. Carries all before him. Let me introduce you. Paul Bryant – young man going places.

"Nonsense," barked Mrs Featherland, regarding me with intense disdain through a pair of exquisite Regency lorgnettes. "What races? Ludlow's over and there's no point to point till Anzac Day."

Despite my discomposure, it was impossible to hold back a tense grin of comedie noire as Chris and the Colonel tried simultaneously to explain matters – especially as behind them, behind the ice tubs, behind the trays of glass, I could see, also joining in the joke, a spectre in the shape of Nemesis.

Or rather her male counterpart. Her profoundly male counterpart, profoundly elegant in his apron and black waistcoat and bold profile,like he'd just stepped out of some doom movie by Renoir, with not the slightest intention of divulging his purpose.

Nor the slightest intention of stepping back.

15: *Plaisir d' Amour*

Does worry go to your guts too? Actually, bladder to be more precise. Or do I mean prostate?

All night long rest eluded me. It was up and down, up and down, and since the route to the bathroom I shared with Miss Frame was now fraught with danger – to wit, its proximity to a certain young gentleman's eyrie – it became a question of desperate remedies. Namely peeing into one's washbasin! What else could I do? The risk of meeting him on the landing was simply too great. Especially as my imagination was playing its usual games á temps du stress. Visions, no less, of the Marsden lair. Of his having fixed up some kind of laser to warn himself of my approach. Of his springing out at me, clad only in a loincloth or a bead jockstrap or a lascivious sou' wester. And – to cap it all – of Murdoch descending suddenly on a halter from the heavens, armed with a brace of submachine guns and trident!

All of which proved needless angst, at least as far as the old termagent was concerned, and at least for the time being. Indeed, when I finally stumbled forth around eleven the next morning, I found him in an unusually accommodating mood.

"It was only on Tuesday I found oot mysel'," he explained apologetically. "At Hoosemasters, ye ken, when they get round to Oxbridge. Before that I'd suspectit nothing."

"So, Marsden's candidacy. Whose idea was it, if you don't mind my asking!"

"Calm yoursel', laddie. Whose would it be but the new Head's?"

"But those grades! I mean, he's well above average, but moneywise he'd need a scholarship – and how likely is that?"

"Dinna forget this TV offer he's expecting."

"Programmes for schools?" I retorted scornfully. "Big deal!"

"Mebbe, but in all probability a damn sight bigger deal than any other hopeful can boast of. Stands to reason, ma friend. It's bound to raise the laddie's profile."

Profile? Thanks a bundle for rubbing that in! And the rest, those shoulders, those legs, the slenderness of that waist! But I tug myself back from disaster.

"OK, OK," I conceded. "So it's a fait accompli! He's coming back for a term, to take an exam he'll fail. Right, accepted! But why the hell give him a room on the private side?"

"School policy; dinna blame me. It's in the prospectus, ye ken. All Seventh term men have to be provided with their own bedrooms, of which, on the boys' side, as ye're dootless aware, Rhodes has a grand total of exactly two. And both already allocated. Hence the old nursery. But I dinna understand the fuss. He'll shower with the other lads. There'll be no inconvenience to yoursel' or Miss Frame. What's this all aboot, Paul?"

And that was that. I could hardly explain, now could I? Just imagine it: 'Look, Owen – let me put this to you man to man. See, not expecting this guy to come back, I sort of started having illegal sex with him. So it might be a teeny-weeny bit embarrassing if one day, en route for my midnight dump, I meet him on the landing, OK? As it were, naked. Me, that is, not him. Or him. Or both of us. Sort of.'

Of course, in an ideal world my boss would lean back thoughtfully and suggest, "Well, couldna you wear a sporran, laddie?" But this is Tolverton where, as far as mores go, we're barely past the old Queen's Jubilee. No words exist which could possibly convey to this self-satisfied Pict one tenth of the maelstrom in my head. The contest between fear and desire – and, perversely, something bordering on a hope of being found out, so at least there'd be an end to suspense.

"Paul?"

Brought back to reality, what option was there but to submit gracefully. "Oh, nothing really," I shrugged. "Just the usual. Bryant making a mountain out of a molehill, I suppose. Don't mind me."

"That's the spirit. Start of term's stressful enough as it is withoot complications. Now here's all the bumph: dorm lists; study lists; rota for hoose prayers; rota for jankers, supervision of. Peruse them at leisure. Ye'll be at new boys' tea this afternoon, I tek it?" My nod sufficing, he continued happily, "Then that just aboot wraps it up. Oh, except for one slight change to routine. Verra minor. Nothing for you to get worrit aboot."

Here it comes, I thought – calamity in sheep's clothing!

"It's just that Marsden's room is a tad far from the boys' landing, ye ken. The morning bell might not carry."

"So?"

"So ye'll have to put your head round his door and give him a wee ring of his own."

"Round his door? Really, Owen – is that necessary?"

"Miss Frame's only a step away, remember? We dinna want the good lady scared oot of her wits."

Wits and nits, I thought, as I wandered off down town – what pests matrons are! Besides which, that morning handbell duty was one I particularly loathed. The top landing, for instance – absolutely pure Dotheboys Hall. Stifling in summer, tomblike in winter, and you had to stand there ringing this bloody contraption while assorted waifs crept past you, pale and twitching, on their way to the bogs. And now there was to be yet more mortification. A wee ring for Andy! Christ Almighty – I'd be lucky if I escaped without having a cricket stump flung at me.

Nor did I have any opportunity to warn him. Hunn had arranged for all the Oxbridge candidates to spend this Thursday visiting their respective colleges and, given the distances involved, it was well late before I heard his return. About half twelve it must have been. I remember switching off at the start of 'Sailing By' and reaching for the new Margery Allingham. A few minutes later and there was that light unmistakable tread in the corridor, approaching softly – and halting, for God's sake, right outside my door!

I sat bolt upright, my heart banging. That crack of his about wine at midnight – surely he'd have more sense. He knew perfectly well that Murdoch's boudoir lay dead underneath, and that the old man was a notoriously light sleeper.

A second or two passed. No sound. My panic grew! Ought I to switch off the lamp? Would that make him less or more likely to leave me be? And anyhow, wouldn't it be playing right into his hands?

I'd already decided the only way to survive the next few weeks was to pretend that all was normal. That nothing untoward had ever happened. For one imperative stood out above everything – no encore! Whatever the provocation, there must be no repeat performance!

Should one's indiscretion, one's bonk on the Brighton line, ever come to light, matters so far might elicit some measure of sympathy from a jury – to fall from grace again, knowing full well that the lad was a current member of one's school, would warrant absolutely zero mercy. I must be firm, I must be masterful. And what could possibly be more out of keeping with such a policy than for yours truly to start acting like a petrified nun?

Normality, that was the menu. Keep up a front. Act ultra bland and boring. Now what does a normal boring youngster do at half past midnight if he's not asleep? Well, apart from you-know-what! Exactly – phone up his buddies!

I reached for the receiver and dialled the speaking clock. "Hi, Toby," I intoned slightly louder than usual. "How's tricks? Oh right – tomorrow? Poor sod. Better not keep you then. I just wanted to say, I'll be down your way at the weekend. No, Trinity actually. But still we could meet up somewhere. Banbury, maybe, or…"

Softly I replaced the receiver. At the mention of Oxford, footsteps had started to recede, and now I heard the sound of his door.

Even so I lay there alert, my pulse still racing, possibilities fighting each other in my brain. What if I hadn't had my bright idea? Would we even now be under my blankets locked in a porno embrace? Trying to make no noise? Pretending that just on the other side of that wall there weren't half a dozen prefects, ears clamped to the plaster – that twenty feet below there wasn't the most merciless gnome in Christendom, ear trumpet aimed at the ceiling?

Frankly such a prospect, or anything like it, was enough to scare me shitless, and I immediately sank into the kind of fretful slumber which promises to bugger up not just tomorrow, but the next fortnight solid!

What, however, had not occurred to me that night was yet another dilemma, approximately no. 55, 618 on the Bryant menu: just as well or I'd have got no sleep at all! Anyhow, first light changed all that. Having crawled out of bed and shaved, I was just about to don my usual jimjams and bathrobe when it dawned on me. Quelle problem! Whom should I bell first, the boys or the bane? I could hardly do them simultaneously, so which way round? And how the hell did one decide?

Without any idea how I resolved things, I found myself outside the nursery door at 7.12 precisely. Pushing it open, I wasn't a bit surprised to find him already awake, lain back on his pillows, a cup of tea by his side. And biscuits.

"Top o' the morning – I'm instructit to give you a wee ring," quoth I in my best Aberdeen. Placing my fingers round the clapper, I waved the bell madly up and down.

He smiled – one of those weary pre-breakfast smiles – and patted the bed beside him. OK, so I ought to have pulled up a chair instead, but which of us can think straight at 7.12 and 34 seconds?

"Like a sip?"

Well, where was the harm in that? Thick and sweet, the way boys like it, the brew began to get my brain going. "Very refreshing – Lapsang presumably?" I volunteered, surrendering the cup and looking round me. Nothing much had been changed to prepare the place for its new exalted role. Still the Disney wallpaper, still the toys stacked in one corner, still the Baby Belling next to the sink, its red light winking. Only the sleeping arrangements were new. Instead of the cots, a bed which – typical of the parsimonious Murdoch – was not quite double, not quite single. Or, you could say it was – safe!

He nodded.

"At least they've made you comfortable."

He nodded.

"So," I ventured after a pause, "how did it go yesterday? My own first visit to Oxford, it rained all morning."

"Afternoon as well?"

"Not as I remember."

"Lucky you."

Well uncanny this feeling, that, every time we met, roles suddenly reversed themselves: he the master, I the boy! I tried again. "Any decisions then?"

"Who knows?" he yawned, brushing the counterpane further down, and stroking his chest. "Much of a muchness, those colleges.

Though there was one I quite liked. Cute chapel and cloisters. And this amazing statue in copper. Some king or other. Saxon, I think."

"Oh yes?" I retorted, unsure whether to be flattered or disturbed.

"Nice easy-going place. Apparently most of its students get fourths!"

"Ah, the Oxford mark of genius," I said starting to rise. "What a pity you're not quite in that league!"

But, swift as a mongoose, he caught my wrist and forced me back. A formidable grip, well exhilarating, and for a moment we paused there in stasis, me wishing I'd spent more time in the gym, he – well, one can only conjecture. But from the expression on his face I'd call it exulting. Relishing the confidence of his toyboy body, its burnish and contours shown off to maximum advantage against the stark-white and patched bed linen, its sheer ascendancy.

And it was of course him who broke the ice. "Listen, when's it to be? No prevarication, OK! When are we going to meet?"

"Meet? What do you call this?"

"You know what I mean. Our return fixture. Meet as in f*ck!"

And yes, as my asterisk indicates, the word was mouthed rather than spoken. Which paradoxically increased its dramatic impact what – a thousandfold? Too much! Much too much! "In your dreams!" I replied stoutly, trying to free my hand and suddenly recalling the time. "Look, you idiot, we'll have Murdoch at the door any moment!"

"Turdoch, don't you mean?"

"If you insist," I grinned. Turdoch! Now why hadn't I thought of that? And how could one be stern with a guy like this, so clearly on one's wavelength?

"So," he retorted, maybe emboldened by my smile, "let's get it sorted."

"Easier said than…!"

"Time? Place?"

"OK, OK," I countered. "How about, after your Mostyn stint next – look, oh I dunno! Um, I'll drop you a note later today. Promise."

"On my pillow?"

"On your fucking pillow," I grinned, giving him, as he freed my wrist, a sort of involuntary pat on the stomach. At which there was this pulse, a slight contraction under his skin. Ravishing, sudden. Another second and there'd have been no escape. As it was I managed to jump to my feet and wave goodbye.

Talk about the nick of time! Already Murdoch, sorry Turdoch, was mounting the stairs, watch in hand. "So what d' ye call this, laddie?" he thundered. "It's verra nearly the middle of next week!"

"Orders is orders – just giving Marsden his wee ring," I chirped, dodging across to the boys' landing, and beginning my peal as if announcing the Great Fire of London. It was only then it occurred to me – I hadn't been offered a biscuit.

Mean bastard! I thought affectionately.

Yet somehow, as time wore on, my mood gan sullen, slowly but resolutely, as though one of those ceilings you see in horror flicks was gradually descending on me, intent on pulping my individuality to oblivion.

It was as much as I could do around five on Saturday to rouse myself from the afternoon's pile of marking and set out for town, having filled up with petrol earlier that morning in anticipation of the evening's revels. At least the contretemps ahead, however sticky, couldn't be worse than the shock of that encounter at Hunn's party. Or could it? The usual sense of foreboding gripped me as I turned from Gagg's Lane into the parking lot behind High Street. What I needed was a decade off people, Andy included. And all honeypots like him. And at least a century off marking.

Oh, for a fucking desert island!

Fortunately, Mostyn's lay almost opposite the barber's and I was thus able to keep an eye on their front door while quizzing Evans on the respective benefits of macassar or linseed oils for an ailing croquet mallet – a conversation which he seemed to find peculiar.

Just after five thirty, the staff across the road emerged, followed by old Mostyn himself who, after locking up, climbed into his Humber with his current beezkneez and purred away. Most of the other girls headed straight for the bus station while Andy lingered a moment, every inch the White Rabbit, before turning back and padding smartly down the side of the building.

Cunning bastard! The area at the back, that was where he must be heading. Entirely enclosed and not overlooked, the ideal starting place for an illicit tryst. Ideal that is if one's mind had not been fixed on an entirely different objective. This whole thing seemed to be heading for the rocks, and no mistake – my only hope was to put my foot down firmly right from the outset. No hesitation, no wavering.

A shilling completed my purchase of a tub of Jacques' Original, as well as eliciting three and a half bows from a flustered Evans, and, after a stroll up to the bridge and back in case of detectives, I found myself entering the red brick jumble of Mostyn's yard – only to pause in consternation. No Andy – just the back door left slightly ajar, its maw a sinister black leading to God knows what. Clearly someone had been cutting keys again!

Not for the first time in recent weeks I cursed myself for my bovinity. My idea had been to wait till the coast was clear, meet up and then whisk the guy off to a remote hostelry in the forest where I could talk some sense into him. Clearly it didn't accord with his. Now, as usual, he'd gained match point, and thus the choice of battlefield. I was going to have to tread warily indeed. Subtly goes it!

Feeling like one of those warriors from Weyburne tump – except I was clothed, thank God – I edged my way into the silence.

There was just enough light to scan my way through the place, but to no apparent avail. Curiouser and curiouser. No sound, no movement, no sign of life whatever. And I was just concluding that this was a typical Marsden subterfuge and that I'd have to search under every counter and behind every roll of lino, when – ping! The unmistakable sound of a Lamson gun. And sure enough, there it was, a canister whizzing down its wire from the first floor. Or rather, what passed for a first floor at Mostyn's – really a kind of bloated balcony, reached by steps from the main sales area.

And then, of course, as way above a match was struck, the penny dropped!

In common with many rural ironmongers at that time, Mostyn kept in stock a small selection of furniture to save folk having to travel to Hereford or Gloucester whenever they needed a bookcase or commode. It was upstairs these were displayed and, query, query – I wondered if, among the tables and tallboys, there'd just happen to be a double bed? Or King size? Or Emperor, God forbid?

OK, time to put cards on the table. Who but the most utterly libidinous of readers – yes, yes, no flinching: if the cap fits don't deny it! – who else will have persevered with a tale like this thus far? And now you must be thinking, here we are at last. Dedication rewarded. Smut coming up. Andy the Dandy sprawled athwart his silky Slumberland, clad in a kimono, a red rose clenched in his teeth! Paul Bryant, all resolve vanished, tearing off his clothes and jumping on the lad like a lascar.

Well, I'm sorry to disappoint, but in devout literature truth must prevail. There was no rose, no kimono – just an old mattress, secondhand, a bit stained, marked down to £7, with Marsden perched on a rustic bench between it and the sales desk. However, he had provided wine – a half bottle of Liebfraumilch, unchilled, which he'd slurped into a couple of plastic tumblers – and had, moreover, attired himself in just about the most shattering rig conceivable.

Guess, can you? Not the pseudness of Aquascutum or Austin Reed. But real bloke stuff. Shorts, striped jersey, socks down to his ankles – exactly the same rugger kit he'd worn that day at Victoria!

Simple – but oh so adroitly judged!

"You took your time," he murmured in a tone of amusement rather than remonstrance, for all the world as though he was acknowledging what time and trouble I'd taken over my own dowdy jacket and cavalry twills.

"One has to be careful." Fighting an intense desire to sink down beside him, I deposited my Jacques' on the desk next to the candelabrum.

"Oh yeah?" – glancing at the label – "what the fuck is that? Lube?"

Can he be serious? Tread carefully, Bryant.

"Ah, well spotted – yes, I suppose you could say that. Now..."

"I'm impressed." Relaxing still further, he pushed a beaker my way. "How about a toast?" We raised our plastic. "To lubrication! And let the fucking puritans howl!"

Sipping the warm wine, and suppressing a natural desire to retch, I noticed a stool nearby on which lay a box of tissues (pretty conventional, I suppose) and a large slab of Kendal Mint Cake (decidedly weird and unconventional!) – what on earth was the guy expecting? A trek up the Matterhorn, or something? Well, whatever he had in mind, disappointment was undoubtedly heading his way. In which case – might as well get it over with...

But, somehow – I dunno, the words wouldn't come. What I actually managed to say was, "That kit and stuff – you look terrific."

"Yuh, well – Mostyn's motto: we aim to please! Actually, I thought it might at least intrigue you – the omission, get it?"

"OK, er – 'fraid you'll have to enlighten me."

"Remember?" With a roguish smile, he tapped his cheek. "Sorry, not a tube of it to be found in town."

"Not even for ready money?"

"Not even for that!"

I grinned. "Well then, where's your ingenuity? You should have tried Bovril."

"Good idea! Or Marmite. Next time I'll get both and you can choose."

"Next time..." The words slipped out kind of involuntarily, tailing away into an inconclusive but intense silence. For a few seconds we regarded each other, I almost guiltily, he with a slight frown.

Finally he glanced at his watch. "Tempus fugit..."

"Uh, sorry," I interposed in as close to my pedagogic style as I could manage. "Daydreaming as always. Apologies, apologies. So how's it all going? Work, I mean. Aiming for a clean sweep, are we? Alphas all the way?"

"Sod the work."

"Oh right. Sod Oxford too?"

"And the whole suppurating universe!"

"Yuh, well – heartless, witless nature! What's the problem? Carver driving you too hard, is he?"

"That jerk!"

"You should have chosen English."

"So you could bugger me three times a day in the stockroom? Thanks a million, Mr Bryant!"

"OK, but seriously..."

"Serious?" Off he jumped from the bench. "I'll tell you serious. It's not English I should have gone for. Nor wasting time at sodding uni."

"Oh right. So what's the flavour of the month now, then? Astronaut training maybe? Professional rent boy?"

"You're getting warm," he smiled. "*Twelfth Night* – remember?"

"So that's it."

"Surprised?"

"Lure of the footlights! A new Irving about to strut his stuff."

"Don't mock, for Chrissake. Look, I've thought it over and over. It's the only thing that makes sense."

"Relax."

"But it's the only thing I want to do."

I shrugged. "You still can. Plenty of actors take a degree before…"

"But I want it now!" I blanched a little at the fury which seemed to be rising in him. "That feel as the lights come up. The adrenalin – the whole universe with your balls in its grasp."

Inwardly I tensed. "Right," I replied cautiously, "I get the point. Sex, drama, classic parallel. Yuh! Like, maybe… I mean, that's stuff I maybe missed out on in the Putney & District…"

"Missed out?" His mood seemed to lighten momentarily. "You, missed out? That's a good one."

"OK, so what's the big joke?"

"Paul Bryant protesting virginity…"

"Now look here…"

"… if that's not the hoot of the century, my name's Kruschev!"

"Even so," I intoned pompously, keen to regain lost ground, "it's vital to distinguish, as it were, between…"

"Vital? Just one thing's vital." Back had surged his former asperity with a vengeance. "One single unnegotiable imperative. I know it, you know it. Why waste time with all this crap?"

Slipping off his watch, he half smiled, half grimaced – and we were back on that ruddy train! In a moment, he'd pull off that jersey and I'd reach out for the heat and silk of his flesh. The strength of his neck. The fragrant harvest of his hair…

But no. I'd refrained once, hadn't I? Just about. OK, I could do so again. Then as now I'd had no choice – que sera, fucking sera!

"Steady on," I snapped. "Look – let's discuss it. I mean, I hear what you say, but isn't that view a trifle, as it were..?"

"Trifle?" Suddenly he laughed. "For fuck sake! There are times you sound about a thousand. Like, totally geriatric. As if your hair's gone, your ears massive, and your poor old choppers can only manage bread and milk. For God's sake, Paul!"

"Or junket," I retorted, trying the only parry I could think of.. "That's even softer."

"You don't say. In which case…" – dumping his glass on the table, he grabbed my jacket, pulling me fiercely to him – "…maybe it's time we talked antonyms?" As his free hand reached for my crotch, I backed sharply away.

"Hang on – whoa Melksham!" I demurred, flustered, out of my depth at the suddenness. "As a matter of fact…"

"Yeah?"

Playing for time, I shook my head. "Just let's, OK – slow it."

"Yeah? And for why exactly? Like, what the fuck did you suggest coming here for? Siesta?"

"Don't be daft!"

"What then?"

"We need to talk."

"Fine, no hassle. Sex first, talk later."

"Or." I retorted, backing away another step or two, wishing I was nearer the staircase, "vice versa?"

"As if."

"Hang on while I mix you a bromide!"

All at once this seemed to faze him, anger mounting in his voice yet again, but to a new pitch. "If that's meant to be a joke, we're not bloody amused. Like, what's with all this? This – act?" Spat out with venom, as if his bollocks had suddenly assumed command and were insisting on tarantara, tarantara – ride to the guns, no retreat, and to hell with finesse!

"What do you mean, act?" I inquired lamely.

"All this time of the month, mind my headache, no rubbers/no sex stuff. What's the game, Paul?"

"Haven't I made myself…?"

"Cut it out," he said fiercely, again grabbing my lapel. "Cut out this shit, for Chrissake! Just cast your mind back! Mega, wasn't it? Out of this world? And no way is it finished – it's there for the taking – we can have it all again. And more!"

"Like Oliver Twist?"

"Like…! A crescendo seemed to shake him, robbing him of words for a second or two. After which, and abruptly, his grip slackened. "Or maybe…"

"Maybe…?"

"You've blotted the whole thing out. Made yourself forget it ever happened."

"Of course not – not exactly," I retorted, brushing his fingers away, avoiding his eyes. "In a manner of speaking, it's true we've heard the chimes at…"

"For fuck sake!" Loud and desperate, the cry rang round the roof. "Can't you ever forget fucking literature for one fucking moment?" Face bloated, fists clenched, for a moment he looked close to losing control. If there'd been a mirror, he'd have smashed it.

"Andrew," I said hastily, with all the emollience I could muster, "don't get me wrong. I know how this feels, believe me…"

"Bullshit!"

"Fair enough, but I'm not shooting a line. All the angst and stuff. I've been through it too. Honest…"

"Shut it!" I quailed at the near scream. "Like all teachers, right, you've been through bugger all. And propose to keep it that way. Which is why you're so sublimely adept at all this shit – hiding behind principles as if they're bulletproof. Morals, principles, whatever. All the crap the God squad peddle. But get this…"

"Andy, listen…"

"It won't wash. Understand?" Now his tone harshened and quietened into a vicious intimacy – almost a whisper in the ear. "Not in your case. Not where you're concerned. We know too much about each other, don't we, *sir*?"

"Or too little," I countered, though wincing at the 'sir'. Tiring of all this, the implied threats, the palpable aggro, I was finding it difficult to quell the resentment knocking at my mind. Sure, strictly speaking I'd offended against the law of the land. But wasn't it an idiot law, smuggled on to the statute book by a gang of Victorian retards who hadn't the faintest idea of what they were letting society in for? Which of us asks to be born queer – why should we suffer for it? Why be forever dreading the stocks and shame?

Moreover, the present situation was obviously none of my making. Anyone could see that. Not even the most blinkered bigot could deny that. If I'd known the lad would return, no way would I have let things get this far. In which case, what right had this bastard to speak to me this way? Hold a pudder over my head? Act like I was some organ grinder's monkey fit only to caper for gibes and dimes?

Christ! At times I do resemble something out of Dickens, don't I?

But then so did Marsden. In his capacity for theatre, at anyrate. The sudden reversal, the melodramatic twist, the sharp veer into the unexpected and unexplored. As evinced, for instance, by his reaction to my previous riposte.

Neither an air of incomprehension, nor a resumption of anger. But a sort of flinch as though he'd suffered a blow. Even a gesture with his right hand as if warding something off.

"Too little?" he queried, turning back to his stool, his tone hollower now. "I get. Yeah, it all fits. Neat and nicesome, as you'd say! I suppose – if I'd read more, I'd have seen it coming."

"I don't quite follow." My frown was genuine – what did it mean, this volte face? More to the point, was it to be trusted? Somehow deflation and Andrew Marsden didn't quite add up. "Trust me," I continued cautiously, "all's well in that respect. Your reading's exceptional – I mean, for your age.."

"For my age!" Again that rueful nod, before turning his face my way. "How fucking patronising! What is this? Some attempt to pick a quarrel? Find an excuse? How conventional can you get? I'd have expected something more ingenious."

By now he'd lost me completely. Ingenious? Quarrels? What the hell was the guy on about?

"You're some dude, that's for sure," he continued. "I kind of admire it – in a way. As an ability. Like, it doesn't take you long at all, does it?"

"Take me…?"

"To tire of people – wipe the slate clean." And now I could hear it, the reproach in his voice. "At least in the movies, guys stay together for a summer or whatever. Not like us – one pathetic bonk, and it's sod off and don't you come back, no more, no more, no more, no…"

"That is," I choked, "entirely out of order! As you perfectly well know!"

"Do I?"

"Fuck you!" The asperity of my intervention surprised even myself – and might well have served as a warning, had I had time to think. As it was, all my pent-up resentment came pouring out in a torrent. "Who was it seduced who in that ghastly train? And what clever dick put us both at risk by coming back to Tolverton having said he wouldn't? And who, even then, can't keep his hands off but has to tart around as if, instead of school, he's part of some Arabian Nights' seraglio?"

The slightest, the very slightest grin had begun to play about his lips. What track on the juke was this? Methinks the lady doth protest too much? Even as I finished my rant, I realised yet again.

Nineteen, and he was in control. Like a crane driver with infinite levers at his disposal, like an author at his Remington, he could scheme and he could deem. All my actions, where I was coming from, where I was inexorably headed. As if I was carrion in a cruel beak, to be played with as it pleased him. He was that confident.

For a moment there was silence. After which he simply returned to the agenda. His agenda. No deviation, no attempt to argue the toss. It was as though we were at a play reading, and had simply moved on to the next speech. His speech.

"What's that Cole Porter lyric you once played me?" he said, a touch of mockery manifest in his voice. "Men grow cold, as girls grow old? Admit it Paul, what you want is a newer number."

"Balls! You know bloody well that's not it."

"Yeah, yeah!"

"Look, in a perfect world, if I had my way we'd be together. I mean it! On, I dunno – some bloody island somewhere…"

"What island?"

"Does it matter? As long as the sea's clear, the beach white, and no other bugger within twenty miles – except…"

"Continue."

"Well," I conceded, swirling the ghastly plonk round my beaker, "there'd need to be a taverna not too far away for supper. And a dentist and stuff. And…"

"Cake. I presume? To have and to eat?"

"Sort of," I replied, wondering all of a sudden where exactly I'd lost control of the conversation. "Sort of." Every moment with this guy was like playing Scrabble in the fourth dimension.

"Anyhow," he continued, watching me closely for reactions, "not to worry. It's not gonna come to that, is it? Exile, and stuff. Nothing theatrical like that.

"Not if we're careful. So – I'm glad you take my point. The wisdom of cooling things – for the time being at any…"

"Incredible!" Draining his glass, he tossed it on the floor. "Look, I was talking in general terms. Altruistically. Paul, what the fuck's your problem? This urge to centre everything on yourself? If you ask me, someone needs a shrink."

"But you just…"

"Brethren, fellow gays, that's what I was referring to. Our generation. Their constant fear. Having to flee abroad at a moment's notice."

"East of Pago-Pago?"

"Whatever. Seriously, there's change coming. Maybe it's not so apparent out in the sticks, in a dump like Tolverton. But this summer's taught me a lot, not that any of it's news to you. You're a Londoner – you know the way people act and talk. Pushing back boundaries bit by bit. It's hard to define but – this new private member's Bill, for instance. You know, to get the law altered."

"All hot air."

"Don't be too sure. It's high time the law changed. Did you know they used to call it the blackmailer's charter?"

Of course I bloody knew, but what alternative had I except to feign ignorance? Or at least keep stumm? There are guys in this world who can only function if they're allowed to play Sir Oracle, and clearly Marsden was one of them.

"It's clear from the papers, the legal columns and stuff. Juries refusing to convict, police holding back where there's been nothing overt. Reading between the lines, there's change in the air. I tell you, unless they're exaggerating..."

"Exactly!"

"...it looks," he continued with a frown, "like it could be as soon as a year or two."

"Pie, Andy love," I said dismissively, "in the sky, OK? No way in our lifetime!" Shaking my head in frustration, I got to my feet and stalked over to where I could push aside the blind, and gaze down through the fanlight on to the High Street. Emptyish already, well desolate, what folk there were hurrying home for Crossroads or The Archers.

I turned back with a shrug. "Look," I said, surprised at his silence, "even if the establishment does relent, even if they do tire of their power games and the satisfaction of making brother humans squirm, how far do you think they'll go? Legalise gay marriage?

Allow us to hold hands in the street, adopt kids, attend each other's deathbed? No way. It'll be the smallest possible concession so as not to offend the wise, liberal, bountiful British voter."

"How small?"

"I suppose they might just allow sex in private between consenting adults over 75."

"Not long to wait then."

"I'm being serious."

"No," he insisted, as though perched on the Woolsack, "childish, actually."

"All right!" Despite another blur of resentment, I stood my ground. "Do you seriously think they'll ever, ever sanction sexual liaisons between a teacher and his pupil? Do you?"

"When the latter's not a kid anymore – why not?"

"Why not!" My grin flicked on before I could stop it. "Still I'll concede this much – your 3rd century Athenian transported to our time might well ask the same question."

"Which makes it all the more valid."

"Which makes it all the more tragic." All of a sudden I wanted, sort of, to put my arm round his credulity. "Surely by now you've realised how life works. That all the religio-sexist stuff, all the blockhead prohibitions which give folk something to live for stem from one thing – fear! A guy can't marry his sister – why? Because they might sire mongols."

"Or geniuses."

"Just as inconvenient. And so it goes on. A jew can't eat pork because of tapeworms. A moslem has to take his shoes off in the mosque because the prophet neglected to invent the hoover."

"And one guy can't sleep with another because…?"

"Because, old love, if the masses ever found out how incandescently pleasurable that particular sin is, there'd be no stopping them. Birth rates would drop, economies falter, civilisations topple."

"Sure, right," he replied, a touch of exasperation now evident, "I get the point. Doom and gloom. Fine, you wallow in Maxwell Fyfe zeitgeist if that's what turns you on. But what's it got to do with us two, here and now, this minute?"

The bell for six o' clock chapel had just begun to ring, its din, sweetened by distance, wafting patchy as smoke over the slates and stacks of the little town.

"See what I mean?" he continued. "An hour to lock-up. All the time in the world. Do we use it or lose it?"

"Haven't you listened to a word I've said?"

With a look too complex for words to describe – fury, supplication, hauteur somehow mixed up in his mind-dish – he rose to his feet. "I'm asking you for the last time. Don't make me fucking beg, Paul. It's totally safe here. There is absolutely no way anyone will ever know. I mean – there is no obstacle except in your stupid, fucking, cautious mind. D' you want it or not?"

"OK," I said, swallowing hard, contradictions flying at me like those bloody bats that time with Marcho, "if you force me – yes, I want it. I want you. Like crazy I want you. And I suspect I'll never stop wanting you. But for both our sakes, and believe me I mean both, I'm walking away. Maybe when you really have left school…"

"No good!" Red faced, on the verge of tears, he was running his fingers through my hair. "It's gotta be now. Paul, don't be like this. Can't you understand – it's gotta be now!"

"I'm sorry," I said, turning to the stairs, in command of myself now, a kind of detachment kicking in, like the credits were about to roll.

"If you do this," he choked, "you'll regret it. For the rest of your life you'll regret it."

"Regret its necessity," I nodded, pausing briefly, "that I grant you. That I certainly grant you." I resumed my descent. "But there's one ingredient of life no kid can ever grasp. Not till he's suffered."

"Kid?"

"And it's with us all the time, sweetie. Like radio waves or magnetism."

"Kid?" Behind me, his voice stabbed out its incredulity.

"Force majeure, they call it."

"Paul…"

"Look it up. Webster, Chambers, whatever." And I was away, blundering through the gloom, pushing past the ladders and stacks of timber.

It's amazing how quickly commonsense tends to evaporate. Almost as soon as I'd heard the lock of that yard door click behind me, certainly by the time I'd reached the Post Office, a conviction had taken hold of me that, although I'd done the right thing, I'd assuredly done the wrong one. And if that seems hard to understand, just try to see things from the guy's point of view.

How difficult it must have been for him to take the initiative as he had. And how about the risks he'd run? And his thoughtfulness in buying candles and wine? To which, what had my response been? A threadbare morality; hiding behind *Daily Express* platitudes; or what Edwardian novelists used to call, and oh so aptly, a blazing blue funk!

Looked at calmly, what risk had there really been? Of being taken in flagrente, I mean? Absolutely none – only old Mostyn had the keys and he'd have been well away with his doxy, the other side of Feyhill. Or, how about the truth somehow coming out later? Pretty minimal – after all, would Marsden want to ruin his chance of Oxford, would I want to fall on the mercy of Hunn and be banged up in Strangeways?

No, painful as the truth was, it had to be faced. I'd simply been unable to cope. At a moment of crisis, when books don't help, when you're on your own with neither credo nor past experience to lean on, I'd caved in. I'd taken the bog standard obvious way out, regardless of his feelings, oblivious to the depth of his pain, intent only on my bland, easy, anodyne cruise through life.

Or so I told myself.

And yuh – that sally of his. All that 'regret it forever' stuff. Well, OK – maybe it was the oldest cliché in the book, maybe it did amount to nothing more than the last fling of his adolescence, still – it had a proleptic ring to it which hit home. Right home. All evening I fidgeted with this and that, unable to focus, aware only of this terrible feeling of contrition I couldn't shake off..

Finally, well after midnight, I fell into one of those disturbed sleeps which presage one of those recurrent distorted dreams of mine. Cesare stalking the firmament.

But this time the streets are completely empty. Only they're not quite the normal streets – of course not. How could they be? Aren't we back in *Caligari*?

My mind's surprisingly calm as I creep along under the angles and eaves. Maybe this is a fool's errand, maybe I should let things take their course. And yet, and yet – while there's night, there's hope.

No light can be seen in Mostyn's, not the slightest chink. OK, it would be commonsense, wouldn't it, to fix that blind again, over the casement? Prudent and admirable? But my heart begins to sink. Looking carefully round for chance revellers, I take a deep breath and begin to head down that side wall towards the gate. At anyrate my agony won't be unduly prolonged. Soon I'll know my fate one way or the other.

A moment and I'm in the yard, groping my way round the emerald tiles, fumbling with the lock and – yes – restraining a whoop of delight as the gleaming glass gives way before me. Unlocked. Amazing, he's unlocked the portal! Somehow, he's thought the whole scenario through, bided his time and patiently waited.

Waited! While I've flailed around like a drowning rat seeking what – solace, safety, deliverance from what I most desire?

But now's no time for debris like that. All thought in abeyance, I creep in and dodge through the lobby, pausing only at the foot of the steps which have now turned into an escalator. As it carries me up, I salute David Niven on the way down – and now, yes, there it is, the faintest gleam of candle. Samarkand! All I have to do is push through the seven silk shrouds, and there he'll be, rising from his bed, beau ideal, naked, smiling, beckoning...

Only – what the hell – he's a beau no longer, but a blasted pixie with a Spitfire moustache, and he's shaking the daylights out of me, his wedding ring cutting into the flesh of my shoulder. "Get oot of your soddin' pit!" he cries. "D' ye think ye're paid to lie there all day?" And now like a conjuror he produces this giant brass cowl thing, flailing it up and down, till its din seems to crack my head into sharp splinters which lunge me sideways, out on to the cold floor. But he leans over, merciless, the brass getting closer and closer, the torment louder and louder till I want to spew out over his face the whole unendurable pith of my head and guts and soul.

16: *In for a Pound*

Mornings after can be keen, crass or all stations in between. For instance, meeting a guy you've slept with the previous night whom you shouldn't – doesn't that reverberate with a certain raffish charm? Whether or not it leads on to episode two, at least it's a bird in the hand rather than nowt in the bush.

Bird, that is, in the sense of what you eat between hors d' oeuvre and the roast. Or you cook for Thanksgiving.

On the other hand, meeting a guy you haven't slept with the previous night whom you should, what else does that resemble but – apologies for the indelicacy – a wet fart? Expectation substantial: outcome pathetic! Best forgotten by all parties concerned, unless of course you're a Queen in the 16th century!

Queen, that is, in the sense of a chick for whom knights lay their cloaks over puddles. Or who takes a horse as her lover.

But the worst hassle lies in the halfway house of which Andy and I, as term sailed on, now found ourselves tenants. I mean, what were we? Proprietors of an erotic past but bereft of an erotic present. Neither one thing nor the other. All the danger, none of the fun.

Nor was it all that much help that the veiled threats made that evening at Mostyn's had as yet come to nothing. What did the future hold? That was the question. That was the worry, the never ending sulphuric worry.

Could he be trusted to hold his tongue and not let slip a chance remark? Could I be trusted to give him rope and not play the bally schoolmaster? No wonder that I began to tread tentatively, almost to the point of obsession – no wonder that his attitude towards me, though not noticeably tinged with acrimony, as might have been expected after the Mostyn encounter, didn't exactly ooze candour. All that cri de coeur stuff, for instance, about wanting to be an actor – he must have been pretty fed up that I hadn't taken it more seriously. That I hadn't responded more sensitively.

Still, on the surface, things pottered along as usual, meeting around the house, the odd quip after one of the wee ring-a-dings – but all the same a kind of spiritual portcullis had descended between us. Reserve ruled. There was about as much flame in our discourse as between two aged aunts in a Sidmouth teashop. Nor were matters helped by Murdoch. Since that debacle of mine over Saturday bell, he'd watched my every mood with morbid suspicion as though I were a KGB agent or something, intent on undermining the perfection of his system

Thinking back on it, the whole situation was nothing less than a powder keg, no two ways about it, though I didn't become seriously concerned until October and the next of those own goals of mine which seemed to have become the norm.

This particular autumn had plunged Tolverton into a period of frenetic uncertainty which in itself was quite capable of driving one's nerves to fever pitch. Gone was the easy-going bonhomie of Eric's reign where our yardstick had been quality of life rather than that most meretricious of delusions, success.

Indeed Hunn seemed to be mirroring himself on those ghastly American presidents whose standing depends on their first 100 days in office! Everything that could be upended was upended, analysed, dissected, and then, whether or not found wanting, changed.

Curiously, not much of this turmoil appeared to affect Chris who bustled on with his admin duties in his accustomed avuncular style. Perhaps a little greyer, perhaps a little more rotund, he remained to all intents and purposes a happy man. Why not? He'd reached the top, albeit briefly. The reins of power had been his for a trice during which, sensible chap that he was, he'd seen through their glitz, and been content to relinquish them to a lesser man. Our beloved Parish Hunn, that is. And lesser, I mean, because the guy had so long craved them.

Strange though that the new Head's choice as fixer to push through all these upheavals turned out to by-pass Chris – nor was he either a Himmler like Murdoch, or a technocrat like Carver, but none other than the Reverend Roy Marchpane, MA, DFC, late of Sidney Sussex College Cambridge, Chaplain and Warden of the Almshouses.

Amazing.

Whether this was some kind of psychotic deference to the 3rd estate, or, on the not unreasonable assumption he'd fail, part of some plan to get rid of Roy from Common Room altogether, was not quite clear. What was undeniable, however, was the avidity with which he took to his new and unexpected status of Development Officer. Proposals began to cascade from him: plans for new uniforms, new syllabuses, new menus, improved links with nearby state schools, weekly boarding – as the days went by, the list swelled like a party balloon. Even that ridiculous hymn book supplement was once again raised, only once again to be squashed at the first planning meeting by Ken – poor chap, one of his rare outings these days, though he never complained.

There was, however, one idea which met with universal approval, or at anyrate almost universal. The Carve found excuses to dissent of course, while Ormulak declared himself too old and fat. But otherwise, to a man, Common Room voiced its enthusiasm and set to work moulding boy opinion.

In favour of what? A so-called sponsored walk, no less.

There had lately appeared on British markets a most peculiar hybrid, half car, half charabanc, entitled the Mini-bus – though

Squash-arse might have been a better description. Given the decrepitude of our Bedford, Marcho's idea was to sell said relic to whatever short-sighted purchaser the local rag could drum up, then subsidise the purchase of one of these newcomers with the proceeds from a sponsored walk. Fifteen miles at ten bob per mile per head, everyone included, would be quite sufficient to defray the cost, plus something over for servicing and petrol.

How apt, how simple, how entirely blameless. The Tuesday before half term was duly selected, parents warned to supply boots for their offspring, and the local police and press alerted.

"Are you lot exempted?" said I to Andy, meaning of course the Oxbridge Sixth. It was one evening a couple of days beforehand, and I'd invited him down for coffee you see, as part of my normalisation campaign, thus far an apparent success. Or maybe one should say, not yet a manifest failure! "I imagine so," I continued, flicking crumbs from my mouth, "considering the proximity of exams."

"Whatever."

"How long before Arnos now, a fortnight?"

"Who knows?"

Not one of his more communicative moods, I agree. But he'd been out all day at Weyburne, doing the final shoot for the Romans in Wales programme, which explained, if not justified, his rather distant manner. Plus also, in those days Oxford colleges examined in groups at different times, so an unworldly candidate might be forgiven for being a bit vague about his forthcoming Waterloo. But there was more to it than that. Something I couldn't quite put my finger on. Something disturbing.

Each of the three or four times he'd been closeted with the Tabor crew, the boy had returned from Cardiff in this kind of limbo. Remote, discontented, not exactly disgruntled but close to it. Who knows what was pissing him off! My part in the film had been confined to one short interview, and I'd thus had no opportunity of seeing what problems arose at the studio. Maybe it was the people, maybe the longeurs? Maybe he was fed up with the whole project?

That maybe he was also getting fed up with me – no, that hadn't escaped my notice as a possibility, especially given our rift over hanky-panky. In other words my, to his way of thinking, unfathomable intransigence.

Like, these days we understand so much more about the quirks and quiddities of the mind – bi-pole, tri-pole, up-the-ruddy-pole – but at that time pretty well all of us were little more than amateurs, and in my search for a solution I'd fallen back on what any modern psychiatrist will tell you is the worst possible remedy.

Humouring the beast!

"Any news about the broadcast date?" I queried.

Shake of the head.

"Work on schedule?"

"Fuck the work!"

I nodded, noting however that he made no move to leave. Whatever distaste was brewing inside him, he was apparently perfectly happy to sit on my floor, eat Osbornes and endure my company. In which case, why not try the Captain Cook trick, and dazzle the dude with trinkets?

"This walk on Tuesday," I ventured. "I'm only dashing around taking pictures. You know, for the school mag and stuff. The archives. I could be finished by midday or thereabouts."

"Bully for you."

"Thought you might fancy lunch at the County. I mean, all work and no play, right?"

At last he looked up with a glimmer of interest.

Of the five hotels in or near Tolverton, the Royal & County was by far the grandest and most expensive, occupying as it did a range of 18th century buildings in buff stone, high above Trefoil bridge and dominating a long curve of the Tolver. Its menus were legendary not only for their prices, but also their quaint mixture of French and Greek, whilst its wine list rendered each sip a memory to be treasured. When you know that, at this precise moment, fifteen shillings is trickling past your tonsils, it concentrates the mind wonderfully. No room for anything but pure, unalloyed bliss – to be savoured to the full.

Altogether, what with the silver, and the whiteness of napery, and the cringing servility of the waiters – their hips appeared to be hinged like puppets – eating at the County fifty years ago was one of those recondite experiences which have all but vanished from our modern 3rd world Britain.

In other words, pure swank – and, I reckoned, just the ticket to cheer up a Marsden. I'd no idea where Mrs Sylvester took him on her rare visits to the marches. It might have been the King's Arms, it might have been the chippie. It would certainly not have been the marble halls I had in mind.

"Ever been there?" I asked.

"Of course."

I smiled knowingly. "Well, how about it then? I could meet you in the bar, say, around five past twelve."

"Sure about this, are we? You don't mind being seen out with a *kid*?"

Closing my eyes, I winced. That word! Or term of abuse as it must have seemed to him! It was the first reference he'd made to it since Mostyn's. What else was festering there in that brain of his? "Do you want to or not?" I said levelly, meeting his sardonic gaze.

"Might as well. There'll be sod all at school."

No, you young brute. And certainly no crème brulée, pheasant in armignac, or soft yielding epoisée inside its creamy rind...

"Jacket, I suppose?" – the query delivered with his best disdain.

"And tie."

"Soup-stained, like yours?"

"If that's all you've got."

Sparring, like two lion cubs spar – and if at moments I was tempted to wonder where it might end, in the future I mean, after school, such thoughts never got far. There was much too much on my mind of pressing import to squander time in conjecture.

The day of the walk dawned bright and clear. Perfect early autumn, with a light breeze which stirred rather than quelled the ground's residual warmth. From half past eight, dayboy cars had been discharging well-booted, check-scarved youngsters into the front quad, and by starting time the whole area was a riot of colourful jeans and chinos and jerkins.

Staff too had entered into the spirit of the day. Otto had borrowed a Polish flag to wrap round his powerful shoulders, Tommo was resplendent in Desert Rat hat and tunic, whilst Murdoch, temporarily at his most human, appeared with bagpipes in some weird tartan slung over his arm. Even the Hunns were in mufti, he sporting Norfolk breeches and a fair-isle pullover, she in ski-pants and blouson, ill-adapted to her lack of figure, but redeemed somewhat by a jaunty cap with a red bobble.

As for me, I was positioned outside the main gates, camera primed, ready to record the start for posterity. I'd already worked out my plan: four vantage points round the course, at Cragfield, Preston, Welsh Medding and Over Tolver, with a quick dash back to school to dump my camera and don a suit. Since the bulk of the participants would take close on four hours over that distance, I'd have ample time for a couple of courses with Andy before belting back to snap at least the stragglers as they expired from exhaustion.

Ten a.m. precisely, and off went the starting pistol, gaudy humanity streaming forth into the streets and alleys to the uncertain & wavering accompaniment of *Land of the Heath and Heather* – doubtless his bagpipes were more adept at the *Horst Wessel* song!

Few could resist a wave at my camera and I must have used up half a spool before the rump of the lemmings had jiven past. Among which, surprisingly, was Marcho, limping along on a stick, Clemmy nowhere in sight.

"Told her to go on ahead," he explained, halting for a chat. "No point in her tottering along with an old crock like me."

"Blister or something, is it?" I asked.

"Gout. Been threatening for a fortnight, and it has to choose now! Port's the culprit. Bear that in mind, my lad. Never forget!"

"What, to steer clear?"

"Not at all," he twinkled. "Drink deep as you can, while you still can!"

"OK," I laughed. "I'll remember that when Lent comes round."

"Do, my boy, do. Oh, and bye the bye. They've published the closure date. Fairford, remember?"

"I see."

"A week on Sunday. Right at the end of half term, so you won't have to worry about Owen."

Nor Hallatrow, come to think of it. How very convenient. "Excellent," I smiled. "Something to look forward to."

"Absolutely. In fact, I thought we might take down one or two of the Blaengwynfi boys. Make it more a reunion than a wake. How does that appeal?"

"The more the merrier."

"Good-oh."

"Tell you what. Why don't we lie down on the track to stop them tearing it up?"

"Why not?" Double twinkle. " This is going to be quite a party."

"Just what I need."

"By the bye," he added, "it might be best if we go down in the daylight. Give time for some filming."

And looting, by any chance? How very zealous! But who could gainsay a guy with a DFC and the gout?

"Ought to be off," he said, grimacing with pain as he shifted his weight a little. "Won't make it before dark otherwise."

"Look, this is daft, OK? Let me drive you part way round. Say, Medding or the Moffat Arms at Preston. No-one could accuse you of shirking, not with a foot like that."

"Out of the question." The old head shook so vigorously, you'd have thought he was exorcising or stuff. "The whole day was my baby and I'll see it through. But, er – thanks for the offer. And if it gets to midnight, make sure it's you leading the search party!"

That image of him limping along and over the cat's-eyes flashed back at me several times during the morning's filming, and again as I sat in the bar of the R & C a couple of hours later. Some contrast! Indeed, what greater contrast could there be between his awkward painful progress, and the ease with which the local scrap metal merchants and building contractors – and their dolled-up tarts – strolled and strutted their way across these sumptuous Wiltons.

The room itself had obviously been modelled on one of the London clubs, with light oak panelling, ormolu lamp brackets, and alcove bookshelves laden with volumes of the kind that seem destined for admiration rather than perusal – and you won't be surprised that I was perched there, on a bar stool, having taken an instant dislike to the place. It was all so – how can I put it? All so glib. As though it had a perfect right to exist like this, an emblem of inertia and excess in a world on the brink. A world crying out in poverty and distress of an intensity which these bitches in their furs, and even the waiters with their comfortable uniforms and three meals a day, could never imagine.

OK, you'll say – how about you with your car and your catamite, about to flash cash at the latter to keep him in tow? What price your social conscience? When did you last spend a day in the slums washing a beggar's sores? When did you so much as give a farthing to charity except as a public gesture to earn you brownie points?

Which is true. And which is synonymous with that inner confusion which stifles the bulk of Western thought and vision at birth. Like, it's headlines when a Cezanne accrues lustre in our eyes by being worth ten million – yet it's insignificant that a mite in Calcutta squirms and starves in mud for the few brief weeks of its life. But how does one reconcile the two? How does one hold them in the mind together sufficiently long, and with sufficient ardour, to even begin thoughts of redress, personal action, involvement? OK, at a given moment I'll agonise along with the poor, but tomorrow I'll still want my bath and breakfast. Two eggs please, sunny side up, and make sure the bacon's Old Spot!

So there I sat, yawning at the Ketélby and Grainger quaintly conching from the loudspeakers, ignoring the slick barman in his slick mess-jacket, expecting Andy any minute to whizz me back to the world I knew. Starter and entrée – they'd do their stuff all right. Sans doubt!

As time was on the tight side, around ten past I moved into the dining room, checking my watch for the third time in five minutes and taking my double Sercial with me. At least I could order the claret and ensure that it reached room temperature. Selecting a window table which would give my guest the best view of the Tolver, I settled myself into the luxurious upholstery and signalled for menus.

River view, Chateau Géste-Dubarre, plovers' eggs to start with. What more could a nineteen year old want? But get this straight, get this very straight – it may look like bribery or something of the sort, but that's not how it seemed then. Not to me at anyrate. My feelings for Marsden, despite his unpredictability, despite our current stand-off, had not really wavered. Except, maybe, time was defining them more clearly. OK, he could be brusque, even rude, whilst his selfcentredness was staggering even by teenage standards. But he had a mind, an exceptional memory, warmth when he chose, and wit – also when he chose. Moreover he was blessed with a body which, if it wasn't quite one to die for, at least surpassed the normal ungainly British carcass by several hundred per cent! All of which amounted, I nodded to myself as the bottle arrived, to someone it was right to make allowances for, give rope to.

After all, you can't enjoy an omelette without breaking the old brown and fragiles!

Half an hour later, I was starting to get irritable. No rope's of infinite length, nor is an omelette worth waiting a lifetime for. Like, what the buggeration was he up to? If he didn't get a move on, there wouldn't be time for so much as a bloody sandwich. I had to be back for the closing ceremony, imperative! Council, Fustians, the Mayor – Hunn would expect photos of all the bigwigs in his wretched magazine. Surely the boy knew that. Why did he think I'd specified the time so exactly? Twelve noon precisely. On the dot. I'd been that clear, hadn't I?

Victoria all over again. That bloody station! As the thought occurred to me, it served both to soothe and, paradoxically, stoke up still further my anger. On the one hand, sure he'd get here – an hour late maybe, but he'd get here. On the other, who did he think he was, playing tricks like this, rubbing the gilt off my largesse, making me look a twerp in public?

For one thing's certain. There's no figure more pathetic than a solitary guy at a table laid for two who's obviously been stood up! He can do what he likes, read his newspaper (I hadn't brought one!), study the boats passing on the river (there weren't any!), sip wine thoughtfully as if about to write a guide on the Loire – none of it washes. The situation's plain. Someone's given him the air, poor bastard! Look at him, sitting there, knowing full well the whole room's savouring his discomfiture.

At which point, one pours another glass, but not, as you'll appreciate, in order to sip!

It was twenty past one as I swept angrily into Rhodes and made for the stairs. I'd given him an hour, hadn't I? Quite sufficient – now for the explanations, if there were any. But, as always, I knew. As always I could predict, not the detail maybe, but at least the outline of what lay ahead. The next scene in the saga.

Even so, deaf to everything except my humiliation, I forged on, bursting into the nursery without knocking. Without speaking. halting, arms akimbo, at the end of his bed.

On which, surprise, surprise, he was lying, rigged out in the selfsame kit as in Mostyn's, silver bracelet, shorts, everything. Even the duffle bag was in evidence, slung casually over the rocking-horse.

Tossing aside his *Spectator* he glanced up at me without expression.

Impasse!

For about a century, neither of us moved or made a sound. Then something inside me sort of flipped. "So?" I queried, beside myself. "What's the sodding game?"

He smiled. "Awkward was it?"

"Awkward…!"

"Sorry about that."

"No, it wasn't bloody *awkward* – just the single most embarrassing hour of my life. In full view of the county, parents, old boys, who knows what – stood up like some pathetic loser. I had to down a whole bottle of wine."

"So I can see."

That got me, that really got me. "Do I have to spell it out?" I fumed. "I might have been arrested, drunk driving, thrown in the clink."

"Doubt it," he said, stretching. "The Chief Constable's a good sort. Besides, I used to be Walmsley's fag. My first score, maybe? Good in the sack, young Mark?"

"For God's sake!" I cried, now comprehensively distraught. So here it was yet again, that spider's web you can't shake off. Cloying, sticky, and now tangled up with sex. The grinning death's-head of sex. Unbelievable. What the hell had I got myself into?

"So what's the hassle, Paul?" He levered himself high on the pillows, folding his arms, still smiling.

"Nothing much. Nothing monumental. Just you – the guy who blights lives like a locust, loves putting the boot in, who doesn't care a toss!"

"Go on."

"What the hell d' you mean 'go on'!"

"Aren't you meant to add 'for anyone except yourself'? Remember, I've had this shit before. Years and years of it. From every crass cunt in my life. Say it, if you want to. What do I care? It's true anyway."

"You admit it?"

"Why not? It's true of me, it's true of you, it's true of moustache man, Head man, the guy who cleans the bogs, the wife who licks his..."

"Enough," I blazed, raising a warning finger. "That's enough! All that scatology stuff – it just makes things worse. For Chrissake grow up, Andrew. Where's the sense in adding insult to injury? I mean, how juvenile..."

"What injury?" he drawled, swinging his legs over the side of the bed, glancing up at me, imperturbable in his disdain. "Where's your evidence, praetor? Cuts, bruises, sockets without..."

"Some scars," I interposed fiercely, "sting inwardly. Deep inside. Like..."

"Being called a kid?"

"Like being made to look an utter fool in the County. Sitting there for an hour, brooding over two place mats, two sets of cutlery, two..."

"Bottles of plonk to keep you company? Tough shit."

"Plonk indeed! I'll have you know..."

"And I'll have *you* know, O sacred heart sore wounded, that nothing you think Paul Bryant's ever suffered compares with years and years of – what the fuck! I don't need to specify."

Chastened of course, but in some remote way that wouldn't focus, I struggled on, loth to give in, unwilling to allow him to strengthen his hold. "OK," I retorted, "so it must have been hell – but why take it out on me? Answer me that. What harm have I ever done you?"

"Harm? The Attorney-General might have something to say about that."

"Now wait a…"

"But anyhow, today was nothing, like – to do with that. I mean, you. Or not altogether. I mean, look at it all – the pissing hypocritical guff."

And then I noticed it, flung over a chair behind the door, his blazer, and a tie, and his regulation schoolboy shirt.

"Got a match?" he said, rising, grabbing the offending neckwear, swinging it back and forth like a thurible. "Make a nice blaze wouldn't it?"

"For about five seconds," I said, calmer now, but increasingly nonplussed. "But what a waste of thirty bob!"

"Think so," he said, rolling the silk up into a tight ball. "To get rid of something as disgusting as this?" And with a sure motion, he hurled it out of the open window as if straight for a wicket at Lord's.

By now I didn't quite know where I was. My anger had abated, but not the wine, and I found myself once again beginning to notice that lithe body, one hand propped against the window frame, staring out to the distant promontory where the Fey meets the Tolver.

He'd rolled up the sleeves of his rugger shirt so my eyes could hardly avoid it, that arm of his, the raised veins that betokened vitality and strength – nor the shoulders, the slimness of his waist, the tightness of his faded shorts. What changes had they seen since bought new at fourteen? Not I mean precisely seen, but witnessed, enfolded, encased, embraced…

He turned. "Got the idea?" he asked as if closing some ledger. "Satisfied? Look, if you must know, like some prat of a model student I'd donned my shirt and buttoned it but – when it came to the tie…" He shrugged. "School uniform's such a pathetic charade! I mean, on campus it's just about bearable, but in town? No way. Even if it meant missing out on lunch."

"And leaving me in the lurch?"

"I've apologised, haven't I?"

"And meant it?"

"Whatever."

"But which – was it just words or did you mean it? Really mean it?"

I know, I understand – you're thinking how cringe-makingly insensitive to push it like that. But it had been, as you'll admit, one of those days and I hardly knew what I was saying. It was like I was following script 5 in some manual for schoolmasters on how to Navigate Potential Crises.

And like most chapters in most such books, it backfired in mega-spectacular fashion.

"What more d' you want of me?" he queried, his voice rising, retreating a step or two, one hand behind his head. "On my knees, for fuck sake? Head on a platter? Like – this is *so* pointless! Get the fuck out of here, can't you?"

"Andy…"

"For that matter, get the fuck out of my life!"

"Look, if any way I've…"

"Just sod off, *OK*?" He turned to the window again, thrusting it higher as though – appalled, I clenched my fists – to throw himself out. Hastily I moved forward, but had only taken a step or two when once more, lazily, he lounged back my way.

"Know what?" Face blank, he tugged at the white cord of his shorts. What did that remind me of? "This is so boring. So utterly boring."

"Well, then…"

"I need a wank."

You don't say! Ten out of ten, Andy. Tactics extraordinaire! Alexander the Great would have been proud of you. So I'm totally upstaged! And cast plumb into one of those spicy dilemmas for which the most avid reading of Jane Austen provides no solution, not of any kind. Do I stay, or do I stamp off in counterfeit ire/disgust/horror? Nor does logic help, flashing its remorseless lure: you're in for a penny, why not the pound?

It would of course have been a help to be able to read the guy's mind. What did he want my next move to be? Then I'd have taken great delight in doing the opposite – or would I? Was I really turning into a Reynolds? Prize bastard, with a skin of steel?

But, time's up. No more questions, no more delay. His shorts slip to the floor. Staring straight at me, he thumbs open the hasp of his bracelet which follows suit. Itself followed by his CKs, but slowly, in stages, as if reluctant to surrender their mandate.

Calmly his fingers begin to pull his shirt aloft and over his head, revealing, kind of episodically, display by display, his array of flesh. The the long slim cream of his stomach, leading down, as it needs must, to his - credential, shall we say? His rather brute credential, brats for the making of. Indeed whole tribes. Not that in his case it's likely to bother with any task so mundane – which, in view of its not inconsiderable resemblance to Cleopatra's needle, both in angle and drama, represents one sodding whopper of an irony. Not to mention, in my case, hyperconfusion..

Quick now. Bugger off or participate?

Eyes, lips (his I mean) brood now with intent as his hands begin to move in familiar rhythm but sinister as they start to speed, invoking an awe in me which robs my brain of the power to act. I'm his puppet, OK? Brain and body consigned to parallel his, lust as he lusts. I can feel my spunk starting to boil as his boils, yearning for the burst into heady air, one aim now, one ambition out of all millions, to heave my stuff forth and coat all the morals of the universe with a truer deeper destiny.

I can't think. I can't see. He's a blur. It's a blur. Any moment. Next thrust, surely next, next, next...

Then – red! Fierce red! Traffic light red! He stops. Abruptly he stops. No spunk, not even pre-cum. Just that mocking smile.

And me? On the brink, on the searing brink Vicariously true, but all the more desperate for that. Speared on my aching need, like a conger writhing, Emerald City still winking over that chasmic void...

Never fear. I got to the tape in time for some snaps, no problem. And found space before the closing ceremony to ring The Monkey's Paw for a table – a table for two that is.

Surprised are we? Gobsmacked that a guy who'd held such a pudder over my head, indeed a double pudder would be no exaggeration, should a couple of hours later be being wined and dined by his victim?

That our altercations that afternoon demanded balm was beyond question, whilst a return to the Royal & County hardly seemed to hit the right note. Apart from anything else, a certain house tie was bobbing sedately on the surface of old Dobson's lily-pond by the back lodge, causing great consternation to the brace of pampered carp who reigned there.

Doubtless there are readers who'll question my judgment in "forgiving" Marsden this readily – his conduct, that is, in standing me up at lunchtime, etcetera – but how about my own? Was I in any position to deem his lapse any greater than mine? No – as we drove off that evening (we'd been careful to meet behind the Post Office) it was like two old lags on an evening out from Parkhurst! After all, the acts were done. No going back.

Seductio ad absurdum!

By seven we'd made it to Preston and were at table picking away at a freebie of curried whitebait and almonds. For Andy, peering solemnly at the menu, it appeared to be seventh heaven. For me it was – well almost. Not having Turdoch's permission was a slight worry, though after the old boy's exertions of the day he'd probably be flat on his back and snoring. More of a downer, though I tried to ignore it, was Andy's costume. There'd been no insistence on my part of anything formal – things had clearly got beyond that stage – but T shirt and torn jeans? Was this really the best he could muster? And how about that heavy wristchain of his that made him look like a rent boy.

In fact, to be fair, had this been Manhattan he'd have been judged drop-dead gorgeous, particularly as he'd just had his crew cut renewed. Agencies would have queued up for him, heiresses offered a thousand a go. But this was Wales, for Chrissake – what the hell did he think he was up to?

Noticing my glances, he broke into one of those slight grins of his. "Thought I'd better please you," he said, twisting the silver around so it caught the light. "Besides, look around. Relax."

So he could read my thoughts, could he – as well as being quite right. At four or five other tables, doting parents were entertaining teenage brats to supper, in each case there being a marked contrast between the garb of sire and scion. All at once a wave of envy swept over me. OK, so why did I have to sit here, trussed up in my waistcoat, and perspiring? What was there between us, two or three years? So why must I obey convention and Andy not?

However, now was not the occasion to pursue such niceties. Our waiter was hovering and time was short. Like, it was more than my job was worth to miss showers – even if he weren't on the prowl, word would most certainly get back to the Turd.

"Pour monsieur?"

"Just coquilles S. Jacques, please, and the lamb cutlets Reform. And I'm afraid we're in a bit of a hurry."

"Va bene! The curse of modern life. And for the infante?"

At first I thought the lad, in his ignorance, was about to protest at the soubriquet, but no. He curbed himself and chose instead to take three minutes over selecting soup of the day (Brown Windsor, for God's sake!) and nearly as long deciding on steak medium rare.

It was quite a performance, indeed bravura, sufficient to blot out doubts and woes, and help start me enjoying myself unreservedly. If only it could be always like this. On the same wavelength, á deux, sharing our youthfulness on an entirely equal basis.

Except for dress, of course, but that could be sorted.

"Know anything about RADA?" The inquiry came suddenly, and out of the blue.

"Not much." An inward groan – why this old chestnut again? What delusions of grandeur were buzzing around in his mind? In whose footsteps was he proposing to follow? Burton's? Redgrave's? And all on the basis of a single Shakespeare part? " Why?" I continued. "Thinking of trying it after Oxford?"

"Certainly not," he retorted with a grin and, as I was later forced to admit to myself, after all the dust had settled, entirely truthfully were one to take each word literally.

"But," I persisted, "something must have made you bring it up again. And don't get carried away. Except for the lucky few, it's a rotten profession."

"Really. That's not the impression I get in Cardiff. The guys at Tabor, they seem to have a good time."

"Ever heard of putting on a brave face?" I began to play with the sugar cubes, trying to forget my own young-guy aspirations. "At Bran's we used to have this annual careers fair where OBs would come back, sit at a stall, and give you advice on how to get in on their profession. OK, so one year this Hollywood star, Louis Hayward, was somehow conned into lending a hand. Long queue, him behind this desk, and as each stage-struck hopeful asks how to get on the first step, guess what he replies."

"No idea."

"Don't!" Shifting my napkin, I looked at him primly. "Just that. Don't! It never varied by a syllable. Don't!"

"Sounds a bit pointless."

"Maybe, but worth remembering, especially as he was one of the lucky ones."

"So might I be – or Pete or Oliver, if any of us happened to have ambitions in that direction."

I nodded, spearing a wayward fish. "Take my tip – stick to your last!"

"Last?"

"Whatever you've worked out with the careers people. Banking, the Law, whatever. Solid joys and lasting treasure."

"And end up with a stroke at fifty!" He shook his head. "Include me out."

I couldn't help laughing. "So – who's been reading up his movie greats?"

"Why not? Anything to alleviate all the history crap. Polish Armada, War of Jenkin's Knob. Who cares a flying fuck?"

"In which case," I retorted, as always enjoying adolescent performance despite my better judgment, "why bother with Oxford?"

"Why indeed!" And said with such vehemence I gazed at him in surprise. "Wasn't it the same with you?" he continued with a sudden blaze of resentment. "On the treadmill because that's what your family wanted? Mumsie, gran, dipso Uncle Bogface, and all the other parasites who try it on. Try to requisition my life – try to wipe out their own mistakes. Their own tossing failures!" Face contorted, all his passion seemed to reach crescendo. "But it's my life." He raised his glass aloft. "Mine!"

I held my breath as he dashed it down, only the folds of his napkin saving it from destruction!

The arrival of a fabulously grave (and deaf?) sommelier provided useful punctuation to all this. Whether comma, colon or full stop, would have to be Andy's to decide – as indeed which wine. Handing the list over, I was happy to have a breathing space to catch up on this new insight into his character. Or was it so new? There'd been that dodgy moment in Mostyn's hadn't there? And that wrestling match in Venice with Travers. But that had been horseplay, a mere tussle, not this kind of thing. Not this kind of violence only just under control. For a moment I'd been convinced he'd smash that glass, so furious was his grip, so intense his expression.

Moreover he'd gone from sun to storm in what – thirty seconds?

Still, perhaps I was reading too much into it, and certainly calm now seemed to have returned as quickly as it had fled. The copiousness and excellence of the food – his and mine respectively, I hasten to add – ensured that for the next forty minutes or so, no further outbursts were forthcoming, and we'd just embarked on coffee, when I noticed a couple of late diners draw up in a Bentley outside.

"No problem," I insisted in answer to a parallel the youngster had just drawn between stage fright and exam nerves. "You managed Malvolio OK – by comparison, three hours on 18th century politics is a piece of cake."

"It's been suggested I need more – practice."

"Oh yes?" – my mind of course turning over at what and with whom? Exactly what, in other words, I was supposed to think, salacious bastard!

" Turdoch's's decided what he calls my interpersonal skills are a bit lacking."

"No comment."

"So what do you think he's cooking up? Only an interview board – some weirdos to put me through a mock."

"Oh yes?" I muttered, my mind all over the place. For into the room had just walked Grufydd Carey and, of all people, the Carve! Fortunately they were shown to a table just inside the door where all they could see of my companion was his back. Even so, the nod I received from Carver had more than a slight air of curiosity in it, as well it might. A stripling teacher at a chic place like this was rare enough – but to be dining with a crew-cut teenager. Now that was something to set tongues wagging. Fortunately, as the boy wasn't in uniform, there'd be no suspicion of a link between him and school, but all the same I'd have to ensure his face wasn't seen. As it happened, we ourselves had entered from the terrace, the French window to which was just behind me. If we made our exit that way, Carver would be none the wiser, and the situation saved.

Quick thinking, huh?

"So what's your opinion? Knock, knock, Paul. Still with us?"

"Opinion?"

"This mock, what d' you think?"

"Mock turtle?"

"Oh yes – mock turtle. That'll really help me to get into Oxford."

"But I thought you didn't want to get in."

"Whatever gave you that idea?"

"Must have dreamt it," I said hastily, more concerned about extricating us from this mess than combating adolescent contradictions. "I say, look at the time. I must fly. Ready for home?" My signal brought a waiter running with the bill.

"Need a pee first," said Andy, folding his napkin.

"We'll go out by the terrace. There's a loo at the end."

"Foyer's nearer, sir," said the waiter helpfully. "That'll be thirty seven and nine, if you please."

"Thanks but we'll go by the terrace," I replied, fishing for my wallet and glancing Carverwards.

"Why?" Andy's question was neutral but crystal clear. No suspicion or rancour, just a request for information. But he seemed to have noticed my glance.

"Keep the change," I said to the flunkey. "Come on, gorgeous. We must get going, OK?"

But he simply turned in his chair, then turned back again. A thin smile crept across his lips. Clearly he'd seen the Carve, though Carver, head averted to his host, had not seen him.

"Now look…" I began.

With all the grace of some predator in the grasslands of Tanganyka, the boy pushed back his chair, rose and stretched – then made casually for the foyer, deliberately taking the route closest to their table. I watched in utter horror expecting any moment the worst to happen. But it didn't. Carey looked up without recognition, Carver continued to expostulate, hand waving, face averted.

Sorely tempted though I was to drive off and leave him high and dry, prudence got the upper hand and I was there outside the loo when he emerged. My expression must have been pretty fearsome since he broke into delighted laughter. "God, you look cross."

"Just," I said, nettled, "just hold it there. Look, it's not just a question of me. How about your future?"

His eyes shone even brighter. "What wimps some guys are!" he replied caustically, brushing past to the car.

The short drive back to Rhodes was undertaken in silence. Wimp indeed? Whom did he think he was talking to? True we'd escaped unscathed. But suppose Carver had noticed – what then? These days of course taking a pupil out to a meal is considered 'grooming' and quite sufficient to have you struck off the teaching register – before, that is, being hanged, drawn and quartered by the press. By contrast, those were saner times when entertaining your charges was considered part of the teaching process. But not á deux, not in mufti, and not inside the school week. Had I been had up before Hunn, explaining matters away would have been pretty awkward, and it surprised me that there was no sign that Andy understood as much.

Or did he?

His manner was genial enough at parting, but his promise to call round that evening had just a taint of arrogance about it, like when someone takes your Queen in the 3rd move of a chess match. And there I was left stuck on my usual high wire with a dodgy pole, flaying myself in his wake. How the hell had I got myself into this position where I had to take a teenager's lip like that? For that matter, why the hell had I chosen teaching? Why not accountancy or one of the cop-outs I'd suggested to him?

Numbers, ledgers, OK they're a pain, but at least they don't stab you in the back. At least they don't build you up high, then knock you flat. And not once, but over and over again, until you're old and washed out and fit only for the dung heap!

A mood which, at least sporadically, coloured the rest of my treadmill to half term. There were, it's true, one or two pluses – an outing to count flamingos with Ormulak on Wednesday, planning the Fairford expedition with Roy, a flying visit to Arnos to sign Julian up for same – but these were more than outweighed by the minuses. All my reservations over Andy together with, I suppose I have to confess, the night by night frustration of not being able to have him. Also, the piles of marking and references now that exams were near, oh and that sticky interview with Igor when I had to explain away the photos. Those of the run's closing ceremony I mean, plenty of frameshake and dodgy focus. I could hardly keep a straight face as I apologised.

So, overall it lingered, this kind of dun feeling, as though it was all too pointless, that nothing mattered, why try? That things could hardly get worse.

Then, miraculously, they did! Which if not exactly a matter for rejoicing, at least provoked me once more into some kind of animation.

The occasion was the half term staff meeting at 6pm on Friday in the library. Under Eric this had been a simple twenty minute review of form orders. Not so with Hunn! By seven, he was just getting into his stride, having embarked on a survey of each department, and thence each sport, match by match, until even Tiny Jarvis could be seen staring at the ceiling in undisguised boredom.

Finally, an interminable age later, it was the turn of the last two files to be pulled towards him.

"It's now my pleasant duty," he began, "to announce some promotions from within Common Room. All well-deserved, and all to take effect as from the end of this term. Quite a welcome Christmas box for three of our colleagues who will be glad of all the support we can give them. So, not in any particular order, we begin with the Art Department where Mr H. Jason Thornby replaces our beloved Ken Tarn whose resignation, I fear, has now become inevitable. Next, Mr Owen Murdoch to take over from Mr Christmas Watson as Second Master, on the occasion of the latter's retirement, although…"

A brief pause, as though acknowledging the buzz which ran round the room, most folk unable to believe their ears, me especially!

"...although from henceforth this post will be known as Deputy Headmaster, with a concomitant increase in responsibility. And, I need hardly say, salary – eh, Owen?"

A smirk on the pixillated features.

"Lastly, Rhodes House, where Mr Murdoch's departure will be filled by Dr Gilbert Carver as Housemaster."

Gilbert the Filbert, King of the Knuts! Could this be for real? With a groan I buried my face in my hands and prepared for more. They say bombshells come in threes, but I knew better. With men like Hunn, disaster has to be comprehensive and all-embracing, and laid on thick like peanut butter. That he'd more up his sleeve I had no doubt. I raised my head. Lord give me strength to hold my tongue!

"Which brings me," he intoned, opening the last file, "to my final piece of good news. The icing on the cake, as it were. As my sainted mother was wont to advise, always keep the best till last."

It was well weird, those pale faces round the four walls. Like quislings awaiting the gibbet. Like atheists on their deathbeds. So what would they be, these tidings of great joy? A return to birching? Lessons before breakfast? Ice showers for all, including staff? After all, these were the things that had made the public schools great. Maybe it was that kind of greatness he aspired to.

But I was wrong. None of my conjectures came anywhere near the Exocet primed on that sheet, held so calmly in those bony fingers.

"I have here," he said boldly, looking round him, " a letter from the Chairman of Council which will be distributed to all parents as they collect their sons tomorrow. It announces an important step in the school's progress. In fact, a vital step. Namely that as from next September, Tolverton will admit girls as well as boys, with a view to becoming fully co-educational within the next five years."

Dead silence. This time no buzz, no turning to neighbours to confer. Just stark silent immobility. As though this were a charcuterie and they'd suddenly been trapped in aspic.

After all we're talking about fifty years ago, before Marlborough had saved its bacon this way and set a trend for the great schools. What mixed establishments there already were, such as Bedales and Letchworth, tended to link the aberration with stunts like short trousers and vegetarian food, and were thus regarded by most of us as amiably dotty. No harm in that, but who wants to be tarred with such a brush if he can help it? Face after face now registered exactly the same sentiment – quelle dump! Can I get out? Where can I bolt to? Is anywhere safe?

After a moment, irritated perhaps by the lack of accolades, Hunn rose to his feet. "Thank you for your enthusiasm, gentlemen," he said drily. "I shall of course communicate its intensity – and unanimity – to Council and the Fustians. Have a good break!"

"Pint of rubbish?" asked Cedric, half an hour later, starting his ritual without waiting for an answer. "You look like death warmed up, old fruit."

"Not surprising," hissed Carver, pausing on his way to the loo. "Packed your bags yet, loser?"

"Get lost!"

"Clock's ticking! Better get organised."

Sudden panic in the entrails. But hang on – he'd not be taking Rhodes over till January, so he couldn't mean that. Or could it be that Carey had noticed something after all? That evening at The Paw? Had Carver been waiting for an opportune moment to spill the beans and dish me to Hunn? Surely not. Why wait so long? But if not – what else? Something maybe far more culpable and damaging…?

"Just sod off!" I said, reaching for my glass.

"In your dreams, sunshine."

"You've got nothing on me."

"Think so? If only you could see in here." He tapped his forehead. "Delivery day – exam reports? Not forgotten, surely!" With a leer, he lounged on his way.

So that was all. I breathed a sigh of relief. No, not forgotten. Not exactly. More like, pushed to the back of my mind along with about forty thousand other incipient clashes of the spheres.

"I can handle it, don't you fret!" I called after him, with a confidence I was very far from feeling. Bloody Weyburne! Bloody Tolverton! My existence was rapidly turning into a three-legged obstacle race – but one with no discernible ending! Maybe that was my destiny: to be a scholastic Flying Dutchman, harried from squall to squall, with Marsden at the wheel, and Carver in hot pursuit cheered on by his posse of Amazons! A life not in any way worth living! In which case, perhaps exposure as a sexual guerrilla would be no bad thing – or more than that. Admirable! In truth, Omelette's consummation devoutly to be wished!

As might have been expected, the bar was a hotbed of debate, table after table in frenetic dispute over Hunn's vision of the New Jerusalem. There was space at most of them, Ormulak, for instance, waving me over to his cabal with Otto and Binks and – wonders will never cease – Mrs Jarrow drinking stout. But to no avail. Just now I couldn't face it. Or, to be more accurate, them. The living dead. Folk who thought all this mattered – who thought anything mattered.

In fact, for the first time in my life, as I parked myself on a stool at the end of the bar, I found myself able to picture how someone like Chatterton felt a minute before take-off.

Well, no – that's facile. To suggest I'd contemplate suicide in any meaningful way was nonsense. There was cash in my account, wasn't there? I still enjoyed orgasm, Bach, the Marx Brothers. I could hop on a plane to Venice anytime I bloody well liked, couldn't I? Or sign myself in at Mount Athos and never meet a human again!

It was just that all those higher aspirations which loom so large when you're lean and young seemed day by day, in my case as in Rowley's, to be moving further and further out of reach. Eluding one's grasp.

OK, so maybe the answer was to forget about them. Live life on the level of the rugger buggers. Let the cannikin clink! Quaff pleasure wherever it glints – no matter if it's fools' gold – and two fingers to eternity.

All very well, but how precisely does one bin the predilections of a lifetime? Or more immediately, where, on a Friday night in the middle of the Welsh marches, does one find a pair of rent boys, cheap?

Intriguing questions which burgeoned, deep and crisp and even, as one pint turned into three and the clock crept round towards nine.

"Better gimme a packet of crisps," I said, beckoning Cedric. "Don't want to risk an ulcer. Or do I? On second thoughts, make it two."

"Sure you wouldn't rather something more substantial?" he replied, gesturing at the cheese roll, and looking rather baffled at my guffaw of laughter, short as it was raucous – though this proved but a speck of an interlude, quickly vanishing at the sudden appearance of Marcho in the doorway, grave of face, leaning on his stick, the evening paper tucked under his arm.

"Thought I'd find you here," he confessed morosely, shaking his head, doing what my father would have called a Robertson Hare. "Calamity, oh calamity! You'll never believe what's happened."

"Have a Lucozade?" I said, keeping my cool, steering him into the empty snug. Compared with the disasters of the afternoon, whatever it was troubling him must surely be a mouse of a problem. Even so, why publish it to the world? Particularly on a day like this when the Tolverton telegraph wires were working full blast.

"Lawyers, damn their eyes!" Unfolding the paper, he turned to the back page. "I mean, Clemmie's agreed to let me have the car, the boys are all excited, and now this." His cigarette holder stabbed a tiny paragraph in the Stop Press. "Talk about a kybosh!"

"Talk about riddles! Roy, could we stick to…"

"Next week's off, is that clear enough for you? Our foray to Fairford. End of story."

"But how, why?" – squinting at the smudgy print.

"They've reprieved it. At the eleventh hour. An injunction in the High Court."

"Reprieved the line? But surely that's great news. Frabjous!"

"For Fairford perhaps. But how about us? All our plans wrecked and in tatters. It really is too bad." Taking a sip of his drink, he coughed on the bubbles.

"Tell me," I said, doing some nimble thinking, "how many people know about this?"

"From the 'Advertiser'? Oh, about fifty thousand, I should say. It's not a widespread circulation."

"No, no. What I mean is, how many people have noticed? Like, rung you up in consequence?" I was blowed if I was going to surrender lightly one of my last dalliances with Andy, despite its unpredictability. The day after would see the start of exams, then there'd be reading leave, then interview week in Oxford, then end of term. It was all drawing to a close, like the end of some predictable baroque opera. A relief, yes, in some ways, but what would ensue?

"I don't quite," replied Marcho petulantly, securing his Sobranie in the holder with a neat twist, "see your point."

"My point is – who bothers to read the Stop Press? One in a million?" I lit his cigarette for him. "Look, there are seven people involved. The two lads, Jazza…"

"Jazza?"

"Sorry – Jason. Your guest, Thornby. That's three, plus my two mates from Oxford, plus we two. As far as the vast majority of this expedition's concerned, that line shuts Sunday week."

"I still don't…"

"Who's forgotten his Gray, if he ever read him?"

"Let me tell you," retorted Marcho a touch huffily, "as a boy I was never without Q in my knapsack."

"Right, then you'll recall. 'Where ignorance is bliss…'"

"Ah!" Suddenly the old blue eyes recovered their accustomed lustre. "'Tis folly to be wise?'"

"Exactly."

He pondered for a few seconds, twisting his holder this way and that, before looking up with a kind of suppressed joy on his face. "But how about Hunn? Wouldn't it be the most fearful risk? I mean he sanctioned it all as a Special Occasion, not just any old outing. Suppose someone found out?"

"Suppose they didn't!"

There we sat like two scamps planning a midnight feast in the dorm – until at last a long slow smile broke over the old features. He raised his glass. "Why not," he grinned. "They can't hang us, can they? In for a penny…"

"Quite!" I said hastily. "Absolutely!"

"You look pale, dear boy. Anything up?"

"Nothing a good long slug of half term won't cure."

"In which case, let's celebrate. And talking of slugs, could you possibly ask that landlord to slip something in this while I'm not looking. It tastes absolutely revolting!"

"Gordon's?"

"Good-oh! And make it a double!"

17: *After the Ball is Over*

Has it ever occurred to you that modern life's a bit like the wireless?

Whoops, forgot myself again! Radio, I suppose you've been dragooned into calling it these days.

What's in my mind is the constant and rapid diversity of register to which it accustoms us. Like, in previous centuries, if you went abroad to sample oo-la-la, it was once in a lifetime and for at least a year. Or a judge, for instance, leaving London on circuit would expect to be away the whole term, and take his butler with him. When you married, you married for aye.

None of this trawling that obsesses post-tech man. The hourly recce over the ether, so one minute you're hep in Ronnie Scott's, the next on your knees for Evensong from Wells, the next laughing your head off with Jewell and Warris.

Or at least, that's how it was in my Tolverton days. Now in the new millennium, with telly and smartphones and the internet, it's ten times worse. Transfixed by yon rainbow screens, you're swept from Robin Hood to Startrek, or Phnom Penh to Bourton-on-the-Water, in less time than it takes to blow your nose!

In other words, we're hooked on the very 'repeated shocks' which, according to Arnold, wear us into the grave.

A state of affairs whose truth never glared at me more convincingly than that October weekend. One evening I was this independent spunky young guy whom underlings twice my age called 'sir' and who diced with disaster like Chaplin with that globe in *The Great Dictator* – by ten the next morning I'd morphed into meek, dutiful son complete with collar and tie, welcoming mum and dad on their long-promised motor tour of the Welsh marches.

Some contrast, huh? As pronounced as those harlequinades of old, except their transformation scenes were grand and glittering, whilst mine was – well, ask yourself! And what a way to spend half-term!

Parents mean so well – and that's the whole trouble. Like mine, for instance, old darlings that they were. Obviously relieved that I'd not only got a job but appeared to be holding it down, they'd clearly decided it was time they did their bit. Doing their bit, in parental parlance, meaning, Flourish the Dosh – high time junior put down Roots!

In each of the towns we passed through, Ross-on-Wye, Monmouth, Hay – those graveyards of the border country – they'd stop and admire a house, discover its asking price, calculate the deposit required, and continue extolling its virtues while stuffing themselves with anchovy toast in the town teashop.

I, of course, kept stumm. It was obvious that had one syllable of praise passed my lips. Dad would have immediately written out a cheque to start the ball rolling, and that would have been that. Paul

Bryant, houseowner. Respectable burgess with mortgage to prove it. Points set, route assured. A scenario made even more apparent by their parting gift that Thursday. A Goblin Teasmade machine decorated in white and pink.

For Chrissake! Twenty three and I'm expected to use a Teasmade? Why not a bathchair, foot muff and ear trumpet into the bargain?

OK, I know – I'm a thankless creep! Of course it was generosity and an expression of love in a way – but what the blazes had it to do with me? The real me? Or to be precise, the gay me?

Bollock naked, facing the storm, a sexual Ché – that, if they'd only known, was the reality of their precious son (at anyrate as it appeared to their precious son) and after waving them goodbye from the King's Arms, I had no other impulse than to get drunk on meths and rape a regiment!

To be fair, I'd have probably felt much the same had their visit been delayed or not paid at all. Quite apart from the traumas of that staff meeting, there was the on-going saga of Marsden, with all its conflicting counterpoint.

That game of Russian roulette he'd so gloried in at Preston – had it been a one-off, or did I just have to cope with his being a loose cannon which might smash me to smithereens at any moment?

And then there were his mood swings, his self-centredness, and now this remove from reality as evinced by his talk of ditching Oxford in favour of drama school. Or was that just another of his poses?

But overall thrummed this other thing, quiet but persistent – my sort of ache of a need for him. What we'd experienced so far had whetted in me an appetite far from just lust, though that was part of it. Remember all that stuff at O level about valency, atoms hooking up with other atoms? It was as if knowing him had kind of charged up some potential in me which could only be satisfied with repeated contact. So that a week like this when he was out of reach represented, for me at anyrate, sheer blue murder.

In those days the school had this policy of requiring Oxbridge candidates to spend the holiday week before exams with their academic tutors, at home en famille – as Carver was unmarried, Andy had decamped to chez Rice, a blameless semi more than fifteen miles away where he'd be ensconced till Fairford. Whether he was having more or less fun there than, say, the English candidates with Trewes was of little moment – as far as I was concerned he could have been on Tristan da Cunha.

Out of reach but so not out of mind. As I say, sheer ruddy blue murder! And what hurt most was the consideration that, almost certainly, he didn't give a toss!

Anyhow, there it was – and with him revising in Gifford Lodge and the Murdochs away in some cut-price bothie in the Trossachs, Rhodes was its usual vacation self: silent, cheerful as the tomb, and possessed of an eeriness which even LSD would have done little to colour.

Gosh, I'd got the hump!

Although – again pardonnez moi – I suppose I shouldn't put it that way, not in view of what's about to transpire. Let's just say I was thoroughly fed up.

Finding something to occupy me had become, without mincing words, an urgent necessity. Something, anything, lest I start to see ghosts, hear voices or push my masturbation rate up to a dozen a day. Fortunately, while plying my razor on Friday morning, an idea both fortuitous and urgent popped into my head.

Though Hunn had welshed on making me boss of Drama, the success of *Twelfth Night* had been such as to persuade the housemasters of Stanley and Clive, both of whom had house plays scheduled for the Easter term, to request my services as director. Having had little to do with Clive, a dull institution, slightly off campus and run by a duller Physicist, I'd opted for the Stanley invitation and had promised Binksie I'd come up with a choice by the end of this half term.

Since a free day lay ahead, why not seize the opportunity and do some research – and do it moreover in a congenial way? At that time, the only really major theatrical bookshop between London and

Birmingham had its premises in Latchfield, and whilst that city's architecture was hardly an alluring prospect, dominated as it was by a large and gloomy cathedral, the drive there was not too daunting, and the place was reputed to boast a lively, though discreet, queer scene.

As I scraped the foam round that awkward bit under one's nostrils, the whole scenario lit up before me. Breezing through Elgar country in the yellow peril, finding a stunning & forgotten play by Clifford Odets or Tennessee Williams, and dining in some canalside bistro where the waiters were butch, blonde and eighteen.

No, I did not in my enthusiasm cut myself, though it was – apologies – a close shave! There were no problems en route and by twenty past eleven I'd found myself a parking space behind Moon Street, and was happily thumbing my way through the Prophater, Davenport & Co's catalogue.

For those of you not acquainted with sixties' Latchfield, the best way of describing Prophater's is to say it bore a strong resemblance to London's then more famous Samuel French emporium in Southampton Row. A long Georgian building with bay windows, its sales area occupied the ground floor, whilst the first floor was given over to offices and a rehearsal room. A further storey, accessed by a spiral staircase marked PRIVATE, added mystery to the already intriguing brew.

Despite his recent death, this was still, of course, the country of Sir Barry Jackson, and the stools and sofas provided by Prophater's functioned as a warm, free and congenial meeting place for the indigent actors who seem to throng wherever a rep struggles on in England. Indigent maybe, but always possessed of that indefatigable verve which drives the Mr Jingles of every age and clime.

Though entirely new to me, I was immediately struck by this kind of foment or eagerness about the place, probably much the same thing that had excited Andy in Cardiff. Also, its sheer physical size, almost surpassing that of its London counterpart.

Immediately on passing through the porter's lobby, you encountered a sort of apodyterium dedicated to magazines, periodicals and the like, plus a rack or two of the vinyl LP records just then coming into vogue. Next, a handsome chamber lit by a glass dome and devoted to sketches, one-act plays, and media texts. Lastly, the main room with its lofty shelves containing, so ran the company's boast, every play in the English language currently in print, and peopled with a considerable crop of youngsters, both young and old, in easy chairs, reading this and that as though their lives depended on it.

Were they actually learning lines, I wondered, without buying the books? How cute.

Here, of course, there was nothing so vulgar as a counter to mar the Green Room atmosphere. Instead, in the bay window at the far end stood an exquisite Regency table on which reposed a telephone, a box of Liquorice Allsorts and a copy of Miss Hartnoll's *Companion to the Theatre*, and behind which, from time to time, could be espied a diminutive clerk who appeared to be there to accept orders – albeit in a loud, shrill voice which carried your business to the four corners of the establishment. The next stage in the process I couldn't quite fathom, but doubtless time would tell.

I'd parked myself on a leather chesterfield, hoping to get inspiration from proximity to its other occupant, a guy of about my age, in scruffy cords and denim shirt, whose profile suggested Hamlet but who was actually perusing *Death at Broadcasting House*. Neither being much use to me – what I was looking for was a satirical comedy with a small cast, all male, plus one set and Victorian costumes – I turned back to my catalogue, which was not much use either.

Victorian costumes, by the way, were what the Tolverton wardrobe abounded in. Mediaeval, Tudor, Restoration – forget it! But if you wanted to kit out a *Patience* or a *Pinafore*, Mrs Jarrow could do you proud.

Which in a kind of way was helpful in my present dilemma. At the back of my mind lurked a play I'd seen on TV a year or two ago by one of those French authors with an unpronounceable name. A rather striking play centred on a love affair between two hunchbacks – its satire, by the way, being directed not at humps but love, a distinctly more intractable deformity. Unfortunately its title escaped me, and after a few minutes scanning the pages for every comedy remotely French, I gave up and approached the table.

"Anything I can help you with, sir?"

"Well actually," I confided as he extracted from the box one of those round bobble-clad sweets, bright blue like a maytime Berberis, "I'm looking for a play."

"Get away!"

"No, really. Only I've forgotten what it's called."

"Any clues to trigger sir's old grey matter?"

"Well, it's one of those modern French jobbies…"

"Sartre, Anouilh, Prevért?"

"Quite probably. And it's about love…"

"Divine, straight, queer?"

"Well, straight – in a funny sort of way."

He cocked his head to one side wryly. "Funny ha-ha?"

"Not intentionally," I said. "More, funny peculiar. It's actually about a love affair between two, er – how shall I put it? Two hunchbacks."

"Anouilh," he nodded, swivelling his chair round forty five degrees and picking up the phone. "Fred?" he barked. "*Ardéle* – any in stock? And hurry it up, gorgeous – gentleman's waiting!"

Gentleman? Abject cringing dope, more like! What was that I'd said? Funny peculiar? Me and my wretched tongue!

For there before me, silhouetted against the light of the window as the guy toyed with the receiver, was displayed the most pronounced and unmistakable hump I'd ever seen. Worse than Olivier, worse than Charles Laughton. I could have sunk through the floor.

Hand over mouthpiece, he swung back my way. "Darling play," he said. "So true to life. It was premiered near here at the Birmingham Rep you know, before its London run. Always radical, old Sir B. Her of course you never see, but the boyfriend – yes, Fred? Yes? I'll check." Hand again over the receiver, he raised an eyebrow. "Copy per character, plus one tech, one prompter?"

"Why not?"

"Sir, you're so amiable!" At which he returned to his phone "That'll be thirteen then, darling – and do hurry them up!"

Of course, I should have guessed! Thirteen, Friday, funny peculiar! And people deride it all as superstition!

"That'll be six pounds, sixteen and six. Like to take a seat, sir? They'll be up directly. Pay the porter."

Feeling every devil in hell was prodding my arse, I retreated to the sofa where Denim Dave was still reading his potboiler. Or at least apparently. Every now and then I felt him shoot a sideways glance at me – doubtless getting a butcher's at the callous cunt who mocks cripples for fun.

At last I could take it no longer and leapt to my feet. "I'll call back later," I said to the astonished desk, offering a pound note. "Will that do for deposit?"

"Sir, you're so…"

I fled, not stopping till I reached the cathedral where I lunched in the safety of the Crypt Café, afterwards catching an unexpected Carl Rosa matinee of *Maritana* at the local Playhouse. All very seemly and English, but just past five found me heading back to Prophater's with undiminished dread. Would he still be on duty, their resident mannikin? Devoutly I hoped not.

In fact I'd taken the precaution of writing out a cheque beforehand, so I was inside the entrance lobby for a mere three minutes or so while the porter wrapped up my books in brown paper, sealing the parcel with red wax and the Prophater, Davenport crest. So far, so good. Maybe all was going my way after all.

You can imagine my surprise, therefore, when a hand touched my sleeve. Gently, no aggro, but even so I flinched before looking round, only to find – my God what a relief – the guy from the couch. Mister Death at the BBC.

Sure, this time he'd shaved and found himself a pair of more or less white chinos, but the profile was the same, so too the eyes and the faintest hint of dope that hovered around him – so faint it was attractive and almost tempting. Moreover, I couldn't help noticing a copy of the Anouilh in his left hand.

"I know this sounds a bit dodgy," he said with extreme diffidence, "but I just wondered if you fancied a drink? On me, I mean."

Now this, hard-bitten old campaigner though I am, was an approach for which I was totally unprepared. I mean, guys simply don't come up to you in broad daylight and offer you freebies. Unless of course there's an ulterior motive, but even then it's done with looks rather than words. Besides I didn't have much cash on me and the guy's face, while interesting, certainly that, was by no means an immediate turn-on. And as for his denim! Why do they wear stuff that covers so much up, in his case a hint of decent pecs? But who can be sure?

I was just about to plead trains to catch, or phone calls to put through, when he hurried on in what was admittedly an engaging voice.

"Don't get me wrong," he said. "It's just that in Prophater's – well, sorry but I overheard you talking."

"Right!" I shrugged. "No problem. I mean, you could hardly help it. What a voice that bloke has."

"Milly?" He nodded, gently steering me into motion. "You should see him in panto. Best Widow Twanky in the midlands."

"I bet."

"Did I get it right? That you're planning new production of *Ardéle*?"

"It's on the cards," I replied, a little perplexed, noticing that we seemed to be turning into a cobbled yard dominated by a small, shabby pub.

"Good for you," enthused my new companion. "Mils was telling me there's been no revival since the Rep did it in 1950. You're on to a good thing there."

"Hope so," I said cautiously, wondering what on earth someone like this could possibly know about the ins-and-outs of public school drama. His next remark, however, put an abrupt end to my musings.

"Should be good box-office."

Box-office? Since when did a school like Tolverton charge for seats? And then of course it clicked, his whole misconception. I only just resisted a laugh. In this bloke's eyes I must seem a mighty impresario, about to stage a lavish version of this crummy play – about which, by the way, I remembered almost nothing except Charles Gray in military costume looking precisely as though he'd just stepped out of *White Horse Inn* – and stage it moreover in the West End or on Broadway or similar. In which case his next gambit would be…?

And was. "Got some excellent parts, that play."

"Oh quite. Something for everyone, as they say."

"Right – though my favourite's Nicholas, remember? Nathalie's boyfriend? Oh, here we are. Hi, Gus – bit early today. Now, er…?" – turning to me slightly embarrassed.

"Paul," I said.

"Ross," he replied, extending a hand and surprising me with a very strong grip. "Ross Farquhar. No relation, I'm afraid. I can recommend the IPA. Will that do? Jolly good. Gus, two halves of Phipps" – selecting a florin from his very small store of silver, from which I surmised both that his career was hardly flourishing, and that Phipps was the local, what Cedric was wont to call, rubbish!

A table found, and the tankards before us, he put a finger to his lip. "Now where were we?"

"Nicholas," I prompted casually, starting to enjoy myself. There was something engagingly provincial about the guy, as though he was ready to be made happy by the slightest favour, gift or gesture. Quite different from some folk I could mention.

"Oh right. Yes, young Nicky, the General's second son. What you might call the romantic lead, desperately in love with, er…?"

"Nathalie?"

"Of course. The General's, um – daughter-in-law."

"You obviously know the play well," I observed wryly, having noticed the pristine state of his copy which gave every indication of having been read but once, and probably that afternoon.

He toyed with the pewter. "Oh well," he retorted, "demands of the profession and all that. One has to have an extensive repertoire." He paused and looked at me almost apologetically. "I'm an actor, you see."

"No, really?" I hope my innocence passed muster.

"Oh, yes. Trained and all, the Central. I've got my card already. Been touring in *Julius Caesar*. Publius. Just closed."

"Publius?" I said with a smile, "well done" – noting for the first time that under that shock of hair this thespian was very young indeed. Hardly more than Andy in all probability. I suddenly felt a pang – that old pang I knew so well – protectiveness, mixed in with the other.

"I could read for you," he said eagerly – or rather with his extraordinary blend of eagerness and diffidence.

"Read?"

"For Nicholas. My room's only a couple of minutes away and my landlady's used to it, me letting my hair down. Raised voices, and so on. I mean, he has to get quite passionate, doesn't he, young Nicky? That final scene where Nathalie makes it clear that Maxim's the only man that can fulfil her sexual needs and her…"

By now, serious alarm bells were ringing. What the hell was I getting into?

Though most of my theatrical experience and all of my theatrical ambitions, except in daydreams, were strictly amateur, I knew enough about that world to see a casting couch approaching. I'd always assumed that particular sport was producer or director led, but when you come to think of it, why necessarily so? Here was a hopeful desperate for work. What might he not offer to get his chance of fame?

OK, OK, dilemma simple, outcome obvious, you might think. But c'est ca? How about Andy? True a liaison like this might vouchsafe insights which would help knock them on the head, those half-baked acting ideas of his – but would that justify my being unfaithful? I mean, after the bliss of that awful train?

Moreover there was something else, wasn't there? Something far worse, as I expect you've surmised, mon guru! Something which meant I'd landed myself in what can only be described as a pretty pickle!

Sure, I needed a shag. Badly. At my age that could still be, and was at this moment, a dire imperative. But there was no getting round the fact that, sooner or later, I must disabuse this tyro as to my status. Come clean that, rather than a C.B. Cochrane or Anthony Quayle, I was just a punk schoolmaster about to stage this epic in a converted gym on a budget of forty quid. So there it was. If indeed sex was on the agenda, exactly when should I spill the beans?

In other words, tell him first and scupper my chances, or confess afterwards and put up with being denounced as a rat and bastard!

Playing perhaps for time, my brain as usual managed to come up with a sort of compromise. Maybe I'd read too much into his approach. Maybe there was no erotic agenda. Why not let him get on with this audition as he'd requested? I wouldn't be expected to give a decision there and then, and could later write him a long and detailed analysis of his rendition which, despite my turning him down, would boost his c.v. for the future. The more I watched him chatter on, the more certain I became. This was really, and no irony intended, a very nice guy indeed.

As expected, his room was meagre. A double bed squashed hard into a corner in an attempt to stop it dominating the place – an attempt which failed signally! A couple of balding armchairs, a desk, a stool, and two sliding doors, one leading to a kind of kitchen alcove, the other to a miniature shower room. The carpet was tiny and oval and much trampled, and the fire was switched off. A very basic habitation indeed.

I declined coffee.

"You sure?" he said. "Well then" – we were still standing – "make yourself at home. Shall I take your jacket?"

So, were my suspicions justified? Well, as I wriggled free, he managed to touch the base of my neck somehow, as well as kind of brush against one of my arms. It was quite enough for me. As he disappeared into the washroom, I parked myself and began to compose an apologia in my mind, ready to articulate before things could go further. But that, I suppose, would have been all too easy. When the Gods have you on the rack, they like their pound of flesh!

In no time at all, he emerged as if from the wings somewhere. I gazed in amazement. He'd divested himself of his T-shirt and belt and was smiling confidently as he stood there, hands in pockets, deliberately defenceless, offering a body slightly skinny and pale although... Well, we'll come to that later, the er - contrast!

So, Mr Cute. But homely with it, as if you were about to sleep with your favourite brother. I was clearly expected to make the next move, despite skeletons beginning their rattle.

"Oh, Ross," I began, caught on the hop, "we need to talk."

Something began to die in his eyes. "Sorry," he shrugged. "I just thought..."

"Yuh, and I mean – great. But..."

"No need to explain. It happens. Crossed wires..."

"As if..."

"What then? Boyfriend at home, warming your slippers?"

"Sod off," I grinned. "You're way off beam. Look, it's a totally different, sort of – obstacle."

"But an obstacle!" He seemed puzzled now, and I suppose it did all sound a bit clinical as though were discussing indigestion rather than sex.

"All I mean is," I replied, getting to my feet, "you've sort of got hold of the wrong end of the stick."

"What, you're not queer?"

"Wrong again!" I laughed. "Ross, I'm not only queer but bloody glad of it. And relaxed and stuff."

By now he was looking well perplexed. "Fine, so what's the problem?"

"This play, OK? This fantastic megashow of mine, cast of thousands and so on – well, things aren't quite how you think."

He nodded ruefully. "You've cast it already. Fine, I…"

"No – look, why jump ahead like that all the bloody time? You're so exasperating."

"Sorry."

"It's just that you don't, I'm afraid, qualify."

"I see. Not enough presence, not enough appeal, not…"

"Balls!" I exploded. "Mate, you'd make an ideal Nicky – you're well fit, you're spirited, intelligent – everything Anouilh had in mind. It's simply that to get into this cast, as Nicky or the hunchback or the sodding wardrobe mistress, you have to be a member of Stanley House, Tolverton. Got it? It's a school production, for Chrissake! I'm a teacher, OK? Not some Val Parnell with a dozen theatres at my disposal."

Now it was his turn to be amused. A broad smile spread across his face. "So I'd make an ideal Nicky?"

"Honest. I meant every word."

"Or a Romeo?"

"I've always thought he's queer."

"Or a Bosie?"

"Be my guest."

"Well now," he murmured, starting to unbutton my shirt, "as to that, I rather think it's the other way round."

"Sounds intriguing" – shuddering slightly as his fingertips found my ribs and began to tease. "So you don't mind – about the play, I mean?"

"Remember your minims?"

"My what?"

"Every Good Boy Deserves Favour?"

"Have I been good?"

"Ask yourself."

"And which particular favour?" I asked, reaching suddenly for his shoulders, running my hands down the silk of his smooth back, feeling the incipient muscle of his arms hot against my cheek, all thoughts of Andy vanished.

But he took a step back, caught me round the neck and pulled my face bodily towards him. "Why not," he whispered, bringing his lips close to mine, "let's cut the fucking script!"

Undressing took about a second and a half – then suddenly my mouth was at the mercy of this sort of asp, writhing this way and that, along and under my tongue, at the brink of my throat, making the blood course through my head, my hands shake at the sheer ecstacy life could pull out of the hat without warning.

Not that this was the youngster's only trick. By no means, though nothing maybe I suppose which would have been deemed world shattering in Chelsea or Casablanca. But in Latchfield? A hudred yards from where they used to burn witches?

It was just that down his left flank, from about halfway between armpit and hip, and spreading south beyond his bum, stretched a bold, colourful frieze of tattoo in the form of a grotesque danse macabre. Folk in lines of antic, like that Bergman film. And skeletons. And scythes. And devils in green and red. The whole mediaeval panorama.

Which, startling in itself, was enhanced by its contrast with the light tan of its canvas. The taut warm skin, lowering itself now on to mine, his mouth biting the side of my neck and left shoulder. And so it began, my second matinée of the day. Not just the usual delights. Like, the feel of the other's body's carnal rhythm, its urge priming your own. Like, the sight of all that power heaving itself and you ever nearer the mindless bloodwild verity of the BB. But this additional – no, this overwhelming – vista of the ages dancing to destruction.

As his movements gained in pace, so did theirs: the thief choking on his gibbet, the recusant in flames, naked maidens writhing in the arms of satyrs leering through the ochre smoke, serpents coiling their whiplash round the crotch of lovers, dragging them into a stifling ultramundane torment of sulphurous vermilion pitch. So that when it finally came, my mind-blow of a Big Bang – why do scientists give stuff such childish names? – it wasn't just your usual, standard, spunk the rafters jobbie, but *ultimate* relief. Annihalation. Collision sanspareil of life and death, in which creation seemed to rage for an instant into the one original sapient molecule.

In other words, about ten thousand and five on the Richter scale, or – roughly approximate, let's face it, to scoring with Andy en route to Brighton.

Andy – me wedged with him between the carriage seats, amidst fag ends and toffee wrappers.

A sobering fantasy and one etched all the deeper as it lay warm beside me, this painting of doom, possessed like me of a name and parents and preferences – and awaiting the same eventual agony.

What actually did I want? Tsunamis like these, marking out my life like milestones, inscribed with people instead of distances? Would that be enough? When the final reckoning came, would that be enough?

Sure there'd be stuff en route, poetry, insight, irony even – like now, that this body next to me which could drive punters to such delirium, was the one body which could never drive itself thus.

But still it remains, the question. Will it be enough? After the break of dawn, after one's last skim through the diary – assuming such a thing's permitted – will it be enough to have enjoyed enjoyment instead of using it, carborundum tip and all, to blast through into what there is?

18: *Come Friends who Plough the Sea*

One's first drive in a new vehicle has always a special exhilaration about it, agreed? The smell of the leather, the sheen of the windscreen, the absence of clutter, old crisp packets, dead gum and the like – everything seems to promise verve and conquest. Just like the first night of marriage. Before, that is, twentieth century promiscuity took off the dairy!

In which case, you can imagine what this first journey in the new minibus was like. KIP 528 had been delivered only two days earlier. A sixteen seater Transit in creamy Cambridge blue with white-walled tyres, she looked a dream, and it clearly cost Roy an effort to concede that, given his gout, it was I that should have the honour of taking her out through the gates. And what a buzz it gave me, especially when we got celebratory waves and cheering from Chuffley and Guy Travers as we passed them coming out out of Old Barn.

"Up a bit early, aren't they?" grunted Marcho, still somewhat miffed at not being able to drive. "Having an illicit smoke, I suppose."

The two best-looking seniors in the school? I should co-co! With an inner smile, I changed into fourth wondering what it must be like to be Roy. I mean, so profoundly naïve. Did it ensure a guaranteed smooth ride, or simply postpone the evil day?

These early Transits had one particularly aggravating feature, that owing to double tyres, their rear axles were considerably wider than the front. With cornering thereby rendered as much luck as judgment, those white Michelins had lost, I'm afraid, much of their virginity by the time we descended into Oxford and its jangle of college bells. Even so, spirits were high as we turned right at Carfax to make our rendezvous with Julian and Jugs outside the late-Victorian extravaganza of Grimbly Hughes. It was just before noon and there they were, on time, in Julian's Morgan, eating cornets.

OK, I confess. Including the pair in the party hadn't quite been the act of pure altruism it seemed, though I'd not seen them for some time and this was an ideal opportunity. The fact is, they'd provide company for Jaz, whom Marcho had insisted on inviting, and would, moreover, contribute a second car to our caravan. A vital necessity had the line really been closing, since the last official train terminated at Fairford, and the return working would not, as we supposed, carry passengers. As things turned out, the extra wheels counted as a mere, if welcome, bonus, allowing us to photograph the line in more varied detail. At least, that was the theory!

Introductions were quickly made – and, I might say, successfully since Jazza was immediately ensconced in the Morgan's dickey and whisked off at high speed stationwards. And thus we all arrived at the Birmingham side in excellent time for the 12.44 departure.

In those days, Oxford had separate booking offices for the up and down platforms, and there next to the timetables for Worcester and the North was a hastily scrawled blackboard, in front of which, arms akimbo, wide smiles on their faces, stood the Morgan trio. "Guess what?" crowed Jazza – at which, like the Red Sea, they parted to reveal the following legend: *Yarnton, Witney & Fairford – Closure postponed pending arbitration in the High Court. Interim timetable during Appeal: down 12.44pm, 6.49pm (not Sundays), 10.10pm – up 6.47am, 6pm.*

With a sly wink my way, Marcho levered himself to the ground. "What's this?" he cried. "Absolute piffle. You scallywags have made it up. Where did you get the chalk? There's a £5 fine for this sort of thing you know. Paul, I'm shocked. Fancy putting them up to such tricks!"

"Naughty, naughty!" whispered Andy, scrambling past the gearstick after Jukes. "Who needs a spanking!"

"Promises, promises," I grinned.

So much for his depression and mood swings! Maybe he'd taken our week of enforced hiatus rather differently to me. But I had no time to think about that now, nor cope with guilt feelings over my lapse with Ross. "What's the trouble, Roy?" I inquired, leaning out of the window with as angelic an expression as I could muster. "Missed it, have we?"

"Don't play the giddy goat. I can recognise your scrawl when I see it."

I had to spread a hand across my mouth to avoid giving the game away, but fortunately Jaz came to the rescue. "Honestly, Chaplain, it's authentic. How could Paul have possibly contrived…?"

"Simple! Slipped it to you rascals, I expect, while I wasn't looking."

"A *black*board?" Jazza's incredulity was a wonder to behold. Again I nearly exploded.

It was now Julian's turn. With that wonderful air of confidence of his, he put a hand on Marcho's shoulder. What terrors did a mere clergyman hold for him? As president of OUCA, he'd handled Head Masters, Heads of college, Archbishops, visiting statesmen film directors and Rajahs, hadn't he? Probably slept with a fair sprinking of them into the bargain! Roy Marchpane must have seemed very small beer by comparison. "On the level, sir. We saw the guy put the board out as we arrived."

"What guy?" retorted Marcho, just about maintaining his mask. "If you mean porter, say so!"

"Look," I interposed, jumping down to join them, "wouldn't the simplest thing be to ask the booking clerk? If he says it's a hoax,

I'll go drown myself in the canal, OK?" So saying, I pushed through the door, the others following.

I'd intended to bring along my tape recorder, but guess what – I'd mislaid the bugger! As usual.

Quelle pity!

For as Marcho launched into contention with the nearest officials, I was once again knocked for six by the ancient lilt of their local burr. Remember, we're talking well postwar. By now, the bewitching tones of artisan Oxford were rapidly giving way to the coarser, more cosmopolitan accents of London and the Midlands, what survivals there were being confined to college scouts and the like, the churches, the market – and of course the railway. It's impossible on a page like this to replicate the sublime sweetness of Oxfordese as the Scholar Gipsy must have heard it – but perhaps it's sufficient to record herein that once, and recently, it did exist, and to remind my older readers of those gentle voices they must have encountered in their youth from tapsters or herdsmen on the borders of Oxfordshire and Berkshire, and to hope that some other aspiring Cecil Sharp will in due course not forget his Grundig!

The gentleman behind the grille that day was a prime specimen of his race, and reminded me of nothing so much as Martha, the very last passenger pigeon, as she must have seemed to visitors to Cincinnati Zoo in 1914. And, by the way, I use the term gentleman advisedly. His hair was a carefully brushed silver, his face was a carefully shaved pink, and he was dressed in a neat seemly suit of charcoal grey. Only the union badge in his lapel belied his trade – that and a certain calm borne of the certainty of his bright steel threads to the cotes and coasts beyond.

"Good morning, sir," he addressed Marcho as the latter began his querulous tirade against the perfidy of British Railways Western Region in not informing the travelling public of this change of plan, and finishing his tirade in fine style: "Seventy miles we've driven," he cried. "Seventy miles over hill and dale, and nothing to show for it. No bunting, no brass band, no mourners."

"Bless you, sir," came the mild reply, "don't fret. You won't have long to wait. South Leigh, and most of they places, Alvescot and Langford, all be wunnerful remote. Cut off every winter at the first snow. That's when Paddington'll shut their line. You mark my words. Come back at first snow, and you'll see yon trains replaced by helicopters a-dropping rations. It's progress, sir. We can't stand in its way."

Before Marcho could reply, Jukes wandered in carrying the blackboard. "Hi," he greeted the clerk. "Sorry, but there's an error here, surely."

"How be that, young master?"

"Fairford's the end of the line, right?"

"As fate decreed. 'Twas intended to forge on to Cirencester, but..."

"All right then, look here. Three trains out, but only two back. Doesn't make sense. Engines and carriages must be piling up there like billy-oh!"

"He be sharp and no mistake," chuckled the clerk to Marcho. "No flies on that one."

"Really, Jukes," retorted Roy, "call yourself a scholar, and can't work out a simple logistical problem. You wouldn't have lasted long in the war, my lad. One of the trains must work back empty." He turned to the clerk. "Isn't that so?"

"Quite right, sir. Due Yarnton quarter past ten of a morning, Mondays excepted."

"But why empty? Why not allow passengers on?"

"Because," explained the old doyen patiently, "it would be too useful. They villagers might catch it to go shopping."

"What's wrong with that?"

Clerk and clergyman exchanged compassionate glances, as if to say, Pity the young – but they'll grow out of it – the Way of the World has to be learnt sooner or later, even by intellectuals!

"It's like this, George," explained the latter. "If the trains ran conveniently, people might use them more. Then the system might make a profit. Then they'd have no excuse to shut it down."

Jukes looked puzzled. "They?" he queried.

"The government!"

"Paddington!" nodded the clerk. "Lord bless us, young master – our job these days bain't to run lines, but close them. It's called Nationalisation!"

"Who's a cretin, then?" said Andy putting his arm round Jukes.

"Cretin yourself!"

Roy reached for his wallet. "Well," he said, still keeping a straight face, "it's a crying shame, but we'll make the journey anyway. That'll be seven day returns to Fairford, if you please."

"Fine growed lads for fourteen, aren't they?" A broad wink at the 6th formers. "That'll be four adults and three halves" – clearly including the horrified Jaz in the latter, though today he did rather resemble a leveret fresh from the nest. "One pound, ten and three in all."

"Tell me, what would it cost now, to upgrade from 3rd?"

"No 1st to Fairford," said the other, franking the green slips. "Not since 1927."

"But," queried Marcho as if haggling in some Eastern souk, "I expect you've got the odd white survivor still in stock?"

A shrewd eye was cocked at Roy and his dog collar. "Let me finish these and I'll see. Tell you what." He lent closer in conspiratorial whisper. "How would a furlough to Lechlade do?"

"First war?"

"Need ye ask?"

We left them to their archives, preferring to inspect our shiny dream express so soon to speed us to the Dim-moon City of Delight – though reality turned out to be a Churchward 2-6-2T plus a couple of abject coaches whose suburban lake was just discernible under several layers of grime. Nevertheless they offered compartments, corridors and lavatories, thus easily eclipsing the buses which would soon replace them.

Into one compartment piled myself, Jaz and, eventually, Marcho – into others some way for'ard the four ingénus. And thus began the last of my expeditions with Roy, though not just that.

In retrospect, there seemed to come over me this sixth sense that here & now was somehow alpha and omega – of my Tolverton days, perhaps the defining one. Of course the future would still, cross fingers, hold one or two rays of sunshine – a last bizarre dinner party at Buggleskkely maybe, or Baffle the Yaffle 2 – but as for that kind of long warm skein of brotherhood that can only be found in schools and monasteries, and instances of which the memory particularly cherishes, this was to be it, finale, finito.

Which is why so much of its detail remains as fresh in my mind as the broken sun and steam of that afternoon over forty years ago. As the train twisted and turned its way through the points and intersections of Oxford yard, as we lurched off the main line at Yarnton, it began to feel as though we were leaving the 20th century behind. The roadless expanses beyond Cassington; the countrywomen in headscarves waiting at South Leigh, all with baskets, one with a piglet; the route right through the middle of Brize Norton aerodrome, with USAF atomic bombers so close you could almost touch them; the goats on the line at Carterton; the bridges so narrow the train seemed to sidle under them like an East End wideboy; and finally, after streams and meadows and haycocks by the million, Fairford itself.

Where four porters rose to meet what would have been, but for ourselves, a single passenger.

Where our help was requested in shouldering the engine round on its turntable because the handgear had broken.

Where a full mile and a half lay between station and town, adorned with superannuated gas lamps which might have come straight out of Dickens's London.

And where, on a rise between market square and the Colne, we encountered St Mary the Virgin, Fairford, commanding in its Cotswold stone, flamboyant with its stained glass of fabulous antiquity – and quietly guarded by an old lady knitting mittens, who was only too pleased to show us the tombs and Parker bible, and who was equally courteous when refusing her half crown tip.

Roy and Jugs, of course, were in their element, the former transfixed by the technicolor gloom, young Fell delighting the organ with some minor but perky Lubeck – though the rest of us, all thoughts of filming trains and track forgotten, were soon loping down through the graves to the river, there to throw stones into the mill race, or feed Trebor refreshers to a suspicious ram rubbing its flank on a stile.

All idyllic, and I well remember deciding that, come what may, here's where, if I fail to buck the trend and eventually do have to die, my grave must be. I even picked out a plot and marked it with a lolly stick.

Thoughts of interment? At twenty three? Well weird, a shrink would say, but how many of us are born cheerful when you come to think of it?

By four, having missed lunch, we were all desperate for tea, the obvious (and, in all probability, only) venue being The Bull, a long weathered hostelry next to the churchyard, which turned out to be the most famous fishing inn in the county. The manageress confessing herself to be short staffed that day, the services of Marcho to slice cucumbers and the lads to light the drawing room fire were quickly procured, leaving Jaz and I to cast amused eyes over the stuffed pikes and perches in their glass cases high on the walls of the bar. At least, mine were amused – his were oddly appreciative.

After a couple of minutes, he edged close to me. "Hoped I'd get you alone for a moment," he murmured.

"Oh yes?" I turned to him with a wry look. "Designs on my honour have we?"

"Not quite."

"I warn you, the answer's invariably yes."

"I'll bear it in mind." He gestured at a sofa and we sat down. "Look Paul, could we speak seriously for once? No arsing about?"

I shrugged. "Lay on Macduff." Could I sense trouble – was this seamless day about to curdle into normality?

"See, I'm in a bit of a fix. On that train coming down, I kind of saw something I shouldn't have. Right?"

"Saw what precisely?"

"Instead of heading straight back from the loo to our compartment, I thought I'd explore a bit. Take a butcher's at more of those sepia prints you were waxing lyrical about."

"Sewage-on-Sea, 1909?"

"Right – well, that's how I passed this compartment where that mate of yours, the one with the curly hair…"

"Toby Copeland?"

"Whatever – well, he and young Marsden seemed to have managed to, as it were, lock their compartment door. I didn't know it was possible."

"You tried it?" I said cautiously.

"I'd no alternative. See, they were alone."

"Yes?"

"And huddled up together. As far as I could see in what the movies call – sorry about this – a clinch."

Wow! I thought instinctively. Jammy bastards! Some people have all the luck! But assuming an air of gravity, I cocked my head to one side. "As far as you could see?"

"I'm pretty certain."

"How embarrassing! Poor you, what an experience on your first school trip! Still, I see the dilemma. Not being 100% certain, I mean. That's the problem – from a distance it's so bloody easy to get hold of the wrong end of the stick, isn't it? And flagrente and stuff, it's a pretty serious accusation. Maybe a touch of the old Nelsons might be your best bet, given…"

"I wondered that, but there's this complication. Just as I moved on, Marsden turned his head. He might have seen me. In which case, can I really risk it? Turning a blind eye? Wouldn't I be on a sticky wicket – if I let it pass, that is?"

"Told anyone else, have you?" I inquired as the manageress swept by with a tray of sandwiches and hot Sally Lunns. Jaz shook his head. "Then don't – not for the time being at anyrate. Let me have a word with the parties concerned, OK?"

"Would you?" His sense of relief was palpable.

"After all, there might be an explanation. Like, uh – were the blinds at all, even partly down? Silly question, but…"

"No, not at all."

"There you are then. Would you risk a spot of hoi-toi-toi with a boyfriend without taking precautions?"

A wary look came into his eye. "With my *girl*friend? No."

"Precisely," I retorted with a kind of post-reckless gaiety. "Give me twenty four hours and I'll get back to you. I expect it's all a storm in a teacup. Talking of which…"

As we joined the others, the fire which had been fitting and fretting suddenly broke into roaring flame, and for the next half hour there was nothing to do but bask in its warmth and eat teacake with salty Gloucestershire butter. Oh, and in my case, of course, relax after what I'd managed hopefully to turn into a damp squib.

Relax? I expect there are those among you who're wondering, how can the idiot relax after his boyfriend's been caught red-handed with a rival? And a younger, fitter rival at that!

OK, of course there was a side of me that felt betrayed, sort of. But remember I'd fancied Jugs long before I'd even so much as noticed Andy. And now the thought of them together – well, there was something profoundly vicarious about it. Almost as if I'd been on that seat with them. Added to which, who was I to preach fidelity? It was barely twenty four hours since I'd been under the sheets with Ross and loving it.

Fair's fair. Let's say Andy's transgression, like mine, had just been the impulse of a moment, a blip that could be sorted out given tact and patience. Besides it gave me a reason to demand a tete-a-tete with each of them, Andy and Toby separately. Delectable!

The former I judged might be conveniently postponed till Tolverton, whilst some opportunity on the train would present itself for the latter. Hopefully. But this time, alack, in a spirit of general camaraderie, everyone squeezed into one compartment, Jukes brought out his harmonica, and a general sing-song began. All the stuff you might expect: *Three coins in the fountain, Horsey horsey don't you trot, Wish me luck as you wave me goodbye*, and that Cavan O'Connor ballad which had had yours truly in tears at the age of seven, *I'm only a roving vagabond*. A memorable party, but one which showed every sign of sustaining itself all the way to Oxford.

I was beginning to get agitato when, having ground to a noisy halt at Eynsham, and after sundry clankings at the front, we were amazed to see our engine reverse past us on the down platform loop.

"Shunting!" cried Marcho in rapture. "Good-oh!" – flinging his stick aside and joining in the general exodus. General, that is, except for myself and Toby whom I plucked aside by the sleeve.

"Can I have a word?"

"Paul?" – trying to free himself.

"Long time, no talk."

"Absolutely, but why not later? This I must see. Just like playing with one's Hornby again."

"OK – shall I drive over to Keble tomorrow?"

"Tomorrow?"

"Or whenever – I could stay the night."

"I see," he replied, relaxing a bit, turning my way. "All right then, out with it. What's cooking? What's got the Bryant on heat and nosey?"

"I'd hardly say on heat," I retorted. "Just, I wanted to…"

"Is this about Julian, by any chance? This ridiculous engagement? I didn't know he'd gone public yet."

"Julian engaged?" I cackled in spontaneous and huge disbelief. "You're pulling my leg!"

"Straight up."

"To whom, for Chrissake?"

"Tina Hatherop – no less."

"You can't be serious. Madam Mascara?"

"Which only goes to prove what they say – handsome gays always marry ugly broads!"

"Is that so? Thank God we're both safe in that case."

"Speak for yourself!" With a wry grin, he reached for the door strap. "Look – if there's nothing else…"

"Hang on," I said hastily. "This won't take a minute, but there are one or two things on my mind."

"Won't they keep?"

"Afraid not."

"Fire away," he said resignedly, lounging against the fire extinguisher. "Numero one? I'd like to get out and see the fireworks."

"OK, OK," I said carefully. This offhand reaction wasn't quite what I'd expected. Where was the playful Toby of old? Always resourceful? Always glad to be of help? Nothing too much trouble?

"It's like this," I continued, "sorry and all that, but one of my colleagues has, well, got this bee in his bonnet. Says one of the lads was seen with you in the train, indulging in – how shall I put it? – in what might have been construed to be…"

"Yuh?"

"Well, a snog, to put it bluntly."

"A snog?" A weird kind of laugh. "Well – that's as good an explanation as any. No problem – guilty! Numero two?"

"For Chrissake, Toby!" I was amazed at his nonchalance. It was like conversing with some shameless St Tropez roué, not young

Jugs. Not the lad I'd been bowled over by at Wartford. "Look," I continued, "we're hardly talking about a fag behind the bogs. If this came out…"

"How could it? Or is this informant of yours intent on wreaking havoc?"

"I very much doubt it, but…"

"Well then, my lips are sealed, no problem. Presumably the same's true of the lad's?"

"Andrew's?"

"Fuck me! Blow job with a laxative!"

"Toby…"

"Which just leaves you, doesn't it? And are you going to blow the gaff? With your track record? I hardly think so! And anyhow – suppose by accident it did slip out. What would it matter? One kiss! By golly, Miss Molly! What's the law going to do? Chop my balls off? Feed me to the lions?"

"Perish the thought. No way. But don't you understand? I'm in what's laughingly called loco parentis. That changes everything."

"It's certainly changed you."

"Bollocks!"

"In which case, why all the hassle?" A shrewd expression came into his face. "Or maybe – have we been up to some caper? In loco copulatis, maybe?"

"That is the most pathetic Latin I've…"

"Hot guy, rabid teacher?"

"Don't talk drivel!"

"You're jealous."

"Sod off!"

"You're fucking jealous!" – uttered with that kind of cynical drawl which, in anyone else, would have set me worrying. Even so, it rankled a bit. Had Marsden been fool enough to drop hints? Surely not, but even so, let's scotch it. And pronto!

"Toby, listen – stow it! You're way off base, OK? By about a zillion zillion miles! I mean, the guy's a minor."

"Technically, but so bloody what? This is the 20th century, remember? Who cares a toss about all that Old Testament stuff. Get a life, man! Before it turns into the proverbial Pumpkin. Which, don't delude yourself, it assuredly will."

"Thanks for the sermon," I shrugged. "What the hell's come over you? All I wanted…"

"Is this numero two?"

"See what I mean. How is it you've got so, I dunno…"

"Radical? Big deal. People do, on the whole. Except for some sad cases who remain stuck in denial, the whole of their pathetic lives."

I nodded as if aggrieved. "Meaning myself?"

"You tell me."

"Toby, what is all this?" I retorted. "Why get your knife into me? I've nowt to reproach myself over where you're concerned. If it was Jules – like, that would be different. But we've got a clean slate, haven't we? We've never even slept together."

"At last Geronimo, at last!"

"At last what?"

"We've never slept together though you were hot as hell for it."

"Ridiculous."

"Like that time at Magdalen."

"You're off your head!"

"When you pissed off to your train. When you preferred to stick to your geriatric schedule, get home to your cocoa. When all the runes came right, but you couldn't cut it. Same as Wartford."

"Wartford?"

"So where's it gone, Paulo, this fabled libido of yours?"

"If you don't bloody mind…"

"Just old age? Or religious conversion, maybe? About to enter a monastery, are we?"

"Don't talk rot!"

"Come on man, see the funny side. Life's a bitch!"

"No way," I began, marvelling that all this had been pent up so long, "it wasn't like that, not at all." Was the bugger on drugs? Had he been reading too many German glossies? Either would fit.

"You don't say!" Cool, assured, he gazed straight at me, with eyes that smiled, but not quite with their former warmth. "So – enlighten me. The floor's all yours."

"Toby, this is absurd." And so it was, and almost literally, since I didn't have a leg to stand on. I mean, that muffed chance at Magdalen – it had, painful though it was to admit, been exactly as he surmised.

Sans doubt.

Evensong over, yes I'd cut and run. And in doing so, what had I been but a Farfrae not wishing to 'make a hole in a sovreign'? Or put it this way, nothing less than a selfish introvert, intent on saving a pound or two instead of reaching out for the horizon – Priapus and all stations West!

Well, what defence had I – what possible excuses which would register with a guy who'd found the knack now, or so it appeared, of taking life on the run? Still, one has to try. "Let's be fair," I continued, "we're talking of what? A year ago, thereabouts? How could I possibly…"

"Yuh," he retorted, blowing a statutory kiss as he turned on his heel. "How could you!"

Stuck in kind of a speechless timewarp, I stood there in that shabby vestibule for a minute or two brooding. Was that how others really saw me? The guy who put comfort and convenience first, who only wrestled with the cosmos if he was sure he'd not get bollocked, financially, emotionally or both?

And how justified was such a view anyway? Like Jonson's Lovewit, my arquebus had gone through with guys a-plenty, hadn't it? Loads of them. Aloysha, Ramon, Andy, Frobisher – no, not Frobisher, come to think of it. But almost. And how about Toby's own brother? Hadn't I taught Julian a thing or two about protocol in the sack?

But maybe – maybe not, as they say, within the meaning of the act. Maybe there was some part of that arcane screenplay called sex whose existence I'd never suspected, let alone sought to grapple with.

And gradually it came back to me. All those times in student bars I'd heard my peers ridiculing great names such as Nietschze and Forster for their sexual inadequacy. And had joined in the laughter, savouring the cruelty. So now was it my turn? Time for my privy parts to be bared to taunts from the mob? Its mockery? All my preenings and pretensions to be laid bare and revealed as the pigmy trivia they'd always been?

Self-excoriation and on a 6 o'clock local!

For a moment or two I festered there, twisting the greasy extinguisher belt round and round my wrist!

By now the crowd was returning and with it a heady joie de vivre which made it impossible to sustain a very long face for more than thirty seconds, especially when Marcho suggested a farewell drink at the Trout after we alighted at Oxford.

Rapids, peacocks, Charrington's on draught – who can resist the headiness of what was, in those days, the world's best pub – though it was noticeable that Jugs steered well clear of Andy on the river wall, and myself on the bench opposite Roy and Julian.

In fact I'd intended to offer the latter congratulations (approximamente, anyhow!) on shacking up with Tina, but didn't get the chance since he'd found other fish to fry: namely, the spry sort of theological dogfight with a priest, so beloved by students and the like: bag-ladies, atheists, and stuff. In my subdued mood it made acceptable entertainment.

"Heaven?" mused Marcho serenely. "Well, of course views vary. There was Muggleton, for instance, a 17th century pundit who believed it was just six miles above us!"

"Why six?"

"Why not?"

"But what's your opinion?"

"And, and, how about Quarles – or was it Vaughan? He insisted he'd seen eternity the night before."

"But have *you* ever seen it?" persisted Julian.

"Unfortunately, dear boy, I don't possess a telescope."

"Now you're taking the piss. Quarles, Muggleton, I ask you! Figments of the imagination!"

"Look them up in DNB if you don't believe me. On the other hand, verifying the existence of heaven – well, that's more chancy. I'm afraid it's hardly a thing one even glimpses unless one's a mystic. It's more a question of sensing. Feeling there's a second chance. A state of being where perhaps – who knows – one has all the time in the world to read the books and hear the music which one only skimmed through in life."

"So then, there'll be a physical presence?" Jukes putting his oar in. "Like, you'd need ears to hear, surely?"

"Does that follow? Does that necessarily follow?"

And so on, and so on, Marcho enjoying himself at the other's expense. I was soon bored and besides there was my forthcoming interrogation of Andy to ponder and think about and savour. Though what had seemed at the Bull a good wheeze – a pantomime third-degree over midnight coffee – had now, after my emotional battering from Toby, lost much of its appeal.

Of precisely what, for instance, would it consist? I mean, how do you sort out a thing like that: who's the busser, who the bussed? Also, the nature of the encounter: lingering or a peck, shallow or you know what? Moreover, what precisely had Jugs meant by that enigmatic comment, 'as good an explanation as any'?

By this time you'll be objecting again that I always seem to miss the main point. Like, my own role in the comedy – as the jilted lover, I mean. Well, not lover, but boyfriend, in a sense.

As I've admitted, once it had sunk in, once the first sexual buzz had passed, the thought of a rival had hurt – and hurt intensely, given the casual nature of Andy's infidelity. But what could I do? Rationally, as I've previously said, I'd long since come to terms with the fact that our affair couldn't be anything but short-lived. A few months maybe, before he went up to Arnos and met friends of his own generation. But a few months is something. And to find it thus imperilled, and by a guy I myself had fancied – well how would you have reacted?

OK, OK, more robustly? Made more fuss? Not allowed myself to be trampled on? Fine, if that's your style. I get the point! It's certainly food for thought.

Ought I to have booted Copeland's arse? Knocked him down? Kicked his balls to shit? Would I have felt better then, more manly? Would Andy have respected me more? Would I have respected myself more? Or – for Godssake – did it matter? Did any of it matter?

Despondently I began to prop beer mats together into a mansion, trying to ignore the first faint indications of a headache.

Why not let the buggers get on with it? Let them howl in the frowst of their faux ecstasy. Better by far to stick to the vintage open to all of us. Most reliable of draughts which never sells you short – wankation in the highest, Amen!

It was close on twelve as the Ford halted outside chapel. Jukes and the other dayboys were staying the night at Buggleskkely, and by the time I'd said my goodbyes, Andy had already let himself into Rhodes. No problem.

By now I'd almost decided to let the whole bloody thing drop. It'd be easy to cook up some excuse for Jaz, and it was clearly all to the good to deny Marsden the satisfaction of knowing that I knew. Besides, tomorrow marked the start of his exams, didn't it? No way ought I to be interfering with the proverbial good night's sleep.

Though the boarders were back, except for a faint smell of socks and burnt toast you'd hardly have known it. Murdoch had done his usual corral act to perfection and not a sound could be heard except the swish of a shower in the basement.

Andy doubtless, washing away the railway grime. No problem. Fun though it would be to third degree the guy while he was covered in lather, better to let commonsense prevail. If I did decide an inquest was necessary, there'd be time après the exams. Besides, I was knackered too and needed my bed.

But not too knackered to pause upstairs with an irresolute yawn, hand on my door. Further along, he'd left his wide open, from which streamed not only light but the faint sound of piano from his radio. OK, unobtrusive enough at the moment, but what if the next track was orchestral and shattering? I shrugged. So? Not my place to intervene, and yet - could I really leave him to the tender mercies of the Frame, or worse still, the Turd?

Since the offending instrument was of Roberts design with a prominent dial, it was easy to silence – after which I cast a fond glance round the place. After all, I'd have few opportunities from now on. There were his jeans and shirt cast over the bed, and smart undershorts in red polka dot. There was a packet of Players, which I slipped into a drawer, just in case. And there, fallen to the floor, was a tiny plastic bag, sealed with a rubber band. Cradling it in my hand, I peered closer, my breath catching in sudden surprise.

So that was what Toby had meant! That was the real reason for locking that compartment door.

As fascination took over from surprise, I found myself undoing the seal and teasing a few of the greeny grey strands into my palm. All too familiar, their provenance, both by look and smell. How many times had I been offered such wares at gigs and stuff? How many times had I striven to find words to accept? How many times had I failed!

Not a dilemma, obviously, which had ever taxed Andy. Yet now a new consideration shouldered into the Bryant mind. How come the lad had been so careful on the train, but so negligent now? Anyone might have come along to turn off that radio, in which case he'd be in quod and no mistake. How could he be so careless!

Or was that it? Not carelessness, but deliberate. Bait, sort of. A lure laid out for the one person he could reasonably expect to be the most likely to…

A sudden rattle of the pipes caught my attention. The basement shower turned off, in all probability. Again I glanced at the shag-like strands between my fingers. One thing was for sure – I had to act quickly.

19: *Black Tuesday*

Have you ever, after the traumas of the night – dreams, hobgoblins, apnoea – woken with profound surprise to find you're actually in your own bed? Not shacked up with some stranger, or out on a heath, or in some black corridor with menace behind the wainscot?

Anyway, that's how it was with me early on Monday.

For obvious reasons, I'd slept somewhat fitfully only to find, at length, the usual fog of coma gradually and harshly invaded by Templecombe Junction at Whitsun, as once described by Marcho. Commotion. Rush and chaos, smoke swirling, the hiss and wetness of steam, and above all the scream of a whistle, one of those Bulleid Atlantics it must be, warning the unwary as it swept down the slope at seventy.

Where was I, on the track or something?

I'd blinked into life, terrified – only to find myself skewed across the bed at an angle close on forty five, pillows all over the floor and, on a nearby table, that wretched Teasmade, lit up and spluttering wildly – shaking and spitting as its superheated arc streamed brazenly down into my best mug and its little mound of Maxwell House.

Ten minutes to bell time, but not, I thought ruefully as I propped myself upright, absolutely not for Andy. No wee ring round the door in that young man's ear today. There'd been no two ways about that unexpected packet last night, nor where it had come from. What was that remark Toby had dropped at Eynsham? 'As good an explanation as any' – something of that ilk anyhow, and I was in no mood yet to expose myself to whatever arcane agenda the Marsden had in mind. Besides, he'd obviously have been up since dawn, memorising the last few dates which would propel him into Arnos, poor sod.

Yawning, I stumbled over to the washbasin and gazed out over the swollen river to Feyhill and the old viaduct. A new week, and, so they say, new horizons. About time too. If one thing had been made clear by recent events, it was that yours truly was not exactly suited to the rigours of bohemian life. Like, sure I'd no desire to descend into a Teasmade and slippers middle age, but neither had I any appetite for living like some adventurer out of John Buchan. There and then I made a solemn vow, that after Andy's departure I'd play it cool. Do my marking, make friends with the Carve, attend chapel regularly – even, maybe, learn the rules of rugger. In short, I'd establish myself as a reliable member of staff, and wallow in the safety such a role provides.

Oh yes, and of course the odd visit to young Farquhar – for tea that is, and plum cake.

I know! Early morning moods. We all have them, but, ridiculous though their resolutions seem by teatime, at least they're a sort of antidote. At least they help restrain impulses which might otherwise get out of hand. Need I specify?

Anyhow, it was thus with a certain fondness I eventually made my way to Common Room where scholarly life was well into its usual Monday routine: Ormulak and Baxter hunting for their gowns, Tiny doing the Manchester Guardian crossword in red biro, and Murdoch roundly denouncing the March for embellishing the new minibus with its first scratch as he turned through the gates that morning – the fact that said blemish was exactly one and one eighth inches long, and shallow at that, seemed to rouse him to even greater fury.

Even Ken Tarn was in the room, come to help with invigilation, all he was capable of by now, poor bugger.

Dodging the throng, I made straight for the mail table, only to find Carver there before me. What a prat the man was! OK, there it lay, fat and threatening – a huge brown envelope marked 'Oxford and Cambridge Schools Examination Board'. Big deal!

"Well I never," he said with that affected sneer of his. "What could this be? Exam reports? Death knell for someone? Hired a solicitor yet, sunshine?"

What lame riposte I could manage was, however, destined never to be heard for, as he pushed off, Watson swept in. "What's this, gentlemen, what's this? Chapel bell ringing, and not in your stalls? Come along, come along. Let's start this half as we mean to go on. Oh, Owen a word if you please."

Picking up my letter, I had to squint to make out the smudgy postmark, not to mention the unknown hand almost obliterated by Old Mother Kent's redirections – and thus found myself overhearing the two of them as they conferred nearby.

"Quick aboot it then. I'm reading the lesson, and havna lookit at the passage yet."

"I'm sorry, but rules are rules. And made to good purpose. It's clearly stated that candidates must be present in the exam room fifteen minutes before the appointed start. It's now eight minutes to nine and there's no sign of your Marsden. It's too bad, too bad."

"The laddie was roused at the usual time by ma hoose tutor here, isn't that the case Mr Bryant?"

"Maybe he's popped out for a walk," I ventured innocently. "Fresh air and all that. Good for the brain cells."

"And mebbe he's gone back to his bed!"

"Whatever the case, if he's not present in seven minutes' time, Oxford is one university that young man will not be attending. You're his housemaster, it's up to you."

"As I said," complained Murdoch, his complexion darkening, "I've noo the time for jankers of any description, being aboot to read from Deuterom… Er, Deutermon… Er, Deuteroniminy!" He turned my way. "Off you go then, laddie. It's your pigeon noo!"

I shrugged. As mentioned previously, I'd administered Andy's wee ring *outside* his door that morning, and had no wish to come face to face with the guy until things had cooled down. However, a direct order from a Housemaster is hardly something to be ignored, and anyway, the errand had one at least one welcome aspect: it enabled me to avoid hearing Owen murder the Authorised Version!

Only – the boy was not at his desk. Nor had any books been opened since last night – or last year by the looks of it! There he lay wrapped in his duvet, one hairy leg stuck out, for all the world as though this was an ordinary day and all he'd be missing was a psalm or two. Or Chalmers Smith.

I parked myself beside him and just for a moment glanced round for more plastic packets, condoms, daggers, whatever. The coast being clear, I heaved a sigh of relief and touched his shoulder. The warm glaze of his shoulder.

An eye or two opened. Incomprehension, the usual struggle with light, then a faint kind of welcome spreading across his lips.

"Paul – I'm honoured." Against my better judgment I began to stroke his nose as he stretched and yawned. Then, collecting himself, he blinked twice before lifting one side of the quilt. "Gonna join me?"

"In your dreams," I shrugged. "Sorry to be a harbinger and all that, but you've got exactly five minutes to get to the exam room. OK, capisco? Cinque minuti!"

I don't quite know what I expected. A howl of despair maybe, as he leapt out of bed and tried to pull on socks shirt and pants, all in one combined time-wasting rant. Or something more orderly, a quick resolute donning of clothes, assembling of pens and stuff – even taking a sip of water.

What I didn't expect was for him to turn over, hug the duvet closer and pull a pillow over his head.

"Andy," I remonstrated, pulling it away. "Five minutes, understand?"

"Fuck the fuck off!" One of those teenage glares, more strident than the basilisk, intended to quail the sternest foe. Not for the first time I found myself wondering why on earth humans couldn't be born at forty!

"Come along, come along!" I joshed in my best Watson. "Four minutes, thirty. Nice easy exam waiting!"

"Can't you," he retorted in sudden savagery, pushing himself up on one elbow, "get it into your thick head. I am not going to any pathetic, wankers' paradise of any fucking exam! Clear? Want it in writing? Now sod off before I get angry!"

Perplexed, I tried again. "Andy mate, what on earth's this all…?"

"Sod the fuck off!" This time loud enough to ring the rafters.

I glanced at my watch and rose. No time for further debate or delay. Regardless of consequences, there was only one thing for it. With a swift flick of the wrist, I yanked his duvet off the bed and cast it on the floor. At which, with an angry cry, naked, enraged, he rolled off the mattress, jumped up and confronted me.

"Bastard!" he cried. "What fucking right have you got – ahhh!"

I'd grabbed his nuts hard with my right hand, as I'd seen in those road movies. Not too much pressure. Just enough to show who's master, and as an earnest of what will follow if compliance does not.

He took a deep breath, raising his arms as if about to strike – but there they stayed, in the air, almost like some gunman surrendering. And at last, mouth open, he was listening. Face but an inch or two from mine, eyes blazing, he was listening.

"Look", I said softly, "no way do I get what crap delusions you're labouring under. But I tell you this. To dodge this exam would be the biggest mistake of your life. OK, you may flunk it. Have to go off to fucking Gateshead Polytechnic or, what's worse, RADA. But you may not. Very probably may not. And if not – doors will open you can't even dream of."

Yes, I know. All the old shit. But it was one of those moments when only neon suffices.

"It's worth the try," I continued. "And if nothing else, for this reason alone: that you'll avoid a lifetime's remorse. That nagging question: what if I'd tried? What if I hadn't played the fucking coward?"

Both his heavy sines-qua-non distinct in my hand, here I upped the pressure slightly. "So that's the score. You're gonna try. Or I warn you, these – won't ever be safe again!"

A threat of mickle might – I was quite proud of myself – but of course essentially empty. Yet it seemed to have a curious effect on him. Like Pistol his fury seemed to abate but, unlike Pistol, without the threat of resurgence.

Apparently.

And it was so – quick! I'd never seen docility come over an actor so rapidly and completely. As soon as I let go, he picked up a shirt, merely observing, "We'll never make it."

"We'll make it all right," said I, looking round for his jacket and tie. Having triumphed thus far, I was in no mood to allow Greenwich Mean Time to stand in my way.

Nine was chiming as we passed chapel, and a couple of minutes more, I suppose, had elapsed before I pushed open the doors of Old School and propelled him in. Fortunately it was Ken in charge, the last man in the universe to give a toss about technicalities. Indicating a desk with his stick, he surveyed the assembled candidates before announcing loudly, "It is now precisely nine of the forenoon – you have three hours, and may God have mercy on your souls."

I certainly hope God accorded dear Ken the same bounty. Though he didn't die till just before Christmas, I never saw him again, and was prevented from attending his funeral by circumstances which will shortly become clear.

Teaching now took up most of my morning – or going through the motions really – and it wasn't until I reached the vestry after lunch that my nerves began to settle. At least there, all was well with the world. The bottle of Camp and a tin of Nestlé's were open and waiting, the kettle was just starting to whine, and Marcho, a jeweller's lens screwed into his eye, was inspecting a small white oblong.

"Exquisite, don't you think?" Handing me his trophy, he turned to attend to the coffee, and thus didn't notice my grin.

What you may ask was this paragon of beauty? Some nonpareil of marquetry? A scrap of elephant tusk? A writing tablet from the court of Marcus Aurelius?

Not a bit of it. White cardboard, actually. A Great Western Railway 1st class single from Oxford General to Lechlade, stamped Furlough. In other words, Marcho's ruddy ticket he'd made so much fuss about a week ago on the Fairford trip. I suppose it was quite sweet with its quaint lettering and price of 1/1d, but it didn't stop me wondering what else he'd brought home that day. Nor how much loot he'd culled over the years. Nor what it had proved worth.

Still how can one have reservations about a man whose box of Cadbury's is pushed one's way three times in the next five minutes? Nor was this all. Today the cornucopia was really dishing out!

"By the bye," he said, as the bell began to ring. "Doing anything this evening, are you? Clemmie's been sent this side of venison from Oakham by Aunt Tabby, and we rather thought we might make a start on it for dinner. Not of course that game's everyone's cup of tea, as it were. Perhaps you've moral objections in that quarter?"

I hastily assured him that I was – sincere apologies – always game for game! And could think of nothing more pleasant than an evening at Buggleskkely. It did cross my mind that maybe there were pieces to be picked up vis a vis Andy – but so what! I wouldn't be back all that late, and what oil I felt inclined to pour upon the waters could wait till then.

And thus it was that seven o'clock found me backing Bird's best out of my garage. As I locked up, my attention was arrested for a moment by noise from the 6th form club. Some rugger victory being celebrated – or the end of exams for the John's, Wadham & Arnos group? I smiled. Good luck to them. Andy was clearly going to be in a mellow mood by midnight!

A state which, it soon became apparent, I was set fair to share with him. I don't know whether it's ever struck you, but hosts fall into two categories. Standard, where a measure of largesse is provided, often generous – and Platinum, where from the start it's made plain that the sky's the limit. For instance, that evening though we were fewer than a dozen at table, the sideboard held no fewer than seventeen bottles: six of hock on ice, eight of claret, and three halves of sauternes. Plus port, madeira and marsala on a kind of dumb waiter to the side. It was the kind of prospect to put the most demanding guest at his ease. Come what may, there was no chance whatever of anyone going home parched.

These were, you'll recall those happy days before the drink-driving laws were foisted upon us by the loathsome puritans, when as long as you could walk a chalked line and recite 'the Leith polith dismitheth uth', you were free to take the wheel. And, sociologists among you, take note – isn't it precisely from the time said laws were introduced that we can trace Britain's descent into third-world status – from, as it were, urbanity to turbanity!

Whether I was particularly early or the final guests, Jazza and a certain Mrs Daubney, particularly late is, I suppose, neither here nor there. The fact is I arrived at Buggleskkely with Clem in a flap, despite enticing odours wafting in layers you could almost see throughout the hall and sitting room.

"For heavens sake, darling," she cried, "why not take Paul out on the terrace for his drink? We could do with the French windows open for a while." And so it was that my host and I, plus glasses and decanter, were shooed out into the mildness of early

November. The garden was a picture, lit by low mercury lamps in various borders, but this time there was no shilly-shallying. The old askew door by the sundial lay already open – and through it, and above the stone of the wall, there issued a very different kind of gleam. Soft, yellow as Booth's, waxing and waning in the slight breeze.

Gaslight!

Stepping over the threshold, I glanced around me in amazement. So this was what it was all about? Snug, had they called it? Nonsense, the place was a miracle, and I half expected to see a yellow brick road curving around through the carefully manicured lawns.

Five iron lamp standards – three of them GCR, one LNWR, and one Taff Vale – cast their bewitching rays over the most extraordinary collection of transport memorabilia I'd ever seen. And every item not just plonked down anywhere, but set meticulously into the contours of banks and shrubs.

There was just so much of it, this pirate's hoard. Old nameboards (including the one filched from Ilfracombe), loo signs, signal arms and a level crossing gate (how on earth had he smuggled that home?) a luggage trolley, one of those Don't Trespass on the Line notices in metal (L & MLR), a pair of buffers, a giant 8ft driving wheel from a Drummond 2-2-4, numerous benches embellished with company scrolls, and – the piece de resistance. A huge platform board with cream capitals picked out against brown, proclaiming TITFIELD.

"I had to pay for that one," admitted the March slightly mournfully as though still bitter over failure, "and a hard bargain Ealing drove, I can tell you."

Chuffed that, at least by inference, I was evidently now at long last a genuine trusty, I put my hand on his shoulder. "Roy, this is fantastic!"

"D' you really think so?" he beamed. "Well, it brings in quite a bit for charity. Society visits, and the like."

"So how long has it taken?" I inquired, quelling remorse at my lack of faith in him – there'd be time for that later.

"To assemble? Let's see – now the very first item was that Spaniard's Crossing whistle sign over there. They dismantled the old Alton & Basingstoke in what – thirty seven? So, getting on for the quarter century."

"Amazing – it's a real labour of love."

"It grew. At first a few knick-knacks in the attic, then as bigger items arrived, the shed…"

"And finally it ended up like this. What an incredible story."

"Ended up?" twinkled the other, striking a match for his Sobranie.

"Beg pardon?"

"You talk as though it's finished. As though there's no more to be done."

"Oh sorry Roy. I didn't mean to…"

"In fact," lowering his voice to one of those conspiratorial whispers of his, "I've a bit of a surprise for you later on. While the others are having coffee, we'll slip up to my study. Ever heard of the Brecon & Abergavenny?"

"Another of your Fal Vale fantasies?"

"Certainly not!" His eyes glistened. "It's a canal!" His eyes glistened more. "They're about to reopen it!" His eyes seemed to brio into futurity. "And we shall be there!"

Clem like so many matrons of her age and class couldn't help being an inveterate matchmaker, dedicated to rooting out bachelor bliss wherever she came across it, and as the meal progressed it became apparent that Claire Daubney was no chance addition to the party. A brisk girl, one of Clem's colleagues at the hospital though no almoner herself, she'd apparently lost her husband a couple of years previously and was obviously keen to find an efficient replacement. Indeed, avid!

With her would come a comfortable four bedroom detached in Gifford Farrar, the remains of a handsome insurance policy, a Range Rover and a ready-made family consisting of two boys heading for Winchester, fees to be paid by grandparents.

By no means a package to be sniffed at – if, that is, you could stomach the concomitant how's-your-father. And as far as that was concerned, well – she might have been thirty, she might have been forty, but with modern make-up does it matter? She was slim, smart and of smart opinions – and was at the moment holding forth on the subject of mixed marriages.

"Not too sure about that," she said thoughtfully. "Isn't it more a question of biology?"

"Quite," murmured Marcho, too preoccupied with carving to listen.

"Or to be more precise, the gene pool. The wider the input, the better the product. That's where Apartheid gets it so wrong. It's not the colour of skins that counts, but the aggregate IQs of the parents. That governs everything, don't you see?"

All the while brief glances were being shot at Jaz and myself as if trying to guess the level of our poor old intellects. Was the woman seriously expecting to breed again? I shifted uncomfortably in my chair.

"I sometimes think," smiled Clem, lifting the lid off the courgettes, "that cleverness is over-rated. Give me kindness anytime. Though of course isn't the ideal both, a cocktail so to speak?"

"Do I hear someone asking for the moon?"

Handing me a serving spoon, my hostess gave me a wink. "Don't mind Daubs. It's her hobbyhorse, you see, brains and all that. Betterment of the sans culottes, as you might say."

I nodded. "Yuh, well – I'm a sucker for brains too, especially when they're served up with black butter."

"Oh dear," laughed Clem. "Back to Apartheid are we? No more politics if you don't mind. Claire, dear. Could you pass Paul the redcurrant?"

The look I was given as Mrs D handed me the jar made it plain that fatherhood for me would have to wait a while longer, at least as far as she was concerned. Tough titty! And at least that left the way open for Jaz though, to tell the truth, so far he'd shown about as much interest as a sack of cement. Something seemed to be weighing on his mind! He was affable enough, at least to the Marchpanes, but the number of times he consulted his watch, and the expression on his face as he ate had begun to get me concerned. As had, now I came to think of it, our one or two encounters after Fairford.

That stupid probe of mine at The Bull, the one about boyfriends – was that still rankling? Or was it just that I'd never really got back to him over the Toby incident? In a sense it was of no great moment, but one never likes to make a needless enemy. I resolved that I'd get him on his own tomorrow and sort things out.

A superb fricassee of venison in jus Pernod was followed by marrons glacé and cream, the banquet crowned with a Windsor Red, ripe fruity and just on the turn. Food for the Gods! Then just as Clem suggested we repair to the lounge for coffee – no separation of the sexes in this liberal household – Marcho gave a little yelp.

"Are you all right, dear? Something gone down the wrong way?"

"My mind must be going! Darling, I forgot to turn off the gas and you know how expensive those canisters are. Paul, you'd better come along and hold the torch."

Yours truly, needless to say, proved to be a complete supernumerary, it taking the old boy one hand and about five seconds to close off the Calor. After locking up its lair, neatly converted from an ex-Glasgow & South Western ballast bin, he led the way round to the east of the house where lay the back stairs. "They'll be well away," he whispered. "Female chitchat. Won't miss us for five minutes."

Amused at the thought of what Jazza must be going through – serves him right for being homophobic! – I followed my host up to his study on the first floor, stopping briefly to admire an Augustus John in a cheap deal frame.

"Could that be an original?" I inquired reverentially.

"Who knows!" he replied absently, thrusting into my hands a crude sketch map etched out on a Gestetner skin. "Had it for years. Now look you here. This'll be our best one yet."

"Can't wait."

"You see, ever since the war, no through traffic has been possible because of a road across at ground level near Tal-y-bont. Military necessity and all that. But now it's been converted to a swing bridge which will be officially opened by Lady Moffat on the 22nd. I don't say we'll actually be the first boat through, but we'll have a damned good try, hey?"

"Absolutely!" I replied, caught up in his fervour. "But do we have a boat?"

"We'll hire one."

"OK, which poses another question. Who else are we going to rope in? To spread the cost, I suppose we'll need half a dozen or so at least."

"Hadn't really thought about it. Boys d'you think, or staff?"

"Lads are less trouble," I ventured, it occurring to me that this might make a welcome post-exam break for Andy. A way of making it up to him for my rough handling that morning. Not that I had regrets about it: how could any schoolmaster have stood by while he wrecked his future?

"Lads it is then. We'll discuss names in the morning. Now, as indicated on the map, the main points of interest are the Ashford tunnel…"

"Hang on – no more tunnels for me!"

He laughed. "Well, you can sit that one out if it bothers you. But what you won't want to miss are the aqueducts at Brynich and Menascin."

"Won't I?"

"Nothing like it, my boy. Floating across in an iron groove a hundred and fifty feet above the valley? How does that strike you?"

"Uh – what one might call well groovy?" I retorted, my quip neither receiving, nor I suppose deserving, anything other than a blink of polite incomprehension!

And thus it was settled. Super! Now there could begin that fabulous time of looking forward to yet another of my Marcho excursions. Since each so far had avoided anything which could be described as mundane, there was no reason to suppose this would be any different, and on the journey back to school I was happy to regale myself with visions of myself with Andy – though I admit in a fast speedboat cutting up the skiffs and li-los off the beach at Copacabana, rather than in a converted coal barge amidst the dews and damps of South Wales!

Jazza had left half Buggleskkely half an hour earlier, bidden, so he said, to the party at the 6th form club – though the Daub's inuendos may have had something to do with it – and I was thus surprised, on returning to campus, to note the lights already out and no-one about. And even more surprised a couple of minutes later to see no gleam under Andy's door, and certainly none under mine!

Which in a sense suited me fine. By adult standards I had bugger all to apologise for, and the self-abasement necessary to keep things sweet would seem altogether more palatable in the bright light of morning. A healthy defiant mood on which to go to bed, and one which was almost immediately to improve still further. For as I emptied my pockets before stripping, what did I encounter, what could I hardly fail to encounter, but that letter forwarded from Abercorn that morning.

What a hoot! It turned out to be none other than an invitation from Rear Admiral & Lady Hatherop to the marriage of their daughter Tina to Mr Julian Cardew Copeland of Corunna Lodge, Wartford, the date some six weeks hence. That is, just before Christmas. My mirth issued forth as inner and sporadic rather than as belly laughs, but was none the less profound for that. And not simply at Copeland's ridiculous middle name, nor the idea of that limp leaf of womanhood having a warrior for a father, but at the date. It didn't take much IQ to work that one out. Clear as day, it must be a shotgun wedding.

Sans doubt!

Julian Copeland, the man in control, the ultimate coper, and now to be a dad by default. What else was that but farce? Turning on my pillow, I chuckled myself into the whirlpool of slumber. And yet, curiously, it was not of Jules I dreamt that night, nor Jugs though he often enlivened the small hours, but Carver of all people. And even more curiously, not of anything to do with the wretched Weyburne debacle so soon to explode in my face, but dancing a tango at The Fox with, of all people, the unspeakable Reynolds.

OK, the mind plays these tricks and I thought nothing of it, nor much of anything else, as, hours later, I blinked fretfully at first light.

First grey light. The slow dawn of what I would ever afterwards look back on, and can with unadulterated justice describe as, my very own dies irae.

Fortunately, feeling a bit shagged I'd decided to defer my morning wank to a double free just before lunch – and thus had just finished shaving, when I was nonplussed to find a visitor at my door.

Murdoch, no less. And already dressed in suit and tie as though about to attend a funeral.

"Doon't bother yourself, laddie," he said reaching for the bell. "I'll be ringing this today. Away aboot your business."

Amazing! I mean, really well weird! That bell had come to stand as a symbol of his domination over my life, and here he was sort of – well it was like a retreat almost. As though he had in mind some devastating campaign against yours truly which required a tactical withdrawal and regrouping before great guns could come into play!

But – nothing seemed amiss as I eventually emerged. No glint of binoculars from spies on the roof – no sinister van with blacked-out windows lying in wait. Nor did breakfast differ from any other Tuesday morning: Baxter chomping his way through three eggs and a rasher, Tiny dribbling coffee all over his Daily Express, Joe, there by virtue of having taken early communion, spreading a smidgin of honey on his Weetabix. All reassuringly normal and I'd begun to think Murdoch had simply flipped or something, when suddenly –

Wham, the mirage shatters! Reality – how things sodding are – abruptly intrudes in the shape of a latecomer, the impossible Carver, with an envelope under his arm. That envelope. That brown brute missile which he hopes will shoot me out of the skies for ever. And which he, ostentatiously as I suppose, places just opposite me so that I can see it's now opened, its contents maybe already in the Head's domain.. And now he gives me the most odious of smiles before lounging off to raid the kedgeree.

As you'd imagine, the Bryant mind now began to devise wild schemes for dealing with that enemy so close to my grasp. If only I had matches, or sulphuric acid, or some monster rodent that could gnaw its way through fifty pages of crap a second! Or ought I brazenly to pick it up by mistake, and bustle out quickly via the boilerhouse?

Not a chance, of course. Before I'd got ten yards, the hue and cry would be raised and I'd have Tiny on me with a flying tackle. Nice one, Bryant! Not only about to be reprimanded for gross unprofessional conduct, but bruised as hell into the bargain!

Quelle fuckup!

A mood of consternation which darkened still further as Chris poked his head round the door. "You bachelors!" he snorted. "Well I never – fat of the land as always! Ah, Carver. After second helpings as usual? Goodness gracious, no time for that" – glancing longingly down at the bubble and squeak with its fat poached egg on top. "Headmaster straight away, if you please." Ignoring protests, he shook his head. "Can't be helped – this morning's gone pear-shaped, I'm afraid. And none of your gobbling. Nothing worse for the digestion. Doris, pop it into the hotplate for him, there's a good girl. Now Bryant, Head at ten to. On the dot if you please. And Marcho. Come along, come along – where's Marcho?"

And so, like a Senecan tragedy, things began their inexorable climb to the rock Tarpeian. And yet – was it really so Senecan? Faking a battle for a monarchist outing – was that really so heinous a crime? Wasn't the real culprit Rudgewick? But for his daftness, none of us would be wasting time like this!

OK – that, understandably, was my viewpoint. But how about Hunn, and the ancient pricks who doubtless ran the exam board? Maybe they'd see it as worthy of the guillotine or malmsey butt or worse. Dismemberment by blunt penknife?

So now, for the first time, I began to seriously ponder it – what my transgression might cost. Suspension? Surely not – the crime was far too trivial. A fine of some sort? Had schools the power to raid your pay packet? Or maybe – yuh, that was it. Way most likely would be some comment in your reference when you wanted to move on. In which case – do your worst, ye mighty ones! By then my cv would be so bursting with honours and triumphs that one tiny slip in my first year would count for nothing. Eton – open wide thy gates!

So brimming was this self-confidence, that I finished my breakfast without haste, before stalking across to the waiting room where I found not, as I'd expected, Carver triumphant with his wheelbarrow of evidence, but a rather woebegone Marcho fiddling with a missal. "Oh Paul, my boy…" he said, holding out his hand.

So he knew. He'd been briefed, Murdoch too maybe. But why? Not that I had time to ruminate on any such oddities since Chris at the door was already beckoning me in. "Storm in a teacup," I winked. "See you in the vestry."

Hunn was standing as I entered, and made no movement except to tug the serge of his gown a bit higher on his shoulders.

Gown? In his study? Who the hell did he think he was? A proctor or something, with Chris as his buller? For the first time, echoes began to ink my mind of an earlier inquisition in this room, with Eric Amberley across that desk and James outside. Not that there was much by way of similarity, was there? Indeed, virtually nothing. Indeed, actually nothing. Even so, a kind of dread blitzed through me.

"Please sit down, Mr Bryant," he said, indicating a plain wooden chair brought in from the office. "I imagine this will not detain us long. Mr Watson will now place a document before you which I would advise you to read carefully."

"No problem," I said with a kind of vestigial defiance as Chris placed a single sheet of foolscap on the desk opposite. Since its contents were obviously well known to me – Weyburne having been in my thoughts almost daily since the day of the exam – I hardly needed to bother, but still. Why not humour the bastards? I pulled it towards me.

"It is as you will see," continued Hunn, seating himself and unscrewing his Conway Stewart, "an instrument of resignation. If you care to sign it immediately, much unpleasantness can be avoided, and there will be no need to involve anybody else. Moreover…"

"Hang on, hang on!" Choking with surprise, I at last managed to find words. "What is all this? I don't understand?"

"Is that so? I rather assumed you'd have guessed by now. Would it help if I mentioned that late last night I was contacted by Mr Thornby on a…"

"Jazza?"

"…Mr Jason Thornby on a matter of the most extreme gravity. Is it necessary for me to go into further detail?"

So that was it! Toby and Marsden caught out on the Fairford line! Nothing to do with Weyburne at all. And Jazz of all people. Quelle prick! Who would ever have imagined a guy as young as him would turn snake in the grass. And over what? Matter of the most extreme gravity, my foot! Two guys having a snog on the quiet? – at anyrate, as far as he knew! Or was that it? Surely…

For a moment, I allowed myself to think the unthinkable. Had the truth of their encounter – the truth on which I'd so haplessly stumbled that midnight as the last of St Tywyn faded away – had that now somehow come out?

"Mr Bryant?"

"Uh? Oh, I suppose not," I answered warily.

"In which case, I take it you'll sign?" – offering me his pen with mock politeness.

"Condemned or not, I'd appreciate time to read the small print, OK?"

Not exactly a reply likely to increase sympathy for me – as evinced by the curt nod with which it was answered – but I needed time to collect my thoughts, didn't I? Anything. A minute or two – a few seconds.

What else could it be? Sure nowadays it's hard to find anyone who's not experimented with grass. It's as integral a part of student life as owning an NUS card, OK? Or wearing jeans, or shaving once a week. .But we're talking fifty years ago, remember? Then it was still a classified drug, using which meant a fine, dealing in which meant prison. How my involvement would be viewed by the law wasn't entirely clear, but was it worth taking risks over? Wasn't it best to go along with what Hunn proposed? Have the whole thing hushed up, and forgotten about? But then, what about Andy? How would he emerge from all this? Hadn't I a duty to…?

"Mr Bryant?"

I looked up. Reverie finito! Igor standing over me, looking more like an executioner than ever. And that bloody pen again, waved at me like a dish of hemlock. "If you please!"

"Whoa – hang on. I haven't said I'm signing yet."

"Then what are your intentions, may I ask? I need hardly point out we haven't all day."

"Intentions?" I queried with some asperity. By now, the first shock having passed, I was starting to find my feet, reach for my scabbard. Who was this little tick trying to push me around like this? Like, of what exactly could I be considered guilty? Even if Marsden had blabbed to Thornby, of what could I be accused? Holding back info, well yes. Not exercising due discipline, maybe. But so what? Was it so major a crime that my whole career should be ruined? Even though I'd not supplied the stuff and, ostensibly, knew nothing about it? And how about Andy and Jugs? OK, a misdemeanour, but nothing more than teenage rite-of-passage – were they to be banged up for life on account of something like that? The whole episode was gradually turning into worse than Kafka.

"Yes, intentions. To put it bluntly, you have two options. Either you sign that paper, in which case you leave the school immediately, without any public stain on your record, and with compensation…"

"Or?" I said defiantly.

"Or I shall have alternative but to institute formal disciplinary proceedings, as laid down in your contract of employment."

"No problem," I replied, courage, Dutch or otherwise, suddenly blazing up. "Do your worst!" There was bound to be some board or committee, and it was inconceivable that they'd agree to my dismissal over a slip where the evidence was so inconclusive.

Wasn't it?

"Very well. I rather expected that might be your attitude, but for your own sake I ask you to reconsider. No? Then let's get on. In cases such as this," he continued, "a member of staff has the right to be accompanied by a friend. Through the formal hearing, that is, at some later date. I take it that one of your senior colleagues will suffice?"

All this fuss? Mountains over molehills, and no mistake! What was the wanker banging on about? Still – best to keep one's powder dry. Fall in with their charade for the time being. So, what's this about a stooge? Who then?

Carver? Joke of the century! No way am I going to have the Inquisition as my so-called friend! Tommy? Great bloke, but no great intellect. Leon – would his English be up to it? Murdoch – a garden gnome as one's advocate?

"I suppose," I said at length, "it had better be Mr Watson, if that's OK?"

"It is not, er – OK, I'm afraid. Mr Watson will be present anyway in his professional capacity. Along with a representative from the Fustians. Now then – your choice from Common Room?"

The Fustians? Why were they being brought into it? This was getting more and more bizarre. Not just Kafka, but Bunuel and Derek Jarman all rolled into one!

"In that case – the Chaplain. If that's OK, with him?"

"Oh, there'll be no difficulty in that quarter. In fact, I rather guessed as much. Mr Watson, will you bring him in?"

By now my mind was totally in a whirl, but I do remember wondering how Chris came into it all. I could only surmise that what was to happen next was some kind of preliminary session. Some sort of Grand Jury. And that evidence would be presented and discussed at a later stage. In front of Fustians, the press, the public – in other words, the world and his wife!

Quite an embarrass des richesses, huh?

Hunn allowed Roy and Chris to find seats before pulling a file out from under his blotter. For the first time he looked me squarely in the eye. "I'm afraid, Mr Bryant, that a charge has been laid against you."

I nodded, almost penitentially. I mean, let's face it, they had a point. No way should I have been such a chump! As soon as I saw the stuff, of course I should have...

Should have what though?

"A charge," he continued, "of some seriousness. Indeed, some gravity, which may, in due course, have to be passed on to the constabulary."

I looked up sharply.

"It is alleged that on August 22nd last, on a railway train, in or near the county of Sussex, you were..."

"Where?" I choked in sudden horror and disbelief.

"...party to an act of misconduct between yourself and a pupil of this school..."

"No way!" I interposed frantically, only just stopping myself adding, Not at that Time he Wasn't.

"...amounting, in fact, to culpable indecency under section 11 of the Criminal Law Amendment Act of 1885."

"This is so weird!" I cried, rising. Like, who the hell's cooked – the whole thing's – like, why the hell would I risk – I mean..?"

"Control yourself, my dear sir. This is not a hearing. In due course, you'll have ample... Oh dear. Watson, ring for the nurse will you? How very distressing. Has he hit his head? The fellow's a graduate, isn't he? You'd think he'd be able to take adversity like a man. That's right, Marchpane. Loosen his collar. Give him air. No chance I take it he's...? No? Pity – still, we can't always expect neat solutions to these things. Shall we say eleven thirty on Thursday? That will give Sir Norwood sufficient time to get here and the Union be briefed. No, no, Chaplain – no brandy. All those wretched fumes! Things are bad enough without more hostages to fortune. Rumours of orgies in The News of the World – Roman romps in the headmaster's study! Beware Fleet Street, gentlemen. Never forget, first last and always – beware the perfidy of Fleet Street!"

20: *The Last Throw*

They say that victims in a catatonic state can sometimes hear what those around them are discussing. Maybe, but, as it turned out, it's not an ability I share. And anyhow, hadn't I a far better Boswell on tap an hour or so later when I found my senses returning in the welcoming environs of Buggleskkely?

"Good-oh, he's coming round. On with the mulligatawny, my love."

Home-made or Heinz, there's nothing, as every reader will admit, so adept at restoring comfort to a man when he's down than a good cup of broth! Plus, of course, bread & butter, a plump sofa and a roaring fire. Having supplied these necessities, Clem, tactful soul that she was, withdrew to allow Marcho his head. And a sorry little scrap of a tale it was too.

Evidently, Thornby had indeed hied him to the bar after Buggleskkely only to find it empty except for a somewhat worried cabal of three 6th formers, Kim Turnbull, Pete Daines and a lad from Clive called, Marcho thought, Jebb. Earlier, carousing at its height, the usual bragging had erupted over sexual prowess and exploits, half exaggeration, half downright lies. Apparently Andy's little tete-a-tete with Jugs had been noticed by others than Thornby and when taxed with it, he'd not only admitted to a clinch (as the lesser of two evils maybe?) but sought to make comedy out of it, insisting that trains brought out the sex in him, turned him on, made him irrepressibly randy – at which of course, in the headiest of moments, out it came, our spunkfest on the Brighton line. Great fun! Shades of Oscar the Awesome embellished with the gaudiest of detail, including, when pressed, the identity of his partner in passion.

Not my name as such, but so many hints it was impossible not to guess. Incredible, I agree but there it is!

All of which, as you might expect, was received as a fine drunken yarn without a scrap of truth behind it by most present – but not these three. To them it had rung true and heinous. And thus had arisen their debate. Whom to inform. Murdoch, the Housemaster of two of them? Or the Chaplain? Or…?

And how chuffed they'd been when Thornby had praised their sense of duty – and offered to deal with the matter himself.

"Not of course that Clemmie or I believe a word of it," insisted Roy gallantly. "Nor will any of your friends in Common Room."

"They don't know yet?

"There's to be a Common Room meeting at break tomorrow."

"And Marsden?"

"Quaratined with Joe till after Thursday's hearing's over. I'm afraid Arnos has been informed already, so that'll be the end of that. Whatever possessed him! How could anyone so intelligent be so stupid? I imagine Mathieson will make mincemeat of him."

Sir Norwood – the hearing! My entrails quailed at the thought. Already notions of owning up, ending all the tension, had crossed my mind – but no way! The prospect of public disgrace, the gutter press, fingers pointing at me for the rest of my life, a future spent stacking shelves at Woolworth's – it was all too much. Besides, who'd caused the scandal? Me or some dope of a teenager who couldn't keep his dick in his pants and his mouth shut?

No, denial was the only course. If I did by a miracle survive, and that meant Marsden branded for all eternity as a congenital liar, so what? He'd deserved it, hadn't he? It was him or me – and as the stuff churned over in my mind, more and more my resolve hardened. To stick it out. No quarter. To be totally adamant that the story was a pack of lies dreamed up by an unstable adolescent, high on booze. And, moreover, high on the other! That'd clinch it all right. That would finish off his credibility. Surely I had at least an even chance of getting off?

Marcho was standing by the grate, knocking ash into the flames. "Don't misunderstand me," he eventually murmured, "but there's still time you know."

"For what?"

"To sign the letter. The Carmarthen sleeper doesn't leave Paddington till ten and I doubt Sir Norwood…"

"Bugger Sir Norwood!" I interposed curtly. "Oh Roy, apologies – pardon the language, but I've had it up to here. Look why on earth should I?"

"To avoid the hearing." His reply was simple and forthright as he stood there in his tweeds, the eternal country parson without an ounce of guile in his body. "And to avoid Common Room being notified. You know what folk are – jumping to conclusions, no smoke without fire. Better they're never tempted."

At the latter, my ears pricked up.

"Nor anyone else, for that matter. Your folk, for instance."

"But how about…?"

"Thornby? The 6th formers? Don't worry – the Head would handle that. And poor Marsden into the bargain. It would simply be as though nothing had happened – no transgression, no accusation. All parties, as one might say, unstained and pristine. Of course, there'd be no question of the boy's ever returning to school…"

"I doubt if he'd mind that very much!"

"…nor of your remaining on the staff beyond today, let alone the end of term."

"Right – yuh, OK, I see that. But listen – how about an alternative scenario? Suppose the guy retracted?"

"Pigs, dear boy, might fly!"

I clenched my fist. "What a howling, bloody mess!"

"Absolutely," he nodded sympathetically. "But look at it this way. Sign that paper and you'll find Hunn starts to pipe a very different tune. All Heads have to deal with this kind of thing from time to time – they're used to it."

"And enjoy it?"

"Your words not mine." Unscrewing the butt, he tossed it into the fire. "Why not think it over? There'd be a plausible explanation. And what one might term, an accommodation."

"Meaning?"

"Salary in lieu, that goes without saying. But more importantly, launching you on some kind of alternative career. Seriously – career, not job. Teaching would be out, naturally. But there are loads of other opportunities for a clever young man of enterprise and…"

"Roy," I interposed, holding up my hand. "Give me credit for some level of acumen, OK? You've obviously something in mind, so let's have it."

He smiled, crossing to a recliner and seating himself. "You're a sensitive kind of chap," he said. "It must have dawned on you that, as a haven from the storms of life, the Church performs an especially…"

"No," I said abruptly, sitting upright. "No way!"

"Hear me out."

"There's no point. It's an absolute non-starter. Seriously, Roy – I mean it!"

"Bishop Geoffrey," he persisted gently but not to be deterred, "would be quite prepared, I'm sure, to sponsor your candidacy…"

"Roy, it's out of the question!"

"…your candidacy, as I was saying, on an ordination course, backed as it would be by an excellent character reference from Hunn…"

"Pull the other one!"

"…a reference which, I'm authorised to divulge, has already been written and which I've seen and, just in case, approved."

Fast workers, these guys, I thought. You have to admire it, the Establishment. Its speed and efficiency. Like some great combine harvester, reaping you, processing you, tossing you out in a neat bale. Your past life erased, your new one formatted, everything brought into line in the best interests of society.

But how about my best interests? Vicar of some ghastly deadbeat church full of old women and mice? Sermons, funerals, roof repairs, the organ fund. What a destiny!

Of course there might be a choir…

"Another thing to bear in mind," he was continuing, "is promotion. No promises of course, but with clergy recruitment at the low ebb it is, you could expect to rise fairly rapidly – barring, shall we say, accidents! I imagine you've a 2.1, haven't you? Well then curate for a year or two, then a first living, then somewhere decent, after which – fifteen years and you might expect to make Archdeacon. Beyond that, who knows. Dean? Bishop?"

"Like yourself?" I retorted, regretting it instantly. "No, look, I'm sorry. That was out of order. Bloody rude."

"Not at all," he said wryly. "Shall we say, I've always preferred the alternative scenario. Cool and sequestered, as our favourite poet says. But it doesn't suit everyone."

"Meaning me?"

"Paul," he replied, grave for a moment. "Just think it over will you? Promise me that at least. In a long life, if I've learned one thing it's this – avoid a hornet's nest when you meet one. Give it a wide berth, no matter how tedious and inconvenient the diversion. It's all very fine to hark to the bugle and opt for battle, but just take a moment to consider the consequences. Maybe – unexpected consequences?"

For a moment we looked at each other in silence

At length, I jumped up and strode to the fire. Though past their peak, its flames were still ducking and weaving in orange embrace against their bed of red. All was as it should be. Nothing aberrant. The universe obeying its laws. Enjoying the ease of conformity.

"Don't think I'm ungrateful," I began, "and, yes, I'll give it my, you know, er…"

"Earnest consideration?"

"Exactly," I nodded, turning back to face him. "But there's just one thing."

"Only one? You surprise me."

"No, not the detail, all the gubbins – we can go over that later. But it would give me peace of mind, make me better able to settle on the future and stuff, if – well, if I could just see Andy once more."

"After what's he's done?"

"After what" – and I oh so wanted to say, 'we've done to each other' but couldn't quite face all the angst and explanations – "he's done, yes."

"Is that wise?"

I shrugged.

"And to what end?"

"I don't know!" I cried, kind of bitterly. "Who knows? Get him to change his story, maybe?"

"Story?"

"Tell the truth then, if you prefer. Look Roy, I just need a chance to clear myself, OK? If it doesn't work, if it blows up in my face, so be it. Then I'll – settle to the halter. Somehow make myself submit. Become a dutiful Parson Adams. But I need that chance!"

"Adams, eh. Not Woodforde?"

"Could never *stomach* him?"

Smiling broadly, he approached me, hands in pockets. "You'll do!" he twinkled. "A man who can keep his sense of humour even in circumstances like these is bound to fall on his feet. Bishop, did I say? You're going to end up Pope if you're not careful!" We both laughed, then he took me by the arm. "Tell you what. As you know, Marsden's at Cragfield till Thursday morning. This evening Joe's due to take chapel here at six, which means he'll be away an hour or more. Suppose I ask him to leave his back door unlocked?"

My heart seemed to skip a beat. "Would he do that?"

"For me?" An ineffable look. "I think so. But Paul, careful does it." Seating himself at his desk, he pulled a notepad towards him and began searching for a pen. "One false step, remember? That poor little cat. See, I do know my Gray."

And so much more than I'll ever know, I conceded to myself as, a couple of hours later, I parked at the end of the drive beside the church, let myself into the field behind, and approached the parsonage from the south. Andy had neglected to draw the curtains and I was able to observe him for a moment or two, sullen of face as he listened to Bach on Joe's old radiogram. A kind of rash had begun to infest his left cheek, and every now and then he seemed to hunch himself round in his chair as if trying to gain more ease.

Gingerly, I crept round to the scullery and silently entered. Although the parlour door was ajar, how to present myself was, as you'll perceive, a problem. I'd no wish to frighten the guy out of his wits by appearing suddenly in the doorway like some devil out of LeFanu, nor alienate him by striding boorishly in like a Carver determined to wring his neck..

So I did the decent thing. Waiting till the sonata had ended, I knocked. Firmly, but not too firm.

"Who's there?" he cried.

"Only me" – I entered, closing the door behind me, keeping one hand firmly against the deal. He'd leapt up at the sound of my voice and was – well, kind of cowering beside the mantelpiece. An abject figure to be frank, not at all the sleek, assured youngster I'd first spotted in class. Then I'd been struck by something inscrutable in his manner – now there was only fear. His hair looked unkempt, and that rash I'd noticed had actually spread from his face down one side of his neck. Only his eyes retained their former brightness, though now it was the kind of brilliance you see in fever victims, not the allure of intelligence or wit. He'd obviously not slept that night, probably not eaten.

All at once, despite everything, my heart went out to him.

"What?" he demanded sharply, looking down at the hearth as if for a weapon, a poker maybe, or shovel.

"Sorry to intrude like this, but…"

"Better watch out – he'll be here any moment."

"If you mean Father Jephson," I retorted demurely, "as you know quite well Evensong never lasts less than forty minutes. Which gives us plenty of time, OK?"

"Randy as always, *sir*!" Insolent and defiant, he backed away a step.

"Time, I mean, to talk."

"About what?"

"Shoes, ships, sealing wax? Take your pick."

"Typical!"

"Well, isn't it obvious?"

Suddenly his face contorted. "As always, the fucking genius. You fancy you're so fucking clever don't you."

"Cleverer than some, by all events! What on earth possessed you? Where was the angle? What the hell were you thinking of?"

"Thinking?" With a pronounced shudder, he retreated to the window seat. "Don't be stupid!"

"Andy, I warn you…!"

"Well, use your stupid loaf for once!" Boiling point already, rank, remorseless, like pitch. "I mean, are you serious? There was no question of thought. How could there be?"

"So…?"

"It was the moment – can't you understand? Guys were bragging, this bitch, that bitch, and then, sort of – eyes turned towards me. My fucking moment. And out it just came. D'you see? It – my high – bingo! It happened. No plan, no premeditation. It was like – I can't exactly… It was just right, like rattling off a speech by Shakespeare you learnt in the 4th form. Boy, you should have seen their faces!"

"I can imagine – you should have seen mine!"

"Come again?"

"When carpeted by Hunn."

"That toad!" he said contemptuously. "What does he matter? Who'd listen to him!"

"The law, maybe?"

"No way. Hunn bring in the fuzz? Wash his dirty linen in public? Not if I know anything about it."

"As to that, I wouldn't count my chickens if I were you. Seriously. I've known cases…"

"So that's it," he interposed, cooler now. "Scared, aren't you? Shit scared! Amazing!" Sprawled against the glass, he was gazing right at me. "Who'd have thought it – smart, young, sexy Mr Paul Bryant intimidated by a tick like Hunn."

"A tick with a sting, don't forget…"

"Sorry – try again! Biological impossibility!"

"But not," I retorted, just about hiding a smile, "a legal one, I fancy. Seriously, you'd be well advised to avoid complacency and stuff. It takes two to tango, as even some dried up old brute of a judge would concede."

"Yuh, right – I've read Agatha Christie too. And as for all the Solomon crap" – he rose, more languid now, and yawned – "which of us more likely to be believed? A jerk like that, all those red robes and wigs and stuff – whose word is he more likely to take?"

I stood my ground, hard though it was in the face of such arrogance. "In point of fact," I replied, "the question's purely academic. The arbiter we'll both be facing tomorrow happens to be Sir Norwood Mathieson, KC. Not a jerk as you so lucidly put it, but a hard-nosed barrister. And, incidentally, Master of the Worshipful Company of Fustian Bollers Trimmers and Weavers."

"Wow!" For a moment, laughter seemed to play about his lips. "I'm shattered! Just leave a revolver on the library table, mon Capitaine!"

"OK," I retorted. "Laugh away while you can. But remember, judges' rules won't apply in that room. Someone like Mathieson wouldn't have got where he is without being a shrewd judge of men…"

"And *kids*?"

"…and without developing a keen nose for a lie when he hears one."

"If he hears one."

"Which is rather up to you."

He shook his head sagely. "Come off it, you're not so squeaky clean. Not if your antics at Arnos are anything to go by, *OK*!"

I flinched – so Toby had been talking, had he!

"Or are you going to perjure yourself when that stuff comes up?"

"If it comes up."

He shrugged in that casual way of his as if to say touché. "Sounds like it's gonna be gloves off in that case. No problem. Let the best man win."

"Why take chances?" I ventured, moving over to the window seat and perching next to him. "Why not be sensible and let both men win?" I was so close, I could have touched his leg – but he didn't move.

"How so?" he replied warily. "Anyhow, isn't it a bit late for that?"

"Depends," I said, assuming my most conciliatory manner. "Depends on how you play your hand. There might be a way out."

"Assuming one's needed."

"Oh you need one all right. More than me, you need one. OK, in the short term, it'll be me who suffers most. Loses his job, loses his friends – some of them. Maybe all."

"Lucky you."

"Cynical sod! But ask yourself this – in the long term, who'll be the one who sticks in the memory? Me? Or the parvenu who turned on his benefactor."

"Benefactor!"

"Who repaid love and affection with treachery and…"

"For fuck sake!" Up he jumped, both fists clenched. "Spare us the fucking melodrama, can't you?"

"I'll tell you something Andy," I murmured, relaxing back against the cushion, "I may have broken the law, but you've broken the code, and in the final analysis that's much worse."

"What code?"

"Decency – human decency. Of all the swine in this world, from penthouse to gutter, there's none so abhorred as – and suddenly recollection gave me the word – as a judas."

For the second time in our interview he looked nettled, his impetigo lurid in the white light from the ceiling. "Talk sense," he said, fingering the pustules uneasily, "it wasn't like that."

"You certain?"

"I've said, haven't I? It was all spur of the moment, not malice, not treachery. Nothing like that intended."

"Yuh, but in matters like this it's looks that count, not intentions," I retorted, my mind flashing back to that label round my umbrella and Berry Wighte, and wondering for the thousandth time whether Marcho had disabused him that day at Lanammerty.

"Says who?" came the childish reply, shrill and nervous as a Woolworth shopgirl.

"Read your bloody history books," I said dismissively, judging now was time to up the ante. "Look, time's short, Andy – there is a solution. What's it to be – dodge or discuss?"

"What d'you mean, solution?"

From my breast pocket I produced the letter Marcho and I had concocted before I set out. "All you have to do," I said, handing him the envelope, "is sign this."

"No way!" he shouted, skimming it back past me. "Fuck off! I'd be a total laughing stock."

"What d' you think you are now?"

"I am not withdrawing what I said, and that's final! Like, I admit – I wish it hadn't happened this way. Or any other. But it did, and that's that. Now stop bloody hounding me!"

By now he was close to tears, but made no attempt to leave the room. Rising, I retrieved the letter and placed it on Joe's bureau.

"Look," I said. "I know how you feel, OK – it's bad for both of us."

"You've no fucking idea!"

"But so far no Rubicon has been crossed, not really."

"Not surprising," he responded, seeming to rally a little. "Neither of us amounts to a Caesar, does he?"

"Speak for yourself!"

A slight smile crossed his face.

"Think of it this way," I continued. "So far your assertion's seen the light of day only twice. First when you were in your cups and not responsible. Second in an interview with Hunn when you were doubtless on edge, and when – let me guess – no third party was present, and no note taken of the actual words used?"

"Correct, but how the hell did you know that?"

"Long experience," I grinned. "What would novelists do without bullies?"

"He might have had a tape recorder under his desk."

"Also beloved by Agatha and co. But in real life? Highly unlikely. In what sort of light would that present him if it ever came out? So, it amounts, you see, to this: everything you've said so far can be explained away as drink talking, or funk in the presence of the Almighty. In both instances, easy to recant."

"Easy? I don't think so!"

"Easy, I mean, compared to later on. Tomorrow, for instance, when no such excuses apply. It's going to be a grilling, make no mistake about that. And if, in front of Sir Norwood, you persist in your story…"

"Which happens to be the truth."

"…you'll have nailed your colours to the mast, good and proper. There'll be no going back after that, whatever the consequences."

"But," he kind of wailed, "it's the actual truth!"

"It's the partial truth," I snapped, rounding the sofa. "Andy, face up to it. You weren't even a member of the school that day in Brighton, and as for afterwards – well, does responsibility really lie on just one pair of shoulders?"

"I just can't," he sobbed. "It's too much to ask."

"You can," I insisted, "and it's very little to ask. You simply sign that rebuttal and it's all over, OK? End of. And let me tell you this – schools are surprisingly supportive of errant teenagers. Oh yuh! They'd be out of business otherwise. Trust me, in a week this'll be a blip in the past, hardly remembered. It might even be possible to get Oxford to reconsider."

"Fuck Oxford."

"OK, OK, change the record, for Chrissake. All I mean is, you can get on with whatever career you choose without – as one might say, impediment.

Picking up the envelope, I extracted the single sheet of notepaper. "Would you like me to read it out?"

Trembling, he shook his head.

"Last chance saloon, Andy. Last chance – for it all to be kept under the proverbial hat. No whispers, no pointing fingers, no need to face your mum…"

"Leave me alone, you bastard!" he cried, turning his back on me.

"Nothing in the press. No hints of calumny. A clean slate."

"No!"

"A totally clean slate, trust me."

"I can't!" he repeated.

"You can – and I'll tell you something else."

"Sod off" – little more than a whisper now.

"You will."

For a few seconds he stood there, shoulders heaving slightly. Then he turned, his face wet and stained, eyes fearful like a child's, breathing unevenly.

"This won't take a moment," I said gently, handing him the letter.

He glanced at the ceiling. "God, I hate you!"

"That's your prerogative."

"And your loss."

Wincing, I shrugged. "I suspect I can live with that."

Again he looked at me sullenly – a minute or a bit longer – before swallowing hard. "In that case," he said reluctantly, "I'll need a pen, won't I?"

With bated breath, I nodded, gesturing at the desk, fumbling for my biro. Crossing the room, reluctantly he sat down and started to read. After a moment or two, he removed his spectacles and looked up at me ruefully. "Any chance of a drink?" he asked. "Condemned man's nourishment and all that?"

"Of course, of course," I crowed, delighted at the way things were going. "Tea? Coffee?"

"Gin and It," he said. "Ice if there is any."

"Back in a second," I nodded, almost skipping my way to the kitchen. Well, of course it was in reality a host of seconds before I'd found the correct vermouth and chipped out some ice, and as I returned he was sealing the envelope.

"There you are," he said, "redemption."

"Know what?" I assured him, noting he'd even initialled the corner, a requirement for internal mail at Tolverton in those days. "There's no way you'll ever regret this."

"Hope it's the same for you." That was all he said as I backed out. No farewells or here's to the next time. Not even a wave.

My elation as I headed back down the drive was so intense, I can hardly put it into words. It was like – I dunno. Being saved from drowning. Winning the pools. Getting your first novel published. I was utterly and completely over the moon, so much so that I didn't at first recognise Joe's yellow headlights as his old Ford bounced towards me. Since they were still carbide and half as bright as anyone else's, I must have been in a right daze.

"Hey up!" he called, sliding back the insinglass as he pulled up opposite me. "Success then, or what?"

"Peace in our time!" I cried, waving the letter, for all the world on the steps of that plane at Croydon.

"Congratulations. Let me see."

"Careful there – no, it's sealed. You can't open it."

"Sure he's not signed it Mickey Mouse or something. Remember that film?"

"Ridiculous," I laughed, but with a tickle at my guts.

"All the same," said the old man. "I'd take a peek, just to be on the safe side. It's probably kosher, but why chance it?"

Frowning, I switched on the light, holding the envelope aloft, all formal and stately, Hunn's name in the centre, Marsden's initials in the corner – then suddenly, seized with proleptic fear, I tore it open and wrenched out the typescript.

Only it wasn't, of course, typescript – or anything clever, ingenious or memorable. Just a blank sheet of paper. A virgin side of A5 destined never now to be written on, or used, or regarded in any way. In a violent burst of anger, I crumpled it into a ball and cast it into the night. Joe said nothing, but, with a grim face, started his motor and resumed his journey, myself close on his tail.

The house was in darkness. Doors locked, completely empty, his bicycle gone.

Within half an hour, I'd signed the letter of resignation, been given twenty four hours to clear out, and accepted a cheque of three hundred and eighteen pounds, seven and eleven, in lieu of notice.

Conditions? Never to contact the boy again. Not to set foot in Tolverton for ten years minimum, nor to make contact with Common Room during that period. Never to discuss the terms of severance with anyone at any future time.

Draconian? Not for those days, I suppose, though now they'd seem harsh – well, some of them anyway. It irked me that there was no opportunity to say goodbye to Marcho and other friends for instance – there was always the telephone, but it's not quite the same thing. I'd have liked to shake their hands and feel their faith in me hadn't been shaken by my sudden disappearance, and all the rumours which would naturally fly around.

Still, over a pint at the Rainbow I calmed myself by reflecting that ten years isn't the end of the world, and that picking up the traces thereafter could mean the biggest thrash the Fox had ever known. Ale by the bumper, music, a bonfire on which Cedric's cheese roll would be sacrificed as appeasement to the Gods, and fireworks – lashings and lashings of starbursts, red and silver and furious orange.

How naïve can you get!

And anyhow, time's chemistry was, as always, on the march. Within a year, for instance, both Joe and Ken were dead, Chris making a third some eighteen months later, in the first year of his retirement. Well, a fourth really, though some folk would disagree. Folk, I mean, without imagination. But that I'll leave to your judgment if you care to read on a little.

And so ended my days at Tolverton, that curious eccentric little town which somehow harboured more of the elect, Ormulak, Ken, the sublime Marcho – you've met them all – than most towns in this drab universe. But before we leave its hills and rivers, one more incident needs to be told.

An incident that can only be explained as a 'there are more things in heaven and earth, Horatio' sort of stunt. If such matters offend your rationality, by all means pass straight on to the last chapter. But if you've an open mind and a life like mine that's never flinched from the quirky – I once slept with a chum, for example, who'd devised a machine to weigh ectoplasm – read on and wonder.

By first light next morning, having packed all I wanted and paid my bills, I found myself heading along the B road past Trefoil bridge. The sky was clear, Colonel Custard pottering along in fine form, my balance at Barclay's way higher than it had any right to be – and yet my spirits refused to budge.

Leaden, impervious to the vitality all around me in the hedgerows and streams and creamy clouds, my mood was one of abject despondency. I'd made a pig's ear of it, hadn't I? Failed. Proved myself inept to the nth degree.

Not regards teaching, I hasten to add, though that might have been the case too, but relationships. Somehow, something in me, something I'd done, had turned a decent (as it seemed) middle-class boy into a pariah. There was no use trying to dodge the fact. OK, he'd probably find his feet again, but no way did that excuse my crimes. I'd put him (as it seemed) through stress that no youngster should ever have to face, and it was right, absolutely right, that I should pay the penalty.

How we flay ourselves at times of crisis, and so bloody pointlessly. All we need is a sage to come along – remind me, by the way, to tell you one day about the night I met an angel on a two-stroke – just some calm, balanced guy to reason things out and set us back on an even keel. But, as Hardy points out, 'Nobody did come, because nobody does' – and anyhow, even if they had, there'd have been no room. Even the passenger seat was piled high with bits and pieces, a mirror, a couple of coats, my toaster, Alex's gloves, and my college scarf – oh, and a leather fire bucket from Dukeries Junction, the latter a gift from guess-who that night at Buggleskkely.

The kind of night which would be notably absent from my life now for yonks. Maybe even for good. And what tale was I going to tell Ombre? How was I going to face the tolerance and forgiveness and understanding I'd find there? Wrath I could deal with – but not those kindly disappointed looks I'd have to wither under from here to eternity.

And so, as the miles passed, my depression deepened. As luck would have it the road was empty and I surged along, almost on auto-pilot until a sharp hill near Combe Asarts brought me to my senses. Third, second, full throttle for half a minute, then back to normal. Thirty, forty, fifty... And there, half a mile ahead, lay the crossroads.

On that route, there are two places where my humble byway crosses a main road, necessitating a halt to make sure the highway's clear. At both vision is obscured by trees, fences, whatever. From time to time, in the bravado of youth, I'd contemplated doing a

Russian roulette: hurtling over without stopping, leaving it to the Gods to ordain whether I was blasted to bits or not.

OK, even as a boyish whim pretty foolish, but doesn't that kind of death gamble turn us all on subconsciously? Chills us but thrills us? And coming out safe – wouldn't that be something? Better than those multiple orgasms German porn mags rave about?

In fact, at one of the junctions I'd once done just that – but at night, so it didn't really count. I'd have seen oncoming headlights and (presumably) stopped. Even so it'd given my balls a good sharp stir and ensured ace release when I got to bed.

Now it came on me again, the lust. The sheer primal urge. Suppose I did lose out, so what? What had I to live for? At best boredom, at worst pity. Some menu! Why not get it over with? At least for a few seconds I'd be living fast again, not suffering this dreary suburban yoke of guilt and self-excoriation.

And no, sorry, not once did I think of the life or lives I might destroy in my selfishness. So deep was my despair that I was it – outside me nothing existed. Zilch all around, like a telly screen on stand-by.

Down went the acclerator to the floor, the engine responding with a roar – well, loud growl really. Remember this was an Austin A30 after all.

My way at the junction was straight over, and even at this distance I could see nothing obstructing me on the other side. All depended now on that main road, that wide main road with its cars and coaches and battering pantechnicons. Clutching the wheel tight, I closed my eyes, to concentrate on and relish my last few seconds of manhood, my complex design of organs, nerves, soul – all functioning so blissfully this instant, but about to be bust into trash in a last thunderous…

Whoosh, we were over! I'd done it! Seventy or faster, and I'd survived. Flicked a V sign at Destiny and got away with it! Defied, cocked a snook, triumphed. What about that! Though maybe it wasn't quite such a signal victory – wide and far the highway had stretched on both sides with not a speck in sight!

All the same, I pulled up in a lay-by, my chest heaving, the one and only thought in my mind being sex. If there'd been a scarecrow in the field I'd have fucked it, honest. And registered it as the fuck of my life! About twenty million on that Lukas scale of his.

As it was, after taking a long cool drink from my thermos, I put madam slowly and sedately into motion once more, fully aware that, four or five miles ahead, there lurked the second of these junctions, vision even more impaired than the first.

Surely this was going to be it! Could one be lucky (or unlucky?) twice in one day? Alert, hard, every nerve in my body jumping, I slammed her into fourth and put my foot down. But not as before. This time not like I was whizzing round Brooklands in front of King Zog or Mrs Simpson.

It had occurred to me that for my next victory to be total, I must approach at normal rate. In the same way there must be no hesitating, there must be no hurrying. And no wimpish closing of the eyes either. This must be a contest worthy of Hector and dudes of that ilk. D' you get my drift? To really claim the bays, I must sail across, eyes open, at a nonchalant fifty – only then could I pat myself on the back, and know I'd never court such fucking lunacy again.

At Gleddly, my lane rises on a slight incline, meeting the main road at an angle of about 35 degrees, the space between occupied by tall dense scrub. Up we purred, revs steady at just 3 thou. This time I was curiously detached, almost an observer of myself, as though death were certain and the best plan was at least to enjoy it vicariously.

But as we swept into the last hundred yards or so, the strangest thing happened. Suddenly I found my right foot forced down hard on to the accelerator, as though old Selby were once more perched beside me with his hands on the dual controls. I even flicked a glance to my left as though somehow my pile of junk had transmogrified into him or some rival. Nothing. No change. Just stripes and crumbs and that absurd bucket labelled NSR.

Still my foot held down the steel with remorseless force. Try as I could, I couldn't wrench it free and swiftly the note of the engine rose. Up swept the needle towards seventy, nor did it pause there. I could only just hold her on the road. And in the midst of my travail, the strangest thing. Something I shall remember as long as I live. A scent, a well-known scent, which all of a sudden ravished my senses.

Coins and glue and old books. Thorntons of Oxford as it used to be?

Across we streaked at eighty, right athwart the path of a mighty oil tanker, huge and blaring, clearing it by an inch, my ears shattered by the sound of its horn. Desperately I wrestled with the wheel, as we bounced along the verge and finally, now that my foot was my own again, came to rest in a gateway.

In tears, I sat there shuddering, trying to understand. Until I remembered. That scent, still faintly lingering. Not of wildflowers or anything in the natural order. Not even Thorntons. But redolent of Madrid, old silk, spent cigars and leather, a warm engaging aroma. Love in blossom, but, like Sullivan's Lost Chord, not perhaps to be hoped for again this side of the grave.

OK, dismiss it if you will. Explain it away as some sixth-sense registering that a crash was imminent and subconsciously taking steps to avoid it. I prefer the alternative scenario.

Wasn't there an Eastern sect which held that, once earthly life is over, all of us are given one final chance to intervene in the human merry-go-round? To redress a wrong maybe, or compensate for some profound lacuna?

If so, perhaps he'd squandered his precious last fling on me, Alex, my Xavier – and at that moment I knew. Not wondered or suspected, but knew. That he was dead, the better man was dead, and I still living. The unworthy still with a chance to make amends, and thanks entirely to him.

For a moment or two, I mused over his face and body, and that lilac shirt of his. And my perfidy, and that last glimpse of him I'd been granted in Venezia.

Then, solemn under the weight of this new responsibility, I eased the Austin back to the tarmac and started her on the way.

Launched her on the journey that requires no map.

21: *Envoi*

And that in a nutshell is that. The story of my first foray into the world of men, a saga which I suppose qualifies for Larkin's label of 'wrong beginnings'. Or were they so wrong? At least they led me here to Latchfield, and thence to an existence that can be called useful, if sometimes tedious.

Still the question remains, do I regret it, any of it? Enjoying myself in that black stream being drowned by Frobisher? Or that first time with Andy on the Brighton line? Or my jape – and if I've not already confessed this, please do remind me sometime – with Alvi in Laceway's potting shed?

Or do I simply regard the whole Chaucerian tale as just one fragment of a human comedy, finely ordained by a supernal Ringmaster whose concept of justice soars so deep that we can but glimpse its faintest outline.

Anyhow, time to tie up loose ends and get this off to the printer.

Despite further encouragement from Marcho by phone and letter, I persisted for many moons in my refusal to take the safe way out and espouse Holy Church. I mean, could you really see me in a pulpit, spouting myths to a gaggle of old bags, half of them asleep, and half trying to remember whether they'd turned the oven on for Sunday lunch? No, religion's too important for that. I have to agree with young Sorley that the only God worth having is the one you've found yourself – though preferably not, as in his case, during a rainstorm!

What ultimately changed my life was that deliverance at Gleddly. I just couldn't get it out of my head. Nor that feeling of Xavier's presence somehow preserving me for a future.

And of course all that talk of his about Lambarene and working far away among the simple and unsung.

Not, don't get me wrong, that I could follow in such footsteps. You have to be realistic about yourself and I knew only too well that I'd never withstand the heat and privation. And the routine. But the more I faced up to where I might fail, the more it began to dawn on me where I might not.

Cathedral life, yes – but as a layman, and eventually a verger – indeed very eventually Head Verger and hence my crimson cloak there, on its great iron hook. And the cottage which goes with the job. And, as I expect you've already guessed, Ross to share it with.

Still, I bore you. This isn't a sociology paper but a novel, and what you want to know about is people.

Well, not exactly people in general, if I guess aright. I mean, is it of any real moment to record that Hunn rose to be High Master of one of the great schools, but expired from a heart attack two months into the appointment while beating a junior for smoking? Or that Jugs, alas, drowned off a Thailand beach trying (and failing) to rescue his boyfriend from a punctured li-lo? Is it illuminating that Roy lived through the Beeching years (just) and willed that his ashes should be scattered athwart the long slope of Shap, handful by handful, from the footplate of an up Scotch express – or that Tiny married Irish – or that Cedric's cheese roll remained unsampled to the last, until indeed The Fox was demolished to make way for Tolverton's first mosque?

No, what you want to know about is Andy. Why not? He's loomed large in this narrative, and anyhow his details are there for anyone to read on-line at the Equity blog.

Unlike yours truly, he had no friends of sufficient pull and, shall we say, subtlety, to persuade Hunn to mercy. On being informed as to how things stood, Arnos as I'd expected still declined to make room for him – ditto Harlech and its schools' programme – in response to which he embarked on a Grand Tour of a couple of years or so, though his meccas turned out to be San Francisco, Sitges, Mykonos and La Paz, rather than Rome and Vienna. Well, as they say – de gustibus and all that. And what better training could there be for drama school?

In case you're curious, I was kept abreast of his doings, as well as all things Tolvertonian, by Marcho via a regular Sunday evening phone call which, whilst hardly the emotional high-spot of the week, came to be anticipated by both of us as a welcome and amiable interface between past and present. And thus was kept alive in my mind, though merely smouldering, never more than that, the question – the rather obvious question, all things considered – why had Andy blown the gaffe so unexpectedly in the bar that night after exams?

Unexpected, at least, by me!

There'd been clues of course, like his grand guignol apologia at Cragfield, but how much water did that hold? Was he really so weak a personality that keeping up with the Joneses could faze him into a course so reckless, and with such unpredictable consequences? No way. It simply didn't ring true. But then neither did the only alternative I could think of: that my actions that Monday, my somewhat forceful method of hustling him into the exam room, had left him with such a profound feeling of humiliation that he'd had to hit back. Somehow, anyhow, but decisively. Was that more plausible? Surely, Marsden being Marsden, his reaction would have been sooner, indeed immediate. Guys who smash glasses don't plot and plan – they strike!

And thus matters stood for month upon month, unresolved & irritating, until an August evening at Hallatrow when the family had motored over to Malvern, guests at Evensong and Common Room dinner there in memory of one of the Housemasters who'd been at Cambridge with Tim, and who'd finally succumbed to his Arnhem war wounds.

I was still at the post-traumatic stage of needing other people to lick my wounds for me, whilst the special delight of seeking such solace at Hallatrow lay, not merely in spending time with James, shades of the Tolver (more or less) forgiven, but also in a most delightful feature - a modern patio to the side of the old house which boasted not one but two open-air hot tubs of the kind which nowdays grace the decks of every ocean liner, but then were a rare luxury indeed.

And so, as the steam rose and the steins emptied, what more natural than to embark on the Marsden conundrum, the nature of his psychosis, though all my queries were, of course, based on the bowderlised account of our relationship with which I'd regaled everyone from Marcho onwards – so much so that I'd almost come to believe it myself. In this, though I admitted there'd been an unusual degree of intimacy between myself and the lad, I insisted stoutly that nether the question of sexual attraction, nor of course actual sex, had ever arisen.

Nix to bodily contact of any kind – ugh!

OK, so it was a lie, but a white one – or at least grey – but what alternative had I? It would have taken just one tiny leak of the truth for me to find myself stigmatised in the hugest headlines The News of the World could muster.

How far people like Roy and Joe had been taken in, I'd always been at a loss to ascertain. Things were rather different here, lounging in the billows.

"As you say," he replied, "it's a mystery all right, but I doubt it's one we'll ever fathom, bro."

"Thanks a million!"

"D' you see why though? It's insofar as it must depend on some cock-up of which we know nothing. Sort of, some extraneous circumstance – follow me? So, no circumstance, no jigsaw. Of course, things would be completely different if, as it were..."

"Go on," I said, sensing what was coming.

"Well, if there was no fib involved – if the two of you really had scored together."

I managed a laugh. "Sounds like material for a confounded novel. OK, proceed. Andy and I have been having sex like crazy all term. What then?"

"Once would be enough – like, just one el bonko, bonko, see? It doesn't take dozens."

"To do what?"

"Unleash guilt, if guilt's there."

"Sufficient to make yours truly the fall guy? Sounds highly dubious."

"Blame Freud, mate, not me."

"But what d' you mean, guilt? What guilt?"

"Who knows. I can hardly remember the bloke, not really. Could be resentment at being gay, if he is."

"He is."

"Could be disparity between parents in early life, loss of a relative or close friend, untoward libido – the list's as long as your arm. But what the hell does it matter? You didn't do a Casanova, so none of it's worth pursuing."

"Exactly!" I agreed, though right on the brink of confessing, getting the whole bloody albatross off my neck, facilitating a genuine discussion on how things had come to this pass.

But, seeming wary of any such intimacies, he reached for his drink and said, "One thing's for sure anyhow, the guy's damaged goods. My advice is forget him. Steer well clear and never be tempted."

"Tempted?"

"To do a Samaritan. Try to help. Try to apply balm to some putative wound."

"Amazing," I retorted, swinging myself upright. "So this is hospice lingo, no less? I thought balm was your whole raison d'etre."

"To the dying – why not? They're beyond doing further damage. Which can no way be said of young Marsden."

A comment which opened up such disturbing vistas that I could only shudder and let it pass. Or hope to let it pass. But James, fresh from all this new training of his, must have noticed something – leaping from his tub into mine, he splashed me hard a few times before a deep double duck.

Here we go again! Crawshaw's Mill mach two...

And then – and then it happened. He kissed me. Not any old cop-out peck on the cheek, but a full on the mouth smooch. And lingering. Well lingering.

So what the hell was this – a Rubicon or just another tributary?

Anyhow, back to basics - how large Andy figured over the next few years in the hinterland of this and not dissimilar encounters - the wild farragos of physical need - it's hard to say. Sometimes, yes, in the last seconds before cum, his face would be there. Or at night some ill-defined phantasm in a dream would call in his voice, and beckon. But by and large he represented a sort of vague but necessary doxology to one's search for sexual endgame, and I was content to leave it at that – and in a sense be grateful for having had the shackles torn away. Or so I told myself as time passed, and intimacy, living for another rather than oneself, became little more than an indistinct memory.

It was, remember, a condition of my exit package that I should never attempt to see him again, and from that I never wavered. Honest. Never *attempted* to see him, savvy?

And so we come to the gods' final spin of the wheel. A cold January night some twelve years after the start of this narrative. Or, as that old booking clerk had once predicted, the night of that winter's first snow.

Hearing that the Fairford line was, at long last and 100% cert, about to close, I'd travelled down from Latchfield to join the last train.

Remember the timetable, by any chance? 10.10pm, OK? Stopping at all stations?

It was, I must insist, a journey of pure nostalgia. There was no chance of meeting anyone there – Roy, for instance, too frail by now to venture out in blizzards such as these, or Ross my lodger (sort of) who was camping it up in the last night of *Dick Whittington* at the Latchfield Playhouse, not to mention the cast party afterwards. But it was pleasant enough to stand on the icy platform at Oxford, warm inside my bachelor overcoat, musing over things past – and to watch the air stir the gas lamps just as in that extraordinary garden at Buggleskkely, and to wonder which of the cluster of aficionados round the booking office would make it, and which be left behind. How massively important that cherished last ticket must have seemed to them!

The train itself, however, was more my cup of tea and quite enough to justify the long journey. An elderly tank engine decked out with bunting and chalked slogans stood ready at the head of her two coaches, steam drifting from her as it had these sixty years past. And as for the coaches themselves – a wry smile ghosted my lips as I realised how identical they were to those at Victoria that momentous long-ago day. Compartments without a corridor, each one with its own door and grimy window.

And so, at the warning whistle, in I climbed, savouring, I suppose, the decrepitude: the teenage graffiti, the broken communication cord dangling from its socket, the ripped cushions with their sticky threads of Wrigley's.

Savouring, but more than that – regretting that things must end this way. The last brief brandish of the green flag – the faintness of the last whistle, knell-like in its shrill solemnity of everything I'd hoped for, and was now beyond my reach.

But, lowering the strap and leaning out of my compartment window, gazing back at the barrier as I awaited the final lurch into motion, trying to quell an absurd sense that the shreds of something exceptional were about to pass from my life, suddenly I started. There he was, Marsden in sideways profile. By all that's holy, Marsden! And looking much as he had all that time ago, though now in leather jacket and white chinos, a lamp directly overhead gleaming on his shoulders.

And all at once it crashed over me, memory like a great breaker, salt and salutary. That day on the Brighton line. When he'd refused to miss the train, the start of all our misfortunes.

Or were they misfortunes?

"Andy?" Forth it came, a cry. Involuntary I swear, and slight. Little more than a whisper really – but enough. Enough for him to turn and spot me. To take a step forward, then hesitate.

I tell you, the whole substance of my being, OK, everything I'd ever been and could be again rose in me like some searing acid reflux as that shabby old local jerked reluctantly forward, halting into motion as if loth to meet its maker. Whistles from the other engines began to screech, firework repeaters on the rail to explode – and miraculously, as though buoyed up into another sphere by the intensity around him, my guy too broke into movement.

My guy. My alter, pace Plato! My altar. My love, my love, my love.

It was platform 19 again, déja vu but tantalisingly real, as his long strides gained rapidly on the carriage. And yes, came abreast, so close I could see those features, even more handsome now, that dreadful impetigo vanished, his eyes kind of pleading, conceding, imploring – and with a depth to them now, experience, knowing man from man.

Out I reached towards the door handle. Quick now, one turn and scoop him in. So slight an action. So obvious a choice. I'd done it once, I could do it again, no problem. But, but…

"Paul," he cried desperately, his fingers almost touching mine. I could hear the harsh retching of his breath, almost the beat of his heart. And I tell you this.

I tell you this.

When my last moment comes, that's what I'll hear, that's what I'll see. The face of the one moment of absolute power that ever touched my life. Two futures clutched firmly like runes in my palm until, with the platform's end little more than a hundred yards away, suddenly I had to act. No more tight-arse delay. This was my Prodigal, loved more deeply than myself, indispensable, inenarrable.

Decisively, yelling his name, yelling my adoration for him, I grabbed it hard, the cold pocked metal of that handle, and turned.

It stuck.

Like Marcho's fucking trafficator, it stuck, it stuck, it stuck!

Straining every nerve and sinew, I strove and strove to lever the bastard round, strove, prayed, cursed, till blood ran from my nails.

Some Avernian end-joke? Summation of all I deserved?

Loud and clear, the last of the whistles seemed to sing through that tempest and bleakness of blind and bitter mockery.

But refusing even now to yield, beside myself, biting back tears, I cried in supplication to all the voids above, and one last frantic time wrenched with all my might and main, all the fury of my soul, at the brass, the hot red smear of that mindless, witless brass…

Alassio
September 2018

Printed in Poland
by Amazon Fulfillment
Poland Sp. z o.o., Wrocław